THE FRIENDS OF RATHLIN ISLAND

A story of hidden wealth and rebellion in
Northern Ireland

Stewart Dalby

ISBN 09544233-9-9

Published by
Polperro Heritage Press
Clifton-upon-Teme
Worcestershire WR6 6EN
United Kingdom
polperro.press@virgin.net

Cover design by Steve Bogen

Acknowledgments

This book grew out of a stint I did as correspondent in Ireland for the *Financial Times* in the late 1970s and 1980s. I was based in Dublin in the Republic but spent a lot of my time in the North. I got to know Rathlin Island as a result of camping and fishing trips there. I found it an interesting microcosm of the cultural divide of the Province and, in a curious way, felt it had something wider to say about the difficulties in Northern Ireland.

When I lived in Ireland full time, the latest phase of the 'Troubles' had been going on for ten or fifteen years. Now, a further twenty years down the line, there is a peace of a kind but the political problems have yet to be finally resolved. This makes Ireland a place of enduring fascination.

The book is set in the near future and inevitably touches on topical events, but it is fiction. Some living people are specifically mentioned (the Rev Ian Paisley, Gerry Adams, John Hume etc.). But any resemblance of characters other than those to any person dead or living, be they Protestant leaders in Ulster, or the politicians and businessmen in Dublin or Scotland, is imagined.

I am obliged to my old friend and mentor at the *Financial Times*, J.D.F. Jones, for persuading me to start the book and encouraging me to finish it. Thanks are also due to Rosemary Kasmir for her valiant copyediting.

I am particularly grateful to my great pal Barney Smith for taking time out from his busy life as HM Ambassador to Thailand to push the project along. He knocked the manuscript into printable form and found someone to publish it.

The book has been a long time in the making and it would not have been possible at all without the forbearance and support of my dear wife Stephanie and my three daughters Thea, Lily and Julia. To them, all my love.

It goes without saying that nothing in the book is the responsibility of any of the aforementioned. The views are mine alone and any errors of fact are down to me.

London, November 2004

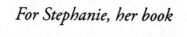

For Stephanie, her book

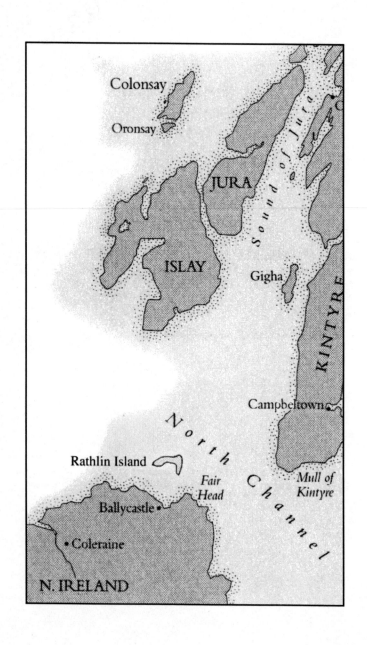

Chapter

1

Dawson pulled back the net curtain in one of the three upstairs rooms in Tony McHugh's guesthouse and glanced out across the bay to the jetty where the *St Iona,* a converted trawler, was wallowing in the swell.

Guillemots circled the harbour. Above, the gorse-clad hill stretching behind St Thomas' church was losing its final touch of yellow, leaving the stiff climb threadbare, brown and dead looking.

The long manor house that occupied most of the foreshore of the little bay looked greyer than usual as the sharp squalls of rain from the southeast trickled down its side like drops from a defective shower.

It was 11 o'clock in the morning, but heavy clouds already enveloped the stark cliffs of the island. Fair Head, the headland that dominated the main shoreline, three miles away, was barely visible in the gathering gloom.

Dawson turned to John (Jackie) Wilson, who rented the next door room. Jackie was stretched out, fully clad, on Dawson's large double bed with its old-fashioned mahogany headboard.

'Another great day,'

'Yup, probably be pitch dark by two o'clock,' said Jackie.

'Looks as if Gerry's taking the boat across, mind. They've winched the cows aboard and the others are already down there.'

'I'd better go now if I'm going. Hey-ho Jackie, I'm off to the bright lights of Ballycastle. Ah, may as well. There will be no diving this weekend, I'll be bound. The drill's the same, maestro. Siobhan's got the letter if I shouldn't return. But, of course, I will. See you, ace, don't do anything I wouldn't do.'

'Chance would be a fine thing,' said Jackie to a disappearing back. He got up from the bed. Apart from a desk that Dawson had especially brought over from the mainland, there was little else in the room. His papers and computer were locked away in the desk. Odd fellow, that Dawson. He'd taken the room indefinitely, but it told you nothing about him; gave no clue to his personality or purpose. He had left no personal signs around, no magazines or books, not even a shaving brush or a dressing gown.

Dawson seemed disciplined all right. Maybe he'd been in the army or prison, thought Jackie, as he watched him walk down the gravel road towards the harbour. They'd never fully discussed his past. He had a Canadian passport and accent, but the bright red hair and creamy complexion spoke of either Scotland or Ireland somewhere in his background.

As he wheeled round the road edged with dry stonewalls, only the top of his body could be seen and then in profile. Dawson would be around six foot four, with broad shoulders and a flat stomach. Jackie thought he was in good nick for a man who must be in his mid-forties.

Jackie assumed he was a Protestant. He had that tense, closed-face look Jackie identified with serious Protestants. There were slightly staring eyes. Yes, maybe he'd been in prison. He was very self-contained. Mind you, thought Jackie, you had to be self-contained on Rathlin, with its population of only 120 and just one pub.

The boomerang-shaped island lies three miles off the nearest point of the most northern coast of Northern Ireland and eight miles from the Mull of Kintyre in Scotland. The journey to the mainland takes an hour even in the finest weather. For the boat must veer away to the east towards Fair Head, then curve round into Ballycastle Bay, an eight-mile journey for a distance of just over three miles. In winter, if the wind is from the north, or west, or both, the stretch of water between Rathlin and the Antrim Coast becomes one of the most treacherous in the British Isles. Heavy seas are thrown up by a vicious tidal rip called the Scheorla. This runs from the southeast around Fair Head and contains an evil strip of water called the Coire, or Cauldron of Bredain, where so many curraghs have disappeared in the past. A queer spot indeed.

In the very depths of winter when even Gerry, the *St. Iona's* captain, cannot take his boat across, the island becomes a prison, cut off from the mainland for days. In emergencies, British army helicopters arrive and take people off.

This time Gerry was clearly going to chance it and Jackie watched the boat pull away and disappear into the mire, climbing the huge swells like a beetle and disappearing into the troughs.

He went out to try to phone Aideen in Dublin. Dear, tempestuous Aideen. She was passionate in everything; in her lovemaking, her friendships and her causes. He could picture her in the Fleet bar in D'Olier Street, opposite the *Irish Times* building. She would stamp her foot to make a point and toss her head causing the mane of blonde curls, with just a suggestion of the renowned Celtic red, to fly in all directions. Her voice speeded up as she spoke so that at the climax of making her case her speech would end in a bubbling gush.

She was beautiful in a very Irish way except the red in her hair had not resulted in the usual white creamy skin. Instead, she had the light brown skin - often associated with darker blondes - that meant any suggestion of sun would turn her into a freckled brown egg colour.

Aideen was tall with broad shoulders and large, high, firm breasts. She had long legs and a wide, full mouth. A small furtive smile would inevitably spread into a large sunny laugh that dominated her entire face. There was a retroussee nose and blue eyes, which somehow did have the cliched twinkling quality.

Maybe she would spread some day when she had the seven children or whatever they still had in modern Ireland. But she would bring the wains up as energetically as she pursued her journalism, her social work and her republicanism.

She was an explosion waiting to happen except, for all the emotional shrapnel packed inside her, there were various currents of kindness, charity and, as with so many Irish, sentimentality. The force of the explosion would be diffused and refracted, coming out like powder puffs. She was like one of those toy guns. They looked real enough, but on firing, a little flag popped out saying, 'I fooled yer, didn't I?'

Phoning Dublin from anywhere in the world became relatively simple once a modern digital switchboard was installed in the 1980s. But telephoning Dublin from Northern Ireland in general, and Rathlin Island in particular, is usually difficult. Northern Ireland is linked to the British system and despite all the political initiatives, cross-border telecommunication cooperation between Northern Ireland and the Republic has been neglected. The links north and south on the island of Ireland are not good. Jackie often thought he had had an easier time with the phones in Borneo where he had done his early fieldwork, long before he started his current study of inter-community relations between Protestants and Catholics on Rathlin.

Jackie pushed out into the swirl of wind and rain, reflecting that the force nine gale was not likely to help matters. Phones usually work less well in the rain. As he struggled to open the new, continental-style, glass booth of the only public telephone on the

10

island, he felt as if he were entering a lighthouse. The blurred light was a strange orange in the all-encompassing grey.

After several attempts, he got through to Aideen. Her effusive welcome quickly melted into false anger.

'Jackie, how are yer? Where the hell are yer?'

'I'm sorry darling. There's a gale. I can't get off the island,' he lied.

'Now don't you be codding me, Jackie Wilson. I know the boats are still sailing.' She lied. She had no way of knowing whether the boats were sailing.

'Tis Thursday now, you were s'posed to be here last evening.'

Jackie sighed to himself. He was attracted to Aideen's passion and life. But he was a cocooned soul and cut off by an English reserve so dense he found it difficult to examine the possibility that he might actually be in love with her. He just wanted to retire to his womb-like room, hole up with biscuits and coffee and consider the interviews he had carried out. He was somehow gripped by inertia. He didn't want to leave the island.

'Look, I've got a lot of interviews to get through.'

'Well, 'tis the parliamentary and press gallery annual dinner on Saturday. We've the Taoiseach at our table. I tink you should be there.'

'Aideen,' said Jackie, trying to sound sharp. 'Point one; do not go into your stage Irish accent with me. Point two; I do not want to eat dinner with your great prime minister. He will only accuse me of being a British spy.' The stage Irishness was something a lot of people like Aideen, who should have known better, slipped into when they met someone like Jackie. It was a sort of defence mechanism against his evident Britishness.

'In fact, in fact, for some curious reason, no one seems to think of you as a Brit spy. Must be your Irish origins.'

'I don't have Irish origins. Not the kind you've got in mind, anyway. I'm part of the Ascendancy, remember? Furthermore I do not need a brainwashing on Irish republicanism.'

'Oh, blah, Jackie Wilson, he's the best prime minister, we've had. He's no need to brainwash yer. Whatever, you should be pleased to sit down with our Taoiseach.'

'Oh, sock it, Aideen. I doubt whether there'll be a boat tomorrow. I'll try to catch it if there is. No promises mind.'

'Oh darling,' she pleaded, 'please try. I miss you so. Would yer ever phone me if you really can't make it. Otherwise, I'll see you in the Fleet Bar eight thirty Friday night. That's settled then.'

'Aideen, Aideen.' But she had gone.

Jackie buttoned up his jacket and pushed out into the gloom. He'd go to his room and think about things. There were too many loose ends to his work. He'd not done enough reading. He needed to talk to more people in depth. He was also, although he barely knew why, apprehensive about going to Dublin.

Lost in thought, he almost bumped into Siobhan, who emerged from the mists like a spirit.

'Got to phone the doctor, Mairead's near her time,' she mumbled, then hurried on.

*

The boat wallowed towards the jetty to the right of Ballycastle Bay, at the very tip of Northern Ireland. Even inside the new harbour wall, the sea was high.

Figures in bright yellow oilskins crept along the jetty with ropes tightened round their waists and the other end tied to the bollards on the shore. The tall mast at the end of the bare landing jetty had fallen over and the backing wall towards the end was broken from a previous storm like some huge giant with his teeth punched out.

Gerry looked as if he was turning in too sharply. The engines were having a minimum effect against the swell but he dare not cut them, since the *Iona* would then be lifted and thrown haphazardly against the jetty.

It had been an arduous journey. At times the bow had plunged so far into the seething foam that the engine's propeller came clear out of the water and the Iona skidded across the water. Gerry pulled the boat out of the skids with sharp movements of the wheel to port and starboard. Now that the boat was in the lee of the jetty, it was the stern that was taking a pounding. It was as if old mother sea, knowing that the *Iona* was about to escape her clutches, was making one last frenzied effort to claim her. The waves, like huge steaming sheets of molten green, crashed down on the stern. The danger was that, if the waves came in too quick succession, the Iona would not right herself. The effect would be of a huge weight holding the stern under and she would founder.

The four other men were crammed tightly in the wheelhouse with Gerry. Although divers, they were not seafaring men like him. They were used to the calm depths, not the violent surfaces. They had stood silently throughout the journey, bracing themselves with their legs and arms against the windows and walls. As Gerry, his face leathery despite his youth, stared into the mist his concentration was almost tangible. He neared the jetty and threw the boat hard to starboard. Too hard, Dawson thought. Gerry said nothing. He turned and looked quickly at the other men. Their faces were red, raw and strained. He had calculated that one wave would pull him round and that the next one would push him into the jetty.

'Two of you rope up, we need the bow and stern ropes thrown ashore, quick, bow first.'

The *Iona* took a sudden surge forward but then a wave sucked the bow into its jaws, not too far though. Gerry cut the engines, held the wheel on its starboard tack and waited for the next blast from the waves. The boat began to come around when another wave lifted it and slammed it flat alongside the jetty. He'd put lots of fenders out, but there was still a sickening thud as the boat collided with the wall and scratched up and down with the heaving of the swell.

Gerry left the wheelhouse and pushed past the men, who were roping up: 'I'll do the bow. One of youse throw the stern rope after I've tied up.'

He slithered forward and grabbed a rail. Then, with one arm round the mast, he threw the bow rope with his free hand to the jetty, where an arm reached out and caught it. Quickly it was wrapped round the bollard and made fast.

Gerry crawled back to the wheelhouse. 'Quick now, make the stern fast.' He loosed the coil and, peeking over the side as if in a trench, hurled the rope up. It found its mark, though. Someone scurried around, picked up the rope and made the stern fast.

The boat fidgeted violently against the wall. 'Youse all get ashore,' said Gerry, ' I'll stay with the boat a while, but we'll not take cows off tonight.' Poor cows, thought Dawson, wonder what state they'll be in in the morning. Still, it was better than being on the open sea.

One by one, the men, clutching their bags, slowly climbed the ladder. Then, grabbing the ropes, they inched along the jetty, bent over like beetles. The four men emerged on the shore. As they straightened and stretched, the tension rolled off them like water off their sou'westers. It was still blowing fiercely but the men started to come back to life. As their fear unfroze, they started to talk quickly and volubly to one another.

'Right, let's go to the Harbour Bar. We'll not make Belfast tonight. We'd better stay at the guesthouse there, or the hotel.

'Aye, but we'll take a wee dram first,' they chattered.

'I'll be with you now,' said Dawson. 'I've to make a wee telephone call first. I'll walk along to the boxes there.' Dawson turned left towards the telephone booths standing out like beacons along the strand.

The Harbour Bar was a low, two-storey building, directly across the road from the jetty. The frontage was of cut glass, half-frosted so that children could not see in. Cut into it, in an ornate pattern, were the words Bushmills Whiskey. The Bar was on a hill, so the little wall beneath the glass was three feet high at one end and only two feet high at the other. The words, Harbour Bar, in blue along a thin strip on the top of the window, seem to slope up the hill. From the outside the building looked like a two-up, two-down, but it did go back a long way. Either side were private houses, their curtains tightly drawn. Further along were the Atlantic Guest House, the Marine Hotel, a fish-and-chip shop with a mini-amusement arcade, then a supermarket.

Inside, like so many dozens of pubs in Ulster, it was ordinary and lacking in style of any kind. There was a long, red Formica-topped counter interspersed with black painted grills going up to the low ceiling. One of the grills had plastic flowers climbing up it. On the bar, there was an artificial pineapple for ice-cubes and behind sat glass shelves against a mirror. There were rows of bottles on the shelves, Jameson's Whiskey, Blackbush, Bushmills, Cork gin, Gordons gin. On the right, as you went in, was another mirror, this one with a picture of a beautiful girl with a large chest, drinking orange juice. The broad grin on her face testified to the qualities and revitalising powers of this particular brand of juice.

Beneath this mirror was a wall bench, usually occupied during the day by old men in exhausted clothes, with their pints of stout and little tots of Bushmills. The young unemployed of the town preferred to drink elsewhere where they could while away the long days playing pool. At the end, next to the back door, which led to the one grubby toilet, was a large poster of Canada showing waterfalls and mountains with spring flowers. Why it should be in a small hostelry in the Protestant town of Ballycastle, Northern Ireland, is a mystery, lest it be for purposes of giving space to the room. The pub was run by the McWilliams, a childless couple in their fifties. Bill was invariably to be found in a white shirt, greying through age, with a red tie and threadbare suit with shiny elbows. Ginty, his waspish wife, was usually to be seen in a flower-patterned, wrap-round overall like a pinafore, tied around her middle. Her hair was often in curlers under a scarf knotted just above her forehead, as in the pictures of plucky wives in the Second World War. She always seemed to have a cigarette hanging from her mouth, and always wore lots of make-up, particularly rouge.

Dawson, who was a regular, didn't think that he'd ever seen her without her curlers. He wondered about the relativities of glamour values, which could combine curlers with the laborious, or perhaps not so laborious, application of make-up. He also wondered what her wispy hair must be like out of curlers. But he did not wonder about silent Billy and sad Ginty that much. They were a mediocre couple in a mediocre bar in a little town, right at the top of Northern Ireland. He found Ballycastle entirely forgettable, save that it was relieved by the sweeping white strand and the views of Rathlin. The south coast of the island consists of a squat range of white cliffs, only 200 feet high. They are peculiarly white and when the sun catches the blue sound in flood, Rathlin can exert a powerful and frightening influence on the beholder.

The three men filed into the Harbour Bar. As they did so, they were observed by a dark-haired young man called Kieran, sitting in the front seat of a car, parked, with its lights off, below the crest of the hill up from the pub. He stubbed out the cigarette he had been nervously puffing and said to the girl in the driving seat of the midnight blue Cortina,

'There they are, let's go.'

'I've seen them wid me own eyes, you eejit.'

'Okay, okay.'

He pulled on a black balaclava with slits for the eyes and mouth, then reached inside his German combat parka jacket and pulled out his 9mm Browning pistol. He laid it on his lap and pulled on the second glove with his teeth. Then, with his left hand, he reached into his pocket and pulled out a silencer, which he screwed on to the Browning.

In the back, Patrick pulled the M16 armalite out of a special golf bag and quietly stroked the barrel. The sensation sent a frisson through him. The only noise was Patrick chewing gum, as if keeping time.

He was a cool one, thought Kieran. Jesus, he said inwardly to himself, an angry frump of a young girl beside me and a feckin psychopath behind.

Kieran, though senior, thought his nerves were beginning to go. Why start all this after so long a gap, when it was supposed to be over? Why him? It was all political work from now on, they had told him. This was a one-off. They really needed to know about these guys from Rathlin. But what a risk they had taken, sitting waiting for forty minutes like chickens trussed for the plucking.

'I thought she said there were four of them.'

'Yeah, well there's only three of 'em gone into the bar right enough,' Patrick said.

'Okay, okay, well maybe one of them didn't make it, his luck,' Kieran added, not realising that, while the curve of the hill towards the sea had allowed a view of the Harbour Bar, it didn't give a clear sighting of the strand where Dawson had peeled off to phone.

'Just the sidelights now, Dolores. You ready, Patrick? Holding three of them is not going to be easy, but don't forget, we just want the papers. No need for rough stuff, no need for any shooting.'

'Uh ha,' chump chump chump.

As the three men from the boat pushed into the bar, a slab

of light shot out into the mire, now thickening into a dark early evening.

'Sure, boys, I never would ha thought I'd be serving ye on a day like this. I'm taken that Gerry wud bring the boat over on such a day. It's the devil's weather, so it is,' said Ginty.

'What'll I get ye. Will I make hot whiskys? Thanks be to God youse are all safe,' she went on.

The three men, the tension rolling off them like clouds disappearing over a hill, started disrobing, putting their oilskins on the long bench. This revealed their shoulder holsters. One took his gun and shoulder holster off and laid it on the bench, another was flinging his arms around himself. The third also unbuckled his gun and harness to lay it down and make himself more comfortable. Two old men sat silently at a table in the corner, near the door.

The two balaclaved gunmen burst in with a crash as the door flew back. Kieran moved to the right of the room by the bench. He automatically went into a crouched position, two hands on his Browning, right eye along the sight. Patrick went along to the left, slightly behind Kieran. He knelt down. If anyone was stupid enough to interfere he'd get the full blast of his armalite, on automatic.

'Now freeze! Youse old ones on the floor.'

'On the feckin' floor,' Kieran's voice rose.

'Youse three, turn around. Up against the wall. Feckin move,' he yelled.

'One piece outta any a youse and youse are dead men,' he said.

Kieran edged forward. Holding his gun in his right hand, he padded the first man and turfed out his wallet from his jacket. He threw out papers from the second man and a wallet from the third man. They had their legs apart with their arms outstretched against the wall. Kieran fell to his knees, lay the gun down and began to sort through the wallets and papers. He put the envelope from the first man into his back pocket.

18

Ginty dropped the bottle of Bushmills she was holding and began to scream: shrill, hysterical, uncontrolled wails. Patrick sprang towards her.

'Shut up, you feckin' whore mother.' He tried to hit her with the butt of his rifle, but couldn't reach far enough across the bar.

One of the three turned around and tried to grab Kieran's gun on the ground. Kieran, frozen, looked up at Patrick, his eyes like a little puppy's, begging and pleading.

Patrick turned round and, at very close range, fired a burst at the first man, now on his knees with Kieran's gun. It tore his chest apart as the Browning flew across the room. He almost fell on Kieran and quickly blood began to run from under him, like dog's pee.

The other two men had turned around. Patrick sprayed his gun at them. They fell down, like sacks of potatoes, crumpled and bloody. So small was the bar, the sound was deafening. Ginty was still screaming. Patrick wheeled to his left, but Billy had pulled her down behind the bar. He blasted the bottles and mirror in a mega-decibel cacophony of breaking glass and crashing bottles. Kieran, still frozen, the three bodies inches from him and the blood now beginning to stain his trouser knees, looked dumbly up at Patrick.

'Get the gun, you eejit,' Patrick screamed at Kieran, who picked up the gun in a daze. Patrick grabbed him by the scruff of the neck, dragged him towards the door and pushed him at it. Patrick backed up, holding the rifle in one hand. He used the other to open the door and dashed through. Kieran scrambled into the front of the car. Patrick threw his rifle into the back and dived in after it.

'Get moving, Dolores. Move!' Kieran screamed. Sweating profusely now, he whipped off his balaclava and yelled at Patrick, 'A right bolex you made of that. Three men dead and we got away wid nuttin.'

'You'll not tell me I made a bolex. D'ye think they'd be waiting quietly in a queue to get plugged in the back of the head while you read their fanmail. They'd have jumped you, sure enough, had I not been there. I saw you, McGuinness. Youse have gone soft. Youse are no longer up to it.'

Dawson emerged from the telephone booth, having failed to make his connection with Whiteabbey. It was then that he thought he heard shots, but he couldn't be sure, because of the rampant wind and rain. His heart started to quicken as he saw in the half-dark a ray of light shoot out from what could only be the Harbour Bar. Seconds later he saw the stab of headlights and heard the screech of a car from the jetty area. His stomach tightened as if an invisible hand had grabbed it. He reached inside his coat and pulled out a snubbed-nosed Biretta. Useless at this range, he thought. He let off two shots at the car which was speeding towards him.

'Kieran, to the left,' yelled Dolores, seeing the flash of light from the gun. Kieran, who was picking the already congealed blood off his denim jeans, jolted.

'On the feckin left,' she yelled again.

Kieran fumbled for his gun, dropped it, and tried to wind the window down. They were almost abreast of Dawson. He took aim.

'Dolores, would you ever slow down.'

'I can't. He'll get us.'

Kieran fired as best he could at the disappearing target. At the same time Dawson let off a shot, then turned round, took two giant paces and dived over the low stone wall lining the strand. He crashed his face, shoulder and side onto the rocks where they just began to give way to the sand. The car sped away.

'D'ye get him? Shall I turn back?' Dolores said.

'Nah, get outta here, the police will be here in no time.'

Dawson faded into unconsciousness as if in a dream. He dreamt of Canadian rivers and his wife Molly making a picnic. He rolled over into the sand and imagined he heard a screaming before blackness came.

Chapter

2

William Carstairs sat in his favourite chintz covered armchair in the study of his house just outside Whiteabbey, watching television alone. The house was a mock Tudor mansion with five bedrooms. In this case it was very mock indeed since Carstairs had built it himself barely 20 years earlier, in the 1980s.

It was set in three acres of immaculately tended gardens. The front lawns were always neatly cut. The hedges were manicured and shaped, and even the artificial ponds, where Carstairs had half-heartedly tried to breed carp, were regularly dredged and cleared of leaves.

The road, or corniche rather, where he lived was often called the Ulster garden route. It seemed to get what sun there was in Ulster. Many of Carstairs' neighbours had tried growing exotic plants; bananas, peaches, palm trees, frangipani, bougainvillea.

Carstairs himself had eschewed such niceties. The flowerbeds consisted of safe reliable plants like hydrangeas, rhododendrons and geraniums. There were roses around the house and some clematis. In the spring there were daffodils, snowdrops and bluebells. It was all very well ordered, like its master.

The corniche along the Lough had become the new heartland of the Protestant middle classes of Belfast, who, at the explosion of violence in the ghettoes in the late 1960s and 1970s, had considered it prudent to up sticks and move from comfortable detached houses along the Malone Road in Belfast's suburbs and live just a little further out.

Down the road from Whiteabbey was the ancient fort city of Carrickfergus - especially dear to the Protestant heart because it was here that in 1690 William of Orange had landed prior to defeating Catholic King James II, and establishing the Protestant ascendancy over Ulster.

But 1690 was a long time ago and the Protestants felt constantly under threat. As a majority within Northern Ireland, but a minority within Ireland as a whole, they felt there was always someone trying to subjugate them - by stealth, by force, by threat, by persuasion, or by political skulduggery. Hence the symbols, rituals, marches and anniversaries to reassure themselves of their identity.

Thus, in pride of place above Carstairs' fire was the coat of arms of the Whiteabbey Orange Lodge, of which he was grand master. There was a picture of the Battle of the Boyne with King Billy on his white horse surrounded by orange and purple sashes. On another wall was a print of Oliver Cromwell, by a Dutch artist. There was a portrait of Sir Edward Carson, the old Protestant leader, with his unsmiling hatchet face above his polka-dot bow tie.

So, surrounded by his symbols and identity badges, in this Protestant sanctuary, within a fortress, within an empire, William Frederick Castlemain Carstairs, self-proclaimed leader of the Ulster Protestants, patted his black retriever Maxwell on the head, and settled down to watch one of the most important news broadcasts of his life.

Mrs Elizabeth Vernon, the Secretary of State for Northern Ireland in the UK coalition government, known universally as Betty, sat composed as the nervous young interviewer, Nicholas Tweesdale ruffled his papers, put his hands together and began.

'Mrs Vernon, Mrs Vernon,' he repeated.

Betty Vernon looked at Tweesdale like a headmistress who was dealing with a not particularly bright pupil who exasperatingly refused to own up to some misdemeanour.

At this point, before they had actually got going, there was a knock on the door of Carstairs' study. Billy Carstairs, eldest son of the house at 21, put his ginger mop around the door.

'Hello Daddy. May I join you?'

'Of course, Billy. Would you care for some tea? You'll need a cup.'

'It's herself, Mrs Vernon on the television?' asked Billy.

'Aye, it's her right enough. About to talk her usual nonsense, I suspect,' Carstairs replied.

'It seems inconceivable that she is about to announce a troops pullout,' Billy sighed.

Betty Vernon, at 45, had only recently become Northern Ireland secretary. She was one of the most senior Liberal Democrats in the so-called Lab/Lib pact, which had succeeded Labour's second term. Despite a huge majority in the 2001 general election, Labour could only now continue in power with the support of the Liberal Democrats. The price of this support was cabinet seats. Like all Liberal Democrats, Betty Vernon had never held government office before. Until she had gained senior status within the Lib Dems she had been a kind of bedraggled throwback to the 1950s, a duffled-coated, college-scarfed all-purpose protester.

But she was clearly now a force to be reckoned with. She was not unattractive. There were piercing green eyes set in an oval face, with high cheekbones, so she stared, or more often, scowled out from a slightly Tibetan face. She did have a lovely smile. She also had a deep throaty laugh, which suggested an enjoyment of, or at least a sympathy with, the seamier side of life.

She had, in fact, been more or less happily married for 18 years to Tim, a former journalist who became a full-time campaigner - Survival International, Friends of the Earth, Greenpeace. You name it, he was in there.

They lived in a small house at the wrong end of Ladbroke Grove, bought with a loan from her mother, which would probably never be paid back. Her two teenage sons went to Holland Park Comprehensive School.

She had, Carstairs thought, considerably smartened up her act in the past year. Her hair had been well cut, in a bob. It shone with health. She wore a pink blouse underneath a blue suit with a brooch and a single string of pearls.

Betty Vernon looked very composed as she waited for the questions.

'Mrs Vernon,' Tweesdale said for the third time. 'I know you have come here to answer questions about your historic announcement on Northern Ireland, but can I first ask you about the new oil tax which has been outlined in the Financial Times today.'

'Answering questions outside my field will probably get me into trouble, but we don't have the spin machine any more, so fire away.'

'Is this some kind of creeping nationalisation or is it some form of stealth tax?' Tweesdale went on.

'No, of course it's not true we are going to nationalise oil, nobody has nationalised anything for decades. No, it is not a stealth tax either. Look, these assets, this income, what is left of it after the oil companies take their cut, was just squandered by the Conservatives.'

'Ah yes, but that reflected the decline in oil production as the North Sea reached maturity,' put in Tweesdale.

Betty Vernon came straight back: 'What do you mean? It is not true that output is falling. It has gone back up. Incremental fields have been found in the North Sea. And we have these exciting finds west of Shetlands. Oil is an important resource and it is madness to give it away cheaply.'

'Ah, but you see,' said Tweesdale, (the 'but you see' showed that he was getting rattled) 'oil men say that without the abolition of royalties and claw backs, the West of Shetlands oil would never have been found. The cost of exploration would have been too high. This is what happened in Ireland.'

Betty Vernon put on a little smile and came back,
'Well Ireland doesn't have much oil. It needs to find some big fields by encouraging exploration. We do have oil. We need to find ways of increasing Government reserves.'

'So there will be an extra tax? Won't this further deter companies from exploration?'

'Mr Tweesdale.' Betty Vernon gave a heavy sigh of

exasperation. 'You have already asked me that question and I have answered it. New exploration will be exempt. Now can we move on please.'

'Can I now turn to the subject of Northern Ireland?' said Tweesdale, 'You have announced you are going to start pulling out the remaining British troops,'

'Yes and no, we are going to withdraw the 11,000 mainland British troops, but we are leaving the Royal Irish Regiment of nearly 7,000 men. There are also the 15,000 members of the Police Force of Northern Ireland, which used to be the Royal Ulster Constabulary. The law and order situation is under control. Since the Provisional IRA declared the second ceasefire in 1997 there has been no major violence for years. Northern Ireland has not known such a period of calm in 30 years. In particular, neither the Republic or the Provisional IRA have recanted on either the agreement, or the ceasefire. The Unionists have been given an assurance that the link with Britain will not be broken. The one stumbling block is Sinn Fein who, having sat in the Assembly all these years, have now withdrawn until the British troops are pulled out, so the Assembly cannot reconvene until the troops leave. Sinn Fein has always said it wanted the demilitarisation of Ireland and has dropped its demand for a united Ireland. Once the troops are gone, it has promised to participate again in the democratic process. It has in the past been as good as its word; I repeat, the violence, at least from the Provisional IRA, has stopped.'

'Ok,' came back Tweesdale, 'What about the suggestion that the Sinn Fein and the Republic are merely playing for time? Once the British troops are gone, they will revert to violence and press for a united Ireland. This will be much easier without British troops.'

'Mr Tweesdale, if you think about it, that scenario is hardly likely. In fact, it is most unlikely.' She was again in the exasperated schoolmarm mode.

'I repeat, Sinn Fein has renounced the claim for a United Ireland, at least for the foreseeable future. It has agreed to re-enter the Assembly, if the troops are removed. It has, in other words, achieved all its immediate aims by peaceful means. Why on earth should it resort to violence at this stage? The Irish Republic has been clamouring for a say in the affairs of Northern Ireland for over 70 years. Now, it has got its say. It has also dropped its claim for a united Ireland'

'Alright,' Tweesdale continued. 'But what about the Protestants?'

'What about the Protestants?' Betty Vernon replied with rising anger, throwing the question back.

Tweesdale said, 'Well the Protestants are hardly likely to take all this lying down. They do have a history of effective resistance when under pressure.'

A really heavy sigh from Betty Vernon this time, 'I think I have already answered this question. Yes, I do expect the Protestants to react equably. They have been given assurances that the Union is safe. That is what they require. All the main Protestant leaders have signed the second Ulster Agreement. They have all agreed to sit in the Ulster assembly.'

Tweesdale would not give up. 'What about Scotland?' he shot at her. 'There is some talk businessmen in Scotland are prepared to support an armed rebellion as a precursor to declaring an independent Ulster.'

'It is precisely that, talk,' Betty Vernon replied. 'Scotland is part of the United Kingdom, a devolved part. There are certainly affinities between Scotland and the Protestant population of Ulster but there isn't any groundswell or stomach in Scotland, or anywhere else, for anything as stupid as backing an armed rebellion.'

In the study these last words were drowned out as Carstairs jumped to his feet, his face reddening, his finger wagging at the television.

'You stupid wee woman. I'll show you what the Ulster people are made of. We will never be sold down the river to Rome.'

Billy responded, 'Now calm yourself, Daddy, she's bluffing, she'll never pull the troops out.'

Officially William Carstairs wanted the troops to stay. Secretly it was the last thing in the world he wanted. What she had been saying was music to his ears. Please God, this woman goes ahead with her plans, he said to himself. He did not let Billy see the smile creeping across his face. When he sat down again it was to hear Tweesdale winding up.

'Mrs Vernon thank you very much.' He gazed into the camera and looking very serious said: 'That extended interview with the Right Honourable Mrs Elizabeth Vernon, Northern Ireland Secretary, was recorded earlier today.'

'Before reading the main points of the news again, we have just received a late newsflash.

'Three men believed to be members of the Police Force of Northern Ireland are reported to have been killed in the Northern Ireland town of Ballycastle. A fourth is thought to be seriously wounded. Hooded gunmen shot the three men in a bar. The names of the deceased are not being released until relatives have been informed. No one has claimed responsibility for the killings. But it is being assumed that it is the work of a nationalist group. This would be the first such major terrorist act since the Provisional IRA announced their indefinite ceasefire....'

Carstairs and his son froze and stared at one another.

'Daddy, d'you think....'

'I don't know, Billy. Go rustle up Joe and the Rover, quickly now.'

Carstairs picked up the telephone and dialled the BBC. 'Give me the Controller, it's William Carstairs speaking.'

An elderly female voice answered. 'I'm afraid the Controller is not here. I'll put you through to someone. Who did you say you were?'

'Carstairs, Carstairs,' he yelled.

Another female voice answered, this time with an English accent. 'I gather you want Mr Broadbent, the Controller. He does not normally take calls from the general public. In any event...'

Carstairs exploded. 'My good lady, I am not the general public. I am William Carstairs, leader of the New Ulster Unionist party. Mr Broadbent is known to me and I to him. This is a matter of great urgency. Put me through, please.'

Her hand went over the receiver and, after what seemed an age, a plummy young voice answered. 'William, it's Nigel. To what do I owe this unexpected pleasure.'

'I want the names of the men killed by the IRA butchers in Ballycastle.'

'Actually, I don't know. I, or rather we, don't even know whether it was the IRA.'

'If you are holding out on me, Broadbent........'

'Now William, please be calm.' Nigel Broadbent was cut off in mid-stream as the phone was slammed down. Carstairs then immediately dialled the Police headquarters outside Belfast.

'It is William Carstairs speaking. I would like to talk to the Chief Constable please.' They would know who he was at the Police Force of Northern Ireland headquarters all right, no messing there.

'I'm afraid the Chief Constable is not here. Can anyone else help, Mr Carstairs?

'Thank you, is Commander MacWhinny there please?'

A little pause, and a thick Ulster accent said,

'Commander John MacWhinny speaking.'

'Mac, it's William. What the hell happened in Ballycastle? Are these men who I think they are? Is Dawson one of them?'

'I don't rightly know, William. We are still waiting for more details. We should know in a wee minute. They came off the Rathlin boat and were Police divers, so I imagine Dawson is one of them, yes.'

'Hell and damnation,' said Carstairs. 'I better get up there. Thanks Mac.'

'You're welcome,' replied MacWhinny, 'Take care now.'

Carstairs opened the study door, grabbed a coat and shouted upstairs. 'Mary, we'll be going out. If Philip or anyone from the party phones, I've gone to Ballycastle. If any press phones, you don't know where I am, okay. Oh be careful about the mobile as usual, they are not secure.'

Mary, in her usual unquestioning way, yelled back down from upstairs, 'Okay. God speed, William.'

Chapter

3

The black highly polished 3-litre Rover purred along looking very official.

'D'you mind if I play some music, Daddy?'

'I'd rather you didn't, Billy. I want to think,' Carstairs replied. 'That alright with you, Joe?'

'Sure enough, Mr Carstairs,' Joe replied nonchalantly.

Joe McMichael, six foot four inches and 205 pounds of mostly muscle, was Carstairs' minder. A former RUC man, he had joined the Ulster Volunteer Force (UVF) when he became disillusioned with the Royal Ulster Constabulary over a lack of firmness in dealing with the IRA. He had an unblinking faith in Carstairs. In return Carstairs was polite and solicitous of Joe.

Carstairs brooded away silently to himself. The night was dark. The roads in Ulster, even after years of the second IRA ceasefire, were still empty at night.

He said, absently minded, 'Better go inland to Ballymena, Joe, the coast might be taking the weather.' Then he returned to his thoughts. If that Dawson has bought it, everything could be ruined. Why now? Why had the IRA returned to violence now? Maybe it wasn't the IRA. Why Dawson? Why now? Who told them? How'd they know he'd be on that boat? His mind raced. Hell, there's no use worrying until there are some facts to go on. He had the ability to compartmentalise his thinking and shut out anything which might upset him. It was a useful trait to have in politics.

Carstairs had a personal agenda. He couldn't believe that the other Loyalist leaders did not have some inkling of what he planned. Anyone, yes, anyone, who thought the people of Ulster no longer had the wherewithal to resist something they did not want, was fooling himself. As Mrs Vernon correctly pointed out, the Protestants had shown what they could do by closing ranks when pushed. They could do it again.

Carstairs had carefully prepared and trained a force of well over 20,000 men, based on the Royal Irish Regiment. They would be the recipients of all the equipment left behind by the departing British army: armoured cars, dozens of Scorpion light tanks and the latest Spartan and Saxon Armoured Personnel Carriers (APCs). There were surface-to-air missiles in the form of Blowpipe, Javelin and Starburst, which could deal with anything the Irish could throw at Carstairs' forces from the air, as well as helicopters.

Not everything would be left behind by a British government anxious to be gone completely from the province. But enough would. What was lacking could be bought on the open market, providing Dawson had done his job properly.

The IRA leaders might imagine that, with the last of the British troops gone, they could gear up and take over the place by force. That seemed unlikely. It would take time to gear up. Anyway, what would be the point? They had spent years preparing the peaceful route; they could hardly go back to violence now. Alternatively, the IRA might be hoping the Irish would do the job for them. They might be in cahoots with the Republic for a swift military takeover. That seemed more possible. But what did the Irish Government have to throw into the game? Not very much.

The Irish army? Well there were 11,000 of them and 16,000 reservists. They were fairly well kitted out. But more than a third of the Irish army was serving in United Nations roles at any given time. They were outgunned and outmanned by Carstairs' putative force.

The Police Force of Northern Ireland, the old RUC? Once upon a time they may have acted in a non-partisan way. There were still 11,000 of them, not 15,000 as the Vernon woman had said. But attempts to integrate them with the Gardai and to have local policing had severely disaffected the almost totally Protestant police. Carstairs was not head of the Police Federation for nothing. He had done a lot of work on the Police Force, particularly their leaders. No, the Police Force would see where its duty lay when it came to it.

Mrs Vernon was right, according to her own lights. The last remaining troops had to go or there was a risk the laboriously constructed political arrangements would collapse. But the threat to withdraw was all grist to Carstairs' mill. With the troops gone, Carstairs would virtually have a free hand. The Provos might have their suspicions about the RIR, just like the other Protestants leaders and for that matter the intelligence services of both Britain and Ireland, but nothing could be proved.

Among his other meticulous preparations, Carstairs had managed to square off MI5, the dominant British intelligence service on the ground. With IRA activity on the wane after the second ceasefire, the agency was targeted more against the Protestants. There were the age-old fears they would arm and mobilise and try and bring down the Assembly.

Carstairs, by an ingenious campaign of disinformation, managed to keep MI5 largely in the dark about his plans. He made full use of his contacts within the Police Special Branch. The Special Branch was unhappy they had come to play second fiddle to MI5, and even unhappier that the police were about to be melded together with the Gardai. As a result MI5 knew nothing about prospective arms purchases and nothing about what was going on in Rathlin.

Carstairs was also absolutely sure there had been no penetration of the RIR. Over a period of time he had won over the key officers and they had let it be known that they were considering ways of safeguarding the future. They filtered down the word of a possible rebellion. Protestant soldiers, like Protestant policemen, were not about to be combined with the Irish army at any price. The Algerian option, as Carstairs liked to call it; a revolt of the military against a settlement imposed on the settlers.

No, everyone might suspect, a lot of people might talk, but nothing could be proved. No-one, save some colonels and his very closest associates, knew the extent of his plans; and this was a tiny leak-proof group.

Carstairs' thoughts came back to Dawson just as the Rover entered Ballycastle and passed the Harbour Bar. There was a heavily armed policeman standing outside and a little clutch of onlookers, even at the late hour.

'Joe, drive on up to the Dalriada hospital at the top of the town. That's where the action will be.'

The Dalriada hospital, set on the brow of a hill above Ballycastle, was a grand Victorian building which looked like a colonial mansion that had been converted into a nursing home. It was, in fact, a working hospital dealing in everything from corpses to emergencies. Like so many of the hospitals in Northern Ireland, it had a very good reputation.

Its grounds were spacious. As the Rover passed through the wrought iron gates and rounded the circular flowerbed, which separated the gates from the main building, Carstairs was brought back to the present by a sighting of the bevy of reporters mingling with at least a dozen policemen. There were two big vans, with BBC TV and Ulster Television written on them, lots of cables connecting the vans to the familiar paraphernalia of boom microphones, and arc lights. Reporters were talking into mobile phones.

Carstairs quickly collected his thoughts.

'Joe, you better help me through this throng, if you would. Billy, would you drive the car off over there somewhere. We'll be out as soon as possible. I'll take the mobile with me.'

'Right you are,' they said simultaneously.

As Carstairs alighted, the arc lights went on and the reporters swarmed around him, blocking his path to the few stairs.

'Mr Carstairs, Mr Carstairs, BBC TV.'

'Mr Carstairs, Mr Carstairs, the Belfast Telegraph.'

It was Jenny from Ulster TV who caught his eye.

'Mr Carstairs, have you any comment to make on the shootings? Dr Paisley has condemned the killings as the work of the IRA.'

Playing for time, Carstairs looked at his watch: fifteen to midnight.

'You're up late, ladies and gentlemen. I really do not have any more information than you do. That is why I am here. I am, as you know, Chairman of the Police Federation. Now if you would let me through, I'll try and find out what is going on.'

The crowd parted with Joe clearing the way. A question was shot at his back: 'What effect do you think this will have on the peace process?' He gave no answer.

At the top of the steps, Carstairs was met by a second cordon of green- uniformed policemen blocking the entrance to the hospital. Behind the cordon the lights of the hospital burned brightly.

'Good evening, officer, what is going on?'

'Your guess is as good as mine. Who is asking?'

'William Carstairs,' he replied in a tone, which said: I will brook no nonsense.

'Oh yes, that's all right, Mr Carstairs. Didn't recognise you there for a minute in the gloom. You go in and talk to Commander Herriott, first off. He is in that wee room there to the left, marked Reception.'

'Commander, good evening. What is the position?'

Commander Herriott looked up distractedly from his papers.

'Oh, Mr Carstairs, hello. I can't tell you much more. There are three men dead and one badly hurt. We've only been able to contact two of the families. We'll probably not be able to release any more details until the morning.'

'But which one is alive?'

'Fellow called Dawson. Not a policeman. According to his papers, he is a marine engineer, whatever that is. Can't tell you a lot else.'

Carstairs breathed a heavy sigh of relief and hoped Herriott didn't notice. He didn't. He just went on, 'We've managed to contact the families of MacTeel and Wilson but we can't get hold of the Ross family. Now you'd like to see the bodies?'

'Er, later, I wouldn't mind a word with Dawson.'

'Aha, you'll be lucky. He's in a coma. I doubt the doctors will let you see him anyroad. Probably best come back in the morning.'

'It's rather important.'

'Well it is also irregular, even for you, sir. He's not a member of the police and if he comes round, we'll need a statement.'

'I really need to see this man,' Carstairs persisted.

'If you must, you'd better go and see Doctor Quinn on the first floor in Emergency. I warn you now, you'll get a frosty reception.'

'You stay here, Joe,' barked Carstairs as he walked up the stairs to the first floor. An angry night sister met him, like some lioness protecting her cubs.

'Yes, can I help you? It is the middle of the night. What do you want?'

'I'd like to see Dr Quinn, please.'

'I am not sure Dr Quinn will want to see you.'

'It's about Mr Dawson.'

Sensing she was not going to get rid of Carstairs easily, she said: 'Wait here, I'll go and see whether he'll talk to you.' She disappeared down the long corridor. After what seemed an interminable wait, she came back and, with a surly look on her face, told Carstairs: 'Doctor Quinn says it will have to wait until the morning.'

'I am afraid, good lady, my business cannot wait until the morning.' He pushed past her and strode off down the corridor.

She ran along after him trying to grab at his arm. 'You cannot behave like this.'

The commotion saw Dr Quinn emerge from his room. A youngish man with thick dark hair, he wore a doctor's white coat, which was open, and a stethoscope around his neck. 'What the hell is going on?'

'I'm sorry doctor, I tried to stop him, he insisted on talking to you.'

Dr Quinn looked at Carstairs. Partly relieved he was not going to have to deal with some midnight drunk, but, also sensing, like the police officer downstairs, that this man wasn't going to be stopped, he said, 'Alright sister, I'll deal with this. You'd better come in. What did you say your name was?'

'I didn't. But it is William Carstairs.'

'Thought you were familiar. Thought this was Paisley's constituency. What are you doing here?'

The minute he said Paisley, rather than Dr Paisley, or the Reverend Ian Paisley, Carstairs instinctively knew he was dealing with a Taig and it was going to be difficult. He tried a soft approach.

'I am really sorry to bother you this late at night. But I am Chairman of the Police Federation. I am trying to establish what went on. I gather one of the men, Alan Dawson, is still alive.'

'Yes, Dawson is alive. That is the good news. The bad news is that he is in what we describe as a concussive coma. There is no telling when he will come round. It could be days, weeks, or never. Look, I really do not see what you are doing here this time of night telling me you are Chairman of the Police Federation. I have worked sixty hours in the past seven days. I am tired and hungry. I really think you should come back in the morning.'

'Did he say anything?' Carstairs persisted.

'No, he bloody well didn't say anything. Now if you don't mind. I need some sleep.'

One last try, thought Carstairs. 'Look I realise you are exhausted. But it's very important to me. Did he say anything at all?'

Dr Quinn gave a heavy sigh. He put his hands to his head and pushed his fingers through his hair.

He stared hard for a moment before speaking: 'Well, he did mumble a few words when he was first brought in. He mentioned your name, actually. He said "Report, Wilson, Carstairs". He repeated it several times. I don't know what it means, do you?'

Carstairs, looking perplexed, said thoughtfully: 'No, no I don't. Thank you for your time, Dr Quinn.'

He left the room and wandered distractedly down the corridor. What the hell did it mean? Did it mean that Dawson had somehow got the vital report through to Wilson for onpassing to him, thinking possibly Wilson would see Carstairs before he did? Oh hell, what a mess. Carstairs got to the ground floor and sat on a chair in the corridor. He took out his mobile phone and switched on to "retrieve" to listen to his messages.

'Could Mr Carstairs ring the *Today* programme in London on ...Could Mr Carstairs please ring BBC Television in Belfast....'

There were half a dozen of these requests for interviews. There was also a message from Philip Sherwood, his political secretary. 'William, all hell is breaking loose here. The entire press corps is after you. Please ring asap about how we proceed.'

'Ha, the entire press corps is here, by the look of things,' he said to no one in particular.

Finally there was the call he wanted. 'Hello William, this is Wilson. There are some developments of which you probably will not be aware of. I am hesitant to speak to you over an insecure line. It is important you contact me as soon as you can.'

Oh, thought Carstairs, my assumption must be correct. But why give the report to Wilson? Carstairs walked distractedly towards the door. Commander Herriott emerged from his office. 'Alright then, Mr Carstairs, would you like to see the bodies now?'

'Er, er, no, in the morning. Thank you now.'

Strange man, thought Herriott. Comes all this way and then does not want to see the bodies. Oh well.

Carstairs pushed out into the night. Again the arc lights, again the reporters closing in on him.

'I am afraid I have nothing further to add to what I said earlier. The names of the deceased will not be released until all the bereaved have been notified. The survivor is in a coma and cannot say anything. I will be making a statement in the morning. Goodnight and thank you.'

Carstairs walked over to the car. Billy and Joe came to meet him.

'Any calls, on your phone Billy?' Carstairs asked.

'There's a clutch of messages from the media. Philip rang. There was a message from a Mr Wilson saying could you call him. Oh, there was one other, could you ring Alexander MacPhee urgently in Aberdeen.'

'Oh really, yes okay.' Carstairs thought: that one is going to have to go on hold. 'Let's get booked in to the Marine Hotel.'

Outside the hotel, opposite the jetty where the *St Iona* was still tied up, Carstairs said, 'You two go ahead, I just want to phone.'

He walked down to the same public booth which Dawson

had used. He fiddled around for some change and dialled a number. He got an answering machine.

'You have reached the Wilson residence. I am afraid your call cannot be answered at the moment. But if you would like to leave a message after the tone, we'll get back to you as soon as possible. Thank you for calling.'

'Humpf, gone to bed,' Carstairs said out loud. 'Couldn't have been that important.'

Still, as he walked back to the hotel, something, he knew not what, was bothering him.

Chapter

4

Carstairs was not the only one jolted into action by the late night news flash. By midnight, telephones had rung, interviews had been given, statements had been prepared, all over the province. In Dublin, London and even Scotland, the wires were buzzing well into the night. Every party involved in Northern Ireland was in action, on the move.

In his Londonderry home, the new leader of the moderate Catholic Social Democratic and Labour Party sat huddled with his assistants. By one o'clock in the morning, he had already given an interview to the *Today* radio programme and spoken to the late-night radio bulletins. Having got dressed hastily - he had missed the news flash - he did spots for the next morning's other breakfast programmes.

The previous leader, John Hume, had been a major architect of the peace process. It was he who had been instrumental in internationalising the process through his contacts in the US and Europe. It was he who had originally opened talks with the IRA leaders. He had been involved in the politics of Northern Ireland right from the time when he took part in the first marches in 1968. He had received the credit for persuading the IRA to give up violence. He was feted in Washington, London and Dublin. He had won every accolade it was possible to win, including the Nobel Peace Prize.

Time was, when Sinn Fein was banned from appearing in the press and radio, John Hume was the main conduit for statements from Sinn Fein. But that time had passed. Sinn Fein now had their offices at Westminster, even though their MPs had not taken their seats in parliament. But Sinn Fein still could not be seen to be speaking directly for the IRA.

The IRA made no direct statement.

Gerry Adams, as President of Sinn Fein, made an announcement on behalf of the party. It was a fuzzy statement to the press saying the IRA had declared a cessation of violence, which he had no reason to believe had been broken. He had no knowledge of who was responsible for the killings in Ballycastle. Why did everyone automatically assume it was the IRA because it was policemen that were shot? Maybe loyalist gunmen were trying to destroy the peace process and keep the British troops in Northern Ireland, Adams implied.

This was all par for the course. Whenever there was any suggestion of nationalist violence, either street protests, or rogue raids on post offices, Adams and his chief lieutenant, Martin McGuinness, tried to turn the tables on the police. They claimed the street protesters were provoked, or that groups within the Police Force were undertaking secret acts of violence to undermine the nationalist community. It was all a Unionist plot to keep the troops in occupied Ireland, they routinely said.

But beneath the Adams bluster, there were always doubts. The distinction between the IRA and Sinn Fein was, as everyone knew, largely a myth. They were all part of one nationalist movement. But, for obvious operational reasons, it was convenient for Sinn Fein, a lawful political entity, to refer to the illegal IRA as a separate organisation.

It had been a long time since either McGuinness or Adams had been involved in military activities, although both had been heavily engaged with the IRA in the 1970s. Once Adams and McGuinness had themselves become convinced that a political course would more quickly rid Ireland of a British presence than continued violence, it had still taken them a very long time to persuade the hard-liners in the IRA to put away the guns.

The Downing Street declaration that Britain had no strategic or selfish interest in remaining in Ireland had been issued as far back as Christmas 1993. It had taken eight months for the political men to talk the hard men round, and declare the first ceasefire in August 1994. This had finally broken down in 1996. A second ceasefire had been declared and this had more or less held. The shootings in Ballycastle were the worse incident in years, although there had been some street violence and a few bank raids.

The ceasefires were very fragile. It was well known that factions within the IRA, particularly the brigades in South Tyrone and Armagh, had never reconciled themselves to the cessation of violence. The arms had never been completely decommissioned, and there was always the danger a small rump would return to the military campaign. The tail was in a position to wag the dog.

History had shown the IRA could divide at times of stress. The great split had come in the 1920s. Michael Collins had led the IRA faction which agreed to the treaty dividing Ireland. Eamon de Valera was the head of the faction which would not agree to partition. Collins was killed during the bloody civil war which ensued. When Eamon De Valera finally eschewed violence in the late 1920s, he formed his political party, Fianna Fail, which right up to the 1990s was committed to a united 32-county Ireland as an article of faith.

Another division had happened in 1969, when the troubles flared anew in Northern Ireland. Gerry Adams, amongst others, decided that the old IRA, led by southerners, could not protect the nationalist communities in the north against Protestant violence. He split away and formed the Provisional IRA.

Now a new split was on everyone's mind. While Adams and McGuinness were too involved in the tortuous peace process to turn back, they were under continuous pressure to hold in line the hard men, whose game was to keep setting Adams deadlines and conditions. The latest was the removal of the British troops before Sinn Fein would sit again in the Assembly. A further problem with the IRA was that there was no such thing as majority voting. Despite the fissures, any decision in the Army Council had to be unanimous. Every single decision, no matter how small, had to be worried through, which was very time consuming.

If the shootings meant that the IRA had split and a return to violence had been endorsed, it would be days before even Adams would know. Alternatively if it had been a rogue element, an armed service unit acting off its own bat, it would again take time before Adams could establish who they were and why they had acted. It was an extremely delicate time in the peace process but Adams' hands were tied. All he could do was stall and hope the process did not unravel.

Weighing all this up, the SDLP leader suggested to his associates a statement which emphasised hope rather than experience. 'Better say something like this: "The SDLP condemns violence, whatever its provenance. The peace process has been punctuated by unnecessary acts of violence. The killings in Ballycastle are among the worst so far. However, nobody has accepted responsibility. We should not rush to judgement until more details are known. We are at a critical time in the peace process. A historic moment has arrived. We are about to see the departure of British troops. The last vestige... no, scrub that last bit, it's too provocative. The Northern Ireland Assembly is about to reconvene. Peace in Northern Ireland is more important than one isolated criminal act, however appalling. The political progress we have made together should not be thrown away. How does that sound?'

'Pretty feeble, if you really want to know,' replied a colleague, Joe McManus.

'I know it damn well does. But what else can we do?'

God, this was no bunch of ordinary criminals, he thought. But who was it? Something's going on. Hell, better go to bed. Can't do anything 'til the morning.

'Okay, Joe, put that out to the usual media people. I am going to bed, goodnight.' Joe shrugged and went to type and fax one of the most anodyne statements he'd ever seen from the SDLP.

On the Protestant side of the divide, there was equal bafflement. The leader of the Official Unionists was roused from his bed in Lurgan. He condemned the killings. They were appalling. If they turned out to be the work of the IRA, then his party would have to re-evaluate its role in supporting the coalition government. No, he did not entirely rule out withdrawing support for the peace process, but he thought it unlikely his position would change. Policy could not be based on a single incident, however terrible. But he did think any idea that the last remaining troops should be pulled out was unwise in the circumstances. He needed to know more details. He would talk to the BBC again in the morning.

The Rev Ian Paisley was his usual bombastic self. The killings were clearly the work of those butchers, the IRA. All the trademarks of the IRA were there to see. The government was now paying the price for surrendering to the IRA. As he'd said all along, leopards do not change their spots. It would be the utmost folly for any British government to pull troops out now. They should be sending more. The whole peace process was one enormous con trick to bring about British withdrawal. Now everyone could see the IRA for what they really were. If anybody thought he would sit down with the murdering IRA trash, they could think again. He called on the Unionist people to resist being sold out to the Republic. Nothing new there.

In London, the Prime Minister got dressed after the news bulletin he had been watching in bed. He phoned one of his political secretaries, Ian Bell and his press secretary, Chris Jenkins, and asked them to meet him at Downing Street in half an hour, at eleven.

He made a telephone call to the head of the Official Unionists, whom he knew to be at home in Lurgan in Northern Ireland. He got only a sleepy response, so he was brief. He then called Sir Roger Jones, the Intelligence Coordinator, on his private number. Leaving the family flat, he went downstairs and waited.

Frantic attempts were made to raise Betty Vernon across the city, in Ladbroke Grove. She had switched the television off immediately after watching herself on the news. Having turned the telephone answering machine on, she had gone to bed and fallen sound asleep. Eventually a Coalition spokesman, Peter Riddlescombe, who fortunately lived nearby off the Harrow Road, was traced and asked to pop around to Mrs Vernon's.

The Prime Minister spoke gravely to Bell and Jenkins. 'You've probably seen the news. This is very serious. It could mean the whole peace process and political settlement is about to fall apart. This is all we need after all the work we've put in. We have worked years for this. Northern Ireland has never been closer to a lasting settlement. But the British people want done with the wretched place. If violence is about to start breaking out, it is certainly not going to help us.'

He went on, 'I've spoken to Roger Jones. He doesn't know what the hell is going on. Says he's spoken to the army and Five (MI5), as well as to the people in Dublin. Could be anything from the Special Branch up to deep mischief, through a rogue element doing some freelancing, to a real split in the ranks of the IRA. All we can do at this stage is a bit of damage limitation. We'll put out a statement deploring the incident, promising a thorough enquiry and saying the peace process is bigger and greater than one isolated incident - that kind of thing.'

'I haven't contacted the Prime Minister in Dublin yet, but I will. Next, I want you to convene a meeting of the Joint Intelligence Committee for six o'clock tomorrow morning. I want Jones, I've already told him, the Army, Five, Six (MI6) as well as Betty Vernon and her PUS.

At this point, John Silver, one of the security men manning the high security telephones, knocked on the door. 'Excuse me sir, the President of the United States on the hot line from Washington. Says he realises it is late here but he would greatly appreciate a word.'

'Hmmm, better take it, I suppose. Oh, you can't put it through here. Excuse me a moment.'

Ten minutes later he was back. 'Our dear American friend just wants to be reassured the political process in Ireland is still on track.'

'Well, is it?' Bell asked.

'Damned if I know,' said the Prime Minister. 'I'll phone the Taoiseach, he's bound to know,' and they all burst out laughing.

Across London, in Ladbroke Grove, Peter Riddlescombe had succeeded in rousing first Tim Vernon, then Betty Vernon, who sat around in the kitchen in their dressing gowns, nursing cups of coffee as they were informed of what was going on. Betty Vernon said, 'Right, Peter, put out an immediate statement deploring the killings; better clear it with Number 10. We are sure this does not herald a return to wider violence. The political process will continue. We will be reviewing our position when we have further information. Better say nothing about the troops for the moment. Can you also get in touch with the PM, the Deputy PM and the various other ministers, home, foreign etc. for a meeting asap wherever they like. Tim, I'm going back to bed. Would you be a love and go through the answering machine and speak to the press. Thanks a lot. Good night.'

*

45

In Aberdeen, Alexander MacPhee paced the study of the stone mansion he had designed for himself, above the so-called Granite City. He was one of the men who epitomised the oil-rich town. Starting out as a diver in the early days of the oil boom in the late 1960s, he had built up MacPhee Marine Services into the largest offshore oil services and exploration company in the UK. The original company did everything from general salvage to servicing the oilrigs, from manufacturing marine equipment to making gas turbines in the US. Towards the end of the century, the company had started to get into oil exploration.

With a total turnover of £400 million, the company was small beer. But if the US oil service companies with their billions in turnover were large, the principal oil majors, like BP in the UK and Exxon in US, were mega-big. Small companies only got a look into oil production by gaining a contract for exploration and "farming in" into concessions - blocks as they were known - which were controlled by the big boys, or which the majors could not be bothered to exploit, either because they were too small or the risk was too great.

It could cost between £10 million to £15 million to drill an exploration well if it was in deep water offshore. On average only one well in ten came good. It was a high-risk business, hence the need to farm in partners to spread the risk.

MacPhee Oil, a subsidiary of the main group, had farmed into concessions in Vietnam and Mexico. Its main area of interest was the UK's North Sea. But the North Sea had become mature, and output was on the way down.

The discovery of oil in the West of Shetlands in the early 1990s extended the possibilities for small explorers like McPhee. It was thought that oil in this area, the so-called the 'Atlantic Arc,' could amount to 500 million barrels, or even one billion barrels, substantial fields by any standards. As late as the 1980s, it would not have been worth trying to exploit these reserves. Because of the bad weather and extreme depth the costs would have been too great. But advances in technology, such as horizontal drilling and floating storage had transformed the situation. These fields had become economic and MacPhee had managed to get a toehold into the area. It could be a big, in fact his main, revenue earner.

Over the years, MacPhee had knocked some of his rough edges off. His shock of blond hair was now smartly groomed. He wore well-cut suits. His harsh Scots accent, which they used to say could strip paint from a door, had been modulated into a mellifluous burr. Now 55, he was still lean and fit. But he was no longer pictured in the gossip columns partying in London nightclubs . He had kept his private Lear jet. But this was more or less a business necessity. Slowly the picture of him as a roustabout and tearaway had faded.

He was still a hustler, but he had refined his image because he needed the money. In the oil business turnover could be deceptive. It was like making films, one smash hit and the returns kept coming in for years. But a string of costly duds and you were soon feeling the pinch. MacPhee's margins were tight.

To realise some capital he needed to float a bit of his company on the stock exchange. At present, he, his brother Angus and Angus' wife, Fiona, owned all the company. Their money was wrapped up in it. They were rich on paper and lived well off the company, but there was not much in the bank.

The West of Shetlands find plus his new image meant the City types would have given MacPhee Marine Services a good reception on flotation. Now the government had threatened to upset the apple cart by effectively seizing his oil with high taxation. Damn it. Not only that, but he suspected that the £10 million he had given Carstairs had not all gone on arms as Carstairs had said. There was more to it than buying and transporting arms. He'd tried ringing Carstairs, but only got his idiot wife and, after that, the answering machine on both his home and mobile lines.

When he got no reply after an hour, he went into action. First, he phoned Fiona. It was midnight. 'Fiona I'm sorry to phone so late. But we may be in trouble. Did you see the ten o'clock news?'

'No, we had an early night.'

MacPhee quickly related the events of the evening. She gasped.

'Now I would like you to convene a full board meeting in the George Hotel in Edinburgh for 10 o'clock tomorrow. Get the non-executive directors from London to take an early flight.

'Me, you and Angy will fly down in the Lear jet. Can you wake up MacNab and tell him we'll want to fly to Edinburgh at eight o'clock. Tell him also to make arrangements to fly to Dublin at 12.30 on Saturday. You'll bring all the necessary paper work for the minutes and so on. We've got to convince those city types we are serious. Oh, one more thing. Somewhere, I think in the office, there is a number for Diarmuid Brogan. I'm pretty sure he still lives in the same place; that Georgian pile north of Dublin. You remember we all dined there when he was convinced he was going to find oil in the Celtic Sea.

'I do indeed. The number is not in the office. I've got it here. Give me a minute. Look I'll phone you back in a moment.'

'Okay, thanks Fiona, you are a brick.'

He was getting nervous about the future. An independent Ulster might sound like a fantasy to some, but when you had seen what had gone on in the Soviet Union, where even the smallest states had wanted and won independence, a go-it- alone Ulster wasn't so far fetched. Certainly no one in mainland Britain seemed to want to continue in Ireland. It was too expensive. It just wasn't worth one more life. MacPhee agreed with Carstairs' calculation that, once British troops had been withdrawn, they would not return, no matter what happened. The British just wanted rid of the place. Besides, MacPhee was passionately behind Carstairs' cause. He was a lowland

Scot, a Presbyterian from Fort William. It was his people who had colonised Ulster. They had every right to be there. He objected to the British government trying to sell his people down the river.

There was also the not-inconsiderable thought of the money. If Carstairs pulled off what MacPhee thought he was going to pull off, then he, as Carstairs' partner, would end up rich beyond the dreams of avarice. He would have no need to worry about the opinion of those city types then.

But it was a very high-risk strategy. There was an awful lot which could go wrong. Okay, if it did go wrong, no blame would attach to him, but he would be ten million pounds down. That was not small change.

Events could just be moving away from Carstairs. He didn't like the way Carstairs hadn't returned his phone calls. He needed a fallback position. Business, after all, was business. He was going to hedge his bets, play both ends against the middle. Yes, it was time to renew his acquaintanceship with Mr Diarmuid Brogan. He was sure Brogan would see him.

Chapter

5

Diarmuid Brogan, master businessman, one time politician, heard the news in his spacious office in Kildare Street, almost exactly opposite Leinster House. Once the palatial home of the Dukes of Leinster, Leinster House now housed Dail Eireann, the Irish parliament. It was right in the heart of Dublin, bordered by St. Stephen's Green to the south and Trinity College to the north.

Brogan was sitting with Dick McGuinness on the black leather Chesterfield couch. Opposite, on the wall above Brogan's large imposing desk, was a portrait of Eamon de Valera, Brogan's political hero. In front of them was an open bottle of Bushmills and a large jug of water. The room was filled with smoke from both mens' constant cigarette puffing. Officially and for public consumption Brogan didn't drink. Privately he loved taking a wet with his cronies.

He had no greater crony than McGuinness who, at 58, was a little older than Brogan, but empathised easily with the younger man. McGuinness was now a backbench TD (MP) but he had been a junior minister in various governments and was still pally with the Taoiseach and various ministers. He cared nothing for administration. He was all politician. He was Brogan's eyes and ears in the Dail and in the Party. His head was a data bank of favours owed and debts unrecalled. His conscience had ceased to be an instrument to assess right and wrong, more a calculator to know precisely what was every man's price. Totally immoral in his master's service, in the buying and selling of mens' (and the occasional woman's) souls, he had an acute sensitivity to market conditions.

What attracted him to Brogan was Brogan's risk-taking brinkmanship. It had always been thought that Charlie Haughey, the Taoiseach for much of the 1980s, was a chancer, but Brogan was in a different league. His wife Maureen had been packed off to live in London and Paris, making only the occasional appearance. There were no children, but there had been a string of mistresses.

Attitudes had changed dramatically in Ireland since Mary Robinson had become the first woman president in the mid-1980s. In the past hypocrisy had overlaid a subterranean admiration for naughtiness. Blind eyes were widespread.

Things had become more open and accepted. But it was still a risky business being a senior politician and a hyperactive lothario in what remained an effective confessional state. It didn't do to be discovered too often. Promiscuity and adultery would be overlooked; getting found out never would.

How had he made his money? One minute he was a junior barrister on the circuit in his native Cork, the next he was a property millionaire with his fingers in every conceivable pie, from oil to fertilisers, to Dublin restaurants. Just about the only thing he had not been able to get his hands on was newspapers or other forms of the media, like radio or cable television. But he had plans.

Rumour had it that his first serious coup was having some agricultural land redesignated outside Cork. It was not difficult. Cork was growing rapidly in the 1980s and some councillors were easily tempted. Land which would have fetched I£5,000 an acre for agricultural use would go for between I£100,000 and I£200,000 an acre, when endowed with planning permission for houses, factories and, particularly, offices.

Later there were suggestions Brogan had been speculating in

property in Northern Ireland and had benefited hugely from the bombing campaign there before the ceasefires. There had also been talk that he had been involved in drugs trafficking. County Cork, with its innumerable peninsulas, harbours and inlets was known to be a main transit area for cocaine, destined not only for Dublin, but also for the British mainland. The Irish navy with only a handful of coastal boats was powerless to stop it. However nothing could be proved about Brogan. He always covered his tracks.

By the age of 40 Brogan was a very wealthy man. He then began his assault on the political system. His climb was rapid. First he gained one of the rural seats for Fianna Fail. He was made a junior minister on entering the Dial. Fianna Fail, for long the natural party of government, as they used to say, ran on patronage. Ireland has too many politicians. There are almost 200 TDs (MPs) for just four million people. The country has a proportional representational system, not a first past the post one.

In the 1980s and 1990s, there were demographic changes, with people moving from the countryside to the cities, notably Dublin. The urban based Labour Party grew in strength. The result was messy coalition governments.

In order to win back a majority, Fianna Fail began to dispense largesse. An unnecessary airport here, a new road there, the occasional hospital, fishing rights on a lough. To keep his seat the average TD had to be seen to be delivering.

As junior finance minister, Brogan was holder of the purse strings. He could go over the heads of cabinet departments and listen to the individual supplications of TDs. To the official back-scratching, Brogan added refinements of his own. TDs were offered trips abroad for research and investigation. Others were given weekends in Brogan's splendid house in Baltimore in County Cork, where he kept his yacht.

By the time the election came around in the early 2000s,

Brogan had assembled enough favours and IOUs to fill a suitcase. He was in a position to challenge for the leadership. But abruptly he decided to quit, to concentrate on business. He did not stand as a TD in the election. His resignation proved well-timed. Brogan had continued to dabble at business while in politics and it once looked as if a scandal would envelop him. In the event it did not, his luck had held. Brogan's luck was like a well-oiled machine. It fed on a diet of other people's misfortunes, weaknesses and naivety. It rarely broke down.

Brogan was very much in the mould of the successful businessman/politician, which emerged in Ireland in the late 1970s and 1980s. As in America, money became an important prerequisite to political office; at least high political office. Two entrepreneurs Charlie Haughey and Albert Reynolds, did go into politics. Both became Taoiseach. Both eventually upset the foot soldiers in the coalitions. Brogan too, might have reached the top, but he decided to get out.

He was different from the others in one very important respect. He was a political throwback. He was fervently Republican; almost fanatically so. He passionately believed in a re-united 32-county Ireland. He regarded the second Anglo-Ireland agreement as a sell out. There was no point in having a Northern Ireland Assembly, even if the Sinn Fein boys had agreed to participate. In effect he had become more Republican than Sinn Fein. An Assembly just meant the Protestants had their own parliament again, their own army and their own police force, whatever you liked to call it. Nothing had changed. Once the British army had left, the Protestants would merely reassert themselves.

No, the only answer was to dismantle all the trappings of the artificial statelet and absorb the huge Protestant minority into the Irish state. Brogan was willing to be flexible. He believed the government should move on the question of freedom of religious worship. There would be no discrimination in jobs. Eventually you would have one secular state, well, semi-secular, and slowly, but surely, the Protestants would be absorbed, the way they had been in the Free State after 1920. He would revoke the decree abandoning Ireland's territorial claim to the North.

Brogan had largely kept his own counsel on these things he would ideally like to see happen. When asked, he mouthed all the cliches expected. The British must leave. There should be weighted representation for the nationalist community in any assembly. There should be cross border bodies on which the Republic should have representation.

Secretly, he never thought the ceasefires would hold. He believed the IRA was just playing for time. He thought it was a clever stratagem to get the British out. Whereupon, out would come the guns and the violence would resume – his own preferred option. He had watched with growing alarm as first the SDLP and then Sinn Fein had agreed to sit in the Northern Ireland Assembly.

He was now out of politics but he could use his financial muscle, aided and abetted by McGuiness' connections, to further the cause as best he could. This included supporting both the mainstream IRA and the rogue splinter groups. He had welcomed the decision by Sinn Fein to withdraw from the Assembly and not to re-enter until the last of the British troops had left. This was a shrewd tactical move for the Republican movement. It appeared to be injecting some backbone into the nationalists at a time when they seemed to be faltering. But most importantly it allowed some time. He knew that the Protestants would be in a strong position to wreck the Assembly and the Republic would be powerless. While he wanted the Assembly wrecked, he did not want it shut down permanently yet. He had got things slightly wrong. He never thought the Brits would agree to leave completely. Damn that Vernon woman.

So while publicly Brogan clamoured for the withdrawal of

British troops, like any self-respecting Irish leader, in reality it was the last thing he wanted. He wanted them to stay at least until he could ascertain what the Protestants in general and that gombeen shit Carstairs in particular, was up to. He didn't like the rumours he'd heard that Carstairs had not abandoned plans to declare an independent Ulster. Following a tip off, he had decided to try to find out what was going on Rathlin.

It was no use going through Adams and McGuinness. Just at the moment, they could not be seen to be involved in the kind of enquiries Brogan had in mind. But there was Tommy McCall in Crossmaglen. Tommy had been a leading light of the old Armagh brigade of the Provisional IRA. He had once been a member of the Army Council. He had always been against the ceasefires. He believed a return to violence was inevitable. He was a powerful local baron and, although Adams and McGuinness had outmanoeuvred him, he had kept all his active service units in a state of readiness. No arms had been decommissioned. No volunteers had been stood down. Surveillance and intelligence had been maintained.

When questioned by the Provisional IRA hierarchy, McCall made the not unreasonable point that it was difficult to keep army volunteers occupied in peacetime. You could not expect young men, who had been used to the glamour of Kalashnikovs and wartime exploits, simply to give up and join the dole queues. In Belfast and Londonderry the volunteers had been kept busy in policing work, which, roughly translated, meant punishment beatings. So, from time to time, McCall allowed his boys to rob a bank or a post office. If anyone was caught or killed he simply denied all knowledge and abandoned the captured to their fate. He would claim they were freelancers.

The IRA leaders knew what was going on. They knew raids on banks could not be undertaken without quartermasters, and McCall's acquiescence. But it was difficult to control McCall from

Derry or Belfast. He was ensconced in bandit country, in his own private fief, and he had his allies on the Army Council. It would be impossible for them to remove him. There was little they could do but accept it, put a brave face on things and deny everything.

Normally Brogan used Dick McGuinness to contact McCall when he wanted a little freelance work done. In this instance he had contacted him through George McQuire, a senior man in C4, the intelligence branch of the Gardai

McQuire had not been happy about being used. But he was 56, four years away from his pension. Through Dick McGuinness, Brogan knew that years previously McGuire had been involved in some unsavoury phone tapping of journalists. It was a large skeleton in a small cupboard and Brogan was about to rattle it.

McQuire was not a wealthy man. There had been the children to educate, and the expensive separation from his wife. It would be a great pity if he were to lose his job just a few years short of his generous pension. Yes, in the circumstances, McQuire would call McCall and see what could be done. It shouldn't be too hard to discover what was going on. Rathlin was a small place.

As an added precaution in case of any fumbling on McQuire's part, Dick McGuinness contacted McCall and suggested the name of a man that he might use in any operation. A former IRA man, he had 'retired' to Dublin. There would be something in it for McCall of course. They had done business before. The usual bank account in Luxembourg? Good.

It was McQuire whom McGuinness phoned when the news finished. He had been watching it with Brogan in his suite just across from the Dail. He jumped up from the sofa and picked up a phone. McQuire's direct line was formatted in. McGuinness pressed one button. McQuire answered it himself.

'You've heard the news,' said McGuinness. The Irish often posed questions in the form of statements.

'Yes, I have.'

'Well, a fine bolex you made of that'

'It was your idea, McGuinness, as I understand it, or was it?' McQuire said sharply, surprised by his own boldness.

McGuinness ignored the implication that he was only the puppet and went on, 'Well, as I understand it, you were asked to find out what the hell is going on in Rathlin Island and perhaps cause enough of a stir to hit the newspapers. I didn't ask you to start World War feckin Three. Now, what in the name of the saints happened?'

'I don't as yet know - I'm waiting to hear through channels. I'll phone as soon as I know, or shall I come over. Are you in the Dail?'

'Er no, no don't do that.'

'I don't mean the Dail. I've a notion where you are, so.'

Again McGuinness ignored this and said, 'This phone secure is it?'

'Certainly is.'

'Be better to phone then.'

'Oh, one other thing,' McQuire said hastily. 'The Minister, he's bound to phone, what'll I tell him?'

'Tell him you don't know anything. No reason why you should know what's going on in Ballycastle, for Jesus sake.'

He put the phone down and said to Brogan. 'I'll get across to the Dail and test the waters.'

At the Dail the Taoiseach was in his grand room, about to phone his press secretary at home in Monkstown, the Dublin suburb.

'TJ, that you?'

'Yes, hello Taoiseach. Yes, I heard the news. What in God's name does this mean?'

'I'm trying to work it out for meself. In about one minute

flat you're going to have every pressman and woman in the feckin country down on your head. Stall. We don't know nothing about nothing. We will be issuing a statement in due course. I will be convening an emergency meeting of the cabinet for first thing tomorrow morning. And don't let the Minister of Justice or any other minister say anything.'

'Taoiseach, hadn't I better come in to your office.'

'I don't think that will be necessary, TJ. We don't know what's going on, we'll be in touch. You'll stay at home? Ring me here in Don Cronin's office.'

The Taoiseach was an upright man to whom not a whiff of scandal attached either in his personal life or business dealings. In fact, he did not have any business dealings. He had been a criminal lawyer. But like some of his predecessors he was keen on surrounding himself with a kitchen cabinet of cronies, to the fury of his officials. Dick McGuinness was one of them, Don Cronin, a legendary political fixer, was another.

T.J. O'Reilly sank down into a chair and said to his wife, who was still watching TV.

'Ring him in Don's office. I don't know why I bother. He never tells me anything. It's like working for the feckin' Vatican, only there they might tell you what's going on. Don's office, always Don. Talk about the Prince of Darkness.'

A similar scene was being enacted in the living room of Richard Leonard, the Minister for Justice. At 50, he thought he had done well to reach the cabinet. He lived modestly with his wife and three daughters. He was a barrister by trade. His wife taught school. He had not become rich as a barrister but felt compensated by his senior position in public life. Leonard, having come from a humble background – his father had been a postman – was interested in status. The problem was the Taoiseach kept him completely in the dark about everything, or so it seemed.

On hearing the news, he immediately phoned McQuire at C4. Not that McQuire was head of the unit. It was just that he was the one that politicians and the press seemed to know. McQuire was short with him, asking how the devil should he know and why didn't he phone Leinster House.

When he finally got through to the Taoiseach's office just before 11 o'clock he was on his third large whisky. The Taoiseach was also short, and, Leonard thought, patronising. If he had known Don Cronin was sitting beside the Taoiseach as he spoke, he would probably have had a heart seizure. People like Don were the bane of Leonard's existence. Always with the short circuit to the Taoiseach, always second guessing people like him.

'Taoiseach, I think we must comment on the events of earlier this evening. This is most serious. I am in the process of drafting a statement. I'll say ...'

The Taoiseach cut in. 'Hang on a second, Richard; we do not know what has happened. I don't know. The Police and intelligence services don't know. I do not want anybody jumping the gun. No statements from anybody but me, please. There'll be a cabinet meeting at 7 o'clock tomorrow. Please don't speak to any press before we've had a chance to make a collective decision. Get some sleep Richard, tomorrow's going to be a long day. Goodnight.' With that he put the phone down.

Leonard exploded with rage: 'Collective decision by the cabinet, what the hell is he talking about. He's never made a collective decision in his life. He treats me like shit. He never consults me on anything. This can't go on. I'm going to resign.'

His wife Oona, not for the first time, thought to herself, whisky doesn't suit you, Richard Leonard. He was a nice, well-meaning, amiable man. But he was fighting out of his league with the Taoiseach.

'Come on Richard,' she said, 'I'm taking you to bed. We can

have a ride. You'll feel better in the morning.' The last thing she needed was for him to resign, just when she'd got the new bedroom suite sorted, and Christmas more or less paid for.

On virtually slamming the phone down on Leonard, the Taoiseach said, 'That was Leonard, silly woman. Now one more call, then we'll transfer to your room, and filter the calls from there.' He phoned Seamus, a young TD who was his political secretary but not yet his confidant. 'Seamus, good evening. You'll have heard the news. The phone is ringing like there's no tomorrow. Would you ever phone round the cabinet, and ask them, ask them, mind, to come to an emergency meeting tomorrow at 7 o'clock. Thanks.'

'Yes, okay.'

'Now, Don, if you would be so kind as to bring the Bushmills, I'll bring the water and we can repair to your room, where we will be better able to field the calls'. The Taoiseach picked up the telephone and called the main switchboard. 'That you, Driscoll? Look, I am moving to Don Cronin's office. Too many nosy parkers have my direct line. I'd like you to catch all the calls, if you would. I do not want to speak to any press. I particularly do not want to speak to the Minister of Foreign Affairs or the Leader of the SDLP. I will speak with Gerry Adams, if he phones. The rest I leave to your discretion. Once they can't get me on my direct line, they'll come back to you. I am counting on you, Driscoll, thanks.'

They walked down the corridor and down one flight of stairs.

'Jesus, I forgot to lock the room. I'll join you now, Don.'

As he walked back, he bumped into Dick McGuinness.

'Dick, how are yer?'

'I'm fine Taoiseach, and yerself.'

'Fine, just step in here for a second.'

They walked into the Taoiseach's office.

60

'Now just what do you make of this, Dick. Your old pals in Intelligence know anything I don't know, or should know?'

McGuinness, apart from his political connections, had a well-earned reputation for operating in the shadowy interstice where intelligence, quasi-terrorist and informers met.

'Nothing at all.'

They talked, parried and thrusted for five minutes, until the Taoiseach had convinced himself that McGuinness didn't know anything he shouldn't. McGuinness, for his part, felt the Taoiseach had not, as yet, cottoned on to the real meaning of the killings in Ballycastle.

In the next half an hour, the Taoiseach answered a call every three minutes. He talked to various cabinet ministers, he spoke to senior civil servants in the foreign ministry and he spoke to C4, who seemed in the dark. He talked briefly with Gerry Adams. With him, he went straight on to the offensive.

'I suppose you are going to tell me it was some freelancers from Armagh,' he said. Adams said he thought it was some Loyalists trying to wreck the ceasefire. Good, thought the Taoiseach, if Adams doesn't know what really happened, it doesn't look likely that the IRA was responsible.

Just before midnight, Driscoll came on and said there was a man claiming he was President of the United States. 'He's got the accent alright,' said Driscoll.

The Taoiseach talked to the President for a few minutes, reassuring him that the peace process would not be derailed and there would be no return to violence. Then, at two minutes past midnight, he took a call from the British Prime Minister. There was coolness between the two men. 'Taoiseach, do we have any knowledge of what went on in Ballycastle, who is responsible?'

'It's your country, Prime Minister, or so you claim. I hoped you might tell me.'

'Yes, well, I do think that kind of remark is not very constructive.'

'Seeing as you ask, Prime Minister, we do not know. There is hardly any reason we should know what goes on in such a heavily Protestant area.'

'Look,' the British PM said sharply,' I hardly think there is any point talking if you are going to adopt that tone.'

'As you like, Prime Minister. I just hope that this will not stop the momentum of peace and you will not be swayed in your decision to remove your last remaining troops from Irish soil.'

'That is the kind of thing we will have to review in the light of events.'

'Yes, but you have accepted the principle of withdrawal at some time, it is very important to us.' There was silence at the other end. Suddenly realising the conversation was going nowhere positive, the Taoiseach sought to wind it up.

'Look Prime Minister; we do not know what happened. If we should find out anything, we will pass it on. Our line is that this is an isolated incident and it is in nobody's interest that it affect the peace process.'

'Yes, that is our line too. We will be in touch in the morning, Taoiseach. Thank you for your time. We will obviously pass on anything we garner this end, goodnight.' The Prime Minister slammed the phone down.

'Bloody Johnny come lately, bring back his predecessor, someone with a bit of experience.'

His two companions chuckled.

'Well, what is it?' said the Prime Minister.

'He's as experienced as you were when you took over.'

'Yes, but he's come from nowhere, I was a long time preparing'. They all laughed at this.

Back in Dublin, the Taoiseach stood and stretched. 'Right,

Don, that's a good evening's work. Come on, I'll give you a lift home. Oh, I nearly forgot.' The Taoiseach rang TJ. 'Hello TJ. what are we saying then?'

'I thought we'd say something along these lines. The Government of Ireland views with grave concern the reported shootings in Northern Ireland last night. We are at a critical point in the peace process in our country and the government, for its part, is determined that criminal acts shall not be allowed to impede the peace process.'

'Hmm, don't like the bit about criminal acts. Why don't you make it isolated acts of violence?'

'Okay.'

'Okay, why don't you issue that and tell your friends in the press we are having an emergency cabinet meeting in the morning. Goodnight.' He phoned down for his official car, a stretch Mercedes.

Dick McGuinness left the Dail and crossed Kildare Street to the office block. He was let in and took the lift to the top floor penthouse where Brogan was waiting for him. Brogan got up from the sofa. He was tall and thin and, at 50, had a shock of black hair without a trace of grey in it.

'Well?'

'Hasn't got a clue what's going on.'

'That's all right. Come on, I'll give you a lift home.'

'No, I'll hang on and make a couple of calls, if you don't mind. I'll lock up.'

Brogan could have stayed in town, but he preferred to drive the road through Phoenix Park to his Georgian mansion in Dunboyne, to the northwest of Dublin.

Chapter

6

Dolores had slowed the Carlton considerably once they screeched out of Ballycastle. They had seen nobody in their flight, but someone was bound to have seen them. They went as slow as their nerves would let them in order to avoid suspicion. But they made good progress towards Belfast. They took the coast road down to Cushenden, cut across to Ballymena, then picked up the M2 to the north of Belfast. The Carlton was not stopped at any roadblocks. Years of peace meant that security had been cut almost to the point of non-existence, with just the occasional flight from army helicopters. Their infra-red beams and night sights had been invaluable in the past since they could project on to a screen in the army headquarters in Lisburn traffic movements in the minutest detail.

By just after ten o'clock the car was cutting across the north circular road and down Crumlin Road towards Ballymurphy. The area was Catholic. The terraced houses of the Falls Road had given way to semi-detached houses, with gardens and driveways and the occasional garage.

Dolores drove the Carlton into the drive of a semi off the Springfield Road. Calmly the two men carried golf bags into the house, where a third man opened the door. A slab of light shot out into the night as he greeted them,

'Had a good day then?'

This was Seamus, the quartermaster for the Active Service Unit to which Dolores and Kieran belonged. Patrick, although known to them by reputation, was not a current member of the Armagh brigade, if he was still a part of the IRA at all.

'We've had a swine of a day,' Kieran said.

'What d'you mean?'

'You'll know soon enough.'

Seamus closed the door. He gave out a stream of orders.

'Quick now, Dolores first. There is a bath run. Give me your clothes. Be sure to dust yourselves with the recordite.' Recordite was a powder the IRA's bomb experts had developed to remove traces of cordite the forensic boys might find if any operatives should be picked up.

Seamus put the golf bags containing the weapons in the false ceiling in the upstairs box room. He then started to burn all Dolores' clothes on the fire he had started. Dolores emerged in a dress, a designer jacket, earrings, necklace and handbag. Ten minutes later Kieran appeared in a suit. By this time Seamus had watched the news and found out what had happened.

'Mother of Jesus,' he said quietly to himself, 'There'll be hell to pay for this.'

'You two, on your way now. Yours is the Cavalier parked four houses down. Here's the keys.'

They walked out, looking a prosperous middle-class couple that had been out for a dinner dance. They got into the Cavalier and drove off towards Armagh.

Just Patrick Hughes left to go. Seamus only vaguely recalled Hughes' reputation as a wild man. But he had been inactive for some time.

'You do this?'

'Had no choice, he panicked.' Seamus knew he meant Kieran.

The matter was closed. Patrick bathed and changed into his well-cut suit. He felt the inside pocket and pulled out an Irish passport with the name Dominic Morris. Inside the passport was another important laissez-passer. He took this out and put it in his other inside pocket. He picked up a brief case.

'I'll take the keys now.'

'Yours is the Carlton on the other side of the road, the one with the blue number plates.' (Blue for Dublin)

He walked out into the night, as Seamus muttered: 'You'll have cost us dear, mister, whoever you are,'

Patrick expected that there would now be some border checks since the alarm would have been raised. But he felt confident he could deal with them. The photographs they had of him were at least ten years old. They showed a young man with long hair and a straggly moustache. Now he was a businessman with glasses and slicked back hair.

Better to take the main road than be caught on some back road with no proper excuse. Sure enough, he was stopped by a police patrol just north of the border. He showed his Irish passport, spoke in a southern accent and made out he didn't know what had happened. He was allowed through and stopped again on the border. A policeman emerged from a breezeblock building.

'Would you like to come this way sir?'

Patrick followed him into the building. The policeman asked to see some identification. He pulled out his Irish passport. The policeman opened it and looked at Patrick.

'Thank you, Mr Morris. When did you drive up?'

'Tuesday. Why, is there a problem?'

'That checks out, we have you driving across on Tuesday. There has been some trouble way up north, nothing for you to worry about. Been here on business have you?'

'Yes and a bit of shopping.'

'Okay, I won't keep you, on your way.'

Patrick then had an unimpeded drive through a sleeping Dundalk. In Drogheda he stopped in the High Street, and went to a public phone box. He dialled another public phone box in Northern Ireland. He was a few minutes late. He hoped she had waited. She answered immediately. A quick conversation no longer than two minutes, then he went back to his car and drove through Drogheda, right down to the north of Dublin.

*

It took Brogan less than 20 minutes to drive to Whitehall, his mansion near Dunboyne. It was an unfashionable place to live. Apart from Howth, the north side of Dublin offered relatively few restaurants. Most people of means liked to live on the south side. But Brogan liked the isolation. He had around 200 acres. It was mostly flat, but good for riding out.

As he approached the gatehouse, a security guard emerged, crouched down, saw who it was, was about to try and say something, but Brogan drove on. Brogan had a private firm look after him. The kidnappings of businessmen had long ceased but you couldn't be too safe. At the top of a long arching driveway, lined with beech trees, another car was parked.

On hearing his car, Jeananne emerged at the front door. Tall and willowy she had auburn shoulder length hair and wore a woollen belted dress.

'You've a visitor,' she said by way of greeting.

'So I see, anyone I know?'

'I put him in the study, save him cluttering up the place.' There was a hint of disapproval in her voice.

The second Brogan walked into the study he felt the tension. 'Who are you, and how d'you get in here?'

Patrick Hughes got up from behind Brogan's desk where he had been sitting.

'Nice place you've got here. I'm Dominic Morris. You might know me better as Patrick Hughes. As to how I got in here, I had a pass made by a friend.'

'I'm afraid neither name means anything to me. Now I'm going to call the guards.' Brogan felt his stomach tightening with fear.

'I wouldn't do that if I were you. I might have some information of interest. Can I have a drink?'

'Why not, since you are here.'

Hughes poured himself a large Bushmills from the crystal glass decanter on the Chippendale side table. He added a little splash of water.

''Tis a hard life being an ex-terrorist. Unemployable you are. Of course you can always rob banks, but they've tightened up such a lot, it's hard work. There is not much profit in it. You usually get caught. No, I'm in the business of selling information these days. I'd like to go and live in the US. The information doesn't come cheap, if you follow my drift. Now, I know you were up to your eyes in the events in Ballycastle. You don't have to say anything. I can take matters further. But, as I say, it doesn't come cheap.'

Brogan said nothing but perched himself on the corner of a Chesterfield settee. Hughes went on,

'The documents you, I mean someone, was so keen to lay their hands on, they were not with the Police boys. I understand that in the event of anything happening to them, one Jackie Wilson, an anthropologist working on the island, was to be given the papers.'

Brogan said, 'That's all very interesting but I can't see what it has to do with me. Now if you don't mind.'

'I haven't finished. Wilson has strong Unionist connections. But he is also walking out with one Aideen O'Connor here in Dublin.

Five will get you ten that at some stage he'll pitch up in Dublin.'

At this Brogan turned around, not wanting Hughes to see his face. He said quickly, 'Well, I am sure that is interesting to someone, but it all means nothing to me. Now if you don't mind, it's been a long day.'

'Sure, I'll leave you now and hope to hear from you. I'll see myself out.'

As soon as he heard the door slam, Brogan punched in Dick McGuinness's number in his own office, hoping he would still be there.

'Dick, is this your idea of some feckin joke?'

After Brogan had explained the proposal made by his nocturnal visitor, McGuinness said

'Our boy's getting out of his depth. Okay, leave it with me, Diarmuid.'

Chapter

7

Carstairs could never help chuckling when he thought of what had happened on Rathlin. The island was part of the North Antrim constituency of the Reverend Ian Paisley, or Dr Ian Paisley, as he insisted on being called because of his doctorate from Bob Jones University in North Carolina.

More than 90 per cent of Rathlin's small population of 120 were Catholics, Paisley's dreaded enemy. Yet Paisley had worked wonders for the island's micro-economy, through his roles as a Westminster MP and a Euro MP. He had dislodged money from Europe to extend and deepen the harbour, which was important because it meant bigger boats could enter. This generated more sailings, which, in turn, meant more tourists.

Back in 1993 he had managed to persuade the European Regional Development Fund (ERDF) to put up half the monies for two wind-powered turbines. This meant that, for the first time in the island's history, there was mains electricity.

Until then, refrigerators were hitched up to car batteries and radios were run by portable batteries. Several years later the islanders had still not got used to the idea of mains electricity. There was only one public telephone on the island and less than half a dozen private ones, as well as a few mobiles. There were scarcely twelve television sets. One of the biggest was in Tommy McQuaig's pub, the only public house on the island.

But the electricity did mean there was now a cold store, which was very helpful to the fishermen, who still fished with hand lines and driftnets. There was also electric light in the diving centre. Diving had become an important minority attraction for Rathlin. But this was Northern Ireland. There were still no tele-commuters and still less any new age travellers.

Paisley's most recent coup had been to prise money from the Northern Ireland Rural Development Commission to refurbish three old barns, two as sleeping barns and one as craft workshops. This was very much in line with UK mainland policy of diversifying the agricultural economy into a more rural economy. The sleeping barns had been finished by one September ready for the following summer's tourists. Few people visited Rathlin between September and May.

The local populace was therefore considerably bemused when word got around in October that a company interested in storage had hired the two sleeping barns on short-term leases - three months.

Bemused they were, but curious they were not. A phenomenon of the Rathlin people was their marked insularity. Many island peoples were insular, but Rathliners were positively secretive. There had been a net immigration on to the island of at least 15 people, three families, in the 1990s, but they had been quickly absorbed.

They were polite enough to tourists, but their forged courtesy masked a calculated cunning. Behind their wild faces, they kept to themselves. The island was barely governed. There was no policeman, no jail. There had not been a murder in living memory. There was virtually no crime. If anyone got drunk, and few of the islanders did, the barmen in Tommy's pub would see them out of the premises to sleep it off. The one incident people could recall was when some off-duty soldiers started to get rowdy, and a police speedboat had to be called from the mainland. There was no town or island council. The only representation was on the Ballycastle District Council, one of Northern Ireland's 26 district councils. Rathlin had one member out of 25, but he hardly bothered to attend meetings. The district councils had few powers.

As Jackie had found initially, the islanders would not easily volunteer information about anything to anyone they did not know. When the M15 man started asking questions about the barns, nobody knew anything. He had, in fact, visited before the leases were taken out, so there was nothing to tell anyway. They called him the Spooky Man. His big mistake was not talking to Jackie Wilson, who was camping at Bull Point at the time of his visit. But he had talked to Dawson and the three Police divers. The divers were not fully in the picture of what Dawson was up to, so they could not have told him much, even if they had wanted to. Dawson was hardly likely to tell him anything.

Dawson's role on Rathlin was two fold. First he was in overall charge of securing a rear base on the island for the arms which were expected. Although the job of arranging the barns for the delivery of the SAM-7s, Kalashnikovs, RPG 7s and Semtex explosive was important, it paled into insignificance beside his second role, which, simply put, was to locate the wealth which was central to Carstairs' grand design.

Ostensibly, the police divers were looking at the sunken wrecks around Rathlin for lost cargoes of arms. There had been a programme of arms decommissioning, and looking for arms on the seabed was logical work for the Police. Most of the wrecks had been well documented by a local man, the late Tommy Cecil, and many were located in shallow water. It was easy work and no questions asked.

But this was a feint. Dawson had convinced them that what he was really looking for was sunken treasure. The oceans of the world were littered with wrecks full of valuable cargoes. Diving for treasure and general salvage had become big business. The rewards could be enormous. In 1942 German warships torpedoed the British cruiser

Edinburgh in the Barents Sea, 170 miles north of Murmansk. It was carrying five tonnes of Russian gold as payment for Allied (principally American) war material. The divers who found it shared gold worth £4 million.

Dawson had told his Police divers that the business was extremely competitive, hence the need for great secrecy. He added that the particular wreck he was looking for was the *Merchant Royal*, a sailing ship which sank in the Atlantic in the Western approaches to Scotland in 1641. The treasure in Mexican silver bars and pieces of eight was thought to be worth over £140m in today's money. The loss was so huge it was mentioned in the Hansard of the day. Dawson had gone to great lengths to impress upon the divers that looking for the *Merchant Royal* was a serious commercial venture; to the extent of hiring a 85 foot deep-sea, ocean-going services ship from MacPhee Marine Services, in Aberdeen, Scotland.

Finding a wreck was now a high-technology activity, offshore oil extraction had moved technology forward at a great rate. The *Northern Star* carried £1m worth of equipment. The computer system divided the search area into a grid with lines spaced 200 metres apart. The information was projected on to a screen on the bridge enabling the ship to steer a course accurate to within three metres.

A vital piece of equipment was the 'fish', a yellow torpedo trawled behind the *Northern Star*, as it searched along each grid line. Inside the fish were four magnometers, underwater transmitters, which sprayed the seabed with a 400 metre-wide beam of sonar signals. All objects longer than 1.5 metres were recorded and simultaneously shown up on a screen in the chart room, producing an exact image of the seabed below. If the 'fish' spotted anything interesting, the *Northern Star* could fix the exact location and check it for precious metals.

With these instruments it was possible to see up to 100 metres under the seabed by bombarding it with deep sound waves. Given reasonable weather the 'fish' could scour every inch of a search area at a rate of 1.5 square kilometres an hour.

If the signs were positive, the *Northern Star* had a two man submarine with TVs and the latest in 'grab' technology. Grab technology was a system of handling and probing which meant the divers could grope around inside a wreck without leaving the submarine.

Dawson kept the divers occupied in and around Rathlin using local boats and poring over the known wrecks. This enabled him to go off in the *Northern Star* by himself for days at a time. When he found something, he would take the divers with him. Meanwhile, the divers' discretion was assured. The crew of the *Northern Star* could be garrulous, so Dawson made sure they never spent a night on Rathlin or Ballycastle, but stayed at sea most of the time, returning to Scotland when necessary to victual and resupply.

But it was another feint. He had worked a double feint, in effect. There was gold out there, off Rathlin, but it wasn't the kind people might think it was. It was the black variety - oil. Or so Dawson earnestly hoped and believed. The techniques for seismic surveys were not that different for oil or gold, just some tinkering with the computers needed. But the seismic surveys were only the first stage. To be sure of oil, drilling had to take place.

On Carstairs' advice, Dawson had taken the precaution of using a different company to MacPhee's to actually drill for the oil. It was a small Canadian independent oil and mining company, not risk averse, as they say, and known to Dawson to have been just marginally the right side of the law in the past. Alexander MacPhee would play a pivotal role in Carstairs' plans, but for the minute there was no harm in keeping him in the dark. Never let the right hand know what the left hand was up to was one of Carstairs' guiding business principles. The crew of the *Northern Star*, MacPhee's boat, might be curious why Dawson should want to be transferred to a strange ship at sea. They might have guessed what he was doing. MacPhee already knew. But MacPhee only had the general outline, it was Dawson and his drillers who possessed the detail.

The possible existence of oil was known to a very few senior civil servants in Northern Ireland. Seismic surveys had been undertaken in the 1970s, when the oil price was high and the need to find new sources of oil seemed urgent. But it was at the height of the Troubles. The oil crisis passed. Although the surveys were promising, they somehow got shelved. But then, by chance, one of the civil servants had mentioned to Carstairs the existence of the surveys. Would he be interested in seeing the surveys as a possible business proposition?

Yes, he would. He was never averse to making money where he could. The surveys were essentially 2D seismic surveys, using the same technology used in the detection of earthquakes.

Sound waves generated at the surface penetrate the earth and are reflected back to the surface from the different layers of rocks. The travel times and reflected waves are measured to within 1/1000th of a second. Anticlines, unconformities, faults and other components of 'traps' that could contain oil can thus be identified and the potential oil-bearing strata projected. The seismic surveys in the areas off Rathlin showed some promise of oil. However, geophysical surveys alone, even 3D seismic, can only identify promising sites. The next step is to drill exploration wells.

This was where Dawson came in. Carstairs knew him from the old days when he was on the fringes of the paramilitaries. He was the perfect man for Carstairs. Not only was he politically committed to the same goals as Carstairs, he also had the professional requirements needed.

Carstairs had managed to track him down to Canada. The situation was explained to him. He didn't hesitate. He devoured the old surveys Carstairs had given him. He conducted new ones from the *Northern Star*. He had completed one well by mid-summer. He now knew the results of his second and third wells.

All the summer Dawson had been preparing two reports. The first was on the wreck-diving, basically the obligatory safety log in case anything should go wrong, with just a hint of the treasure hunt. The other report contained the drill results. This was the vital record that Carstairs and, in turn, MacPhee were waiting on.

Dawson had typed the two reports on two separate floppy discs. He did not need to label them, for he could distinguish them by their colour. The red one contained the diving findings, and the blue one, the oil results. The diving findings he had kept updating on the computer. When it was finished, he printed out one hard copy for Siobhan, with instructions that, if anything should happen to him, she was to pass it on to Wilson.

He could have given it to Wilson direct. But although he liked Wilson well enough, he thought him fey and vague. He knew from their conversations that Wilson had a determination to stay clear of Irish sectarian politics, even though, in a sense, he was born into them. He knew also that, insofar as he was involved, his interest manifested itself in an animus towards people like Paisley and Carstairs.

He suspected as well that, if Jackie couldn't resist the temptation to tear open the report and read it, he would spot some obvious holes in it. It only required a rudimentary knowledge of diving to espy some inconsistencies. Wilson was not stupid. No, he would only use Jackie Wilson in emergencies.

The other, more important, report, was not quite finished. He was in the last stages. Indeed, if he had not had the chance to slip away to Ballycastle for a break, he would have finished it off, printed it out and taken it to Carstairs.

He hadn't. He had left the disc locked in a secret compartment in his desk on Rathlin. Later Dawson was to reflect that his failure to finish it had cost him and Carstairs very dear.

Chapter

8

'Jackie, would you ever wake up? Jackie, Jackie,' Siobhan repeated, shaking Jackie's recumbent frame violently. 'Whenever are you going to wake up? The helicopter's here.'

She went over to the window and pulled at the rose patterned curtains. It made just a little difference to the light. For at eight o'clock in the morning the dark night was just beginning to make its daily armistice with the grey murky dawn.

The wind was quietly whistling. ''Tis a wonder the helicopter made it across. It's been blowing something fierce,' Siobhan said. 'You'll not have heard the news Jackie. I put my head in last night but you were sleeping like a lamb. I thought it best to leave you.'

Siobhan was talking over her shoulder. She was looking through the window where she could make out the large green Westland, its main rotor idling, its little back rotor, to avoid torque reaction, now silent. It was in the meadow by Church Bay, close to the newly restored barn. She moved across the room and switched the light on.

Behind her, Jackie slowly emerged from a deep dream about the Indonesian rain forest and the Dyak people who lived there. Siobhan was like a disincarnate voice making disjointed statements. Shielding his eyes from the sudden light, Jackie said, 'Siobhan, what, eh, hang on a second, what helicopter?'

'You'll not have heard the news, you were asleep,' she repeated.

'Siobhan, one thing at a time - helicopter, news.'

'The helicopter's come for Mairead. There's more wind predicted but there's been a lull. You're on the list for the helicopter.'

Jackie gawped at Siobhan. With her beaky nose and sharp red face she looked a typical islander. Framed against the window, wrapped in a hand knitted multicoloured shawl, she was like something from a Jack Yeats painting adorning the cover of a Synge paperback book about the Aran Isles.

The Rathlin people seemed shy compared to the mainlanders. They tended to swallow their vowels. It was said the winds were so fierce they pushed words back into peoples' mouths. Whatever the reason, the Rathlin people were quietly spoken. Their accent was without the harsh declamatory bark typical of Northern Ireland. The mildness of their speech delivery gave the Rathliners a standing-back quality, a reserve.

Siobhan was handsome rather than beautiful. She was tall, but not gaunt, and had an athletic body with muscles rather than a buxom figure. Though in appearance she had taken on an islander's persona, she was not. Jackie, who fancied himself an expert on accents, thought he caught a trace of Belfast in hers. But she said she came from Ballycastle, so Ballycastle it was.

She had married Tony, came to live on the island, and had two children. Tony had bought the house next door to his own and converted it into a guesthouse, one of several on the island. Some of the farms were also doing a little bed and breakfasting. Tony had a boat. He did some fishing and took out divers. They also jointly owned a little trinket shop for the tourists up the hill near the Church. It sold painted rocks, postcards and pictures, some linen, cheap jewellery, ornaments made of seashells and T-shirts with a map and the words "A Friend of Rathlin Island" written on them.

Tony and his friends had renovated the guesthouse. It was really just bedrooms and somewhere downstairs to eat. There was a television, but it was next door, in the main house. Watching it meant sitting down with Siobhan's sub-teenager children who survived on a diet of soap operas. Jackie felt he could do without this. He rarely watched the news, or current affairs, but did have a weakness for nature programmes.

There was no phone. This may have seemed odd for a small business. But apart from oddballs like Dawson and himself (the policemen stayed at the diving centre), the clientele of the McHugh's guesthouse were the birdwatchers, walkers and fishermen.

The lack of a telephone suited Jackie perfectly. It increased his feeling of remoteness, which was vital for his sense of professionalism. He had always steadfastly refused to have a mobile phone. That would be ridiculous. Here he was, an anthropologist dealing with tribal peoples, and he would be walking around with the latest in twenty-first century technology. It would be like Wilfred Thesiger dismounting from his camel in the desert each evening and catching an air-conditioned Mercedes back to a hotel for the night. No, Jackie liked to simulate local conditions for himself as best he could.

There was no real reason why he should know about the events of the previous evening unless someone had purposely awoken him to tell him. Siobhan clearly did not think it was worth the effort.

He was now properly awake. He got out from his bed. He had on a huge red and white striped nightshirt, which reached to his feet. The nightshirt went with him everywhere. He had nothing on underneath. He reached for some underpants and then pulled on a pair of thick brown corduroy trousers. He was about to take off his nightshirt but hesitated when he thought Siobhan might be embarrassed. She took the hint and turned away. He pulled off his nightshirt and put on his red and brown woollen shirt.

'Now what's this about a helicopter?'

'Ah look, the sijer's coming for you now. Says you're on the list. Did you ask for a ride to the mainland?'

'No, I most certainly did not.'

Jackie went over to the window and saw an officer striding across the paddock towards the guesthouse. Behind him, soldiers were putting a stretcher on to the big Westland. Around the proceedings hovered two islanders, Mairead's husband, Tim Carten, and her brother-in-law, Vincent Carten.

Jackie went out to the wooden landing. He descended the spiral wooden staircase barefoot and finished buttoning himself up. Siobhan tailed behind. Jackie always thought all the wood made the guest house seem like an alpine ski-ing chalet.

There was a knock, and when no-one answered, the door opened. A red bereted head poked in just as Jackie reached the bottom of the stairs in his bare feet.

'Hellagh, you must be John Wilson,' a plummy voice brayed. Before Jackie had a chance to answer, it went on,

'Major Ben Trubshaw, good to see you.'

The red beret advanced down the hall and the major removed a cigarette delicately from his mouth, where it was clenched between his teeth, with his index finger and thumb. His little finger stuck out as if he were drinking tea from some fine bone china. His head was thrown back and slightly to the left, so, if he were not a good five inches shorter than Jackie, he would be looking down his nose at him. With his free right hand he grasped Jackie's hand in a bone-crushing handshake.

Jackie blurted out, 'Yes, but what....'

'Orders to take you off the island, old man.'

'Wait a minute. I didn't ask to be taken off the island. I'm not even sure I want to leave the island at all just at the moment.'

'Don't know about that, old chum.'

With that he put the cigarette back between his teeth, rolled it around and half closed his eyes in a squint to protect them from the thin film of smoke rising from the cigarette. He reached across to the breast pocket of his combat jacket, took out a folded piece of paper and shook it open.

'Says here to pick up one Mairead Carten and her husband. Seems the poor gel's three weeks overdue. It's a bit dicky. She might need a caesarean. Also to pick up John Wilson staying at McHugh's guesthouse.'

'Look, I know nothing whatsoever about this,' Jackie said, 'can I see the order form?'

'Certainly old man, but I should come if I were you.'

The major was insufferably hearty and jolly for this time of the morning. Jackie expected a huge thump on the back at any second.

'That was a nasty little scrap on the mainland last night,' Trubshaw said.

'What I, I...' Jackie mumbled and concentrated on the order form, OM/4-7 W7G 0800 Rathlin, it was headed. Jackie's eye went down to the bottom of the page; it was signed Colonel Charles Wilson, battalion commander, Royal Irish Regiment.

'Damn! I might have known. Charlie's behind this.' Jackie said under his breath. God damn him. God rot his cotton socks. Would Charlie never leave him alone, he thought. 'I'm sorry, what did you say, nasty scrap?' He asked Trubshaw.

'Yes, nasty business last night over in Ballycastle. Three divers caught it, a fourth badly mauled about. Seems Pira was responsible.' (Pira was the army's name for the IRA.)

'What! What!' Jackie was incredulous.

'Didn't you know, old man? Sorry to shock you, thought you'd be bound to know. Chaps got off the boat from Rathlin, went into a bar and rat-a-tat-tat, Pira mowed them down like nine pins.' Then, turning grave, he said, 'It looks like a return to the bad old days.'

81

Jackie replied, 'I didn't know. I didn't watch TV. I had an early night. Who were they?'

'Don't have the names and pack drill, old man. Look here, I think you'd better come along. Might be some questions the intelligence chaps want to ask you.'

Ask a stupid question and get a stupid answer. It was obvious who they were. His mind started going into overdrive. It could only be Dawson and the others. But why should they be shot? There had not been any violence for months, no, years. They were harmless enough. They were mucking around diving in a remote corner of Northern Ireland. They were no danger to anyone, were they?

Jackie's first instinct was to refuse. Presumably the army could not force him to go. Apart from anything else, it would be embarrassing. It would make his work more difficult with the islanders. He wanted to thumb his nose at Charlie who had no right to keep interfering in his life. He tried to control his anger and stalled.

'Look I can't come now. I'm not ready. I'll come on the boat.'

'Fraid there's no boat today,' said Trubshaw, then, with rising firmness, 'Look, you'd better come.'

Jackie did a complete U-turn. He thought, well, I've got to go to the library in Belfast and get down to Dublin. At least Aideen would be happy.

'Okay, look I'll have to get some things together. How long do I have?' he said.

'I'd like to be away pretty swiftly, before the wind gets up again. Get your skates on, will you, there's a good chap.'

How Jackie hated this bantering-everyone-in-the-rugby-club-drinking-beer style. It implied a complicity, which was both false and patronising. Trubshaw was trying to score points crudely. He wouldn't call an Irishman in the street, "old chap", or "my dear fellow". He obviously knew who Jackie was, and of his relationship with his commanding officer.

Jackie walked back upstairs where Siobhan was standing with her hand on the bannister.

'Did you know about Dawson and the others?' he asked her. Of course she did, he then thought. He was still in a bit of a daze.

'Heard it on the news. I was about to tell you when the sijer knocked. You'll be going to the mainland, though? Whenever you go, I've to give you a letter from Dawson. They've not mentioned his name on television, but it'll be him all right. He said to leave a letter with you, if anything happened. Wait now, I'll be gone to get the letter.'

Jackie went back into his room and finished getting dressed. He pulled on his long red woollen socks, hikers socks. He had a pair of calf-length brown boots. They were French paratrooper's boots, which he had bought second hand in a army surplus store in Wexford when he been at the Opera Festival in that pretty little Irish seaside town some years before. Jackie loved army surplus stores. He was a sucker for kit and gear, and bought lots of things he did not need: mosquito nets, camping equipment, old maps and sea charts.

He tucked his corduroys into his socks and put on the boots. Into his green holdall he put some clothes and his shaving kit. He thought he had better pack some black shoes, but then thought, hell no. I've clothes in Dublin, in Strangford - where hadn't he got clothes? He could hire some evening dress if it came to it.

Into his leather briefcase-cum-satchel, which he had had specially made by a ship's chandler, he stuffed a sheath of papers marked 'Rathlin-History.' He zipped up the plastic container, which was inside. In another compartment he put a different file marked 'Gage Family'. He scooped up various papers and bills lying on the solid oak table he had brought from the mainland and used as a desk. He put his binoculars in their old battered leather case. He placed his word processor in his metal trunk.

He was about to lock the trunk when he thought he would like a book for the journey. He picked up Adrian Cowell's *In the Heart of the Forest; A journey into the Amazon rain forest.* The book was written in 1960. It was pop anthropology but he was fond of it. He locked his trunk, dragged on his red Guernsey sweater and put his waterproof on over that. He then did a mental check: money, passport, driving licence, yep, all in his briefcase.

He went bounding down the stairs and Siobhan emerged from the kitchen door, like a brightly coloured peacock darting out from a hedgerow.

'Here, Jackie, take this. 'Tis Dawson's letter to you.'

'Oh yes, do you know what it is about?'

She hesitated for a moment then said quickly, 'No, no I don't. I was to give it to you. That's all I know.'

'Must be his diving log, he mentioned it vaguely to me.'

Jackie put it into his briefcase and walked out into the mire. The drab grey sheets of light drizzle almost blotted out the autumnal brownish hillside. Major Trubshaw, standing by the door of the Westland, waving vigorously as the rotors whipped into life, forced the prospect of the journey into the foreground of his thoughts.

Jackie buckled himself into a rear seat then looked at Mairead. She was asleep, and looked enormous strapped against the side of the chopper. The rotors started thundering, and the helicopter veered off to the right at a 40-degree angle. It passed over the harbour where the moored fishing boats bobbed violently like toys in a child's bath. The sharp basalt cliffs above Church Bay disappeared behind his right shoulder. The rotors cut through the puffs of cloud, and the white-capped deep blue of Rathlin Sound slid away as if he were watching a panning shot from a fast car.

Noisier, but slower than a jet, it was just possible to see the detail of Rathlin, despite the clouds. Jackie looked at the Crook-na-

Screichen, the 'Hill of Screaming' at the southern tip of the island, and its bleak cliff reminded him of Rathlin's bloody and dismal past.

In 1642 a governor was appointed to the island, a Campbell, the Marquis of Argyll. He was charged with putting a stop to the civil war in Ireland, using Rathlin as home base. He appointed his cousin, Sir Duncan Campbell, Deputy Governor, and, instead of concentrating on Ireland, Sir Duncan began to murder and massacre the islanders. From the Crook-na-Screichen, women and children watched as the Campbells butchered their menfolk in the Lagavriste, or Hollow of the Great Defeat. Nearby are the cliffs known as the Sloch-na-Calliagh or the Hollow of the Old Women and here, it is said, all the old women were herded over the cliffs on to the rocks below by the bloodthirsty Campbells.

It was only three miles to Fair Head as the crow flies. Through the gloom Jackie could now see beyond Fair Head into the hinterland and the odd shaft of golden sun striking through the cloud, indicating the storm was passing.

He turned from the window and looked at Mairead. He then gazed at Trubshaw who was looking straight ahead, jaw jutting, arms folded across his chest, legs straight out in front of him across the aisle of the helicopter, his two black boots like anchors at the end of his stubby legs.

Jackie gazed at Vincent and his brother, both leaning forward, wringing their hands. He looked at the soldiers, fully kitted up, even though there was peace. They were young and expressionless.

Trubshaw, the soldiers and the Cartens brought his jumble of thoughts back from the bloody history of the island's past to its current brief moment in the news, Dawson, his own brother Charlie, and the interest both had in Ulster in general and in Jackie's involvement in Rathlin in particular.

He again thought the enforced journey had some blessing. After he had given Charlie a piece of his mind, he could whistle back

to Belfast, go to the Linenhall Library, then proceed down to Dublin...
A weekend in Dublin, eating and drinking, making love to the great
soft girl, would be enjoyable, if only he could keep her off Ireland's
tragic past, and, for that matter, the current turn of events.

Why had Charlie acted so swiftly? Perhaps he was worried
about Jackie's safety? Hardly, Jackie chortled to himself. There was
little love lost between them although most of the animus came from
Charlie. Colonel Wilson found it difficult to understand Jackie's
chosen role in life.

Jackie had gone from Harrow to Cambridge where he
had taken the best first class degree in his year in History and
Anthropology and automatically become a fellow of the Scott-Polar
Institute. Having taken his Master's degree on Shamanism and the
role of the Shaman among the Dyaks of North Borneo, he followed
this with a Doctorate on the Maoris of New Zealand and their land
rights. Without knowing it, Jackie had picked his moment well. The
Maoris were resurgent and land ownership was the burning issue of
the day.

His thesis became a best-selling book and the basis of an award-
winning documentary; at first in New Zealand, but then in Britain.
It was pop anthropology, like the work of his role model, Adrian
Cowell. The notion of being a populariser had intruded a little on
his reputation in rarified academic circles. But it had given him an
income of sorts, allowed him to tramp around the borderlands of
his science with freedom, and offered independence from his family
inheritance and obligations.

It had also given him a place in the politics of the environment
and tribal peoples. He became a luminary of Greenpeace and Survival
International. Select Committees in the British parliament asked
him to give evidence. Jackie became quite well known within certain
circles, and it would be churlish to say he didn't enjoy the status of
minor celebrity.

He stood out on two counts. He was not upper middle class. He was a titled member of the aristocracy. In his case, it was the Anglo-Irish aristocracy, or the Ascendancy, as it was known, which had run Ireland for centuries.

Jackie was not unique in being an aristocrat who became an academic. People were always quoting Lord David Cecil at him or, further back, Lord Byron. Jackie did not place himself in Lord Byron's league, but it was unusual for the scion of a noble family to become an academic. By the late twentieth century, the blood and the intellect had normally become a little thin. Sons either went into the services, like his brother Charles, or estate management, or other country pursuits, like his youngest brother, Jeremy.

Many Irish aristocratic families had developed a slightly raffish image. The Wilsons were no exception. There was plenty of land, much of it worthless, and a crumbling manor house. The 14th Earl of Portaferry, Jackie's father, had largely run through what money there was. Now, arthritic and curmudgeonly, he sat in his pile, keeping up appearances and moaning about the state of the world. Jackie's long-suffering mother immersed herself in good works. Jeremy tirelessly tried to revive the family fortunes by taking visitors into the house, promoting conference facilities and breeding racehorses.

Jackie's refusal to participate in the family in the normal way or, 'take his proper place in Ulster society', caused Charlie great chagrin. The Wilsons were, after all, a leading Protestant family, Anglicans in fact. There was a long tradition of service to the Crown and country. Yet here was John, heir to the ancient title, behaving like some anarchist gypsy tramping foreign jungles on airy-fairy projects, as if he had no responsibilities at all.

Charles' problems were compounded by the fact that Jackie's return to Ireland had coincided with this minor celebrity status. It was one thing for him to go off to foreign parts. If he was out of sight, he was also largely out of mind.

His absence could always be explained away with a nod and wink. Gone off the rails. Slightly dotty eccentric. Thinks he's a nineteenth century explorer. Every family has one. Such a pity he's the heir. But we all have our crosses to bear. Black sheep and all that. But right here on Charles' doorstep! Really! It was more than embarrassing. He would appear on Irish television, or sometimes Ulster television, not often, but enough to get noticed. Wearing a Shetland sweater, he would hold forth on any environmental issue, from recycled paper to the rainforests, everything except, mercifully, until now, the Northern Ireland situation, which he had turned into an intellectual no-go area for himself.

He was habitually hob-nobbing with the great and good of Ireland, whenever he deigned to leave Rathlin. At a time when Charles believed he was embroiled in the endgame for Ulster's very existence, it was insulting. When, on one of his campaigns, Jackie met and took up with Aideen, it was almost more than Charles could bear. It was bad enough parading around like some bearded hippy in sandals. People from his background just didn't behave like that. But to take up with some Fenian trollop from Dublin, with Republican leanings, well, it was little short of treason in Charles eyes. It was betrayal - betrayal of his family, his class, and his heritage - of Ulster. Now Jackie had really got himself in at the deep end, messing around in Rathlin. The bloody idiot had placed himself right slap bang in the centre of events.

The irony was that Jackie had chosen Rathlin in a genuine effort at rapprochement with Charlie and his own past. From his early teens, Jackie had deliberately eschewed any emotional involvement in Northern Ireland. He could not help but know of the situation there. He had spent his childhood living a Swallows and Amazons existence in the old house on the Ards Peninsula, with the lake and the woods. He had gone back for holidays right until he had left university and relations had become strained.

He knew how the Protestant parliament for the Protestant people had discriminated against Catholics in housing, education and jobs. He knew how the B-Specials, and later the UDR, were a brutal paramilitary force acting as a Protestant army. He knew how effective apartheid was. Some of the Catholic workers and their children had virtually never come across Protestants apart from people like the Wilsons, who employed them. He knew how the genuine civil rights grievances exploded on to the streets and how the struggle turned in to a nationalist one as the IRA took over the agenda.

But he had sensed early on that any involvement in the province would be the start of a destructive course. His fine intellect, whose provenance he knew not - certainly it did not come from his father or grandfather - had been a passport to a world of rationality. This held that, at bottom, all problems were capable of solution. He regarded himself as a scientist with an analytic approach to life. To become enmeshed in Northern Ireland, with all its bigotry, narrow-mindedness and intractable conflicts would have been, for him, a cancerous process.

He was capable of genuine friendship and had a capacity for hedonistic pleasures, but he rarely lost control. This deep reserve stemmed not so much from an aristocratic froideur, or public school-inculcated-code that feelings should be kept in check, but from his distrust of rampant emotion, from his belief, honed through study, that logic should usually triumph over intuition. This remoteness, combined with his lean good looks and easy charm, had made him irresistible to Aideen. He was seemingly unobtainable, clearly heterosexual, but still single in his forties. He was antithetical to Aideen. Where her surface effervescence masked a core of seriousness, his outward calm concealed a wild strain of impulsiveness. His sleeping around in Borneo and his interest in Aideen, suggested it. But it was well locked away. She suspected passion hidden deep down, but needed to find the combination to the lock.

89

Having established distance from his family and the province, he thought that Rathlin would represent a nice soft landing back into Northern Ireland. He had been there on camping trips as a boy, and had always found its quiet, menacing quality, attractive. He thought at first he would study kinship patterns and the organic working of a small island community, but found this had been done to death by other anthropologists. His experience in New Zealand had persuaded him that his work could have a practical usefulness. He moved on to the idea of a behavioural study in a mixed community. Of the population of 120, there was only one Protestant family. The rest were Catholics, but there was no history of sectarianism. At Harvest Festival the Catholics went to the Protestant church to help fill out the numbers. This was unheard of on the mainland.

Here were Catholics right in the Protestant heartland of Northern Ireland, represented by Protestant politicians, insofar as they were represented at all, yet who had no ill-feelings towards the other religion.

Rathlin would be a good elliptical way into Northern Ireland he decided. It could turn out that little could be extrapolated from a small island community about sectarianism in places like Belfast. On the other hand, it could well be that thorough investigation into attitudes could throw up some useful ramifications for the wider communities in the province.

But, by starting with Rathlin rather than with an inner-city area, Jackie could avoid accusations of Johnny-come-lately presumptuousness. He would not be seen as yet one more know-all, masquerading as a prodigal son, who magically had found the formula to end the province's troubles.

There was another reason for starting with the island. New Zealand had whetted his appetite for land title and searches. He had started a sub-career as a land researcher/historian.

It was not generally known that the Doomsday Book, set up by

William the Conqueror to establish just what he had conquered, only really covered what is now England and Wales. Scotland and parts of Ireland were left with an approximate system of land registration.

The arrangement of land ownership started by the Doomsday book was known as subinfeudation. William, in order to consolidate the loyalty of his nobles, gave them presents of land. In return they would be obliged to supply knights and archers should William need them. They in turn did the same. Land gifts like this were passed down the line until the level of yeoman or squire.

Thus the lords could surround the 'manor house' with tenanted farms which paid rents. The system of subinfeudation was abolished in 1289, but those ancient rights remain legally recognised.

The other aspect that has survived is common land. This is not, as is widely supposed, land held in common ownership. The owners set it aside for common use. In the olden days, everyone had the right to graze his or her sheep on this land. But no matter how many walkers or sheep went across the land, the ownership always remained with the man who held the lordship of the manor in which the common land stood.

What this means is that someone owned every bit of land, every scrap covered by the Doomsday book, somehow. Even if over 900 years estates had been dismembered to build towns, factories, housing estates and whatever, this still left strips of land not needed for development. The sell-off of land over the centuries has been likened to a rolled out pastry. The best bits of land were cut out the way that a cook carves the best piece to cover a pie dish. The pieces of pastry left on the rim would be rolled up and used for something else.

But you cannot roll up land. It just lay there and was assumed to be useless. But these strips, 'ransom strips' as they came to be known, turned out to be far from worthless. Once the Commons Registration Act came into effect in 1965, it became clear that every jot of land that was owned had a potential value. Anyone who built a pylon, ran a sewer, or an electricity cable across a motorway hard shoulder, for example, became legally obliged to pay the owner something. If Jackie could establish that the system of subinfeudation had been extended to Ireland in some form, even though the Doomsday Book had not, then it could be worth money to his brother Jeremy.

Rathlin was an intriguing place to start his researches. It was Northern Ireland's only inhabited island and in the traffic lanes of history. The Scots, in particular, have used and abused it. Jackie had decided that the best chance of proving the case lay in the detailed study of the best documented tenure, that of the Gage family, who bought the island from the fifth Earl of Antrim, specifically the period of Rev John Gage, who lived in the last part of the nineteenth century. Fortunately the island's past was recorded in numerous documents, now mostly kept in the Linenhall Library in Belfast.

Jackie liked most libraries, especially antiquarian ones. But he loved the Linenhall Library, built by prosperous Victorian businessmen for the city, because of its mustiness. He was looking forward to going there and losing himself among its shelves, after this business with his brother, and presumably Dawson, was sorted.

But would it be sorted? Was Dawson dead? What should he do now? It was becoming increasingly apparent that his wish to remain neutral as a scientist, as a doctor almost, was irreconcilable with his return to Ulster. He could see that, with his background, it was inevitable that he would be drawn into the debate. Now it looked as if he were suddenly thrust at the heart of a new wave of violence.

Oh well, nothing I can do about it for the minute, he thought. He would have to roll with it, at least until he got to a telephone. He reached down casually and took the package Siobhan had given him from his briefcase. He rummaged in his pocket and, with his

Swiss army knife, slit open the top and pulled out several sheets of paper. He started to read.

Dear Jackie,

In the event that anything should happen to me, i.e. that I should meet with an unfortunate accident, I would be grateful if you ensure that the enclosed documents reach Mr William Carstairs. His telephone number in Belfast is 614532. It is ex-directory, I think, so you better note it well. His office number in Belfast is 623178. That is in the book. He also has a mobile and a car telephone. The numbers are 07835 72654 and 0835 729100, respectively.

I think I get the impression from talking to you that you do not wholly approve of Mr Carstairs. However, I assure you there is nothing sinister in what we have been doing. He is Chairman of the Police Force of Northern Ireland Federation. At his request I have been helping with a project. What with the peace and all, the Police Force has had less and less to do. Making an inventory of the wrecks, some of which might have had arms, seemed like a useful exercise. A log like this is standard procedure for safety reasons.

You are not stupid, so it would be foolish of me to try and disguise the fact there is another reason for our presence on the island. Carstairs is also a businessman and we are examining the possibilities of salvage. Treasure hunting has become big business in the world. There are known to be at least twenty wrecks around Britain from the days of the Spanish-American empire. There must also be a chance that some of the ships from the Spanish Armada which tried to sail round Britain foundered near Rathlin.

You will see from the log, if you decide to read it - you do not have to read it, by the way, but I am betting you will - that we have not found any yet. However, given that it is competitive, I would be grateful if you would be as discreet as possible about our activities.

Thanks a lot,

Yours ever,

Alan Dawson,

Jackie was just about to start on the report when the helicopter began to vibrate and wobble as it danced to land behind the Dalriada hospital in a clearing especially made for such emergencies.

Once down, the soldiers quickly jumped out. Mairead was lifted out and hurried into the hospital. Her husband and brother-in-law trailed behind with the white coated doctors. Trubshaw spoke to Jackie from the ground.

'Shouldn't be two ticks old man. Do jump out and stretch your legs if you want to.' Trubshaw wandered off in the direction of the hospital, lighting a cigarette. Jackie took him at his word. He put his papers back in his briefcase and climbed down and looked at the lowering sky and the sun shafts to the west. He decided to walk to the hospital, if only to get out of the rain. It was still only nine in the morning.

Chapter

9

By the time Carstairs had left the hospital and returned to the hotel, he had been up for two hours. This was unusual for him as he was not an early riser. He hadn't slept very well. Again, unusual. He never had any trouble sleeping.

He'd watched the breakfast news on television. The names of the three dead Police Force men were given, Ross, MacTeel and Wilson. A fourth man, Alan Dawson, who apparently was not a member of the Police Force, was in a coma. There then followed an interview with Commander Herriott, who said the police had advanced no further in their inquiries.

The cat's partly out of the bag, thought Carstairs. He phoned down to reception and, in his truculent Ulster politician's voice, ordered an Ulster fry and some tea for breakfast. Yes, he wanted the lot, sausage, bacon, eggs, tomatoes, and some white pudding, if they had it. He would also like some newspapers. The *Newsletter,* the *Daily Telegraph* and the *Times.* He did not know why he was sharp with the receptionist. It was usually part of his code to be polite to ordinary people.

He phoned Billy and told him to rouse Joe and join him downstairs in three quarters of an hour. He'd be taking breakfast in his room, since he had some telephoning to do. He walked over to the window and threw the curtains back. There was a view overlooking the harbour, but nothing to see in the grey, early morning drizzle

He phoned Wilson and got his wife. She gushed, 'Oh, I am so sorry, William, he's left for the barracks.'

As a senior officer Charles Wilson was allowed to reside outside the base and lived comfortably in a large detached house in an acre of garden with his wife and two children, when they were not away at school across the province, in County Down, near the coast.

'He did get your message. He should be at the barracks shortly. Have you got the number? Can I get him to ring you? I know he is anxious to speak to you. Where are you? Somewhere comfortable I hope. How's your wife...'

At this Carstairs cut in, 'Yes, everyone's fine, Mrs Wilson, I'll phone your husband at the barracks.'

He'd known the Wilsons for years, but it was never Charles and Sally. It was always Mrs Wilson, and the Colonel, or your husband. Carstairs put the phone down, went to his briefcase for his electronic diary and phoned a number in Lisburn. He would like to speak to Colonel Charles Wilson please. Officers did not normally take calls direct, he was told. Would the caller like to speak to the press office? He would not like to speak to the press office. He was William Carstairs, and he needed to speak to Colonel Wilson urgently.

'Just a minute.' Seconds later, a fruity English voice came on the line. 'Hello, Mr Carstairs. Andrews, press department, can I help?'

'I am most anxious to speak to Colonel Wilson.'

'I'm awfully sorry, Colonel Wilson is here but he is tied up in a meeting with the General. Can I help? What does it concern.'

'Oh it doesn't matter. Please ask him to contact me when he is free. He has my mobile number - or I am staying at the Marine Hotel, Ballycastle. Thank you now.'

He put the phone down and Andrews spluttered into the dialling sound.

'Yes I'll make sure he gets the message.'

Carstairs went downstairs just after 8 o'clock and found Joe and Billy. They were just finishing breakfast. 'Good morning to you both. I think if you have finished we'd better get right over to the hospital.'

It took less than five minutes to get to the Dalriada Hospital. But there had been a change of shift. There were new police, a new officer and a starchy replacement ward sister.

Carstairs managed to negotiate the police easily, but he was kept waiting on the ward. Patience was not one of Carstairs' strong suits. He registered the noise of a helicopter but thought nothing of it. Finally after nearly 20 minutes, an iron-grey matron emerged.

He was told tersely that a note had been left about him. There was no change in Mr Dawson's condition. The doctor would not be in until later that morning. No, she did not know what time. She was sorry she could not be of more help. But there was little point him hanging around the ward. Perhaps he could come back later. Yes, perhaps he would come back later.

As they arrived back at the Marine Hotel, Gerry, with his mate and some others, were making an attempt to winch the cows ashore on to the quay from the *St. Iona*. The cows, more dead than alive, it seemed, reeled like drunks and one nearly fell into the sea.

Joe went to park the car, while Billy and his father walked into the Marine lobby. 'What'll we do now, Daddy?'

'We wait.'

They walked into the lounge as a message came over the crackly tannoy. 'Telephone call for Mr William Carstairs please.'

Carstairs rushed up to Reception. 'Yes, I am Carstairs.'

'Right you are, sir. There is a call for you. You can take it in that booth there.'

'William? Charles.'

'There you are, Colonel, I've been trying like hellfire to get you. What on earth is going on?'

'You probably know as much as we do. Have you managed to speak to Dawson?'

'Dawson's in a sort of coma. He's not speaking properly. He kept mumbling my name and your name, it seems.'

'Aaaagh, that's why I have been trying to reach you, William. It may be he is talking about my brother.'

'Your brother! What on earth do you mean? Can you explain yourself Colonel?'

Charles Wilson swallowed hard before speaking: 'Well, you see, my brother, John Wilson, is working on the island. He is an anthropologist, if you know what that is. He's sort of interested in the environment, and other worthy causes. I gather he and Dawson became quite friendly. It may well be, I don't know, well, it's just possible, that Dawson may conceivably have left some documents to John in case of accidents. Dawson vaguely mentioned this to me, but, as I say, I really don't know.'

Wilson waited for the predictable explosion. Carstairs had a vague but rapidly growing cognisance of who Jackie Wilson was. 'Let me see if I understand you correctly, Colonel,' he started quietly. 'A vital document on which all our futures depend may have fallen into the hands of your brother, a man, who, you will excuse me saying, is of dubious political leanings.' Then came the explosion, 'God in Heaven!'

'Please be calm, William.' Wilson thought what a melodramatic man Carstairs was, vital documents ... fallen into the hands of.. such was the currency of Carstairs' life. He was a little concerned himself, but didn't want to pander to Carstairs' inflammatory tendencies.

'I am just guessing, William. I do not have anything to go on. I have had no contact with my brother, or, for that matter, with Dawson. What was he doing in Ballycastle anyway? I thought you didn't expect him for some days yet?'

'I don't know, I just don't know.'

'Look, be calm, William, everything is in hand. I am arranging to have John flown over to the barracks where I can give him the third degree, so to speak. He should be here shortly. I'll get back to you as soon as I know anything, all right? Good.'

'When might that be?'

'Oh, round lunchtime I expect.'

'Well, I do not have a lot of choice. But it is vital...'

Wilson cut him off. 'William, there's no point in panicking until we know something.'

Even now, Carstairs made no connection with this recent news and the helicopter. If he had got back in his car and driven to the Dalriada, he could have found Jackie Wilson and relieved him of the documents, which were addressed to him. He would have saved himself a lot time and anxiety. Instead he slammed down the phone, strode out into the storm and across to the quay.

He shouted at Gerry, 'Excuse me, excuse me. Would it be possible to take passage across to Rathlin Island?'

Gerry, annoyed at the interruption, recognised who it was and answered, 'No, it would not, not even for you.'

'I'll make it worth your while.'

'The only thing that'll make it worth my while is the storm dropping. You go away now back to your hotel, and I will contact you when it's safe to cross.'

'When will that be?'

'Who knows, tomorrow may be.'

'Blast!' With that, Carstairs, his coat gathered around him and in a semi-crouch, made his way back to the hotel.

*

Earlier that day in London, in the cabinet room at Number 10 Downing Street, a small group of men and one woman had gathered. Besides the Prime Minister and Sir Roger Jones, the Intelligence Coordinator, there was Lieutenant-General Sir William Sander, the Commander of Land Forces (UK). (Although he was the number two man in the army, he was widely regarded as the most politically attuned) Also present were Betty Vernon, the Secretary of State for Northern Ireland, Sir Timothy Avery, her permanent secretary, John Stonehurst, the head of MI5, the domestic counter intelligence agency, and Sir Charles Pont, the head of MI6, the foreign or espionage agency.

The Prime Minister spoke first, 'Well I gather we are no further along than we were last night. Sir Roger perhaps you'd like to give us a brief update?'

Sir Roger had had one hour's sleep. At 59 and close to retirement, it showed. He sighed, 'We really are no further on. Of the three possibilities outlined last night, one, the Police Force up to tricks, can now probably be ruled out, although Mr Stonehurst might to able to enlighten us further here. Seems that the Police Force are shocked and totally taken aback. Of the other two, either that the IRA has genuinely split or that it is some freelancers, rogue elements, well, who knows? It always takes a little time for the facts to emerge when the IRA is involved. But our chaps are tending to dismiss the possibility of a split. The peace process is too well advanced. That leaves rogue elements or freelancers. Though we still need to know why and who put them up to it. But the good thing is that, if it is freelancers, it will blow over. We all know Northern Ireland. One minute it's all over the front pages; the next, nobody gives a damn and you can't find a line in the public prints.'

'What do you think, Betty?'

'Well, I agree with that. It might seem sensational tonight, but unless they find the culprits, it will fade from the consciousness pretty swiftly. It always does in Ulster.' She was noticeably reserved.

'Sir William?'

'There is something here that, even by the bizarre standards of Ulster, doesn't smell right. Why now, why right up there in the Protestant heartland?'

Stonehurst cut in: 'We may never discover, but I can say I am confident that it is not the Police Force. We're pretty close to those boys, and killing their own is just not on.'

Sir Roger, looking very owlish, came in, 'There is one more thing.' He savoured the moment and looked around at all the faces before going on, 'Seems that one of the four, the one that is still alive, is not a member of the Police Force. He is some kind of marine engineer. Seems also that there is a chap on the island called Wilson, a Northern Ireland Protestant who has gone sort of native, an anthropologist, or environmentalist.'

The Prime Minister responded, 'I am not sure we want to start getting into the beards and sandals brigade. What has he got to do with it anyway?'

Sir William spoke up, 'Yes we know about this one. He has got relatives in the army.'

The Prime Minister, in a pre-emptory fashion, butted back in, 'So what is his significance?'

Sir Roger said, 'I have not quite finished. He may be part of the Ascendancy, but it seems he has an Irish, very Irish, girlfriend. Spends a bit of time in Dublin. Our people there have been keeping an eye on him. One of our chaps in the embassy was a direct contemporary at Cambridge. Knows him a bit. There might be some profit in having a word with this man, assuming he turns up in Dublin soon, see what he knows.'

Sir Charles Pont, determined that his agency was not outshone by either Jones or Stonehurst, was quick to agree: 'Capital idea.'

'Right, you do that Sir Roger,' said the Prime Minister unconsciously awarding points to the senior man. 'In the meantime we will put out a bland statement saying inquiries are continuing, and hold our breath. Good, thank you gentlemen. S'pose I'd better brief the enemy at some stage.'

'What will we do about the troops, Betty?'

'Stay as we are for the moment, I think, don't you?'

'Yes, I suppose so,' said the PM looking around the room, and, getting no dissenting nods, he wrapped up the meeting.

'Betty, have you got a minute?'

She knew what was coming. In a room opposite the cabinet room he tore into her. Why on earth did she exceed her brief on TV? She knew what friction it would cause with colleagues. Did she want to be in opposition, or on the backbenches? It was not her job to talk about oil or energy policy. She hung her head. She tried to comply with the rules, but sometimes she couldn't help herself.

A stone's throw away, in his room in the Houses of Parliament, the Leader of the Opposition, his deputy, and the shadow spokesmen on Northern Ireland and Home Affairs were thrashing around with even less knowledge than the government.

It was a curious place for it to happen, the leader said. He thought Dublin might have had a hand in it all. He came as close as anyone in discerning what had really gone on. But he didn't realise it. And his colleagues then led him off the trail. There was no Question Time to speak of in the House anymore. He hoped the Prime Minister would have the decency to brief the Leader of the Opposition at some stage.

The meeting of the full cabinet in Dublin was stormier than the earlier gatherings in London. Predictably, the Foreign Minister and Richard Leonard railed on in an emotional fashion. It was all an MI5 plot. The Unionists had conspired to get MI5 to do this so the British troops would not leave. Surely, the Irish Government was not going to be thwarted by the treachery of the Brits when the island was so close to a solution, and so on and so forth for about three quarters of an hour. The one scenario that no one mentioned

— and everyone had their say, including the ministers for health and labour, who barely knew how to find Belfast on a map — was that the IRA had split and the peace process was falling apart.

The general drift of all speakers was that it had to be the Brits' fault. The Irish Government, or governments, had invested too much in the notion that the IRA had sincerely wanted peace and power sharing to even countenance the idea that the terrorists, or some of them, might have been playing a long game and still wanted a united Ireland brought about by violent means.

The cabinet wanted some lead from the Taoiseach. But, as was his way, he let the steam run out, whilst thinking to himself, will I never learn. I should have done this myself. He made occasional interjections and, when he felt that the more emotional members had fully unburdened themselves, he attempted to sum up. He said nobody knew what had gone on up in Antrim. It was Protestant country. He had spoken to Gerry Adams. He really believed that Adams did not know who was behind the shootings.

All that could be done for the moment was to issue a strong statement saying how much the Government condemned the killings. The Irish Government would not be diverted from playing its part in achieving the historic settlement which was at hand. The best policy was to stay calm and await events. No point fanning the flames.

When he finally got the cabinet to disband, after their unaccustomed early start, he went to his room. He punched in Don's number and blurted, 'Don, you got a minute?'

When Don Cronin arrived three minutes later, an angry Taoiseach let out his pent-up frustration at the need to consult with his cabinet colleagues. 'That lot really could not organise a piss-up in a brewery. Why I bother getting them together I'll never know, ah me.'

'Now, now, Taoiseach, you must be seen to be observing the democratic niceties.'

'I suppose so, Don, but you can never get anything done. I don't know why I don't just send the troops in when the Brits leave.'

'Because you haven't got enough troops.'

'It's a joke, Don, a joke. No need for any bloodshed.'

*

Over the road at his penthouse office, Brogan was gathered with McGuinness at an early hour. He admitted he was shaken by the nocturnal visit by Hughes. McGuinness had reassured him that everything was under control.

'Now, where do we stand with this document business? We didn't get any documents, so we still don't know what Carstairs is up to. I told you what Hughes said last night about this Wilson fella and his girlfriend. Small world eh? Hughes seems to think Wilson'll be on his way down here.'

'Haven't had a minute to find out yet. But I see that Miss O'Connor is down for the dinner-dance tomorrow night, so there must be a good chance he is coming to town. I should bump into her during the course of today.'

'Good, okay, you'll keep me posted. Oh by the by, Dick, I had a call last night from one Alex MacPhee. Ring any bells?'

'Certainly does. What in the devil's name does he want?'

'He's coming to Dublin for the match on Saturday, wonders if we might have a chat. Says he might have something to interest me.'

'Ha, you know what that means. Mrs Vernon is about to snatch his oil, so he wants some of ours.'

'You always see the best in people, don't you, Dick?' Brogan said sarcastically. 'Well we haven't got much oil, yet. But a chat costs nothing. I told him I'd have a few minutes after the match. Let's see what he is up to.'

*

At that moment, Alex MacPhee's private jet was touching down at Edinburgh Airport. It carried Alex, his brother Angus, Angus' wife Fiona, and Willie MacIntosh, an accountant and businessman from the local Aberdeen firm, Fry, MacIntosh.

Willie was important because it meant that the MacPhees and friends outnumbered the London business types Alex had felt constrained to put on his board. There were three of them and they were due to arrive in Edinburgh imminently. When they did, they were not in the best of tempers. They had had to get up too early, and it had been a filthy drive through the murk in from the airport.

Sir Myles was particularly querulous. Why had he been dragged from his bed? He didn't see why this could not be done on the telephone. After he had been given some coffee, he calmed down a bit, and just after ten o'clock, they sat down around an oak table. Fiona handed everyone a single sheet of paper. It had just two items on it; the minutes of the last meeting and the effects of the government's oil proposals.

Alex MacPhee opened the meeting. 'Can we dispense with the minutes? We take them as read?'

Everyone nodded or said 'Aye.'

MacPhee continued, a trifle nervously, 'Obviously the reason I have asked you here, and I apologise to the non-executive directors for the inconvenience, is Mrs Vernon's statements of last night. I should like to make two points. First is that Mrs Vernon is the Northern Ireland Secretary, not the government's energy spokesperson. The government has not made up its mind yet, it seems. It may well be the proposals she has tentatively outlined about oil taxes will not come to pass. Second, we are not entirely dependent on oil in British waters. We are a diversified group, less than half of our turnover comes from oil extraction.'

'Hurrumph,' said Rodney Wyatt. 'Nice try, Alex, but it won't wash. Okay, I'll concede Betty Vernon may not be speaking for the government in this instance, but you'll get few willing punters to say these ideas won't materialise. The government needs money. If these new oil taxes go through, you are in trouble, Alex. Not terminal trouble maybe, you will survive. But you can forget a stock market flotation.'

Alex MacPhee began to redden, a sign he was getting angry. 'That's what I like about you, Rodney, always prepared to look on the bright side.'

Wyatt started to backtrack. 'I'm sorry, Alex, but we must be realistic. What is proposed is very serious for all companies in the oil sector. Wouldn't you agree, Oliver?'

Oliver Templeton nodded slowly but said nothing.

Wyatt went on, 'You have put a lot of chips down on the West of Shetland field. According to your own figures, something like £150m will come from it. That is more than a third of your group's turnover. It is not all your eggs in one basket. But it is as near as dammit. The stuff in Mexico and Vietnam is not really relevant.'

At this point Oliver Templeton broke in gravely. 'You say you have a diversified group. But the West of Shetland field is the jewel in the crown that would have given you sufficient cash flow to look for other assets. Most of your other business is oil support. If the government does what I think it is likely to do, your companies will be servicing a pretty lame industry. I can't see anyone making much money after such swingeing taxes, though a higher oil price will help. Of course, there may be something we don't know. Have you got any cheery news for us? Anything in the pipeline? Found oil somewhere else outside British waters?'

MacPhee looked at his brother, Fiona and Willie. They were blank. They always let him do all the talking. He was rattled. He said, without much conviction, 'There is the general salvage. Sunken treasure is becoming big business,'

'Piffle. Sorry Alex, but that's a non-starter. It might amuse you as a former diver to go in for that sort of thing. But the biggest find would just about equal one medium sized well,' Templeton said.

Non-plussed, Alex went on, 'There could be oil off Ireland. They have a very liberal tax regime these days.'

'Oh is there indeed, well I'd obliged if you would tell me where it is,' Templeton asked.

'They could be about to pump oil from the Connemara field in the Porcupine basin in the Atlantic. The operation is similar to the West of Shetland,' MacPhee said, a trifle defensively.

'They could be about to pump 20,000 barrels from the Connemara field. That is very small potatoes. All the evidence suggests that there are a string of puddles in the Atlantic's Porcupine Trough. You will not hit pay dirt there,' Templeton came back.

'Gentlemen, gentlemen,' Sir Myles broke in. 'This is getting a mite overheated. What, after all, has happened? Mrs Vernon, presumably without the Government's authority, has announced it is thinking about new taxes. This is par for the course. The company is not being nationalised. It's not going to be wiped out by this. All right, you might have to delay the flotation. But you were not planning to float until next year anyway. I do feel we should not panic.'

'Precisely, my view,' Alex said, 'I just feel that we should show a calm front.'

Sir Myles said to himself, we could have done this on the phone. Then aloud, 'Can I ask why you thought it necessary to bring us up here in the middle of the night if that is all you wanted to say?'

Alex nearly said, 'You are glad enough to collect your directors fees.' but instead said, 'I have apologised for the inconvenience. I felt it important that the non-execs as our representatives in the City of London, so to speak, should be close at hand.'

Sir Myles said, 'Look Alex, we are all men of the world here (ignoring Fiona). I think we should stay calm, say nothing, and see which way the wind blows. Oliver, Rodney and I will soothe any fears in the City, right chaps?'

'Absolutely,' they chimed.

'Well, I think that wraps it up, Alex, what?' said Sir Myles.

Alex looked at his brother. 'Well, all right. I've organised a late breakfast, brunch, for eleven o'clock.'

'Splendid', said Templeton, 'That'll give me time for a bit of shopping, then back on the afternoon flight. What are you up to, Alex?'

'We're staying here today. Going to Dublin tomorrow for the match.'

'Good on you. Very nice.'

On a wave of such banalities they went off to eat their scrambled eggs, smoked salmon and kedgeree.

Chapter

10

The helicopter gently lowered itself on to the pad. The deafening roar had reduced to a regular chopping noise.

'Hey ho, old man,' Trubshaw said to Wilson and jumped down first. Jackie waited for the squaddies to disembark, then threw out his bag. He sat on the edge of the door and, with his briefcase in one hand, levered himself off with the other. The squaddies dispersed and the two men crouched and walked across the grass to a large wooden hut. Inside, two unsmiling men stood behind a counter like in a police station. A third sat on a bench to one side and stared at a screen. To his left was a small baggage scanner, common to most international airports.

Trubshaw went to the counter, saluted and pulled out the order paper from his pocket. 'Trubshaw,' he said, 'brought Wilson to see General Tim.'

Jackie started at this. There had been no mention of the General. He thought he was coming to see his brother. But he said nothing. The corporal handed over a wooden clipboard. Trubshaw squiggled on it and turned round, leaned back against the counter and pulled out his pack of cigarettes.

'Smoke, old man?' he offered his packet to Wilson. He resolutely refused to call Jackie, Sir, or Mr Wilson, or anything that might hint at deference. It was like an act of compliance with Colonel Wilson's disapproval of his brother.

'Er no, no thank you.' He was slightly bemused, wondering what he was going to say to the General.

'If you, sir, would follow me,' the stony faced corporal looked at Wilson, but saw nothing. It was not a look of assessment. Wilson was taken to a back room, where he was photographed. He was escorted out again. They waited. The corporal came out with an identity pass, which he stuffed into a plastic wallet with a clip.

'If you could wear this at all times, sir. Could you pass through the check. If you give me your bags.' His two bags went through the X-ray machine, and Jackie set off the bleeper.

'Mind if I go over you with this, sir. Got any metal objects in your pockets?'

Jackie emptied his pocket of his Swiss army knife and keys. The soldier ran the scanner over him. 'That's alright, sir, through you go.'

Jackie picked up his bags, and went through a side door. Not wishing to engage Trubshaw in conversation, he thought to himself that this seemed a bit unnecessary many years into a ceasefire. But he supposed you could not be too careful. Besides, army camps were like international hotel chains. They had a set formula wherever in the world they might be, save that in hot countries they had air conditioning, and in cold ones, central heating. This camp in the cold grey drizzle could only be in Britain. But in its uptight uniformity it could have been Aldershot, or Inverness.

The officers' bungalows had drives and little square gardens without fences. The tall trees in the compound were shedding the last of their leaves, and they lay scattered over the sparse grass. Joggers criss-crossed one another. Uniformed soldiers, spending four long months on a tour of duty, walked slowly. There was no need to hurry, time hung heavy on their hands.

The main Operations Centre was a squat, two storey building, not unlike an airport control-tower. It was built of reinforced concrete to withstand shells. There was a radar scanner on the roof. The whole complex had fences and wire grills around, like layers of protective hair-netting. The approach road had ramps and concrete blocks studded along its route. Crouched in the bushes on either side were soldiers in full combat rig, their faces blackened, guns at the ready. Again, this struck Jackie as over the top, but he was only passingly acquainted with this world.

They walked to the Centre. Once inside there was a desk and, to the left, a cell-type door, which gave on to a staircase. A corporal saluted. Drawing himself up, Trubshaw saluted back, 'John Wilson to see Colonel Wilson, in the first instance.

'Can I see your pass, sir'?

Jackie was slightly overawed by the surroundings. It felt like he was entering a prison. 'Pardon, yes,' he fumbled in his pocket and pulled out the plastic wallet.

'If you could wear your identification, sir.'

'Yes, of course.'

Trubshaw said, 'I'll leave you then.' They did not shake hands this time.

The corporal punched some numbers into a combination lock and the cell door swung open. At the top of the stairs stood Colonel Charles Wilson, DSO, Jackie's younger brother. By his own lights Charles had done very well indeed. Still in his early forties, he could hope for further promotion. He was one of the youngest full colonels in the army. He had won his gong, his Distinguished Service Order, while still a captain, in his twenties, in the Falklands.

Next to Charlie stood a man of similar age, who Jackie noticed was a half-colonel, a lieutenant-colonel. The corporal put down Jackie's bag, saluted, turned round and walked back down the stairs.

'John, it's good of you to come,' Charlie said expansively, extending a hand of welcome. Quickly, as if to cut off Jackie's reply, he added, 'Can I introduce you to my colleague, Colonel Dave Curtis. This is John Wilson. You are still plain John Wilson are you?' Charles said sarcastically.

'Dr John Wilson to you,' Jackie came back, equally sharp.

'How do you do,' Curtis said grabbing Jackie's hand

'Hello,' Jackie replied, then turning back to Charles he said as tersely as he could manage, 'It was not good of me at all. I had little choice. You virtually hijacked me. Now, what is this about, as if I didn't know? I have got better things to do than go around the same old Mulberry bush with you, Charles.'

Jackie realised they would want to glean any information about Rathlin and Dawson they could get, but he also knew that Charles would never miss an opportunity to try to work him over along familiar lines; honour, family responsibilities, couldn't understand him. It was if he were the errant little brother. Jackie again felt a mixture of humiliation and anger welling up.

'Oh, come now, John,' Charles said with a nervous giggle, 'even you must realise the events on Rathlin are of concern to us. General Tim would like a quiet word. After, we'll talk and have an early lunch, if that's all right. Now why don't you give me your grip and we'll get things underway.'

Charles picked up Jackie's bag and walked off down the corridor. Charles didn't want to meet General Tim, even though he was an old family friend. But he didn't have a lot of choice; he was now a prisoner in this citadel. He trailed off behind his brother as if he was off to his prison cell. They passed blown-up photographs of soldiers in action: soldiers in tanks, soldiers swinging from ropes, soldiers driving piggies, the slang for armoured personnel carriers, down rubble-strewn Belfast streets.

Charles pressed the intercom on the door of a corner room at the end of the corridor.

'Sir, my brother Dr John Wilson is here.'

'Show him in,' came the disembodied reply.

There was a buzz and Charles ushered Jackie in. Jackie still had his briefcase, but Charles kept hold of his grip.

Lieutenant-General Sir Timothy Ruskin, KCMG, DSO was sitting behind a large desk, silhouetted against a window, affecting to study some papers. Charles coughed slightly. The General rose to his feet and came round the desk, broke into a tight little grin and, hand extended, said, 'John, how awfully good to see you.'

The general was small and wiry, a touch over 5' 6". He had grey hair, neatly combed. His foxy features and sharp nose were above a salt and pepper toothbrush moustache. But his most dominant trait was two small, lively, coal black eyes. They almost pecked into you.

'How are you,' he said with a heavy emphasis on the are. 'How are your parents? Have you seen them recently?'

'I'm fine, thank you, sir. My parents are well, although Charles has probably seen them more recently than I have. I do slightly wonder what I am doing here.'

'Yes,' the General said, as if to himself.

'Look Charles, would you give us a few minutes? Perhaps you could give John a snort of something after.'

'Certainly, sir.' With this Colonel Wilson saluted, did a mock three foot turn and left the room, taking Jackie's grip with him.

'Do come in and make yourself comfortable,' the General said to Jackie, motioning him to a sofa. Behind the settee was a cabinet full of silver cups from the General's clay shooting days. To the side of it were two flags representing the General's regimental colours and in front was a long coffee table with *Country Life* magazines and a silver cigarette box. On the facing wall, covering all of it, was a large-scale map of Northern Ireland.

'Cigarette?'

'I don't smoke, thank you.'

'Can I offer you some tea or coffee or a soft drink. It is a bit early in the day for anything stronger, hey?'

'Coffee would be fine, black, no sugar, thanks.'

The General walked over to his desk, pressed an intercom and said, 'Corporal, bring some coffee for Lord Strangford, and some for me, please.'

Jackie winced at the use of his title. He said, 'Sir, I do not use my title. I am trying to renounce it in favour of Charles.'

'Are you really. Mmmh, yes, mmmh. Earl approve does he?' He did not wait for a reply.

The General was wearing battle fatigues and a green pullover, with leather shoulder and elbow patches. The three red stars on his shoulders were his only sign of rank, apart from his mien of authority. For a small man he managed to ooze a terrific sense of power and concentration. His eyes fixed on Jackie as if to hypnotise him, and, without waiting for a reply to his question about the earl, said.

'Look, I've asked you, well, had you brought you here, because I am a friend of the family and I wanted a quiet word about this Rathlin business. I'll come straight to the point. What do you know about this Dawson fellow?'

Jackie wondered for a second why it was Dawson everyone was interested in. What about the others?

' Not a great deal, actually. He said he was diving for the police. Looking at all the old wrecks. He had been living in Canada, but came from the province originally. We saw quite a lot of one another.' He chuckled. 'You could hardly do anything else, actually. It's a small island. We stayed in the same guesthouse. Winter tends to lock you in. I didn't see so much of the others - they were away at the diving centre. Dawson did not tell me much. He was pretty reserved. We never talked politics. It's a house rule of mine while in Northern Ireland. I am sorry he is dead. I couldn't work him out. But he was nice enough.'

The General stared straight at him, and said matter-of-factly, 'Dawson's not dead, actually.'

'Not dead? Well I'd better go and see him.'

'I'm afraid that will not be possible. He is in some kind of coma. Is there anything you can think of, anything at all, as to why someone should want to have Dawson out of the way?'

Jackie was about to pull the documents out of his briefcase. But then thought better of it. If Dawson was alive, then they were his property. Besides he had read them on the helicopter, and in his methodical, academic, way there were one or two points he wanted to go over.

Instead, he said, 'There were various hints that the divers were not searching known wrecks for arms caches. Dawson vouchsafed that they were looking for sunken booty. One night he was telling me the oceans are strewn with wrecks entombing millions upon millions worth of treasures, not just bullion. He said some of the wrecks around Rathlin could be from the Spanish Armada. Dawson said searching for bullion with new techniques had become big business. Perhaps it's like the drugs trade. Perhaps Dawson stepped on someone's toes.'

Jackie thought there was no harm in talking about the sunken treasure theories. But it was not the answer the General wanted to hear. It was not an avenue he wanted to walk down. 'What are you doing in Rathlin, John?' The General suddenly asked.

'Well, well, I'm, I'm... Charles must have told you.'

'I'd like to hear it from you.'

'I am a professional anthropologist, studying sectarian relations in a small Northern Ireland community. Perhaps there are lessons to be learned from Rathlin which have applications for the rest of Northern Ireland.'

'Mmmh, yes, mmmh.'

The General sprang to his feet and walked round the sofa.

His right hand was across his chest, cupping his left elbow, and his left hand cupped his chin. With his sharp nose looking towards the ceiling, he started to bob like a rabbit. Talking into the middle distance, he began, 'John, these are dangerous times in which we live. I expect you feel it is strange these kind of questions coming from me. I imagine you might think it would be the police or Special Branch that should be talking to you.'

'Hadn't really thought about it, tell you the truth. It's been a bit sudden,' Jackie interjected.

'As an old friend of the family, I thought I might take this opportunity for a quiet word. As I say, these are dangerous times in which we live. In a short time there could be a troops pull-out. Mrs Vernon has indicated as much, and I've no reason to think she could be persuaded to change her mind.

'Now a lot has been achieved here. We have just about seen things through; but not quite. If we pull out precipitately, it could create a dangerous vacuum. Our departure now would leave Irish troops inside Northern Ireland. None of us, not even Charles, know what the RIR will do; which way they will jump. The Police, well, their loyalties are severely strained. It could all end in tears. Now this incident on Rathlin illustrates exactly why we should stay.'

'Sounds like you are plotting a coup', Jackie said irreverently.

The General shot him a look so fierce it was like being pushed in the face.

'That's not very funny. Not funny at all.'

Jackie was beginning to feel like a mole. He had peeked above ground, and the more he learned, the more he wanted to burrow back in, and forget all about Northern Ireland. 'Sorry sir, only teasing.'

The General returned to his cupped arm posture and went on, 'This Dawson chap, we've checked him out, very little to go on really. Seems he was in the UDA a long time ago. Then emigrated to Canada, was in the police there for a while, don't know why. Describes himself as a marine engineer. Took some kind of degree out in Canada. Then dropped out of sight. Had a wife, she came back to the province, it seems. Suddenly pitches up on Rathlin. Has some kind of connection with William Carstairs.'

'Now there has been some talk that Carstairs is planning UDI, a Unilateral Declaration of Independence, when we go. You can discount that. Wouldn't have the wherewithal. The Loyalists used to get arms on the market from Russia and South Africa. What with the blacks taking over in South Africa and the collapse of the Soviet Union, the Loyalists haven't got a friend in the world, bit of support in Scotland, but not enough. No, you can forget UDI. But there is something going on, now what is it Jackie?'

'As I have already said, General, I can't help you very much. I'm surprised to learn he was in the UDA. He never mentioned a wife. We talked a lot mostly about trivial things. As I told you, I try never to discuss Northern Ireland politics.'

'God damn it man, people you know, people you have associated closely with over a period of months, have been killed in cold blood, for no apparent reason, and you sit talking as if you had just been out on a summer's picnic. Don't you care?'

Jackie again thought about the report in his briefcase at his feet. He could pass it all over to the General, together with his doubts about its contents and his growing feeling that there was more to the attack on Dawson than met the eye. But his sangfroid held.

'Of course I care, it is just that, that, well, I am trained not to get hysterical about things.'

He could have added that if his outer reserve crumbled, as it did occasionally, the General would be surprised by the violence of his emotions, but that was his business. All he said was, 'It is obviously upsetting when something like this happens. I have said I am relieved to hear Dawson is alive, but there really is very little I can add to what I have already told you.'

The penny then dropped about why he had been hauled up in front of the General; the tight security, the state of readiness. General Sir Timothy Ruskin clearly did not want to leave the province. For him, the war was not over. He lived in a time warp of his own making.

Jackie wanted to leave this vacuum world, but had a growing feeling that he would not get out without a further session with his brother. As if reading his thoughts the General looked at him hard and said, 'Okay, John.' It was John again. 'Sorry to give you the third degree like this. But you will appreciate we are concerned. Why don't I get Charles and David to take you down to the mess? Have you got time for a spot of lunch? You'll have to excuse me, I'm afraid. I would join you in the ordinary way. I have got to go up to town for a meeting with the Police Commissioner and the Secretary of State. It is a regular chore.'

Jackie got to his feet clutching his briefcase. The General, who grabbed him by the elbow, guided him out of the room. They walked along the corridor on the dull grey lino until they reached Colonel Wilson's room. Both colonels jumped to their feet.

'Charles, David, why don't you take John down to the mess and get his nose into the feedbag, what?' General Tim had become a jovial blimp again.

'Just give me a minute first, would you, Colonel,' addressing Charles Wilson.

David Curtis said to Jackie, 'What are your plans? Fancy a spot of lunch?'

Back in his room, General Tim wheeled round on Charles, who had closed the door and rapped out, 'I've not managed to get much out of him.'

Charles, who had a slightly different - well, wildly different-agenda to his commanding officer, thought, good. But he said nothing. He had let the General think it was his idea to get his brother to Lisburn.

'Strange chap, your brother. Seems to want to inhabit some kind of emotional no-man's land. Kept saying he didn't want to be involved.'

He suddenly blazed, 'Well he bloody well is involved. We all are.' Then calmer, 'Oh well, we better get on. I think he knows a little more than he's letting on. Probably not the whole story, but a little more'

'What is the whole story, sir?'

'Aaah, if I knew that, we wouldn't be going through this rigmarole. I don't know. There is something going on. The politicians are fools. We can't leave now. Why should these people be shot in Ballycastle, of all places? Take him down to the mess and see if you shake anything else out of him. That will be all, Colonel.'

'Yes, sir'

Charles went out and walked to his own office where his brother and Curtis were waiting. He addressed Jackie,

'Well John, Jackie, my Lord Strangford, what are your plans?'

'I'd like to put as much distance between you and me as possible, as soon as possible. But, as you have me prisoner, I suppose I have few options. Now that I am on the mainland, I intend to go down to Dublin. I need to go to Belfast to do one or two things. I could catch the 5.30 train to Dublin. Some lunch wouldn't go amiss.'

'Good,' David Curtis said, 'that's settled then.' He picked up the phone, pressed one button and said, 'Captain, have you got room at the officers feeding trough for three in half an hour, say? Yes, early lunch, the works. Good, thanks. John, why don't you leave your things here and we'll give you a quick tour of the communications room.'

Jackie twirled the combination lock on his brief case and gave it to David Curtis. He put it with Jackie's grip. The three of them walked down the corridor. Charles and Jackie were of similar height, both around 6'2". Both were slim and fairly taut. While Jackie's hair was black and flopped down over his forehead, Charles' fair hair was brushed severely back off his forehead and grew longest at the nape of his neck to cover his collar. Off-duty, he was the type you would see at a point to point in a cravat and tweed sports jacket, cavalry twill trousers and suede shoes, all underneath a Barbour.

He had deep blue eyes. His brushed back hair tended to emphasise his angular features, and his small, tight mouth. It was as if years of talking in a tight clipped accent had actually reduced the size of his mouth. Like a Frenchman, the sounds wouldn't come out right if the mouth were too big.

Jackie's face was a little more rounded than Charles' and gave him an air of being more comfortable with himself. Charles' long, stern face was an army face, with obedience and restraint etched into it like tribal scars. Whereas the tautness of Jackie's persona made him a picture of outward reserve, often mistaken for arrogance, in Charles it translated into an air of suppressed energy, of violence almost.

They had been close as children, with just three years between them. They could recall idyllic childhoods in Strangford and Portaferry. They had played in the woods, building camps and houses, cruelly excluding Jeremy, their much younger brother, in the rough politics of childhood. Occasionally they would take the ferry across from Portaferry to Strangford and then buses right down south till they reached the Mourne Mountains. Children could travel safely then. They would visit the bird sanctuaries on the islands of Strangford Lough and collect birds' eggs. They would go to Skettrick Island and collect mussels and oysters.

The return journey to Portaferry was magical. The ferry would dog-leg across the narrow mouth of Strangford Lough to counter the strong tidal rip and then Portaferry came in view, white and almost Scottish looking, with its steeply roofed houses alongside the seashore, with three pubs and the Portaferry Hotel next to the marine station. Further along the shore was a derelict boathouse.

Each year in July, Portaferry had its Gala Week. There would be yacht races, a fete and a swimming contest across the mouth of the Lough. This would only be possible when the tide turned; otherwise the children would be swept out to sea. Jackie sometimes won. There was competitiveness between the two brothers but little real tension. That came later.

Nor had Jackie overshadowed Charles academically at first. They had both gone away to school early. Both to Harrow, and then, unusually for someone destined for the army from an early age, Charles had followed Jackie to university. Charles had gone to Oxford and although he did not distinguish himself academically in the same way as Jackie, he did well enough, with a second class degree in history. He then took up his commission.

Seeing Charles now, the memories formed a queue for Jackie's attention. As their different personas closed in around them, they grew apart and eventually estranged. Jackie found the atmosphere at Cambridge uplifting and liberating. It enabled him to cut the cords from what he came to see as a parochial and stultifying past. He would not look back, at least for many more years. Charles, on the other hand, seemed to have some atavistic calling to go back and serve the cause, as he saw it. The rough and the smooth, the tough and the gentle, one son a warrior; the other, an environmentalist.

Jackie's reverie was interrupted when Curtis asked, 'Fancy a quick squiz in the operations room?'

They entered an aviary-like room with banks of computers, and chattering printers. Huge maps lined the walls. The centrepiece was a large screen, tilted at 45 degrees, which resembled a blood circulation diagram. This, in fact, was a map of all the roads in the province and those going into the Republic. Even the small minor roads showed up like capillaries. By moving a lever, an individual car, or stretch of road, could be isolated and magnified by a factor of up to 100 so that it became almost life-sized.

Curtis started, unasked, to explain to Jackie, 'You see, with the choppers criss-crossing the Province and using unseen infrared scanners, we can trace all the cars in the province simultaneously. We can not only establish the make and ownership of the car, but get an instantaneous print-out of what speed the car is going, when it entered the province and so on. Bit like a bugging device really. Look at that little ant on the road from Derry. We've been tracking that beauty for half an hour. It's the Keenan brothers. They'll be up to no good, I'll wager.'

He picked up a hand microphone and spoke into it: 'Delta Charlie to Oscar Foxtrot. Pick up Escort reg E 345 YDY, at Strabane. It's the Keenan Brothers. Over.'

'Wilco,' came the disembodied reply.

'Like the code? Devised it myself, based on the Americans' alphabet', Curtis said, almost preening himself. He was like a little boy showing off his best train set.

Jackie said, 'There has been a ceasefire for many years. Why are you picking people up? Anyway, I thought the police did these things nowadays.'

'Oh, well they do, but, as you have seen from Rathlin, you can't let your guard slip for a moment, you've got to remain vigilant. It's bad enough the way they have cut down on the helicopter flights, especially the night ones. Can't let things slip altogether.'

Charles interjected, 'Seen enough? Let's go and get some scoff.'

They left the operations room and walked down several corridors and stairs, painted pale green like any hospital. Finally, they came to the hermetically sealed officers' mess down in the basement.

The bar looked like a cross between a Costa Brava beach-hut and an old-style colonial hotel. After some peremptory introductions, they found a corner of the bar to themselves. Curtis, who seemed to be acting as host, asked, 'What'll you have, sherry or something else?'

Jackie was not a great boozer, but he enjoyed social drinking when in civilised company. Unusually for him, at this early hour he felt in need of something stiff.

'Gin and tonic, thanks.'

'Good idea. Charles?' Charles nodded. 'Three large G and Ts, steward.'

They chitchatted about nothing in particular until a white-coated waiter told them their table was ready. He led them to a corner table out of earshot, hopefully, of others. Jackie took his gin and tonic and still clung to his briefcase, although a waiter had tried to relieve him of it, as if they were in some Pall Mall club. With rising trepidation Jackie knew what awaited him. Charles would start off smoothly, with a stance of hurt miscomprehension, which hinted at lack of consideration on the part of his elder brother. He would rise through an arc of irritation and end in frustrated anger. Jackie, meanwhile, would go through a similar process. He, too, would become angry. They would reach a standoff and start again. The conversation would take place amidst lots of sighing and shaking of heads as they united on a front of mutual bafflement about each other's motivations. This time the encounter would be spiced by recent events on Rathlin, and there was Curtis to referee, of course.

With a picture of the Queen smiling down above his head, Jackie got in first before Charles could speak and opened the bowling with, 'Look, Charles, I do fully intend to renounce the title and devolve in favour of you. Apparently I can do this now. I have spoken with father. He was not entirely happy, but I think he understood.'

'Well, I can't say that I do, but there you are. It's up to you, I suppose.'

Charles was thrown, as always, when the subject came up. He had to admit he was attracted to the idea of succeeding as the earl. There would not be much money, obviously, and Jeremy already had de facto control of the land. But he simply could not understand how anyone could want to renounce his family name and renege on his responsibilities in this way. He almost accused Jackie of being a coward. But he had other fish to fry, and he didn't want to inflame him at the outset. Instead he said, 'Let's get the order out of the way. I can recommend the Rioja, both the white and the red. The white is quite light. Shall I get some of both?' No reply was seen as yes.

'We'll have some fizzy water too,' Charles went on.

Curtis wrote this down on a chitty. In officers' messes, as in London clubs, no money changes hands at the time of eating.

Curtis then said, 'I'm easy to please. I'm going to have the fish soup and the rack of lamb. Anybody going to join me in the lamb, it's for two?'

'Yes, I'd be on for that, and I'll start with the melon,' said Charles. 'Why don't we get a selection of vegetables and some minted potatoes?'

'What about you, John?'

'I'd like the oysters to start and then the plaice. I'm a very fishy person.'

'Good, done,' said Curtis.

Charles then launched straight in, 'Now, Jackie, just what are you doing on Rathlin?'

Jackie gave a deep sigh before speaking, 'You know full well what I am doing on Rathlin. I'm conducting an inter-community study. I'm hoping it will offer some rational explanation as to why, if Catholics and Protestants can rub along peacefully on a small island, in a small community, they can't do so on a larger scale. You know what my work is. I've already explained this to the General. I am beginning to sound like a cracked record.'

'Very interesting, I am sure,' Charles said sarcastically, then exploded. 'Why for God's sake man, do you have to do your studies here, now, in this part of the world?'

Charles leant forward, almost glaring at his brother. 'You know as well as anyone, unless you are completely naive, that very shortly all hell could break loose. It could have already have started. The Irish army is at the gates, well, it's already here. There could be complete mayhem and you are fiddling around asking irrelevant questions and poking your nose in where you shouldn't.'

Jackie was equally heated. 'Now look, Charles, this is gratuitous rudeness. I have been around this particular course many times. I do not have to answer to you about my work, or, if it comes to that, about my politics, insofar as I have any. I resent any suggestions I am poking my nose in. Perhaps if you hadn't poked your noses in, the place wouldn't have exploded. Now if you will return my bag and get someone to see me out, I think I will be going. Thank you for the drink, Colonel Curtis.'

Curtis intervened at this stage. 'Gentlemen, gentlemen, this is all very unnecessary. Let's just all calm down for a second.'

Jackie sat back down as the first course was served and the wine poured - and the rest of the room pretended not to notice the kerfuffle.

Curtis went on, 'Look at it this way, John. You are Lord Strangford. You may not like it, but that's who you are, scion of one of Ulster's oldest and best-known Protestant families. You must realise you are also a well-known figure in your own right. You say you have no politics. I've seen you on television many times taking positions on various issues. That's politics isn't it? Moreover, your brother is a colonel in the Royal Irish Regiment. How do you know the gunmen were not after you? You do also have friends in Dublin.'

Jackie looked at both of them in turn. He could read their thoughts. Here was a completely naive, unworldly figure bringing trouble down on everyone's heads through his meddling. What was it that Graham Greene said about the 'idealistic innocence' of Homer Pyle in *The Quiet American*, his novel about Vietnam. 'I never knew anyone with better reasons for all the damage that he caused.'

Jackie then sighed, 'I can see you regard me as naive in the extreme. But try and look at things from another perspective; a less straight jacketed approach, if I may use that phrase. There have been two IRA ceasefires in the past decade. This current one has lasted for some years. Life has returned to normal in many respects. You, here, in the army camp may still be in a state of readiness. But you are unusual. Most people, including me, are going about their normal, legitimate business. I have - or had until yesterday - no reason to believe I was in any way behaving in a meddling fashion or being provocative. I was just getting on with my work in a calm atmosphere. You and your commanding officer might still think you are at war. But virtually no one else does. As for Aideen in Dublin, to whom I suppose you are referring, she has nothing to do with anything. She's a friend. I have lots of friends.'

Charles was just about to say something when Curtis put his hand up to stop him and said, 'Fair enough, but what about Dawson? Anything you could tell us about him?'

'I don't know why everyone is so preoccupied with Dawson. Three others were killed you know.' He sighed and went on, 'As I said to the General, there is very little I can add. Seems he was diving for wrecks around Rathlin. The Northern Ireland Police Force is doing some kind of audit of arms, and there were a number of wrecks known to have contained guns. Seems a bit like make-work, but there you are. He was pleasant enough. We chatted in generalities. I knew nothing about his background, except that he had been living abroad and had come back to live in the province recently. I didn't even know what religion he was, or is, rather. Certainly we never discussed politics, or the state of Northern Ireland in anything but the vaguest terms. In fact, the General knew more about him than I did.'

The two colonels looked at one another then said simultaneously, 'What did the General say to you?'

'He said that Dawson had been a member of the UDA a long time ago. He thought there was some connection with William Carstairs. He said there was a lot of talk Carstairs was planning a unilateral declaration of independence. But he dismissed this, said that Carstairs did not have the wherewithal.'

Charles gave a nervous giggle. 'Quite right, absolute nonsense.'

Curtis cut him off again, saying, 'I don't mean to be disrespectful, but our General does have some flights of fancy from time to time. Is there anything else you can add about Dawson?'

The drink was beginning to work and Jackie was starting to chill out after the initial encounter with Charles.

'Dawson did go on in his cups one night about the amount of treasure, salvageable treasure, that lay strewn around the ocean beds of the world. He said there were literally tens of millions pounds' worth of sunken treasure waiting to be claimed. Modern technology made this possible. There were no known wrecks from the Spanish Armada off Rathlin, but it was always possible.'

Curtis jumped in, 'Ah, that was what he was up to. That would explain the Carstairs connection. Carstairs is a businessman. He obviously has his eye on the main chance. Well, that is most helpful John. That certainly clears some things up. Curtis was about to wind up the lunch, when Charles asked, 'Did he put any of this in writing, as far as you know?'

'As a matter of fact, he alludes to salvage techniques in his report.'

Jackie had finally let it slip. Curtis then smoothly enquired, 'What report is this?'

'Dawson drew up a diving log, as he is required to do under the rules of the diving clubs in the province. It was a record of dives they made. What they had found, diving depths and tide currents, nothing out of the ordinary. Bit about the famous wrecks, like *HMS Drake*. There were some passages about recovery techniques.'

'You've obviously read the report. What became of it?'

'I was asked to look after it in the event of an accident. I was asked to give it to William Carstairs. So you are right, there was a Carstairs connection.'

'You were what?'

'Dawson had the impression that William Carstairs was not my favourite person, although, as I have said, we never really discussed politics.'

'Have you still got the report?'

'Matter of fact, I have.

'We would like to have a look at that, if you don't mind'

'I think I do mind. Why are you so excited? What is this? I have been given custody of a straightforward report. Now, I accept all you say about the circumstances being rather dramatic and unusual - but I ought to hand it over to Carstairs, shouldn't I, or at least give it back to Dawson. It is presumably confidential.'

Curtis at his blandest said, 'Again, John, we, you, cannot pretend that nothing has happened. In the ordinary way if the report were as straightforward as you say, then of course the correct thing would be to pass it on to Mr Carstairs. But, given the extraordinary circumstances, we ought to have a look; there might just be something, which could give us a lead. Something, which you, no disrespect, might just have missed. Dawson is in a coma, so there no point trying to give it to him. Moreover, we can get the document to Carstairs more easily than you.'

Jackie thought for a minute. It would make life easier to be rid of the bloody thing and what harm could it do.

'Oh, very well.' He picked up his briefcase, fixed the combination and handed over the envelope. Charles took the report, got up and left the room, saying he would get a copy made. He came back minutes later with the original. The meal was quickly wrapped up.

'Jackie, what are your plans?'

'I'm going to Dublin, but I need to go to Belfast first.'

'I'll organise a car,' said Curtis.

'Don't worry, I'm happy to take the train. If you could get me a lift to the station.'

'Consider it done.'

As Charles and Curtis watched him get in the car, Charles remarked, 'Off to see his floozy in Dublin. Fenian whore.'

'Now Charles, that really is his own business.'

Within in a few minutes, Jackie was sitting on the platform of Lisburn station.

Chapter

11

Once on the train, Jackie went through Dawson's document again. It was straightforward enough. There were thought to be something like 180 wrecks around Rathlin. Most of their histories, their provenance and their depths, as well as their cargoes, were well established. Some had interesting pasts like the *Arlow Hills*, which went aground in 1989. It certainly had been carrying guns. But it had never been established whether they were Protestant or Catholic guns. According to Dawson's log, the police divers had started with the *Arlow Hills* and worked their way through fifty or so more wrecks over the months. They had, inevitably, found very little apart from a lot of conger, ling, dog-fish, cod and some tope, or small sharks. They had not found any new wrecks, still less any trace of treasure-laden wrecks from the Spanish armada.

From what Dawson said, all the easy wrecks, in relatively shallow water, not only around Rathlin, but in many parts of the world, were fished out, so to speak. It was only in deep water that further treasure was to be found. Even in the absence of any evidence, it remained possible that there was some Spanish treasure in the deep water to the north of Rathlin. When Drake scattered the Armada, some ships were known to have gone right round Ireland to find a passage home through the Atlantic.

A section on deep-sea salvage followed the initial log. This mentioned the *Merchant Royal,* a seventeenth century sailing ship, originally thought to have sunk in the Atlantic off the Isles of Scilly. Further archaeological research by the maritime detectives - and there were a growing army of these, poring over charts at Admiralty House - later placed the *Merchant Royal* in the western approaches to Scotland.

Jackie noted that when the vessel went down in 1641, the treasure in Mexican silver bars and pieces of eight was thought to be one-third of the national exchequer. The more he read, the more it seemed that this was the vessel that Dawson was really interested in, behind the screen of police diving.

The twenty-minute train ride had been enough to read through the report and Jackie was just coming to the end as the train pulled into Belfast's Botanic station. Students in overcoats, anoraks and scarves milled around on the opposite platform, waiting for trains to take them to Belfast's faceless suburbs and satellite towns. Jackie stayed on the train for the two-minute ride to Belfast Central station.

The report was interesting enough. But it was hardly something to get killed for. Certainly it showed that the arms audit was a cover for a treasure hunt. But the treasure was theoretical. The report just said there could be untold wealth on the seabed and the means existed to recover it. Hardly exclusive information. Moreover, the whole thing read as if it were recycled. It gave Jackie a definite sense of déjà vu, as if he had read it all before somewhere. Very strange, he thought. He put the document back in his satchel, got off the train and climbed the stairs to the station exit on the bridge over the railway.

Back in Lisburn, Charles Wilson, having run off another copy of the report for Curtis, read through it. He looked at Curtis: 'That looks pretty innocuous, don't you think? The only thing you could read into it is that Dawson, and, by extension, Carstairs, are not doing on Rathlin exactly what they say they are doing. There is no crime in that. You couldn't deduce from this document that there is any plan to import arms. I do not think this document implicates us in any way.'

Curtis said nothing for a long thirty seconds, then he looked up and, staring hard at Charles, said slowly, 'I think someone really devious, or really acute, would realise this report is a fabrication. Let us hope your brother is as naive as he seems.'

Charles got up from his chair, walked to his desk and dialled a number in Ballycastle.

'Hello, Marine Hotel.'

'I'd like to speak to Mr William Carstairs, it's Charles Wilson speaking.'

'Just a minute, trying to connect you.'

Two minutes passed. That's a long time to wait on a phone. Come on, thought Wilson.

'He's not in his room.'

'Well, page him, please.'

At last, Carstairs came to the phone. He had been lunching in silence with Billy and Joe.

'William Carstairs speaking.'

'William, it's Charles Wilson. There was indeed a report. My brother John was given it to look after in case of accidents.'

As he spoke, he could almost feel the tension rising at the other end of the phone. He hurried on, 'But don't worry. It is perfectly harmless. It just deals with the salvage of possible bullion. There is a little about wrecks which might have been used for gun running. It suggests that Dawson was not there for quite the reasons he was supposed to be, hence the need for some secrecy. But it is a perfectly plausible cover. There is no hint of any transhipments of you-know-what, or any suggestion of any other kind of wealth. There is no law which says you cannot make a bit of money.' Wilson spoke circumspectly, you never knew about phones in Northern Ireland.

Carstairs could not contain his anxiety, 'Why in the devil's name has your brother got mixed up in this? If there is nothing in the report, the report I knew about, that means there has to be another one. Where is it? Are you sure he hasn't got it? How do you know your brother is not stringing you along?'

'William, we've had him here for hours. He has even seen the General, who, of course, knows nothing of our plans,' he added hastily. 'John is either the best actor in the world, or he genuinely does not suspect our real purpose. I doubt it has even occurred to him.'

'I'd feel reassured if you would interrogate him again. There has to be a report on the other thing. Dawson had to write something down. You cannot commit that kind of detail to memory.'

'Fraid I cannot do that, William. You see he's gone to Dublin, well, by way of Belfast first.'

This was almost too much for Carstairs, who became paranoiac as easily as most people caught the common cold.

'He has gone where?'

'He is on his way to Dublin. He has a lady friend down there.'

'Who might she be?'

'She is Aideen O'Connor, actually.'

Carstairs knew who she was. In his mind a conspiracy clicked into place like a combination lock.

'Your brother,' he yelled,' has gone off with a document containing important information, to see his girlfriend, who is a well-known republican journalist. In the name of all the saints, do you want the whole world knowing what we are up to on Rathlin. Have you now got the document?'

'No. I took a copy. But William...' He didn't get a chance to finish.

'You took a copy. Well get the original back. I don't care how you do it, just get it back.'

Charles Wilson was beginning to feel like a little boy who had been sent to the corner shop and come back with the wrong thing. 'William, I really feel you are being a bit overdramatic. There is nothing in that report that gives any hint at all as to our true purposes on Rathlin. In fact, quite the reverse. In a sense Dawson has done his job well. It gives a perfectly plausible explanation as to why Dawson is really there. I would stake my life that John does not know anything he shouldn't.'

'Colonel Wilson, if I make the assumption that you are not a complete idiot, will you repay the complement? I repeat: your brother has gone off to Dublin with a secret document to stay with his girl friend, a journalist. I can see the Sunday newspapers now. There will be a huge display speculating that the Police Force men may have been killed because of some kind of industrial sabotage. Who is this man Dawson they will ask. There will be lots of hints about buried treasure. Is anyone going to believe that? Fish may fly.'

'Before we know what's hit us, we will have every journalist in the world crawling over Rathlin, buying drinks for the locals, trying to get what they call an angle. Rathlin will become the most televised island in the western hemisphere. Something is bound to come out. Already we are under siege here from the local press. The Dublin gang is most certainly on its way. There is also the very key question of where to find the data we need. If it is not with the report, then where in God's name is it? No, my dear colonel, we, or rather you, have got to get back in touch with your brother and relieve him of the document. We, or rather I, since I am here, have got to get to Rathlin before everyone else does and establish what went wrong.'

'How do you suggest I catch up with my brother?' Wilson said. 'Ireland is a foreign country. We have no jurisdiction there.'

'Yes, I know it is a foreign country. You must have some apparatus down there. Now I have to get on.'

Colonel Wilson put the phone down and said to Curtis, 'Did you catch all that? Says we, or rather I, was stupid to let John go without relieving him of the document. Says it will be all over the papers, the island will be crawling with pressmen and our best-laid plans will be blown. Also says that the data has got to be somewhere, where the hell is it.'

'He has got a point,' Curtis replied. 'Even if your brother has not put two and two together, it won't be long before the place is overrun with the press. The idea that Dawson and the others were bumped off because they had found buried treasure, or someone thought they had, won't hold for five minutes once exposed to harsh sunlight. We should have relieved him of the documents when we had the chance. Ah me.'

'Yes, but that would have immediately raised his suspicions.'

'Suppose so. The only thing we can do is get hold of Ollie in the embassy in Dublin. Six has been known to do the occasional chore for Five. No reason they can't help us out.'

'Smart thinking, David. If memory serves, Ollie was a direct contemporary of John's at Cambridge. That might be an added bonus.'

*

Jackie thought about a taxi, but decided to walk. From the bridge outside the station you could see the crane symbolising the Harland and Wolff dockyards. They probably weren't called Harland and Wolff any more, but the dockyards were still there in some shape or form. As in many old industrial towns, an attempt had been made to tart up the riverside. The Lagan had been a particularly scruffy little river. Now it had widened walkways and themed towpaths, and a brand new five star hotel.

In the foreground stood the imposing Central Criminal Court. Still with barbed wire on the top of its outer walls and armed policemen on the gates, it stood like some muscle-bound bouncer separating the Lagan side developments from the city centre. Perhaps things would never be completely normal in Ulster, there would always be reminders of the fault-line running through the province.

But Jackie always marvelled at the changes whenever he entered Belfast. The images embedded in his mind were those of his teenage years, when the street troubles were no longer at their height, but were still ongoing: a mass of soldiers scrambling on to a piggy armoured car, the scream of fire engines, police moving forward behind rows of plastic shields, with rubber bullets thumping against walls, small boys digging up roads and hurling bombs made from milk bottles, women banging dustbin lids on the streets and ululating almost Middle East style, burnt-out buses overturned and used as makeshift road blocks. Always, it seemed, there was a lowering, grey, autumnal sky and always the smells of acrid tear gas and burning hanging over the town like brown halitosis.

The surrounding Belfast hills were bleak and scarred with rows of uniform pink houses. Bombed property was just left, so that in some of the ghetto streets the little two-up two-downs were like a drunk with some teeth knocked out. Other houses had bricked-up windows so that, in Dervla Murphy's deathless phrase, they looked like corpses. Belfast was an ancient prize-fighter who had taken too much punishment. Bruised and battered, it had bits of its anatomy missing. For years, the central shopping area around Royal Avenue, which Jackie now approached, had had all its entrances sealed by a corset of steel gates, topped with barbed wire. Security checks were made in wooden huts, which you had to pass through to get to the shops.

How different it was now. Part of the shopping precinct had

been pedestrianised. Royal Avenue was thronged with shoppers. Many would be up from Dublin and the Republic to take advantage of the lower prices because of lower taxes. With its baroque town hall and other Victorian buildings, you could have been in the middle of Leeds, or Manchester, or any of the other great cities of northern England or Scotland with roots in the nineteenth century.

But it was brighter and slicker than some other cities which had developed a certain shabbiness in their post-industrial life. Their age had started to show, but Belfast had had a lot of cosmetic surgery. Successive British governments, in a void of real economic and political policies, had reverted to just throwing money at the problem in the hope it would go away.

In education, housing, employment and health, as well as security and policing, the province was not only the most subsidised part of the United Kingdom, it was amongst the most heavily supported parts of Europe. Before the countries of the former Soviet Union had started to climb aboard the gravy train, only the Republic of Ireland had received more handouts from the European Union in Brussels.

Northern Ireland has always had a huge public sector bureaucracy. With the first flush of peace, Government departments, previously crammed into temporary buildings that had somehow become permanent, were rehoused in gleaming new office blocks with more glass than had once been deemed prudent in the city. The streets leading south from the centre to the Queen's University area had come alive with bistros, renovated pubs, teashops and bijou craft shops, without one security grille between them. Dinky designer houses with gardens replaced rows of burnt-out terraces. Belfast, indeed, had some of the best, award winning, public housing in the United Kingdom, courtesy of the British taxpayer.

People no longer walked singly and briskly, looking anxiously to either side. Drinkers no longer lined the walls of the few pubs, looking silently at the doors to watch for strangers who might walk in. It was as if, with the second ceasefire, people had to be out on the streets to reaffirm their lives; a ritual to exorcise the ghosts of disappointment and despair.

Jackie passed one such group of young men, in boots, jeans and leather jackets, as he entered the portals of the Linenhall Library. Once, if they had been there at all, they would have gazed at him intently; now, self-absorbed, they totally ignored him.

As Jackie climbed the winding staircase, holding the brightly polished brass hand rail, his brother had finally managed to contact Oliver Sweetman at the British Embassy in Ballsbridge, Dublin. Back from a good, vinous lunch with an opposition politician in Bailey's restaurant in central Dublin, Sweetman brayed down the phone, 'Colonel Wilson, my dear fellow, to what do I owe this pleasure?'

Ignoring the condescending tone, Charles Wilson explained the situation and suggested it might be a good idea if Oliver Sweetman and his colleagues could somehow relieve Jackie of the document. As Charles spoke, Sweetman saw his early cut on Friday and long weekend on the west coast vaporising before his eyes. He responded cautiously:

'I'm not sure this comes within our bailiwick, old boy. We can't go meddling in the affairs of a foreign country. You know how sensitive they are down here about us poking our noses into the north.'

This was a standard Foreign Office line; we are only guests here, etc. etc. Wilson knew, and knew that Sweetman knew that he knew, that Sweetman was playing for time. This was a good sign for Wilson. Officially Oliver Sweetman was Counsellor, or number two, in the large British Embassy in Dublin. He nominally reported on economic and political developments in the Republic. Unofficially he had, as they say, links with the intelligence services. He wasn't part of MI6, still less MI5, but, yes, if pushed, he did have 'chums' who might do him the odd favour from time to time.

'Do our friends in the other branches of Her Majesty's loyal services know anything about this?' By this he meant either MI5 or the Police Special Branch. Army intelligence clearly did, since it was Charles Wilson who was telephoning.

'Not from us they don't. Of course, with the Rathlin events, everyone and his brother is devilling around. But, as far as we know, knowledge of the document is fairly restricted. Look, Oliver, I know I can trust your discretion on this, but it is vital that this doesn't get into the press. You probably know - Dublin is a small place - of John's friendship with Aideen O'Connor. It would be unfortunate if any details from this document should find their way into the public prints. The bottom line, of course, is that John is a British citizen, and a friend of yours.'

'I wouldn't call him a friend exactly, but yes, I do know him. Look, this is most difficult. Why don't you leave it with me and I'll see what I can do.'

'I'd appreciate that, we'll be in touch, and mum's the word okay?'

'Of course, of course.'

When Oliver Sweetman put down the phone, his immediate thought was, how the devil am I supposed to relieve John Wilson of a document. Sweetman had been slightly economical with the truth on the phone. That morning a telegram had come from London. It was addressed to the Ambassador from the head of MI6 suggesting that if Dr John Wilson, aka Lord Strangford, were to turn up in Dublin, it might be useful for someone to have a quiet word with him. He had been on Rathlin, and he might be able to shed some light on events. As with most cables of this type, the nuances spoke volumes of possibilities. The Ambassador and Sweetman had agreed that Oliver would do a trawl of the most likely watering holes and try and have a word with John Wilson.

Yes, Sweetman did know Wilson. They had been exact contemporaries at Cambridge. But he could hardly call him a friend. Sweetman had thought him a bit unsound even then. What was the word they used at the time, a bit flaky? Wilson would have been known as a bohemian if he had gone up to Cambridge a decade earlier. He dressed casually and was interested in all the fashionable causes, environment and so on.

Oliver was bestowed with all the certainties of his background. His father had been a diplomat. Oliver, who was small and wiry, did not excel at sports but like a lot of small people, he was intensely competitive in other ways. It was as if he could add a few inches by always being top of the class. He emerged from Cambridge with a double first and had been not only chairman of the Conservative Association but also President of the Union.

He had considered going straight into politics by the traditional route of researching at Central Office or joining one of the think tanks. He had also thought about reading for the Bar. But his father had persuaded him that the Foreign Office still offered a good career, even though, like so many of the professions, it had been downsized and thrown open to competition. Curzon would roll in his grave, but some of the top positions had been given to businessmen. It was like America; if you had made enough money you could buy a plum posting. Officially the argument was that as foreign missions now had primarily to deal with trade matters, it was good to have ambassadors with a business background. What did the traditional mandarin know about selling goods abroad?

Oliver had moved swiftly within the office. His first posting was to Tehran (he had the advantage of being good at languages.) After a stint in Brussels, where he began to move into the fast lane, he returned to London, was promoted and started his connection with MI6; another posting followed, this time to Dublin.

Ireland was not everyone's cup of tea. It imposed restraints on personal lives. Marianne, Sweetman's wife who towered over him by some four inches, found life in Dublin confining, although, God knows, compared with Belfast, it was fairly relaxed for diplomats. But the constant security, guards at the house etc, were a bore. Marianne spent more and more time in London (there were no children) and the marriage came under pressure. Oliver might have anticipated all this. Nevertheless, he opted for Dublin when the opportunity arose because it offered rapid promotion, and it could prove useful later when, and if, he decided to make the jump into politics. He had the rank of under-secretary and he was still only 40.

Oliver reflected on his phone call; there had been no mention of any documents in the telegram from London. This put rather a different complexion on matters, gave it a greater sense of urgency. There would be no weekend away. He would have to track Wilson's whereabouts. First he needed to know a little bit more about Aideen O'Connor's habits. He telephoned a hotel in Galway and cancelled his reservation. Then he called a journalist he knew on one of the posher Irish dailies.

*

In the Linenhall Library, Jackie went up to the circular desk and asked for the copy of McCahan's Local Histories - a series of pamphlets on North Antrim and the Glens. It was published by the Glens of Antrim Historical Society. A leather bound volume, it was not a genuine antiquarian book, since its publication date was 1923. It was unique, however, in that it was a compilation of a series of pamphlets compiled in the late nineteenth century by Robert McCahan, a staunchly Protestant bookseller, local historian and publisher, born in Ballycastle in 1863. Pamphlet H was called *History of Rathlin Island*.

The tiny, bird-like lady behind the counter came around and

unlocked the glass cabinet and, holding the volume carefully like a pack of cards that was about to splatter, gently handed it to Jackie.

'Do you want me to sign for it?'

'No, we know you well enough. It'll be all right.'

Jackie went off to the small reading room, which he was glad to see he had to himself. Although his real objective was the references to the Gage family he was, as usual, diverted from his path. The History began with a general description of the island's geography and location, together with a section on bird life. Next was a long passage on the Norwegians and the Danes, the Abbots they installed and the tangled web of marriages and alliances of sons and daughters to establish hegemony. It is not until King John and, later, Robert the Bruce, that the history comes alive with constant wars, skirmishes and the granting of Rathlin to various barons to secure loyalty with the gift of ownership.

After John, King of England, had landed at Carrickfergus in 1210 and suppressed Hugh De Lacy's rebellion, Rathlin was included in a grant of lands which he made to Alanus De Galweia, Earl of Atholl. By Elizabethan times, Rathlin seemed to come under the sway of the McDonnells from Kintyre and Arran in Scotland. The McDonnells appeared to be simultaneously involved in warfare against the Irish in Ulster, the English in Ireland and in constant raids on Rathlin by Elizabeth's generals who wanted to establish garrisons there.

In 1575, Walter Devereux, Earl of Essex, recommended that a garrison should be stationed on the island. He believed that a permanent garrison would strengthen English power in this part of the country and overawe the Irish, as well as the MacDonnells in the Glens of Antrim and along the coast. The MacDonnells decided not to tamely submit to such an arrangement. Sorley Boy MacDonnell reinforced the island with men. He thought the island would be a refuge, but unfortunately it turned into a death trap. His own side betrayed him and Captain John Norris, Essex's commander, massacred more than 600 people, including members of Sorley's family sent to the island for safety.

But by 1603 the MacDonnells were back in control of the island. It was included in a grant of lands given to Sir Randal MacDonnell.

In 1617, however, after the death of Elizabeth, one George Crawford of Lisnorris in Ayrshire commenced an action against Sir Randal MacDonnell claiming that in 1500 the island was granted to his ancestors (the Redes) by James IV of Scotland.

His case was that: 'All the cosmographers account the Hebrides or Aemonae insulae to belong to Scotland, like as all of them consider Raughlin to be one of the same, that the island belonged to John, Lord of the Isles, by whose forfeiture it fell to the crown of Scotland, that James IV, AD 1500, granted to Adam Reade and his heirs; that his grandson, Adam Read, dying AD 1575 seized of it, left four daughters; that Henry Stewart, the husband of the eldest daughter, claimed it and also obtained from the King a new grant for it. That he afterwards sold his title to George Crawford of Lisnorris.'

Jackie loved digging into the history and this was all fascinating stuff. But he was being diverted. Guiltily, he reminded himself that his real purpose was to look at the question of who owned what.

One way and another, the MacDonnells seem to have lost control to the Campbells during the period of the Jacobite uprisings. It was a Campbell, the Marquis of Argyle, who perpetrated the massacre at Crook-na-Screichen, the 'Hill of Screaming.' But the MacDonnells must have regained control, since on March 10, 1746 the fifth Earl of Antrim, Alexander MacDonnell, sold the island to a Mr Gage.

Ah, now I'm getting warm, Jackie thought. Even though the history was not very well written and the subject matter swerved all over the place, the chronology was vaguely in order. He ploughed on. The rental paid to Mr Gage was £600, and in the same year barley valued at £600 was sold. The Gage family, he read, traced their descent from a Norman knight named Da Gaga. There was then page upon page about who married who, and how the Gages intermarried with the Lovats in Scotland.

Jackie looked at his watch. Damn, ten past four. He would have to move fast if he wanted to catch the train. He hadn't found what he wanted. He packed up quickly and, thanking the lady, bounded down the stairs. He walked briskly to the station and bought himself a ticket for the Enterprise Express. This was a bit of a misnomer. It still took three hours for a journey of just over 100 miles. There had been talk of speeding up the service and having trains every two hours, but as with so many areas of life, the Dublin and British authorities had been unable to agree on who would pay, so there were three very slow trains a day.

Nor was the train very enterprising, if the restaurant car was anything to go by. Jackie treated himself to a first class ticket on this line because the normal class was, as they say, not well appointed. At least you could get a meal in first class. But it was very standard fare, with bullet peas, soggy chips and dried out fish. This came with a choice between a rough red wine and two kinds of white wine, one impossibly sweet. It would undoubtedly be a long evening in Dublin, so Jackie took it easy on the drinks front. He ordered fish and chips and half a bottle of the dry white wine, paint stripper as he called it, and settled down with his book for the gentle amble to the Irish capital.

*

In Ballycastle, Carstairs was fuming to breaking point. A further trip to the jetty had yielded nothing. In fact, when he finally located Gerry in Blake's Bar (the Harbour Bar being closed), he was curtly told: 'Won't be going today. Tomorrow, early. Storm's dropping.'

With this, Carstairs returned to the Marine Hotel, picked up his phone and dialled a Belfast number.

'Philip. It's William. Without going into too much detail, I want you to activate one of the units in Dublin. Dr John Wilson, you know, the environmentalist fellow, has a document belonging to me. Just relieve him of it, would you? I'm told he is in the company of the Fenian whore, Aideen O'Connor. You know the one. Well, find her and you'll find him. Tell our men to be discreet. No violence. I don't want this reaching the newspapers.'

'Right you are, William. Can I tell the lads what they are looking for?'

'They'll know right enough. It's about Rathlin.'

'Okay William.'

After the phone call Carstairs paced round the room, mentally preening himself about his organisation. The Loyalist paramilitaries were always being written off. Not only did he have the Police Force wrapped up, he had cells in Dublin and London. Up 'til now he hadn't had to use them. If the IRA could have cells, Active Service Units, then so could he. He left his room and went down to the lobby looking for his son for company. It was six o'clock and dark outside.

Chapter

12

Aaah Dublin! Jackie's spirits never failed to lift as he stepped out of Connolly station. Belfast was an austere, Victorian gentleman of a city. Dublin was feminine, like a high-class whore, beautiful but a little battered; elegant yet slightly tawdry.

Belfast remained provincial; Dublin had become a European capital city, exuberant and nonchalantly living beyond its means. People in Belfast were pasty faced and despite years of peace still looked as if they had unmanageable overdrafts at the bank, or arthritis, or both. Dubliners were ruddy cheeked, and wore their troubles lightly, determined, as the popular song had it, to face the music and dance, despite the troubles ahead. Jackie patted the stone wall as he walked down the cobbled drive from Connolly Station towards the River Liffey. Two old freighters were on the river, looking like stranded, dirty swans amid the reflections of the neon lights of the city.

Dublin, like most modern cities had suffered its share of redevelopment, with its Internet cafes, waterfront restaurants and flats. But there was simply too much of Georgian Dublin extant to change the character of the city. Just below him on the banks of the Liffey, was the Customs House, now a successful financial centre. In the middle of town were Trinity College and Dublin Castle, immovable and indestructible. There were any number of squares and terraces dating from Regency times. And there were the pubs. Dublin pubs, the traditional ones, had managed to avoid the invasion of jukeboxes and fruit machines and pool tables. They often had live Irish music, fiddles, drums and pipes, and remained spit and sawdust affairs. Irish public houses had become fashionable in London and other British cities in the early 1990s, but these were the originals, McDaid's, Mulligan's, O'Donoghue's, and Toner's. Years on, they were still redolent of literary Dublin with the lingering ghosts of Yeats, James Joyce and Brendan Behan.

Jackie cut through the labyrinth of streets next to the station, emerging just behind the Abbey Theatre. This was the inner city. Early in the 20th century this area had been so poor it was compared with Naples. Seeing two young people propped up against a wall outside a dilapidated hotel, not far from some vomit, he was reminded that Dublin had developed one of the worst drug problems in Europe, with the police seemingly powerless to arrest it. He hurried on and emerged into the garish lights of O'Connell Street, the main strip on Dublin's north side, with amusement arcades, cinema complexes, hamburger joints and orange buses, almost stately in their progress up and down the wide boulevard.

At 8.30 on a Friday evening, the street was packed with people, determinedly bent on pleasure, despite a sharp wind and drizzle. Definitely a soddit factor operated in flatulent, hedonistic Dublin. Jackie marched across the bridge and cut into D'Olier Street, just before the walls of Trinity College.

He climbed the narrow stairs to the first floor bar of Fleet's which was packed to the rafters. There was a buzz of chatter with the occasional shriek or yell breaking it up. The customers stood in their overcoats and mackintoshs, or sat at low tables, with their Guinness glasses making dark rings on the glass tops. The suffused light gave the bar an intimate air, people jostled and swayed easily. Jackie fought his way towards the bar and, as he forced apart the last two people in his path, Eamonn, the barman, saw him.

'Ah, Jackie, message for you from Aideen, if you were to show, yer to go straight to Buswells where herself is taking a drink with Dick McGuinness. You'll take something yerself first?' It was a question rather than a command. Jackie replied, 'No, no, thank you, Eamonn, I'll push on.'

Jackie felt crestfallen. A long evening of social drinking and chatting loomed into prospect, when all he really wanted to do was be alone with Aideen. The weeks of celibacy and isolation on Rathlin with Siobhan and, less frequently, Dawson for real company, had taken their toll, he now realised. It was fine when he was actually there. He really enjoyed himself in his work. It was like drinking, once you stopped, non-drinking became addictive.

Now that he was away from the island and in Dublin, the tension of the past day ran out of him. He proposed to put everything on hold and surrender to a nice, hedonistic weekend with Aideen. This assumed, of course, he could wrench her away from the *craic*, the constant round of talk and revelry, which was integral to Dublin life. He would inevitably be cross-examined, which was going to be boring. What was she doing with McGuinness? It was her work, he supposed.

Now that he had actually left the island, he realised he probably had another reason for wanting to leave. Siobhan was beginning to irritate him. He constantly found her watching him. She seemed to lurk behind doors monitoring his comings and goings. Hope she didn't fancy him. Tony was away a lot on the ferry and with the fishing. She was attractive enough, he had to admit that. But it would never do, not on a small, close knit island like that.

Jackie fought his way out of the bar and walked around the entrance to Trinity College. The railings were festooned with posters, 'Brits out Now.' The huge wooden doors, studded with painted iron, were locked shut, apart from a little doorway in the middle. The

Bank of Ireland building opposite, with columns, a sculpture and fountain, was newly scrubbed.

Jackie swung around the other side of Trinity and cut through South Frederick Street, with its rows of brass plates announcing firms of solicitors. He emerged into Molesworth Street and to Buswell's, opposite the Dail or Parliament.

Buswell's was a natural watering hole for politicians and journalists. Upstairs an attempt had been made to evoke a fine Georgian atmosphere, with chintz floral seats set among Sheraton tables. Irish matrons would take their afternoon tea from silver pots under ornate chandeliers. Downstairs was a long bar. There was a staircase inside and another staircase from the street.

He saw Aideen halfway down over the shoulders of a smaller man who was standing with his elbow resting on the bar. She was jabbing with her fingers when she saw Jackie coming. She did a double take, then grinned widely. McGuinness half turned around, thought better of it and turned back to Aideen. Jackie pushed his way through the crowd.

'How are yer darlin'? 'Tis good to see yer. You know Dick McGuinness, he used to be the minister for security. Dick, this is John Wilson.'

McGuinness didn't wait for the niceties but dived straight in. 'Yes indeed, how are you Mr Wilson, or should I call you Lord Strangford? Have you just come from the troubled province? That was a nasty piece of business up on Rathlin. I hear tell you were actually on the island at the time. What do you make of it all?'

Jackie looked at the chubby, red veined face and the brown, wiry hair turning grey. He thought, you are very well on, you drunken bum. But said, 'The incident happened in Ballycastle, I was on the island. I probably know as much as you do.'

Jackie never ceased to be amazed at the informality of the Irish generally and of Irish politicians in particular. Here he was conversing with a former minister in the company of a journalist, being asked sensitive questions only seconds after meeting. McGuinness was two parts drunk already and undoubtedly would be very drunk before the evening was out, but there was no embarrassment, no guilt attached to having a good time and being uninhibited. Jackie came from a world where politeness could be a substitute for good intentions. Nevertheless preliminary small talk was a necessary rite of passage before anything beyond the superficial could be discussed.

The strangest thing of all was that if he were to see McGuinness at Bewleys, the coffee house, for breakfast the next day, McGuinness would act as if nothing had happened. He would make some remark like, 'Sure, didn't we have good craic last night.'

On the unlikely assumption that Jackie were to find himself in a similar situation with a British government minister, it would be all circling and embarrassment. The next day it would be something along the lines of, 'I may have got slightly out of hand last night, old boy. Been under a lot of pressure. I do hope you will overlook any intemperance and forget about it.'

McGuinness ploughed on 'But surely..' when the small figure of Oliver Sweetman joined them, coming as from nowhere, a whiskey in his hand.

'Thought it was you, how have you been, Jackie?'

Jackie, taken by surprise, responded, 'Fine, thanks. Do you know Aideen O'Connor and Dick McGuinness?'

Sweetman's arrival had caused an instant frosting in both Aideen and McGuinness.

'We've met,' they both said.

'Sorry to butt in like this, but it's so long since I've seen you, thought it would be nice to say hello.' Sweetman said.

McGuinness almost burped out, 'Well, I'd best be off then.'

'Oh Dick, please don't go, Jackie's only just got here,' Aideen pleaded.

'No, must away,' and with that he was gone through the door leading to the street. It wouldn't do to be seen supping with Sweetman, who himself was unfazed by this. He was conscious of Aideen glaring at him, but continued, 'Oh dear, I don't seem to be very popular this evening. I am sorry to break up your party but it would be nice to catch up.'

Jackie let out a roar of laughter: 'Oh, sure it would, I suppose you want to catch up on racial relations on Rathlin Island, with a little bit about Ballycastle.'

'Oh come now, I hope I am not that obvious.'

'Fraid you are. Look Ollie, I've got to come into town tomorrow morning and do some things - why don't we have a jar in Doheny's about twelve?'

'Fine, twelve it is then. Good, I'll be off. Good night Miss O'Connor.'

Aideen just nodded then turned on Jackie,

'Why in God's name are yer fixing to meet him? Everyone knows he is a British spy.'

'Well, I got rid of him didn't I? In fact I arranged for him to come up so that I could get rid of McGuinness and have you to myself.'

'The hell you did.'

'Anyway he's gone. I think I'll have a drink now. Make it a hot whiskey.'

Jackie looked at her properly now. She wore a three-quarter-length tailored brown corduroy skirt, which stressed the slimness of her long legs. This was over high-heeled leather boots. A long woollen cardigan came down to her thighs and under this her cream silk blouse was provocatively unbuttoned to her cleavage. It hung easily on her large round breasts emphasising their firmness, then fell away down to her small waist. Jackie felt he wanted nothing more than to put his hand inside the blouse and bra and fondle the breast until she became aroused. Lay a hand on Aideen and she was away.

As if reading his thoughts, she flushed. He broke the intimate private moment with a question: 'Did you miss me?'

'I s'pose.'

'What do you mean, s'pose? I thought you were panting for me, couldn't wait to get your hands on me.'

'Panting for you, was I? Away with you, Jackie Wilson. Would you ever stop being so crude. How a well-brought-up gentleman like yourself can be so vulgar I'll never know.'

'Precisely. It is because of my public school upbringing, shower room chat amongst the chaps and all that, boys only. I intend to be very crude, intimate and obscene."

'Well yer just embarrassing me, you shit.' She paused. 'Maybe we can be a little of all three, but later.'

They both started giggling.

'We've to meet Brian and Fergus in Doheny's for a jar, then go for a meal. You know you like those two, now don't cha?'

'Aideen, I've had a hell of a day, can't we just go to your house and fornicate?'

'Oh, come on, I promised. They'd love to see yer.'

'Oh, very well.' So they hauled themselves up and walked out the front entrance into the street.

'Can I at least put my grip in your car. I don't want to be lugging these bags through every crowded street in Dublin.'

'Sure, Okay. I'm parked in the Dail, one of the privileges of my position don't cha know.'

They walked across to Leinster House. She flashed her pass, was waved on and he dumped his grip in the little Renault. He was about to put his briefcase in too, but thought better of it. Unnoticed, Dick McGuinness was watching all this from Brogan's office.

Jackie and Aideen walked back out up Kildare Street, swung

left into St Stephen's Green, past the Shelbourne Hotel with its green awnings and uniformed porters hailing taxis, and into Baggot Street. In a distance of only a couple of hundred yards Aideen saw at least four people she knew. It was ever thus, it was a small town and you couldn't move without someone asking you for lunch, dinner, a drink. Jackie always found this unsettling. When they got to Doheny and Nesbitt's, it was jam-packed.

People were passing pints of Guinness over the heads of those nearest the bar, as if in some rescue operation. Jackie suddenly couldn't face it. The combination of drink, strain and travel made him decide he'd almost had enough. Jackie didn't mind Brian and Fergus - they were academics like himself- but he needed to go somewhere quieter.

'Why don't you go in and get them and we'll go off somewhere for a bite.' Jackie had already eaten but he knew he wasn't going to get off without at least seeing these two. Aideen plunged into Doheny's and was soon swallowed up by the crowd. The three of them emerged minutes later like corks from wine bottles.

'Jackie, how are yer?' said Fergus.

'I hope you don't mind if we go off and eat. I thought we might try Bernardo's,' he replied

'Not at all. Will we walk?'

The four of them turned around and went back the way they had come, right the length of Kildare Street. Even now there were only a few very good restaurants in Dublin. But a place like the Mirabeau out in Dun Loaghaire was fiercely expensive. So too, was The Bailey in town. The curve of demand then went plunging down until it met the straight, unyielding baseline of supply, in the form of McDonald's or Chinese and Indian restaurants of variable quality.

There were one or two exceptions on the way down the curve, one of them was Bernardo's. It was an old-fashioned Italian restaurant, like Bertorelli's used to be in London. There were ancient family waiters and crisp white tablecloths and napkins. Aldo, the maitre d', was pleased to see them. Jackie thought he knew before he even reached the table the way the conversation was going to go. So he was pleasantly surprised when Fergus, who was an economist, opened up with, 'How is your study going, Jackie?'

'Oh, you know, slowly, slowly.' He then put his own foot in it. 'Things are not helped by the dramatic events of the past twenty-four hours.'

'I think it is all a Protestant plot to discredit the IRA,' said Brian.

'Sure it is,' said Aideen. Jackie looked at her sharply, not sure whether she meant it or was trying to provoke him.

Here we go again, thought Jackie. Amazing. These were Dublin intellectuals, not stupid people. But though they were far from the scene, with no possible way of knowing what had happened in Ballycastle, they gave in to the kind of republican or "green" fascism that even at the end of the twentieth century was inculcated into every schoolboy in the Republic. Ireland was a young country, barely 90 years old, with young institutions, yet it was locked into an ancient cosmology of interconnected bardic myths and Catholic confessionalism which held that back in the mists of time there was one united, happy, artistic, democratic island.

'I might expect some kind of inane remark like that from you, Aideen,' said Jackie, putting her down. 'But Brian, how can you possibly know what happened? I have just come from the area. I knew one of the victims reasonably well. And I sure as hell do not know what went on.'

'The way I see it is this,' said Brian. 'Things were going too well for the IRA. They have got almost everything they want. If yer woman pulls out the troops, then the game is virtually all over for the Prods.'

'Don't you believe it,' came in Fergus. 'The Prods won't just lie down. They'll think of something. But it is difficult to believe that this is it. On the other hand, it is also difficult to imagine the Ra (his name for the IRA) would pull a stunt like this at this point. What could they possibly gain?'

Aideen said, 'I wouldn't put it past some of those extreme Prods like Carstairs' lot to orchestrate something like this; it could result in the Brits staying and we're back to square one.'

Jackie had had enough. 'For God's sake can't we talk about something else.?'

Aideen reacted instinctively. 'Mother of the Saints. Can't you see Jackie, this is vitally important to us. This is the future of our country. Do you really expect that people are not going to ask you what you think? You've just come from there.'

Aideen had begun to anglicise her speech. This always happened when she was in his company. She started off taunting him with extreme and often silly views, not truly passionately held (she was too intelligent for that). She liked the irritation bordering on anger it produced. But she was so besotted with him she was careful not to push it too far. The longer she spent with him, she always found her persona dissolving into compliance with his mien of dispassionate rationality

'Who says it's your country?' Jackie said tauntingly and uncharacteristically, but, before they could respond, he quickly added: 'Look I have spoken to God knows how many people about this today. I really don't know what happened, and I have no theories. Can we please talk about something else? How's the Irish economy, Fergus?'

Seeing that they were going to get no further and not feeling particularly strongly about the issue on a Friday night, Fergus replied, 'We are all excited about the oil find in the Atlantic.'

'Yes, I heard about that. What is it? A big gusher like the North Sea?' said Jackie, relieved to be on neutral ground.

'Heavens, no. The Connemara Field is pretty small, probably about 60 million barrels. That means it wouldn't even fill half Ireland's needs, let alone leave anything for export. We've always known the stuff was there - it just wasn't worth getting it out. The water's very deep and rough and we've no infrastructure, pipes, refineries and the like, and it's a hundred miles from shore. But now, with horizontal drilling and moveable storage, it's become economic to exploit. The interesting thing is that geologists think that the Porcupine Trough, which includes the Connemara Field, is part of the same structure as the West of Shetland fields. It comes round in a great arc, if you follow me. Now, if that is true, then there could be a lot more out there. Connemara is only a puddle. If there are some large fields, then Ireland could become a player in the oil market. Okay, I know the oil price is volatile but even so, it could be important to a country like Ireland, with no real energy sources save some gas. Anyway, be good for Galway.'

'Perish the thought,' said Jackie, who had seen other Klondyke towns, where a discovery of oil had suddenly transformed little sleepy backwaters and wiped out their charms.

The evening then proceeded gently on its downward slope. Jackie had sardines, while the others had fritto misto, pasta, cheese, the works. They all had a lot of Bardolino red wine, for which Jackie thought they would all be paying the next morning in terms of thick heads. But they had all started to relax. At about 11.30 Jackie called for the bill. They went Dutch. They said their goodbyes outside Bernardo's, Aideen put her arm into Jackie's and they walked slowly up to Leinster House and the Renault. Aideen showed her pass.

'Wait now, I'll put my briefcase in the boot,' said Jackie. Then, again, he thought better of it. 'Oh it's only a short hop, might as well keep it.'

When they got into the car, Jackie grabbed Aideen's face with his two hands and kissed her fully on the mouth,

'C'mon Jackie, let's get home.'

Dick McGuinness was again watching from his window. As they left the grounds, McGuinness turned away from the window and dialled a telephone number. No reply. Damn, he thought.

Aideen turned right out of Leinster House, back down towards Bernardo's, then up Merrion Square, left into Baggot Street, down the hill across the little hump bridge which straddled the Grand Canal with its locks, houseboats and leaves floating silently on still, deep water, and towards Ballsbridge.

A couple of hundred yards before the roundabout and the Berkeley Hotel, she turned right into Waterloo Road, opposite Sarsons, another traditional pub, Aideen had a spacious flat on two floors of one of the large Georgian houses in Waterloo Road. The ground floor had flagstones on the floor, an Aga stove and lots of pine chests. French doors gave on to a little stone staircase leading to an overgrown garden with climbing plants against a whitewashed wall. The front room, the living room, had a huge fireplace, a leather settee, books and paintings and lots of newspapers strewn around.

The two bedrooms, one of which she used as a study, were on the upper ground floor. They had high ceilings with mouldings. In Aideen's bedroom there was a large fireplace which had a gas fire in it, and an armchair with a tall plant standing over it. Jackie loved this room in the mornings, when he drew back the curtains and the light flooded in across the double bed.

Aideen lit the gas fire. 'D'you want a nightcap or something, a whiskey?'

'No, I want you.'

He put his hands around her waist and began nibbling her ear. With one hand he began to unbutton her blouse and he reached around with the other and unbuckled her bra.

'Hang on, Jackie, let's get undressed.'

They got undressed in a frenzy, clothes left where they dropped, shoes and jackets thrown haphazardly.

Aideen got into bed and stretched. Jackie got in and settled between her long legs which were thrown wide open. She was very wet and Jackie penetrated her easily. She let out a gasp.

She liked to be in a fixed position in the early stages. She grabbed the brass bedstead above her head and allowed herself to be buffeted. She went into a trance-like state straight away, moaning softly. Then, as she approached her climax, her legs and arms suddenly grasped Jackie round his middle and shoulders, holding him tighter and tighter. His tongue lashed into her mouth and her legs flayed along his back and into the space above him. They came together and as she came down, like one long sigh, she gasped out.

'Oh, Jackie, you darlin, you darlin.'

They lay entwined for some minutes with just the red glow of the gas fire illuminating them. Then Jackie got up and went to the window. He sort of peeked through. He didn't know why. There were three or four cars parked. By the light of a street lamp a little further down, he saw that one of the cars had someone sitting in it.

'You expecting visitors, Aida?'

'No, why, what do you mean?'

'Well, there's someone sitting in a parked car over there.'

'Oh, it's probably nothing, someone just finishing his pint.'

'What, at ten past midnight?'

'It's nothing. Leave it Jackie. Come back to bed, I want more of you.'

'You are an insatiable sex maniac. Must have been all that repression in the convent.'

He tumbled into bed and as he did so, the man called Dominic Morris fired up his engine, let out the clutch and slowly drove away.

'There, you see, whoever it was has gone. And what do you

mean repression in the convent? You don't know when you are well off. I've friends who were at school with me who still can't get undressed in front of their husbands.'

'Oh, really? I have a professional interest in sexual mores, tell me.'

'I have a theory that Irish women, or most Irish women, have a deep sense of guilt about sex and contraception. Perhaps it is the illicit nature of sex in this country that makes the idea so exciting."

'I know, it's like drink, go to confession and all is forgiven, so you can start again,' Jackie said.

'Oh, you're codding me?'

'Not at all, I'm just glad I have a liberated, thoroughly modern woman, that's all.'

'Do you love me?'

'In the morning I will.'

With this she picked up the pillow, and begun to hit him. 'You are an insensitive swine. You're the one who's repressed around here. Keep a stiff upper lip. Never show your feelings.' They then slipped into sleep, he in a foetal position and she on her front, spread out.

Chapter

13

Jackie woke up first. He looked round for his bag and remembered he had left it in the car. He got up, put on his shirt, picked up his trousers and threw open the curtains. It was a nice, clear, crisp morning: the clouds and rain had passed. The kind of winter's day he liked - cold and sharp but bright - was in prospect.

He walked out into the hall, was about to go downstairs, but then, instead, went to the front door and picked up the thick wodge of Saturday's papers. They weighed a ton. The dew and overnight rain was silver on the cars.

He went downstairs to the kitchen and looked at the time. It was half past eight. Coffee, he thought. He put on the percolator and then pulled on his trousers. He sat at the table and started browsing in the papers. Aideen came down about twenty minutes later.

'I was hoping you were going to wake me up properly.'

'Not likely, you'd want sex in the daylight. Whatever next.'

'There, you see, you are repressed.'

She had her dressing gown wrapped tightly round her. She looked firm and lovely and he put his arm around her bottom and kissed her tummy.

'Only teasing, we can go back upstairs if you want.'

'Naagh, we're up now.'

'Just as well. I've been reading in the paper that we should use a condom. I thought you couldn't get them here.'

'Yes you can, but it's a bit late for us isn't it? I just hope you haven't been two-timing and there's nothing nasty in your past.'

'My past! What about yours, all your politician friends?'

'Vile, unsubstantiated rumours. D'you want some breakfast or you happy with toast?'

'I wouldn't mind some boiled eggs. But could I have your key - I need to go to the car and get my grip from the boot.'

'Okay, the keys are upstairs in my bag.'

He skipped upstairs, rummaged in her bag for the keys, put his boots on and went out across to the car. When he got there, he had some difficulty in opening the boot. He had to pull and tug. He got it open and noticed the catch was bent. Someone had been trying to break in. Nothing was gone. Hey ho, he thought and went back to the house. He threw the bag on the bed and got out his shaving things. Jackie always liked to shave. He wasn't so fussy about other things, but had an obsessive need to be clean.

'Aida, how long before breakfast?'

'Five minutes.'

'The hell with it, I'll shave afterwards.'

He picked up his briefcase and trundled downstairs, where the smell of coffee and toast came up to meet him.

They sat down with the eggs, toast, coffee and newspapers all around, like a bubble bath.

'Funny, I couldn't get the boot open. Looked as if someone had tried to break in.'

'Now why would anyone want to do that? It's a cheapo car, nothing of value.'

'Maybe they were after my clothes.'

'Aagh, you are mad. First a man is looking at us from a parked car, now someone's trying to steal your clothes. You getting paranoia or something.'

'By my standards, I've had a stressful twenty four hours.'

'Frankly, if I may say so, you should slightly drop this pose of naivety and it all having nothing to do with you.'

'It's not a pose. I genuinely believe in detachment about Ireland. I do not want it to become an obsession, like it is with you.'

'That's not entirely fair.'

'It is fair. You Irish are totally obsessed with your past and the situation, inverted commas, in the North. You remind me of an anthropologist friend who worked in South Africa before they ended apartheid. When he used, occasionally, to come up for air somewhere else, he would be asked how things were and he would say, "it's always a relief and a pleasant surprise to learn that people talk about things other than race". That's what it is like here. Total obsession. Ireland is a goldfish bowl of a country. You breathe it, eat it and sleep with it. It is all so emotive.'

'See, that's what I mean by naive. Here we are at a truly historic moment in our history. We are only days from a likely withdrawal of British troops from Ireland, something that has been an aspiration of our people for literally hundreds of years. Suddenly the balloon goes up. Three, maybe four, Prods are killed. No one knows why. No one can even guess why, really. You are virtually the only witness to the events leading up to the shootings. You are almost a player. You are not only an anthropologist and a well-known environmentalist; you are also Lord Strangford, a big honcho in a leading Ascendancy family. Last, but not least, your brother is a leader of the Royal Irish Regiment. Do you really think that people are not going to want to talk to you? You are an intelligent, articulate man. How do you know it was not you they were after? Whoever they are. It is all very bizarre, and you come over like some innocent who acts surprised when he gets wet because he has forgotten to take his raincoat into the storm. Come on Jackie. Of course people wonder what's going on. Of course they want to know what you think. I'd like to know what you think. You can't stay out of this one.'

'You sound just like my brother, although your perspective is different.'

'What do you mean?'

'He said more or less the same thing. I must be involved. Can't understand why I am not involved. Mind you, it has been one of his things for years. Family honour and all that.'

'When did you talk to him?'

'That's the thing. See, the reason I have been able to make this assignation with you is that Charles sent a helicopter to get me. Ostensibly it was to pick up Mairead Carten who is overdue. But I was press-ganged on to the chopper and flown to the army HQ in Lisburn. I was taken straight in to see General Sir Timothy Ruskin. He is an old friend of the family. Very worried about what went on. I had to see him, Charles said. It was the only way Charles could get me on to the chopper. Seems that the RIR boys do not have control of the helicopters and all the heavy-duty stuff, at least not for the minute. They have been training up some of their men and there's going to be a handover. But Charles was not on about his usual themes, my responsibilities, and obligations. Instead he was most anxious to secure a document I had. There was another chap with him, Colonel Curtis, very spooky-type individual.'

'Jackie, document, what document?'

'Wait on now and I'll tell you.'

Jackie was beginning to slip into a kind of Irish vernacular; it was part of the strange chameleon role reversal they engaged in.

'I vaguely knew about it. Officially Dawson has been diving for wrecks with the Police Force. It was to keep them busy during the peace. To do this, under the rules of diving, he had to keep a record. This was straightforward enough. But he vouchsafed to me during one of his rare moments of indiscretion that he might be up to something else. He was diving in search of sunken bullion and all that. It is very big business. Thus, I'm woken up, there is an army major yanking me on to a helicopter and Siobhan McHugh, she owns the guesthouse, as you know, shoves a package into my hand. When I open it, it says, in the event of anything happening to me te da te da, I am to deliver the package to William Carstairs.'

'Yer what! This is beginning to get interesting. Did you read it? Did you give to Carstairs?'

'Yes I did, and no, I didn't give it to Carstairs. I didn't get a chance. Charles took a copy and said he would get it to Carstairs easier than I could.'

'So you handed it over to the British army. Typical.'

'Now hang on, Aideen. What was I supposed to do? Dawson is in a coma and how am I supposed to contact Carstairs?'

'Carstairs has got telephone numbers, hasn't he? I could've given you them. But no, I take your point. What's in this document anyway?'

'That's the thing. It is completely innocuous. I can't see why Charles is in such a lather to get it. I've read it twice. There is nothing in it worth killing for, if indeed that is why these men were killed. Also, there's something else. I have the strangest feeling that I have read it all before somewhere.'

'Yes, but those after it weren't to know it was innocuous, were they? This could explain the whole thing. I'd like to read it.'

'If you must, but I wouldn't waste your time, I can tell you what it says.'

*

Meanwhile, William Carstairs had finally got under way to Rathlin with Billy and Joe and a host of others. There were plain-clothes detectives from the Police Force's Special Branch, several uniformed policemen and a veritable army of newspapermen and women, television crews and reporters, cameras, microphones.

Gerry had enjoyed himself, holding everyone up by sending off to the shops for things he had ostensibly forgotten. Finally, just after 9.30, the *St Iona* pushed off into a placid millpond. In other circumstances, it would have been a magical day. Bright and fresh, the last wisps of an early morning mist danced in the air.

Gerry irritatingly hummed *What a Difference a Day Makes,* and intoned every now and again, 'Funny thing the weather. Who'd have thought it would turn out like this.'

One or two of the journalists tried to question Carstairs. He said he could add nothing to what had been said. When one asked why in that case he was going to the island, the famous scowl came over him and the journalists backed off. They then tried to talk to the police, but again, getting nowhere, decided to drop it.

After a while, Chief Inspector William Marshall came over for a talk with Carstairs. Although not a close confidant, he was senior enough to have an idea of what was planned. He didn't know the details of Dawson's activities and didn't care to know, but he could make an intelligent guess. He, and virtually all his senior Police Force colleagues, would be there when it really mattered. They were as much a secret society as the senior echelons of the IRA. They would get short shrift from their communities if they went against Carstairs.

'Morning, William, nasty business last night.'

'Aye.'

'What brings you across, if I may ask?'

'I was associated with Dawson and the lads, through the Police Federation. Thought as I was here, I might as well see if anyone knows anything.'

'Aye, well I don't think we'll get anywhere. But we've got enquiries to make. Can I give you a bit of unsolicited advice, William?'

'Of course, Billy.'

'I wouldn't think of importing anything to the island just now. These media people crawling over the place are bound to come up with something. If you see what I mean.'

Carstairs looked at the squat, lined policeman, then stared out to sea. 'Hmmm,' he murmured.

*

Aideen put down the report: 'I take your point that there is nothing in this worth killing for.'

'It's all theorising, isn't it?' Jackie agreed. 'It's like a little story about treasure hunting. He hasn't actually found anything. Even the stuff about the known wrecks is a bit old hat.'

'Yes,' came back Aideen, 'but I'd like to repeat my point. Whoever it was wouldn't have known it was innocuous. Maybe it was just a straight bit of villainy that went wrong, a simple robbery. I read a book once which was all about salvaging a wreck almost in the Arctic Circle that had gold that Churchill had sent to Stalin. You read in the papers all the time about sunken treasure being auctioned off for millions. I'd like to put it in the paper for tomorrow. It could help ease the situation a bit.'

'Hang on a second, Aideen. First, it was given to me as a matter of trust. It was not meant to be spread over the Sunday papers.'

'Yes, but it was given under circumstances which could not possibly have foreseen what would happen. People have died. Your brother already has a copy, that means it won't be long before Special Branch has it, probably already has.'

It was then that it hit him. He almost jumped up in the air. 'Aideen you're a genius. What an idiot I am. That's where I've seen it all before. I read the same book as you. It was called *Stalin's Gold*, by a journalist called Barrie Penrose. The McHughs had a row of books downstairs. There's where I saw it. There was nothing else to read apart from some Catherine Cooksons and Mills and Boon stuff. But there was a clutch of books on diving. There was another one I read called *The Harsh Winds of Rathlin*. A local man wrote it. It catalogued all the known wrecks, depths, tidal strengths, diving possibilities and so on.'

'So,' said Aideen, 'I'm not quite with you.'

'Don't you see? Dawson's report is pure invention. He's taken everything from the books.'

'Yes, but again I say, who was to know?'

'Yes, yes, but that is not the point. Why would he make up a whole report? Think. Think hard.'

'As a cover for something else?' she volunteered.

'Precisely. But what on earth is that something else? And why is it worth killing for? Why is everybody, including my brother who is in the British army and not directly involved in crime and jollity of this kind, desperate to get hold of a worthless report? How did he know about it?'

She did not answer directly, 'I still think we should put it in the paper.'

'Do you? You might end up looking a right eejit, if it turns out Dawson and his pals were on Rathlin for other reasons.'

'How do you mean?'

'If this is a fabrication, you would be putting a cock and bull story about sunken treasure in the paper. It would seem you were trying a cover up.'

'I s'pose you're right. I'll hold fire. But how are you going to find out what the something else is?'

'That I don't know. I'll think about it.'

He looked at his watch. 'Look we had better get on. I've got to go and hire a monkey suit, then meet Sweetman. What are your plans?'

'I've to do a bit of shopping and get me hair done. But you go ahead. Will I see you at the Unicorn for a bite of lunch.'

'Good idea, then we can fall back here and watch the match.'

He got up and went to shave. She picked up the report, flicked through it, then put it on the sideboard with some other papers, next to the telephone.

*

At the George Hotel in Edinburgh, Alex MacPhee had risen slowly, and breakfasted in his suite. He had ordered the newspapers and read systematically through the news, business and sport, disregarding the lifestyle sections. He found nothing he didn't already know about Rathlin and Carstairs. He decided to go for a quick constitutional. He thought he might cross and go up the Royal Mile but decided against it and walked along Princes Street instead.

He had tried several times during the course of Friday to get hold of Carstairs, but to no avail. Carstairs' wife had been evasive. His political office also claimed not to know his whereabouts. He couldn't even get Carstairs on his mobile. His son answered the mobile and said his father was not available. Why was Carstairs avoiding him? The news had initially given out the names of those killed. Dawson was not among them. He was in a coma. It was all a bit worrying. No, it was more than a bit worrying. Carstairs should have been in touch. Well, he would see what Mr Brogan had to say. He returned to the hotel. There was a message waiting. A Mr Carstairs had phoned. He said he was going to the island and would be in touch later. He said Mr MacPhee would understand what he meant. The hotel receptionist added that the message came late last night. Unfortunately it had got mislaid with the changeover from the night manager.

MacPhee said that was alright and breathed a small sigh of relief. That's a bit better, he thought. But he would still proceed with plan A to go to Dublin. He then called up Fiona and Angus and asked them to meet him in his suite. Everything was quickly arranged. He and Angus would fly to Dublin in about an hour, in time for lunch. They were booked into the Shelbourne. After the match, they would see Diarmuid Brogan. He couldn't give them long but he would certainly see them. It would be at his house north of Dublin. A car would pick them up at the Shelbourne at around six o'clock.

*

William Carstairs stepped on to Rathlin Island half an hour before Alexander MacPhee called his meeting. He had explained to Billy Marshall that he needed to get to the McHughs' guesthouse, and have a word with the McHughs before the hordes got at them. Billy had agreed, suggesting the best way to approach it was for him to go in first and talk to them and pave the way. He assumed that Carstairs would not need long and his officers could keep the press off.

The press did not all immediately converge on the McHughs. Some trekked up the hill to the Church. Others headed for the diving centre at the end of the Manor House, as did some of the detectives and police. Still others lingered on the quay, trying to chat to the fishermen and get what in the jargon is known as vox-pop. One detective and two of the uniformed constables also stayed on the quay. But there was still a squadron of journalists to follow Carstairs and the police round Church Bay to the row of terraced houses where the guesthouse sat.

Chief Inspector William Marshall disappeared into the house and came out after a couple of minutes. 'The man's not there, William, away on the mainland on business. She's there. She says she will talk to you, but I warn you she's none too friendly.'

He then turned to the throng, 'Why don't you media types go and inspect the island. I am going for a cup of tea.'

He strode off towards the little teashop, past the public telephone. None of the press moved. Three uniformed police stood guard. Carstairs had a quick word with Joe and his son Billy, then knocked. When Mrs McHugh opened the door to Carstairs she shied up like a startled horse and stepped back.

'Sorry to trouble you, good lady, but Mr Dawson was an associate of mine, I wonder if I might have a word. I am William Carstairs.'

'I know you well enough. You'd better come in.'
She had a cross look on her face.

Carstairs said, 'Is Mr Wilson at home?' knowing full well he wasn't, but trying to break the ice.

'He's away on the mainland.'

'So there no-one next door?'

'That's right, there's no-one next door.'

'Do you mind if I have a look? You see there are some papers relating to work Mr Dawson was undertaking for the Police Federation. I am the Chairman of the Police Federation.'

'I gave some papers to Mr Wilson. Mr Dawson said I was to.'

She spoke in short, shy, sentences like a schoolgirl in front of the teacher.

'Still, I would like to look, there might be some other papers.'

'There's not. Yer man is very tidy.'

'It is possible for me to get a search warrant. In fact, I am pretty sure Chief Inspector Marshall already has one.'

He was bluffing but the mention of the word 'warrant' jolted her.

'Tony wouldn't like it, but I suppose there's no stopping you.'

She went into the kitchen and came back with a key. As they left the house to go next door, Chief Inspector Marshall was walking up the path. The uniformed police were keeping the journalists at bay. They were muttering that it was curious that Carstairs was first in, but Marshall ignored them.

'Alright, William?'

'Aye.'

Siobhan let them in, and they marched upstairs, past Jackie Wilson's room before reaching Dawson's. She opened the door and Carstairs went into the Spartan cell. A double bed and a large desk against the window. There was little else. Carstairs tried pulling at the middle desk drawer. Locked.

'Do you happen to have a key?'

'No. It was his desk. Bought it himself. He has the key.'

Carstairs pulled and tugged, then pushed.

'Hey, what are you doing?' Siobhan said.

'Sorry about this, but there could be very important information in here.'

After further struggle, the drawer gave way. But, as Carstairs strained and pulled, with his head thrown back, he did not notice the blue disc pop out of the makeshift slit Dawson had made at the back of the central drawer. It fell and lodged behind the bottom of the curtain. Siobhan saw, but kept quiet.

In the central drawer was a sheaf of papers and a red floppy disc. All the other drawers had also come free. Carstairs pulled them out one by one. In a bottom drawer were Dawson's computer and printer with a tangle of wires and a number of batteries, a reminder that Rathlin had not long had electricity. Carstairs was surprised to find just one floppy disc, without any apparent form of back up. But then he thought to himself, there would be another system on the boat. Better to hope the red disc contained the secrets. He turned to Siobhan.

'I will pay for repairs to the desk. I am really sorry, but the situation is unusual. I'll take these papers, if you don't mind.'

She shrugged. 'It's all the same if I do.'

Carstairs went out and Siobhan locked the door behind him. He walked down the path to Joe and Billy and the press. William Marshall went into the house, saying that he wouldn't take long but there were some questions he had to ask. Strictly speaking, he should not have let Carstairs walk off with material which could contain clues as to why Dawson was shot. But he did not want, or feel inclined, to cross the politician. Carstairs surely knew what he was doing. If there was something he needed to lay his hands on, that was okay. There would be no account to be rendered to any superiors later. When Siobhan complained about Carstairs' behaviour - she had no love of Protestant politicians - she was fobbed off with the line that Carstairs was acting in concert with the police, as he, technically, had been Dawson's employer.

Marshall said he would like to see Dawson's room and afterwards John Wilson's. He was joined by another detective and they spoke to Siobhan for half an hour over cups of tea back in her kitchen next door.

Carstairs meanwhile was surrounded by the press, who were beginning to get restless at being kept away from the guesthouse. One of them asked why Carstairs had gone in before the police and why, if he was so concerned about the dead policemen, he had not gone down to the diving centre where they had been staying. Carstairs would normally have roared at this impudence. But since he was effectively cooped up with the rat pack until Gerry deigned to take them back, he let it go and said that he was proceeding to the diving centre forthwith.

Gerry had been disinclined to make a return trip until a fellow islander pointed out that it was a better option to take them back than have them loitering around the island. Where would they all stay for one thing? And Gerry would not be out of pocket, although it would mean he would have to stay over in Ballycastle. He was secretly beginning to enjoy all the fuss. He had been interviewed by several television stations and been bought drinks by many reporters. He said that he would take them back no later than two o'clock in the afternoon, any time beyond that and the light would begin to fade. This gave the assembled corps of press, police and politicians, around three hours to kill.

After half an hour Marshall emerged and said that Mrs McHugh would not be speaking to the press, she had little to say anyway. This did not stop some of the reporters laying siege and banging on her door. The rest of the media scattered. Some followed Carstairs down to the diving centre where he enquired politely about the murdered divers. Others went to the teashop and post office. And the rest went to Tommy McQuaig's pub. This was the only pub on the island, although it was possible to get alcoholic drinks at the diving centre. The three dead Police Force divers, it transpired, were quiet, family men. They rarely drank and went home to the mainland at weekends, weather permitting.

Dawson was pleasant enough alright, but didn't really say much about anything. He was known to take a drink with that boffin fella, who, rumour had it, bore some kind of strange title. No one really knew what either he or Dawson were doing on the island, although the Wilson fella asked a lot of strange questions, about ancestors, cousins, aunties and the like.

The TV crews did stand-up pieces in front of Siobhan's guesthouse, in front of the pub and in front of the diving centre and manor house. One of the crews had got as far as the bird sanctuary at West Point on the tip of the island. The reporter was a keen naturalist and wanted to get some shots. Just before two o'clock they all trooped back to the *Iona* for the journey to the mainland, with no one any the wiser about the events of Thursday night, not even Carstairs, although he did not yet know it.

Chapter
14

In his room in Pearse Street, near the dockland area of Ringsend, Gerry Watson was going through a telephone directory he had borrowed from Mrs Murphy, his landlady, who had had the tall, old, crumbling, Georgian house converted into a number of bed sits. It was what used to be called a tenement. She continued to live on the ground floor. The flats were small but self-contained. There was no lift. Gerry lived on the fourth floor. He had one big room, which was a sitting room/bedroom and a little kitchenette and dining area. There was a shared toilet and bathroom on the landing. There was no common room as such, people kept to themselves. He had a radio, a small CD player and a portable television.

Pearse Street and other parts of Ringsend had been transformed in recent years. The street used to lead to a row of car workshops and a gasworks. The area had had a transient, down-at-heel population, like so many dockland sites. But like other riverside areas in Europe it was being regenerated. The gasworks had been cleared and had been replaced by a four star hotel. Where the Armstrong motorcycle factory used to be, there were new apartments. The first bistros were beginning to appear. But there was little you could do about the likes of Mrs Murphy's establishment. The buildings were listed, so couldn't be knocked down.

Watson had been in Dublin eighteen months now. He was

leader of what Carstairs like to regard as his elite undercover unit in the heart of the Republic. There were two others in the unit, Gary Malloy and John McWilliams. In former times they might have stood out. But the years of peace had relaxed suspicions about Protestants from the North. Gary lived across the river in Gardner Street in a small hotel, John McWilliams in the Rathmines district, again in a small hotel. There was nothing elite about any of their pasts. They were electricians. They had been apprentices, and drifted into crime and terrorism as the work had dried up in Belfast in the late 1980s. They were gunmen, pure and simple, although Watson liked to kid himself he knew something of explosives.

Watson was now in his late thirties. He had been a member of the UDA, and had done a spell in prison for possession of arms. Like the other two, he had neither risen very high in the UDA hierarchy nor achieved notoriety as a paramilitary. Watson, however, had more blood on his hands than was often assumed. He did not boast about his killings.

Officially, his story was that he couldn't get much work in Belfast. Recently he had been on the mainland, but now that everyone was getting on better in the Republic, Dublin was more convenient for him to get back to his family. He had become a member of the small army of jobbing plumbers and electricians, many from the North, living in suburbs like Swords to the north of the Irish capital. He did get some work sub-contracting, but he was basically supported in his ostensibly dull, routine, uneventful life by Carstairs.

He turned the pages of the telephone directory. Aideen O'Connor had to be in it. Sure enough, she was. Now he had the number, he would go out to phone, for Mrs Murphy had flapping ears. He rang John and Gary from the booth on the corner of the street. He told them both the same thing. Yer woman lives in Waterloo Road. There's a pub at the top, just where Baggot Street becomes Pembroke Street. They were to meet in there at 11 o'clock. McWilliams was to bring the get-away car, a 2.9 litre Granada that he kept in Rathmines. It wasn't new, so it wouldn't be out of place. Watson drove a small van, but Waterloo Road was close enough to walk. Molloy was also on foot.

Watson believed his cover was secure, for the three of them had not yet done anything. While they waited, they led normal, if lonely, lives, meeting occasionally for a drink in pubs where they were not known. But Watson was on the computer. Carstairs' instructions that Watson's records should not be sent to the Garda had been overruled. The Garda did know about him.

*

When John McWilliams was driving the Granada to the rendezvous, he could almost have touched Dominic Morris. For Morris was getting into his car in Leinster Road just as McWilliams was driving along North Kenilworth Road. They lived in remarkably similar circumstances, in cheap, shabby lodgings, existing on Chinese takeaways and fish and chips. If confronted, they might even have recognised one another, since they had drunk in the same pubs. Now it was as if Morris was following McWilliams up to the Waterloo pub.

Morris was finishing his preparations. He had made a discovery. Between Waterloo Road and Waterloo Avenue, which ran parallel, there was a small lane, on to which the rear gardens of the houses on both roads backed. Such was the level of crime in Dublin that the doors on the gardens were locked and barred. Aideen hardly ever used hers. Had no need to. But the garden wall was not that high and Aideen had never had any broken glass or barbed wire put on it, unlike some of her more nervous neighbours.

Morris was convinced the rear would be the easiest way into

her flat. He parked his car in Waterloo Avenue and walked round to the lane. He needed to see the house in daylight. From behind he wasn't sure which was Aideen's, so he doubled back, walked around to the front and counted the houses. Aideen came out as he was approaching her door. She did not look at the man with his hands in his overcoat pockets. He walked up and down until she drove off. He turned round and looked into her window. He saw right through because Aideen had opened the doors between the ground floor rooms. In the garden he glimpsed an identifying pear tree, now looking bare and frail. He went back to the alley and counted the houses again. There was the tree peeking above the wall. The tree would make life a lot easier

*

John, Gary and Gerry sat over their pints of Guinness in the corner of the Waterloo. The bar was empty except for them. Gerry Watson started his briefing. 'Sherwell said Wilson, the Lord fella, would be at Aideen O'Connor's. Well she lives down Waterloo Road, number 14. Sherwell says that we are not to cause any fuss. He says the intelligence is that they'll be out tonight, so we can go in then. We've to pick up some documents. John, do you have any kit with youse?'

'I've got a bag in the boot. I don't have me piece with me,' said John.

'No, I don't mean your piece. What you should do is take your bag and knock on her door and say you're the electrician. When she acts surprised, take out a piece of paper. And then say you've got the wrong address. That'll give you a chance to take a look at the lock. See if you can crack it. We'll wait here for you, okay. When you get back, Gary and me'll go and have a look just so we know where it is.'

*

Jackie loved walking in Dublin, providing it was not too grey. He strode briskly up Baggot Street, on to the hump bridge over the Grand Canal. Then up the hill to St Stephen's Green. Once in Grafton Street, he looked at his watch and decided he had time to go into Bewley's for a coffee before going to get his hire suit and other rig from Swift's. Inside, he ordered a large black coffee and reached into his satchel-cum-briefcase. Damn, he thought, I've left the document behind. Instead he went to the central table and picked up a copy of the *Irish Times*. The shooting of Dawson was all over the front page and splattered across three inside pages. There were pictures of Carstairs outside the Dalriada hospital and scenic pictures of Rathlin Island. He started to read, and then got bored with it. A cursory glance at the inside pages showed there was no reference to him anywhere. He didn't think of it, but this meant that none of the journalists had yet reached the island.

*

John McWilliams inspected the lock. From the outside it seemed to be a standard five lever mortice. He needed to get a look at the inside of the door frame to see if there was a lip which would stop him getting a crowbar in. He pressed the bell above Aideen's, labelled O'Riley. Seconds later he heard a light footfall on the stairs. A pretty, dark girl opened the door.

'Morning ma'am, electrician for O'Connor.'

The small be-jeaned figure replied with just an edge of annoyance, 'You've the wrong bell, see there, O'Connor.'

'Oh yes, sorry, my mistake.' As he said this, he put his left hand on the door frame where the lock was. Good, he thought, no lip.

'She's not here.'

'Okay, well I'll come back later. Sorry to have bothered youse.'

The girl, who was called Ethna, thought there was something odd about the man, but couldn't immediately put her finger on it. John McWilliams walked back to his car, put his bag of tools in the boot and then rejoined the two others in the Waterloo. He took a pull at his pint.

'It's okay. Simple job to get in.'

'Keep your damn voice down. Okay, here's what we'll do. Gary and me'll walk down the road so as we know which house it is, then we'll split up. Best we don't meet at this same pub. We'll meet at that one up on the corner, what you call it, McCrae's, about nine o'clock. Usual drill. Bring your piece and make sure the car's got some petrol.'

Gary and Gerry got up and walked down Waterloo Road. John finished his pint before he too left and went to his car.

*

Jackie picked up his bags from Swift's and made his way to Doheny and Nesbitt's. He was still a little early, so he walked slowly. He gazed in the shop windows in Duke Street, the antique silver, the clothes. He turned into Kildare Street, and passed the Shelbourne. Doheny's was only beginning to fill up. Although he was early, Oliver Sweetman was already there and got up to greet him. 'Jackie, good to see you, what'll I get you?'

'Let me just put these things down.'

'Oh, yes, right, I am over there in the corner. Nice to get a seat for a change.'

Jackie returned to join him at the bar and said, 'I think I will break a rule and have a pint of stout' - by which he meant Guinness.

'Good idea, I've already got one in.'

They settled in the corner table in a sort of snug. There was an embarrassed silence and then they said together, 'I...' Then Jackie continued, 'You go on.'

'Well, I, I just wanted to catch up really.' He paused and then changed tack. 'Look, there's no point beating about the bush. We are obviously interested in knowing what went down on Rathlin Island. It is a very sensitive time. Wonder if you can shed any light.'

'Nothing went down, as you put it, on Rathlin Island. These guys were shot in Ballycastle, on the mainland.'

'Yes I know, but they had come from the island. What's so mysterious?'

Jackie was now beginning to get use to Aideen's idea that people wanted to talk to him about Rathlin. But he wasn't quite sure why he was talking to Oliver Sweetman.

'Until the day before yesterday nothing was mysterious. We were all minding our own business. What is your interest?'

'HMG,' (funny how the diplomat had never shaken the habit of referring to the British government as HMG, it was like referring to oneself in the third person.) 'HMG,' Sweetman repeated, 'is obviously concerned about recent events. The peace process is very delicately poised. Tension is high in the Protestant community, with the likelihood of a British troop pull out. We were just wondering why this incident should have occurred now. I know the Dublin government is very concerned. Just wondered if you have any thoughts.'

'Fraid not,' Jackie said tersely.

Sweetman went on, 'You see, I saw your name mentioned in connection with Dawson.'

'My name, where did you see my name?'

'Oh, in one of the papers.'

'Which one.?'

'One of them, I can't think which. Perhaps it was the *Irish Times*.'

'Ollie what are you up to? I am just after reading the *Irish Times*.' He was slipping into the Irish vernacular again. 'My name is not mentioned anywhere in the *Irish Times*. Come to think of it, there is no reason you should even know about my presence on Rathlin Island.'

'Oh, come now old man, you are pretty well known. I've seen you on the television many times. Anyway, we do have our channels, you know.'

'Come clean, Ollie, what is the real purpose of this meeting?'

'This is all most delicate. I must try and be discreet. Northern Ireland is still the responsibility of the British Government. I am a representative of the British Government in a foreign country, which - how shall I put it - does not always see eye to eye with our own on these matters. Is it possible these appalling killings are an attempt by our Irish friends, through the IRA perhaps, at sabotage?'

Jackie looked at him slightly incredulously. 'Why on earth should the IRA, or the Irish government, want to sabotage the peace process. It is all going their way, isn't it? After the troops pull out there will be no impediment to a political peace, will there? By the way, my brother is seconded to the RIR.'

'Yes, how is Charles?'

'I didn't know you knew my brother.'

'As I say, we have our channels.'

'Ollie, you are a devious bugger. But I s'pose you all are.'

Sweetman ignored this and went on, 'OK, maybe it is not about sabotaging the peace process. Maybe it is about sabotaging future arrangements.'

'Sorry, I'm not with you.'

'There has been a lot of talk of Carstairs fiddling around and trying to make political capital out of the situation. It would be unfortunate if Carstairs thought he could get away with ruining the new arrangements in some way. Embarrassing all round.'

'Surely not. Charles said there simply wouldn't be the wherewithal.'

'Well, to coin a cliché, perhaps he would say that, wouldn't he?'

'What do you mean?'

'All right I will come clean with you. Our information is that Dawson had written up some documents and given them to you to onpass to Mr Carstairs.'

'Those bloody documents. Why is everyone so interested in this report?'

'For the obvious reason that it could give a clue as to what is going on'

Jackie stared at Sweetman and thought, what a serpentine mind. He had opened one line of thought and doubled back on it, then doubled back again. It was impossible to tell whether he was trying to find out what happened on behalf of good old HMG, or suggesting that Carstairs was planning something involving his brother, or just trying to spike the guns of the Irish government. His true intentions were hidden behind a mosaic of theories. Talking to him was like playing snakes and ladders.

He sighed, 'I don't know why I am telling you this, Ollie. Yes, there is a document and, yes, I was supposed to pass it to Carstairs. But I didn't. Charles got it first. He said he would pass it on.'

'Interesting, very interesting,' Sweetman pretended he didn't know and continued, 'So you are saying your brother has got the document. This gets more and more interesting.'

Guilelessly, Jackie replied. 'He took a copy, actually.'

'So you've got the original. Be fascinating to take a peek.'

'Well it doesn't say much. It's all about diving for wrecks.

The Police Force were doing an inventory of all the known wrecks looking for arms.'

'That all?"

'Well no, actually.'

'What else?'

'I suppose I can tell you. There was a whole lot of guff about diving for sunken bullion. Seems new technology means you can get at wrecks that once lay too deep to be salvaged. It appears sunken treasure can be big business worth millions.'

'Ah, there you are, you see, that's how Carstairs will finance a rebellion.'

'Unfortunately for that theory, the report is bullshit from beginning to end.'

'How's that?'

'It's all made up. It's taken from books, and secondary sources. Carstairs is no more likely to find sunken treasure than I am to fly to the moon.'

Sweetman decided he had gone as far as he could and said, 'I must get on. I wouldn't mind having a look at the report, if possible.'

'Why not, everyone else seems to have, and as I said, it is all bullshit.'

'Even so, it might be useful. Where you staying?'

Jackie started to tell him, then thought of Aideen's reaction and didn't. 'Look, I can meet you tomorrow morning, while the lady's at mass. What about Bewley's around eleven?'

'Fine. Now I really must go.'

'Hang on. I'll come with you.'

As they went out, Sweetman said, 'Where are you going? Can I give you a lift anywhere.'

'No, it's okay, I'm only going across to the Unicorn for some lunch.'

'Aargh, the Irish mafia eh?'

Sweetman turned to face Jackie, giving him a firm handshake, and, looking meaningfully at him, said, 'Tomorrow then? Let me give you a little tip, Jackie. Don't dismiss as totally fanciful the notion that Carstairs has got some crazy scheme in mind. Another chat with your brother might repay. 'Bye for now.'

Jackie walked across the road to the Unicorn, thinking what the devil is he on about. He left his bags with the waiter at the door and said, 'I am John Wilson. Has Miss O'Connor booked?'

'Yes, you are, sir. No, she hasn't, but no worries, we'll fit you in alright.'

*

As Jackie was shown to his seat, a taxi was drawing up at the nearby Shelbourne Hotel. It decanted Alex MacPhee and his brother. The porters in long grey coats and peaked caps took the bags into reception.

Alex said, 'Let's sign in and go straight to lunch, Angy. The porters can take the bags up.' Alex MacPhee was used to having someone do everything for him. So with that, he walked to the Carvery, along the corridor from reception.

*

Aideen had returned to the flat at around 12.15. She unloaded her shopping, including the extra stock of whiskey and decided to go straight back out. She met Ethna at the door, also on her way out.

'Oh Aideen, yer man called, the electrician.'

'Electrician. I'm not expecting an electrician.'

'I'd say it was odd.' Ethna said, and remembered what it was that was odd. 'Funny that, he had an accent from the Nort.'

*

Aideen arrived at the Unicorn shortly after Jackie, having parked her car in Merrion Row. It took a good five minutes to reach Jackie's table since she table-hopped all the way, stopping to talk to the politicians, the journalists and a well known actor.

'How was yer Brit spy then?' she said, sitting down.

'So-so, he talked in riddles most of the time. Surprise, surprise, he wanted to know what was in the report.'

'How'd he know about it? You told him, I suppose.'

'Not at all, he told me he knew through channels. Seemed to know Charles.'

Just then, Geraldine McCory, a Fianna Fail backbencher, and her husband Ronan came up and said, 'Hi, mind if we join you?'

'Not at all,' said Aideen, without consulting Jackie, who had been cut off in mid-flow.

Jackie had met them before, so there was no need for introductions. Barely had they sat down when the conversation fell into its usual predictable pattern. 'Tis a terrible business in the North. It's all a Brit plot. No, the IRA has lost discipline. It is just a renegade IRA group. No, it's the Protestants, they are the ones to watch. It's a complicated double manoeuvre by the Police Force. Don't be ridiculous. The Police would never harm their own kind. Saw that man Carstairs was interviewed on television. He's trouble if ever you saw it, and so forth and so on.

Aideen, for her, was subdued. Certainly, she was less voluble than she had been the night before. She was chewing over what Jackie had said about the fake report. Always a one for conspiracy theories, she was trying to link Carstairs with the island. The image of an electrician with a northern accent kept swinging in and out of her thoughts.

The lunch didn't drag on for hours the way it would normally have done because everyone wanted to watch the match. They quickly ordered coffees. At twenty to three they were out on Baggot

Street. The pubs along the street were either very full or very empty depending on whether they had a television set. Many of the traditional ones like Doheny's hadn't.

When Jackie and Aideen turned into Merrion Row with its empty government offices, it was deserted. The streets to Waterloo were empty and they were home in five minutes. They got into the flat and walked down the corridor and into the bedroom. Jackie let his parcels drop. Aideen closed the door behind her and lent against it. She had taken off her coat and began to unbutton her blouse.

'Jackie, we've time for a quick ride before the match.'

'Aideen, you're insatiable. I want to watch the match. It's important.' He went to switch the TV on.

'There's nothing as important as sex.'

'Sex is wonderful before rugby and even after rugby, but not simultaneously.'

He turned round to face her and almost gasped when he saw her blouse hanging loose with her full breasts packed into a white bra. She threw off her blouse and advanced on him. She put one arm round his shoulders and kissed him, with the other she grabbed his penis and began rubbing it. It shot up.

'You sure?' she said. She unzipped his fly and with her hand massaged his penis. She undid her jeans and levered them down over her hips. She then sprawled on the bed on her front, her arms grabbing the rails of the bedstead, her legs spread as wide as she could get them.

'Fuck me from the back, Jackie, fuck me quick.'

He took his jeans and pants off. He put his arm under her and lifted her up so she was on her knees. He thrust himself into her. She let out a moan. He pumped rhythmically, she pounded the pillow with her fists and cried out. 'You're good to me. You're good to me,' then a long 'Aaah,' as they both came and she collapsed on to her stomach. He rolled off her and she turned over and stared at the ceiling. 'Jackie, something strange happened this morning.'

'What's that?'

'A man came to fix the electrics. Ethna said he was from the North.'

'What's wrong with that? They have perfectly good electricians in Belfast. Don't be prejudiced.'

'No, you eejit. I didn't ask for an electrician.'

'He must have got the wrong place.' But he was not really listening. His mind was on the game, he had switched on the corner television.

Aideen got up and picked up her clothes. She started to dress. 'Jackie do you love me?'

'Absolutely. What's the phrase, truly, madly, deeply.'

'You shit. Look why don't we go downstairs and watch the game properly in the living room. I'll put the kettle on for a pot of tea.'

'Okay you go on down and I'll join you.'

She went downstairs and put the kettle on and opened the wooden doors to the living room.

*

Oliver Sweetman had gone straight from Doheny and Nesbitt's to the British Ambassador's residence at Glairnduff. It was like a fake imitation castle, with bushy gardens, now a bit skeletal, and a fake tower as the centrepiece.

O'Toole received Sweetman. He was not a butler as such. There was a husband and wife team. Mrs O'Toole did cooking and cleaning. O'Toole was the handyman and helped out with the gardens. They were all the full-time staff. The downsizing of the 1990s had had its effect on the Foreign Office, as elsewhere. Other staff were bought in for functions and dinner parties. There were, however, plenty of security men around the grounds and on the gates. A previous ambassador had been killed just outside in 1976.

'The Ambassador is in the library, Mr Sweetman. Can I take your coat?'

'Yes, thank you, Mr O'Toole.'

The Ambassador was of the old school. At 61, he should have already retired from the service. He was kept on because he had been with the peace process from the beginning - almost a decade - and was a steady hand. His full head of iron grey hair was slicked back. He had a nicely weathered face. He was seated behind a desk and got up and walked around to greet Sweetman.

'Oliver, hello, had a good morning?'

The Ambassador, who wore a tweed jacket, cavalry twill trousers, check shirt and woollen tie - regular weekend rig for a country gentleman - made towards the drinks tray on an old oak sideboard beneath the window which looked out to the garden. The other three walls were lined with books. This room, with its high moulded ceiling, always reminded Sweetman of a London club. This was presumably what it was supposed to do, since Sir Robert Dawney was a great one for Pall Mall and would undoubtedly be spending a lot of time in the Travellers Club when he did retire.

'Can I get you a snifter before lunch, a sherry, gin or something?'

'I shouldn't, really,' replied Oliver. 'I've just had a drink with Wilson. All in the course of duty you know.'

'Go on, be a devil. It is Saturday.'

'Oh, very well, you twist my arm. I'll have a gin and tonic.'

'Good, so will I. Great minds think alike.'

They sat down with their drinks in two leather armchairs round a little table.

'Any joy with Wilson?'

Sweetman thought for a bit. There were some things that Sir

Robert should know and some things that might need to go straight to London. Sir Robert was a canny old bird, Sweetman would have to tread carefully.

'I managed to get a quiet word with Wilson by himself. His lady friend, Aideen O'Connor is rather hostile, actually.'

'And?' prodded Sir Robert.

'It seems that he was given some documentation by this chap Dawson. Ostensibly it was about diving for wrecks to do an arms audit. The Police needs things to do apparently. But they were also looking for bullion for salvage. They could make some big money.'

'Ah, so that would fit in with your theory that Carstairs is trying to finance an insurrection.'

'Yes and no, this man Wilson is either extremely naive, or he is as cleverly devious as a snake.'

Sir Robert spluttered into laughter at this.

'Not like you, hey?'

'Well, that's as maybe. He then went on to tell me that the report in his estimation was a load of codswallop. That it was completely fabricated, from books.'

'What do you deduce from that?'

'He is either in cahoots with his brother in some plot or other, or is genuinely disingenuous in the extreme.'

'How so?'

'It's difficult to work out his brother's role in this. Why should he haul him up to Lisburn, then, having secured the document, phone us and ask for a favour?'

'That's simple enough. He realised he made a mistake in letting this fellow hang on to the original. Presumably that's what he has done.'

'That is precisely what he has done. Colonel Wilson took a copy. But what is the Wilson-Carstairs-Wilson connection? Why is Colonel Wilson so interested in Dawson and the others?'

Sir Robert again gave a small splutter. 'I swear Machiavelli had nothing on you, Oliver. It could be much more prosaic than that. The Wilsons are brothers after all. He may have been genuinely concerned for his brother. He may be doing Carstairs a favour. They are all very thick up there, you know. The army, the police and the politicians.'

'Precisely, they could all be in it together. We have received information that Carstairs has plans to launch an insurrection. To do this, he needs not just men, which presumably he could get. He needs money. Big bucks. John Wilson could be just trying to throw me off the scent, of course.'

'Oliver, Oliver. We have been asked by London to find out what we can about three, possibly four Protestant murders, in Ulster. It might be very simple indeed. Carstairs and Co were devilling around trying to make some money, for whatever purpose. Someone wanted to find out what he was up to and things went wrong. No one was to know what was in the document.'

'That would not explain why the British army is so anxious to get hold of all copies of the documentation.'

'I know your concerns about a possible unilateral declaration of independence. But we do not know that. Let us take this step by step, not try and run before we can walk and all that. What we do know is that three men have been killed and a fourth lies in a coma. They were in possession of potentially important commercial information, that could explain why they were killed.'

Sir Robert Dawney, in trying to keep things simple, was protecting his back and his embassy. He knew Sweetman was perfectly capable of outlining a long conspiracy theory to Sir Roger Jones in London. He was inclined to believe there was something in Sweetman's theory but he didn't want him jumping the gun. He wanted to head him off and await further developments.

'Now, how shall we proceed?' Sir Robert said.

'I did arrange to meet Wilson again tomorrow, and get a peek at the document,' Sweetman replied.

'Well, there you are then. We will be able to take a better view of things tomorrow, and you can send a cable then. Now, what about a spot of lunch?' He rose.

Chapter

15

William Carstairs got off the *St Iona* in Ballycastle in a very businesslike mood.

'Right now, Billy, Joe, let's book out of the hotel, go and check on Dawson at the hospital and then get down to Whiteabbey quick.'

He went to his room and packed. In reception Billy was settling the bills. Increasingly he acted as Carstairs' private secretary, although he was not involved in what Carstairs referred to as his higher plans. A few minutes later they were at the Dalriada. He got past the first hurdle of the police easily enough and then tried to see Commander Herriott. He was no longer there. Instead he found an Inspector Regan.

'Good afternoon, I am William Carstairs and I'm enquiring as to the health of Alan Dawson.'

'Yes,' Regan, a tall thin man with a gaunt grey face, rose from the makeshift desk as Carstairs filled the little room. 'I was told you might be coming. I am afraid I can be of little help. As I understand it, he's still out, but go on up and check if you want.'

He found his way to the ward, but, at five o'clock on a Saturday evening, Dr Quinn was not there. He discovered a sister who herself had only just come on duty. She was irritated to have this big man towering over her this early in her shift. She didn't know how Dawson was. Couldn't Carstairs come back later? Anyway it was strictly only next of kin who should be enquiring.

Carstairs was not a man to be deflected from his purpose. He insisted, but quietly. He explained that he was a close associate of Dawson's, that Dawson was working for him. In a way he could be regarded as the next of kin.

She gave in: 'Wait there now, I'll go and look at the notes.'

Carstairs stood there for a good fifteen minutes. He read the chart on the wall explaining blood circulation, red for arteries, blue for veins. He read the caution against Aids. He sat down on one of the row of chairs opposite the semi-circular reception desk. He got up and paced up and down.

'I am sorry to have kept you. Mr Dawson has been moved up to the Sir Edward Carson ward. I am afraid I cannot let you see him. There has been no visible change. He is off the ventilator and life support, but he is being fed intravenously and it looks a bit of mess with the drips and all. He has not come round so there is not a lot of point anyway.'

Carstairs, seeing there was little more to be done, thanked her, for her help, turned on his heel and went back to Inspector Regan's little hut.

'Inspector, it does occur to me that Dawson may have had visitors, next of kin and friends.'

'I haven't been here all the while, but no one has   visited that I know of.'

'Who is his next of kin, do we know?'

'Yes, we do, as a matter of fact. According to his passport, his wife's a Maureen Dawson, who lives somewhere in Londonderry. Our boys have been trying to contact her. But no luck so far.'

'There's no one else?'

'No one as far as we know.'

'You'll let me know if there is any change in the situation.'

'I'll be certain to do that, yes. Do I have your numbers?'

'Let me give them to you now.' He scribbled three numbers and walked out to his car.

Joe said, 'Right now, Whiteabbey is it?'

'No, hang on a moment, pass me the mobile will you, Billy.'

Carstairs walked back into the hospital and then thought better of it. He walked round into the gardens by the side of the hospital and, using the light from the ground-floor windows, began to dial a series of numbers.

Joe he didn't mind, but he did not want Billy hearing his conversations. Children could be very indiscreet. In quick succession he dialled nine numbers. Six of the nine numbers belonged to senior Police Force members from the six counties of Ulster. Carstairs thought of them as his county commanders. They were not at the very top of the Police Force, they were just below, but they were all superintendents or inspectors, and their loyalty was assured, Protestants to a man. The other three were from the Royal Irish Regiment, including Colonel Charles Wilson.

To the six he managed to contact he uttered the same coded message. 'Martha will be visiting tonight at nine o'clock.' This, translated, meant the insurrection executive was to meet at an agreed safe house in Bangor. It was a small upmarket hotel, called the Town House. Carstairs had paid his friend, John Duffy, the owner, to close it down for a year so that it could be available exclusively for Carstairs' 'business matters'. John Duffy was a totally discreet Protestant, a supporter of the cause. Bangor was a big enough seaside town to house a gathering of important people without anyone noticing.

To his coded message each replied, 'Right you are', meaning they would be there. These key people would not like being called out on a Saturday night, at short notice, as winter was closing in. But this was an emergency. There was little time to waste. With six of them he had a quorum. Nine o'clock gave them enough time to get to Bangor even from the far reaches of the province. Carstairs folded the aerial of the mobile and walked back to the Rover. 'Right Joe, Whiteabbey it is, and don't spare the horses.'

*

Aideen got up after watching Ireland lose the rugby game 22 points to 9, stretched and said, 'Right, now I am going to have a big fat bath. I only had a wash this morning.'

Jackie replied, 'Good, can I watch?'

'Didn't know you were into voyeurism. I don't perform in the bath you know.'

'I'm not. On second thoughts, it's a big bath - perhaps I'll get in with you.'

'Okay, wait now 'til I run it.'

The bathroom was an add-on to the living room but you had to go out into the hall to get to it. One of Aideen's luxuries was a huge old-fashioned bath, which she had bought on a trip to the West of Ireland. It had brass feet and taps. Jackie often joked you could get the entire Irish rugby side in it. It was big enough for these two big people to get in together. As she walked back into the living room unbuttoning her blouse, Jackie said, 'You know the trouble with your lot, they are sixty-minute players, they are not fit enough.'

'Oh, spare me the clichés, Jackie Wilson. I suppose you are going to tell me next that they train on Guinness.'

'No, I'm going to tell you that you are highly desirable.' With that he leapt from his seat, picked Aideen up in his arms, and walked into the bathroom. He held her over the bath - she still had her jeans and bra on - and said, 'Now, unless you come clean about your past loves, I am going to drop you in the bath.'

'Jackie, Jackie, now stop it, you're messing.' she wriggled. 'I'll bite your nose Jackie.'

'I wouldn't, you'll get lockjaw. Now did you, or did you not, once have an affair with Diarmuid Brogan? Did he seduce you as a young girl?'

'Now that would be telling. No, Jackie, don't, don't, you'll ruin my hair, aahhh.'

With that he lowered her down and dropped her in the bath.

'You swine. You brute, I'll look awful.'

'No, you won't, move over.' He undressed. She got out and dumped her wet clothes and they both got back in, one at each end.

They splashed and frolicked and washed one another.

'Sure, it's none of your business who I've slept with, Jackie, I don't ask you. It's you I love.'

'Sure you do.'

'Jackie, after we're ready, I'd like to go and have a drink before the dinner.'

'You want to be seen in your finery? Where do you want to go? The Clarence, with the young trendies? We are going to the Berkeley Court for dinner.'

'No, the Shelbourne.'

'Why not. It'll take me no time at all to get ready.'

Inevitably it was he who was ready first. He looked every inch the cool aristocrat in his dinner jacket and large bow tie. His shirt was very white. His black shoes, which he kept at Aideen's along with various other bits and pieces like his Burberry raincoat, were very shiny.

He sat down at the kitchen table and picked up a newspaper. Minutes later Aideen emerged looking ravishing. She wore a sheer full-length black shift, with long sleeves and a plunging neckline that showed off her cleavage. Not a trace of underwear showed through. Around her neck was a chunky silver choker matched by drop earrings. Across her arm was a red military style overcoat. Her hair had not been affected by the bath and she had teased her curls a little more. Her face had just the right amount of make-up.

'How do I look?' she asked.

'Sensational.'

'You don't look too bad yourself. You look as pretty as a brandy advert.'

'Oh, come off it. Shall we go?'

They drove off in the little Renault, round Merrion Square and up to Merrion Row. They then walked around to the Shelbourne. Outside was a long black stretch Mercedes.

Aideen said, 'Look now, that's Diarmuid Brogan's car. I wonder what he's doing here?'

'How do you know it's Brogan's? They've all got them.'

'The number plate. It's got a one in it.'

Once inside the lobby, Aideen made a detour to talk to Brogan's chauffeur. 'Hello Edward, what's himself doing slumming in a place like this?'

He laughed, 'Oh, it's not himself. I'm to pick someone up.' At that instant Alex and Angus MacPhee emerged from the lift. 'There they are, I think. Excuse me, Miss O'Connor.'

As Alex MacPhee walked past Aideen, they both did a double take. They were vaguely familiar to one another. But Aideen could not immediately put a name to the face. She went on into the Horseshoe bar, which was pretty full. Heads turned as she came in. It was said of the Horseshoe Bar, named because of its shape, that if you stayed long enough you would see everyone you needed to see in Dublin's political and business life. Sure enough Aideen said hello to at least six people before reaching Jackie who had secured a little stretch of the bar on the far side.

*

The MacPhee brothers were whisked down Grafton Street across the bridge leading to O'Connell Street, then left along the quay out towards Phoenix Park. After twenty minutes through the dark countryside, they reached the village of Dunboyne, which was shuttered and closed apart from the light in the pub.

On the north side of Dunboyne, they stopped at the gates, the security guard came out of his gatehouse and, seeing it was Edward, waved them through into the curving drive, lined with beech trees like silent skeletons. Edward rang the front door and they were met by Jeananne. She wore a long green silk dress, her hair was newly washed and shiny with brushing. This evening she was being allowed to go to the ball. She showed them up to the study, where Dominic Morris had recently intruded. As they came in, Diarmuid Brogan got up from behind his desk and Dick McGuinness hauled himself up from the deep sofa into which he was sunk. Both were wearing dinner jackets.

Brogan said, 'Gentlemen, to what do we owe the pleasure? Before you answer, let me get you a drink. What'll it be?'

'Got any Scotch?' said Alex MacPhee.

'What, here, are you mad?' replied Brogan.

'I was joking. I'd like a Bushmills, please, with some ice.'

'Same for me,' chimed in Angus.

'You're okay, Dick?' Brogan said to his crony. 'You two know Dick McGuinness. He's a TD, a member of parliament.'

MacPhee said, 'We've not met,' and walked over to shake McGuinness's hand.

The drinks poured, Brogan said, 'Let's all sit down. The place is not bugged. As I was saying, to what do we owe the pleasure? Dick here seems to think you are after our oil, seeing how Mrs Vernon is about to pinch yours.'

MacPhee pondered for a second before replying, 'Not exactly, but he's in the right area. We were in Dublin for the match, and, remembering our past association, thought we might have a chat.'

'Okay, chat away.'

'Has it occurred to you, that there might be further oil to be found around Ireland?'

'We've been looking a long time and we are just after finding some in the Atlantic. Not much, mind, but it's a start.'

MacPhee continued, 'I'm not talking about the Atlantic. I am talking about nearer to home. Like in the North.'

'Naah, the Brits, someone, would have found it if it was there. You are talking about the North of Ireland, I presume?'

'Yes I am.'

'I can tell you from my own days in the oil business that there is no oil up there. The Brits had a look.'

'Did they? You sure?'

'Now you come to mention it, I am not so sure. I can't call to mind any prolonged search. But they must have looked. What with their own oil running down and all. What do you say Dick?'

'I am just listening,' McGuinness said. But then added, 'What makes you think there is oil in Northern Ireland?'

Alex MacPhee said, 'I don't know for sure that there is oil in, or around, Northern Ireland, but I don't know there is not. If there is, presumably it would be yours. Mrs Vernon is pulling out.'

'We'll have to wait and see about that,' Brogan came in. 'Mrs Vernon hasn't done the deed yet. What is your interest anyway, Mr MacPhee?'

'We are involved in general salvage, wrecks and that, as well as oil. But I'm always interested in new fields. It occurs to me, if there is oil off the Shetlands, and oil off the Isle of Man, there could be oil off Northern Ireland. It is a question of finding it and deciding who it belongs to. I, or rather we, are interested in concessions wherever we can find them.'

McGuinness intervened, 'I bet you are, particularly as the Brit government is about to pirate your British oil. But I ask you again, what makes you think there is oil there? Surely the Brits would have found it by now?'

'As I say, I do not know whether there is any there, but it is worth thinking about.'

Brogan said, 'Thanks for the tip. Now we better be getting on. Where are you boys heading? We'll give you a lift. If you could just give Dick and myself a minute or two.' He walked to the door, opened it and yelled, 'Jeananne, would you ever give these gentlemen a drink in the drawing room, we'll be down directly.' He ushered them through the door and down the stairs where they were met by Jeananne who lead them off to the drawing room and offered drinks.

In the study Brogan turned to McGuinnesss and whispered, 'Now, in the name of the saints, what was that all about?'

McGuinness stroked his chin. 'He's trying to put an idea into your head. The question is why.'

'I should think it is obvious why. He is losing his oil and wants to find some more. Ours.'

'Yes, but why should he pitch up now after the Rathlin business? We've known for some time what the British planned to do with their oil.'

Brogan said, 'That's a point. We'd better get a look at that report.'

'It's in hand,' said McGuinness.

'Let's go, shall we.'

They went downstairs and asked the MacPhees where they wanted to go. On learning it was the Shelbourne, Brogan said, 'That's easy, I am sure we can fit five in the Merc.' He grabbed his overcoat from behind the front door, and picked up the telephone on the small oak table. It was a direct line to Edward's cottage. 'Edward, we're ready to go now.'

On the drive into town, they talked about the match, a little smugly on MacPhee's part, Brogan thought, and about the dinner ahead. It was the annual press gallery dinner, where the assembled hacks slugged it out with politicians of the various parties. Not all 168 TDs, many did not want to come, but it was a sizeable gathering none the less. Brogan was invited partly because of his eminence as a businessman but also because of his political past. The Taoiseach would normally make a speech extolling the importance of a free press and wishing it would behave more sensibly at times, concentrate on the issues and less on tittle tattle.

Edward dropped the MacPhees outside the Shelbourne. Brogan said, 'Okay, on to the Berkeley Court please, Edward.'

*

Inside the Shelbourne, Aideen and Jackie had moved to the morning room in the front of the hotel, as the Horse Shoe Bar had become impossibly crowded. They were with a Fine Gael deputy and his wife, who then left to go to the dinner.

Jackie said, 'You know Aideen, It occurs to me I should have tried to get hold of Carstairs, or at least phoned Dawson.'

'I'm sure you would have heard,' Aideen was fairly tipsy on two gin and tonics and the adrenalin rush of the prospect of the night ahead. Nothing was further from her thoughts at the moment than Carstairs and Dawson. 'Come on, we'd better be going.' She said.

At the Berkeley Court, the large entrance and reception gave way to stairs which wound up to a large mezzanine with a balcony looking out on to the street. There were bars at either end and lots of seats. Here the party goers would foregather at 7.30. Waiters would weave in and out with trays of drinks and canapés. Then at 8.30 the doors at the back of the mezzanine would be thrown back to reveal a vast chandeliered dining room with dozens of tables for eight.

*

As the revellers started to take their seats, Dominic Morris was parking his car in Waterloo Road. He walked up and down twice. The house was dark apart from a light from Aideen's front room. The O'Briens, who lived on the second floor, had gone away. Ethna, however, was at home with her boyfriend Ronan. Ethna was a convent girl who didn't like making love during daylight. She had switched the bedroom light off and started to undress. Ronan, who had already undressed, was in the bed. 'Sure Ethna, I'm going to ride yer all night.'

'Be my guest,' she replied as she dashed to the bed, pulled back the covers and crawled in beside him.

Dominic Morris stood at the back of Aideen's house, looked either way and behind to the back of houses on Waterloo Avenue. Lights were on but no-one was hanging out of any windows. He looked both ways again. No-one. He hauled himself up on the wall at the end of Aideen's garden. He sat astride for a second, threw his leg over and jumped softly, swinging on the branch of the pear tree. The wall was barely seven feet tall so there was hardly a thud. He was guided towards the back of Aideen's flat by the light coming from the front room of the basement. Aideen had left the double doors inside the flat open.

Morris walked down the steps to the French windows. He took out a rolled scroll from the right pocket of his overcoat. It contained a folded newspaper, a roll of adhesive tape, a screwdriver and a glass cutter. He cut a little six inch square on three sides next to the lock. He then taped the newspaper over it. With the handle of his screwdriver he bashed the newspaper. The glass gave, but did not fall. One side of the tape held in place. He gently pulled the glass out and laid it on the York stone beneath his feet. He put his hand back in and turned the key. Easy, peasy. He was in. He had done some burgling in his time had Dominic Morris, when he was Patrick Hughes.

He reached into his left pocket and gripped, but did not pull out, his torch. It was an army torch with a clip for putting on his belt and, most usefully, an L-shaped top which meant that the light shone down rather than forward if you held it normally. He walked into the hall, which was not completely dark because of the light coming in from the street from the fanlight. He crept softly up the stairs. At the top he stopped to listen. Nothing save a rhythmic creaking from above. The ceilings were high, but Ethna had an old fashioned metal bedstead she had bought in a junk shop. Morris smiled.

He let himself into Aideen's bedroom and switched on his flashlight, making sure it faced down and he had his back to the window. He quietly drew the curtains. He grabbed Jackie's satchel. It was unlocked. He opened and upturned it. With one hand he sorted through the papers. Nothing he wanted. He grabbed hold of Aideen's big workbag. He emptied that out on to the bed. There was all kind of bric-a-brac, pieces of make-up, notebooks, address book, calculator and magazines.

Morris went into the back room. He had been told the document had been printed out. On her desk next to the computer was a pile of papers. He started going through them. There were court reports, press releases. He hurled each one to the floor with increasing frustration. Nothing.

He retraced his footsteps, and crept back downstairs. He could still hear the creaking. My, the girl's got stamina, he thought. Maybe they had stopped for a cigarette break while he was in the bedroom.

Once downstairs, he went into the front room. The light was on, but no one could see from the street. He stared at the rows of videos and cassettes. Damn, he thought, it's got to be here somewhere. Think, Hughes, he said to himself. He wandered out to the kitchen. There was a large pile of newspapers on the sideboard next to the telephone. He began to pick them up and there, amongst the newspapers, where Aideen had left it and Jackie had failed to retrieve it, was what he had come for, Dawson's report. He began to read.

At the front door John McWilliams was expertly inserting a thin bar into the front door. For a shooting, McWilliams would normally have been the driver. But his skills at breaking and entering meant that it was Gary Molloy who sat in the Granada almost exactly opposite the house and about four parking spaces down from Dominic Morris' car.

Gary Watson stood with his back to McWilliams, nervously looking up and down the street. The door gave easily. They moved quickly inside and quietly closed the door. They heard the creaking of the bed and the shrieks of Ethna. They didn't turn left into the bedroom but went downstairs, attracted like lumbering moths to the light. Neither had masks. Watson had his hand on the 9mm Browning pistol in his right hand pocket. When he saw Morris, he stopped. McWilliams bumped into him.

Morris looked up. 'What the feck?' He automatically reached into his inside pocket. But it was too late. Watson already had his gun out. He could not take aim though, because McWilliams had pushed him forward when he had bumped into him. Still holding the document in his left hand, Morris up-ended the heavy table with his right. It fell on to Watson. Morris made a dash for the French windows, barged through them and ran up the steps to the garden.

Watson pushed the table away and ran after Morris, who dived for the branch of the pear tree The document dropped. Morris thought to retrieve it, but heard Watson behind him like a savage dog intent on biting his ankles. So he mounted the wall. Watson was only yards away. He went into a crouch position and let off three shots. The force of the bullets pushed Morris off the wall into the lane.

One pierced his lung, another chipped into his aorta, a third entered his stomach. It was the bullet that hit his aorta that did for him. He was bleeding internally. He crashed down on to the floor of the alley. He picked himself up and clutched his side, blood seeping through his fingers and leaving a trail as he limped towards the end of the lane, turned right into Fleming Street and staggered the last few yards to the Waterloo Road. Sheer willpower was urging him on. He collapsed a hundred yards from the junction with Baggot Street. His eyes closed and a huge red cloud rose up in front of him before he lost consciousness.

With the sound of gunfire, lights had come on and windows had been thrown up in Waterloo Road, Waterloo Lane and Burlington Road.

Ethna was still coming down from her rapture when she heard the bangs. She did not immediately register, but went to the backroom, switched the light on and went to the window. She threw it up to see a man in the garden. She was still bleary. Watson grabbed the document and ran back into the house.

Ethna, hearing the noise from below, put her dressing gown on and went out to the hall. She turned to the top of the stairs and pushed the light on. Watson was at the front door. McWilliams was behind him. When the light went on, he turned around and looked up. She stared straight at him.

She yelled, 'Ronan, Ronan it's him, it's him.'

McWilliams was taking a shot when Watson grabbed his collar and dragged him through the door. The bullet went up through the ceiling. Ethna shrieked.

The two men ran across the road and into the back of the Granada whose engine was already running. There was nobody on the street. People were looking out of their windows, but nobody got the car number.

Ronan grasped Ethna who was shaking uncontrollably: 'What do you mean it's him?'

'It's him. It's the electrician.'

*

As Dominic Morris/ Patrick Hughes was drawing his final breath, the Taoiseach was winding up his speech. He was sitting at the same table as Jackie, Aideen and Dick McGuinness. Jeananne had come in with Brogan, but they sat at separate tables. Her arrival had caused some sniggers and a scowl from Aideen, who whispered in Jackie's ear, 'Getting bold isn't he, appearing in public with his trollop.'

'Now, now, miaow. We mustn't be bitchy, must we?'

Aideen just said, 'I wish he'd hurry up and finish. I want to eat, I'm hungry.'

The Taoiseach sat down opposite Jackie and said 'My, what distinguished company we find ourselves in, tonight.' Jackie winced. The Taoiseach saw this and changed tack. 'Lord Strangford, we've not met, you're most welcome.'

McGuinness, meanwhile, turned his attention to Aideen. She was sat next to him. He wanted to pump her about the documents but realised it was the wrong setting. After a few minutes he said, 'Look Aideen, you've been wanting to interview Diarmuid for some time. Can you make it tomorrow? He'll see you at his office about eleven after mass. He'd invite you out to the house. But you know how it is. People might talk.'

Aideen thought it would not be me they'd be talking about and, why does Diarmuid want to see me now? But said, 'Yes I'd like to do that,' then turned to the man on her left with some small talk. Aideen winked at Jackie.

*

At the Town House at nine o'clock, six men were still waiting for the arrival of the seventh, Bill Tomkins from Londonderry, a superintendent of the Police Force. They sat in a large vestibule making small talk, with William Carstairs noticeably nervous.

Tomkins rushed in after fifteen minutes. 'William, I am sorry, it's very dark tonight.'

Carstairs replied, 'Well, you're here, let's get on.'

They got up and walked into an old-fashioned room, with some hunting prints on the wall, dominated by a long table with a dozen chairs. John Duffy had christened it the Boardroom. Only he and his wife were there. The gentlemen would not be disturbed.

William Carstairs solemnly opened the proceedings, 'Gentlemen, I have asked you here this evening because of crucial developments which might affect our plans. You will all have read, or have knowledge, of the events in Ballycastle. I think that it is now impossible for us to make the planned shipments of arms to Rathlin Island. It is still too much the focus of attention.'

John Strange, a Police Force inspector from Enniskillen, which had an evenly balanced Catholic/Protestant population, came in: 'Is that all? I always thought it was a stupid idea anyway. Bringing the arms into Rathlin, then distributing them again. Apart from anything else, Rathlin is full of Taigs.'

Strange was considered a bit of a cynic. He was about to continue when Carstairs cut him off: 'No, it is not all. Some of you know the full picture, some of you don't. I will now brief you and then we will review our arrangements and we will decide what alterations we need to make. Rathlin is vital to our plans for one simple reason. It will be the source of the wealth which will make it possible for us to sustain an independent Ulster. Dawson and the others were supposed to be diving for wrecks. What he was really doing was drilling for oil.'

Strange again cut in. 'I don't want to appear dumb, William, but what has oil got to do with our plans? We are planning an armed insurrection in the near future. You led us to believe that the arms needed, beyond the ones we've already got, would be available. The men are all in place.'

'Frankly that is a dumb question, John, if you don't mind me saying so. Ulster is virtually bankrupt. It is kept going by a huge subvention from the British. They even pay your wages. The idea of the wee whore, Mrs Vernon, is that Ireland should take over the cost of running the place. In reality that means the European Union and their handouts. Ireland is half owned by Europe. We can have our rebellion. But how long will it last? We could be cut off. Never mind sanctions, we could be brought to our knees in weeks. But with our oil wealth, we would have friends, friends we don't even know we have, beating a path to our door, trying to exploit us. The Brits might have abandoned us to joint sovereignty. But they would soon want to come back.

'So,' said Strange.

'Unfortunately, the only person who knows where the stuff is Dawson and he's in a coma.'

John Strange again spoke. 'Let me see if I understand you. As things stand, we have enough resources to mount an insurrection, but not enough to maintain an independent state?'

'Exactly.'

Charles Wilson broke in: 'I say we go ahead anyway, we can't back out now. Everything is prepared.'

Carstairs then said, 'Colonel Wilson, I am not proposing that we back out, as you put it. I am merely trying to brief everyone on the situation at hand. I came back from Rathlin Island thinking that I had the floppy disc with the vital information on it. It turned out to contain only the data which you already know about.'

Charles Meredith, a flint eyed inspector of few words from

Banbridge, said, 'You are not making sense, William.'

Carstairs looked at him for a second. He was stared down. 'Inspector Meredith, let me fill you in. Alan Dawson was looking for oil and preparing Rathlin Island as a rear base for our activities. To mask his activities, he was searching out wrecks and pretending he was preparing salvage of wrecks known to, or thought to, contain treasure or bullion. This is, of course, big business nowadays. He drew up one report about this diving for gold and another report about his research on the oil. The first report has come to light, in fact, it is in the hands of Colonel Wilson and others. Of the second report, there is no sign.'

'What do you mean, others?' said Meredith.

'Well, an anthropologist on the island, who happens to be Colonel Wilson's brother, has a copy. Dawson gave it to him for safe keeping.'

'And?'

'He has gone to Dublin.'

Meredith then said, 'I am sorry William , you are talking in riddles.'

'Let me make myself clear then. A report detailing the possibility of bullion off Rathlin Island is in the hands of persons in Dublin. Given the murders, people could put two and two together on Rathlin and conclude that something is amiss.'

'Does the report detail the arms shipment?' asked Meredith.

'No, it certainly does not,' answered Carstairs.

'Well then why are you worrying? All the world knows is that there have been some sectarian killings on the coast close to Rathlin Island. Should the report gain wider currency, what difference does it make?' Meredith asked.

'Only that the report is addressed to me,' said Carstairs.

'So what?' said Strange.

'So the conspiratorially minded might conclude that there is something wrong, and that there is truth in the rumours that we are plotting a coup.'

'Coup, smoo,' said Strange. 'There are always rumours of coups. The air is thick with them. Nobody but us knows what the Police Force will do. We know our duty. Nobody can prove anything.'

'Yes, but in the light of recent events, is it wise to import weapons into Rathlin Island?'

Charles Wilson said: 'What weapons are we talking about, William? We, that is the regiment, will be left with armoured cars and helicopters. The idea is to integrate with the Irish army at some point. Like never, ha!'

'We are talking about rifles and ammunition for the volunteers. Lots of them and some missiles.'

Derek Ironside, who had been very thoughtful throughout, spoke up, 'I think Mr Carstairs has got a point. No advantage in flagging our intentions. There's still a lot of press and media hanging around Ballycastle. Why don't we bring the goods into Port Rush. As for the other thing, we go ahead anyway. If you are convinced the oil is there, we can confirm it later.'

Carstairs said, 'That's a good idea, Superintendent, let us bring them into Port Rush - anyone disagree?' Nobody spoke. 'As for the oil, I'd rather have the evidence, if only to mollify our backers in Scotland. Also, that way, no one can call our bluff.'

'It'll be too late for that anyroad. The deed will be done,' said Ironside.

'Very well,' said Carstairs, 'let us review our arrangements.' He spoke first, followed by Charles Wilson and then Superintendent Ironside. Once the British troops had gone, the Royal Irish Regiment would not proceed with any integration with the army of the Irish Republic. They would disarm the Catholics in the Regiment. In the event of the Irish army trying anything, the Regiment would be responsible for sealing off the border, namely the roads, and securing the airport and the ports. They would be supported by the volunteers - the men secretly trained by Carstairs, and consisting mostly of disaffected UDA and UFF members.

'Are we satisfied with the loyalty of the Regiment? It is thought to be one third Catholic,' asked Strange.

He was reassured by Charles Wilson that the Catholics were out of the game, on the border. He had spent a lot of time preparing his soldiers. Not every man jack knew, but the key officers were in on the plot and they would ensure loyalty.

That left the Police Force. Several of the men tried to speak at once. Ironside pointed out that in times of stress, the police acted in the unionist cause. Look at 1974, the police had refused to break the power workers' strikes, and the province had become paralysed. The Police instinctively knew where their duty lay. They came close to revolt on their own accord during the 1990s. They were answerable to their communities. There were virtually no Catholics left in the Police Force. No, the meeting was assured, when the time came, the Police Force would be there.

With this, Carstairs called the meeting to a close. He would arrange for the arms to come into Port Rush on Monday evening and they would have one more meeting, as soon as possible thereafter. The meeting broke up. It was late, but Carstairs had business to do. He had originally arranged for the weapons to be shipped from Campbeltown on the Mull of Kintyre to Rathlin. They now needed to be diverted to Port Rush. This was comparatively simple, the shipping company was another ally in favour of the Protestant cause. The arms were all safely stored. It would be a relatively easy task to load them and bring them across. The Police Force would ensure there would be no interference at Port Rush. It was a solidly Protestant town, almost Scottish in its demeanour.

He would also need to contact MacPhee and give him the bad news. It was late when Carstairs phoned, almost midnight, but all he got was an answering machine. Finally he spoke to Fiona, Angy's wife. She vouchsafed that Alex and Angus had gone to Dublin to watch the rugby match. At this news, a fear clutched at Carstairs' stomach. There was so much that could go wrong. Maybe the others were right; it was too late for MacPhee to back out now. But he had an uneasy feeling about MacPhee. Carstairs would have to get hold of him as soon as possible and steady him. Damn that Dawson.

Chapter

16

Oliver Sweetman went straight from lunch with the ambassador to the embassy where he drafted a telegram for the personal attention of Sir Roderick Jones, the head of M16. This was the text:

"Following from Sweetman.

Based on intelligence received from Northern Ireland, it seems that Colonel Charles Wilson, in cahoots with business leaders like William Carstairs, plans to mount some sort of coup, or even declare independence, possibly with the help and connivance of the Police Force.

The ambassador will be reporting separately about John Wilson, the elder brother of Charles Wilson, who was on Rathlin at the time of the killings. At first sight, it is difficult to see what link there is between the two Wilsons. John Wilson is known to have no Northern Ireland political interests. Moreover the two brothers are said to have become estranged.

But John Wilson (Lord Strangford) told me today that he is in possession of a document given to him by Dawson, one of the men attacked, which establishes a link between Dawson and William Carstairs. I am not yet completely clear about the contents of the document, but, if what John Wilson told me is true, (Sweetman was pleased about this bit. It showed he was on the ball.) then the document could provide the missing link since it was about searching for bullion on the seabed. Successful salvage operations could provide the wherewithal to mount a rebellion. However, I should know more on Sunday as John Wilson has agreed to show me the document. He himself feels that the report is bogus and is meant as a cover for other activities."

As soon as he saw the Sunday morning newspapers, Sweetman heartily wished he had never sent the telegram. Splashed across the front pages was the story of how, for the first time in decades, sectarian violence had broken out in the streets of Dublin. A known IRA man, Patrick Hughes, who also went by the name of Dominic Morris, had been shot dead in a Dublin street. Three men, believed to be from Northern Ireland and with known links with the Ulster Defence Association, had been arrested and were being held in Dublin's Central Police Station. This was the first occurrence of sectarian violence in Dublin since 1994 when two bombs planted by the UDA had failed to explode.

It had all been very simple from a police point of view. There had been a number of phone calls about shootings down by the Waterloo pub. They had quickly identified Morris. He had been obliging enough to have his passport on him. Through a computer link up with Belfast they soon found this was an alias and learned his real identity. Once Ethna had talked of the Northerners, it was a question of rounding up the known suspects. Gerry Watson was picked up without difficulty in his flat, together with his gun and Wilson's document, which a sharp-eyed detective had seen and started to read. John McWilliams was arrested on the border and transported back to Dublin and Malloy was apprehended in his hotel.

When Sweetman read the papers, he groaned inwardly. It

now looked like a straightforward sectarian tit-for-tat. The killing in Dublin in return for the killings in Ballycastle. This could herald a breakdown of the peace process. Perhaps there was a conspiracy, but his telegram made it look as if he was wildly wide of the mark and had got the wrong conspiracy. Ah me, he said to himself, might as well go ahead with things, meet with Wilson and get a peek at his document.

What nobody cottoned on to, at least initially, was the connection with Aideen and Jackie. This was partly because of a fluke. Since it was thought to be a terrorist act, C4 had been involved almost immediately and relieved the homicide division of responsibility for the Wilson document. It thus reached McQuire, who had passed the information, on a hunch, to McGuinness. He had quickly said it was to be kept under wraps. As far as the press was concerned this was a straightforward sectarian killing.

McGuinness had followed Brogan back to his office while Jeananne was being driven home. When McQuire arrived, he was shown into Brogan's smoke-filled room. He came straight to the point. 'I imagine this is what you have been looking for.' He passed the document to Brogan and who flicked through it and then passed it on to McGuinness.

'Have you read it, McQuire, what does it say?'

'It says that really Dawson was looking for bullion and sunken treasure, rather than being involved in police work. The interesting thing is, it is addressed to Carstairs.'

'Yes, well, Carstairs is a businessman as well as being a bigot. No reason why he shouldn't try and make some money,' said Brogan. He went on, 'More to the point, how did you come by it?'

'We lifted it from one of the Prods.'

'They presumably got it from Dominic Morris, or Hughes, or whatever his feckin name was.'

'That is the point I was coming to. It seems the document

was in the possession of John Wilson and it was taken from the flat of Aideen O'Connor. We know this because a young woman living in the flat recognised one of the Prods, and phoned us. Is this what we were looking for all along?'

Brogan ignored this question. 'The hell of it, they were at the dinner with us. What have they got to do with this? Has the government seen the document?'

'Not yet, but they'll have to.'

'What happened, McQuire?'

'As far as we can see, the two parties were after the same thing, only the Proddies won. Morris was the same man who did the Ballycastle job. I don't know how Wilson or yer woman got hold of the document. It's not looking good.'

'I'll be the judge of that. Now look, McQuire, how long can you keep this under wraps? It is a straightforward sectarian killing. Jesus that's feckin bad enough. If Wilson comes into the picture, God knows what the gombeen journos will do with it. No one is to leak, so, right.'

'Is that wise? Once the girl starts blabbing, someone's bound to pick up their involvement. We will be accused of a cover up. The government will have to know before morning.'

'I don't feckin give a gombeen shite whether it's wise to keep things quiet. Is it possible? Whaddya say Dick?'

Dick McGuinness looked up from his intense study of the document and asked: 'Who knows about this, apart from us three?'

'So far, the Gards who picked it up and their superior officer,' replied McQuire.

'The Government can slap the 1994 Terrorist Information Act on them, and the press too, if it comes to that. Any paper that prints it could be liable for prosecution,' said McGuinness.

'OK. The Government has to know. But how do we keep

Wilson and O'Connor quiet?' asked Brogan.

'They can be persuaded. They are being pulled in right now,' said McQuire.

'Is that wise?' said Brogan, almost aping McQuire.

'It'd look pretty odd if they were not brought in. McQuire can pursue the line that a robbery at their flat, or rather her flat, seems to have a connection with the terrorist shooting. Would they care to enlighten the Garda. He can spiel them the line that he is involved in the questioning because of the terrorist nature of the killing,' said McGuinness and went back to the document.

'I don't like it. It's only a matter of time before some journo puts two and two together and gets the connection. I don't know whether the government will want to keep the lid on,' said McQuire.

'Yeah, well you persuade them, make sure you do, McQuire. You can get along, thanks,' and thus was dismissed this most senior police intelligence officer, a man who knew all about Dominic Morris and his involvement in Ballycastle, and a man who bore a grudge.

When he had gone, Brogan got up and exploded. 'Jesus, feckin Mary and feckin Joseph. This is one hell of a mess, Dick. A simple operation in the North of Ireland to find out what that louse Carstairs is on about and we get civil feckin' war. Can you just see what the press is going to make of this. Sectarian violence in Dublin! This surely is the end of the peace process. Ireland is descending into civil war. When the Prods can rove the streets of Dublin with impunity, shooting innocent Irish citizens, etc etc. Surely the Brits can't pull out now. What is our government doing negotiating with the Brits at a time when Protestant paramilitaries are allowed to roam free in the Republic. Ah Jesus, what a mess. That's to say nothing of the Wilson thing. I knew I should never have trusted yer man. Now Dick, are you sure? Are you positive? Swear on all the saints they cannot trace this Hughes, this Morris, or whatever his name is, back to us.' He was beginning to repeat himself. 'What does the feckin document say anyway? Was it worth our bother?'

'Diarmuid, Diarmuid, would yer ever calm yerself, so.' McGuinness always called Brogan "Diarmuid" whenever he was rattled and nervous. It seemed to bolster his confidence. 'Hughes is dead, and good riddance. A dead man can't talk. Who else knows, McQuire? McCall? Well, they ain't going to say anything. No, we're clear. On the other thing, the press. Yes, well they'll huff and puff about the peace process. But the press do not know what we know.'

'Which is?'

'That this was not a tit-for-tat for the Ballycastle killings. It was an unfortunate accident.'

'What do you mean?'

'Our friend Hughes was trying to get this document at the same time as Carstairs was trying to get his papers back.'

'So, how d'you get to that anyway?'

'McQuire told me he had those Prod boys on file for the past year. They work for Carstairs. So it was an accident. There won't be any more killings. This is not the start of a spiral, as they say.'

'Hmm, I see your point. Now what about this document?'

McGuinness had reached the same conclusion as Jackie Wilson. 'The document doesn't add up. It was not worth killing a mouse for, let alone three, now four, men. We've got to find out what is going down on the island. What did yer man say about oil? There has got to be more to it than that load of bolex in the report.'

'Okay,' said Brogan, 'but no more types like Hughes, or whatever his name was. Got any other ideas?'

'Yes, yer woman Aideen O'Connor is coming to see you after mass. You can start with her. She must know more. Push. Use your charm.'

*

Across the road in the Dail the Taoiseach was again sitting with his crony Don. They had heard the news.

'What'll we say now, Don?'

'What'll we say? Why don't you wake up TJ and tell him to say the Garda are continuing their enquiries and until we know more, the government will not be making a statement. We can hold this until tomorrow lunchtime, at least.'

The Taoiseach did not need to ring T.J.O'Reilly because, at that moment, O'Reilly rang him. 'Taoiseach, several of the press are ringing wanting to know about this shooting. There are rumours that it was a Protestant gang who shot the man in Waterloo Road.'

'Yes, so I've heard. The best thing, TJ, is to put out a statement saying the Garda are continuing their enquiries. We will make a fuller announcement in the morning when we have more information. Okay. Right.' He put the phone down. O'Reilly stared at the phone, and thought what a strange man, but he did as he was asked.

The press the next day was very much as Brogan had predicted. The morning newspapers had screamed that sectarian violence had returned to Dublin. Commentaries had declaimed wildly that this was the end of the peace process. The more nationalist newspapers wondered how an Irish government could possibly negotiate with the British under these circumstances, asserting, as always, that the Protestant community was the same thing as the British.

In Northern Ireland, the Protestant press was noticeably silent on the matter. They reported little of what went on in Dublin and the Republic. The Protestant leaders, including Ian Paisley, had said nothing. It was always difficult to get Ian Paisley to say anything over a weekend anyway because of the sabbath. William Carstairs could not be contacted on Saturday night.

The nationalist press in the North while reporting the Dublin murder, was more concerned with another killing, just outside of

Armagh, of a former IRA member, Kieran Williams. The single bullet to the back of the head had all the hallmarks of an IRA punishment killing. But, unusually, the IRA had not claimed the shooting. Indeed, the solitary death of Kieran Williams, in a lonely glade outside the cathedral town, after a terrifying kangaroo court in the nondescript back room of a shabby bar, went unclaimed by anyone. It did not go unremarked, though. John Hume was on the radio saying how he regretted the murders in the North and in Dublin. He condemned sectarian killings of any kind. He called for restraint. The peace process must not be jeopardised by these acts of gangsters.

In London, the media gave the Dublin killing little attention. It rarely gave extravagant space, or time, to Dublin events. The newspapers in particular were, like the government establishment, loath to credit the Irish government with any real influence in the course of events in Northern Ireland, whatever they might say publicly. Sectarian killings in Dublin just didn't rate, they were more like drug wars.

Certainly the Prime Minister was in that kind of mood when Sir Roderick Jones, who had requested a meeting, arrived at number 10 Downing Street a little after ten o'clock. 'Morning, Prime Minister.'

'Good morning, Sir Roderick, what can I do for you?'

'Have you seen this news in Dublin?'

'Yes, I believe I have.'

'Well, of course, early indications are that they are in uproar. How dare the kind of violence we are so used to in the North spill over to Dublin.'

'I should say that that was their problem, wouldn't you?'

'What do you mean exactly, Prime Minister?'

The Prime Minister looked Sir Roderick straight in the eye as he replied, 'I get sick and tired of the bleating from Dublin about a united Ireland. They rant and rave, then, the second they get a hint of the enormity of the problem, they wet themselves. Let them see what it is like to have a terrorist minority in their midst. Only it will be a large minority. They want a united Ireland. Well, let them live with one million Protestants in a population of five million. Moreover, a minority of one million who don't want to be part of a united Ireland. The place will sink like a stone. Serves them bloody well right. No doubt I'll have the Taoiseach phoning up whining before much longer.'

'Actually it is not about the events in Dublin that I asked to see you, although they could be related,' said Sir Roderick. 'You will recall at our last meeting about the Ballycastle shootings, one avenue we were looking at was this man John Wilson, or Lord Strangford, who had been on Rathlin and seemed to have some connection with one of the attacked.'

'Yes, vaguely, the beards and sandals man.'

Sir Roderick continued smoothly, 'He has duly turned up in Dublin. Our man there has made contact.'

'And?' said the Prime Minister, wanting to get on and back to his leisurely Sunday morning.

'Our man, Sweetman, not the ambassador, seems to think there is something very fishy going on at Rathlin Island. But he can't quite get the connection.'

'What do you mean?'

'It seems that this John Wilson is the brother of one Colonel Charles Wilson, who is in the Royal Irish Regiment. Sweetman says that, based on intelligence, Colonel Wilson and others, notably our old friend William Carstairs, are plotting a coup, some kind of UDI. Rathlin Island could provide the wherewithal, something about sunken treasure worth millions.'

The Prime Minister weighed this for a moment and then said, 'That sounds preposterous to me. Sunken treasure, coups, what on earth are you talking about Sir Roderick? Sounds as if your man has lost his marbles. As long as I can remember, there has been talk of independence for Ulster, or some bunch of nutcases is going to declare UDI, or launch a coup. Now you talk of sunken treasure. This is fantasyland surely. What do you think?'

Sir Roderick also pondered, then replied in measured tones. 'Sweetman's a reliable chap, had a good career. Doesn't usually let conspiracies run away with him. At a time like this, I suppose we are going to get all kinds of rumours of plots, secret armies and so on. On this occasion it does sound as if he has got a bit carried away. Dublin is that kind of place, of course.'

'So what do you propose?'

'I just felt that you should know Prime Minister. The last thing we need is for the British troops to be pulled out and a bunch of do-it-yourself Protestants to claim the state for themselves.'

'So again, I ask you what do you propose?'

'We should know more shortly. Sweetman tells me he has a meeting with John Wilson this morning. When he gets back to me, I will update you. What I think we should do is authorise Sweetman to pull out all the stops. We need to find out just what is going on in the Police Force and the Royal Irish Regiment.'

'Good idea. Okay I'll leave it with you. Check it out with Betty Vernon, but keep me posted.'

'Okay, will do.'

The Prime Minister showed Sir Roderick out into the hard sunshine, which had not yet dulled into a grey cloud, laden day.

Betty Vernon, informed that morning by her press secretary, reacted in a fashion not dissimilar to that of the Prime Minister.

'I really can't see what this has got to do with us. This Irish government, like other Irish governments, have pushed for reunification, or for joint sovereignty. It is up to them to deal with any terrorism problem on their soil.'

Chapter

17

The person who reacted most violently to the night's events was Jackie Wilson. He and Aideen had returned before midnight to find the street as if in the aftermath of a carnival, and Aideen's flat as if hit by a tropical storm. At the top of the road television lights illuminated the corner and the pub. Several police cars were in the streets with their lights whirring and people were still hanging out of the windows as if waiting for a parade.

Aideen was calm when she walked into her bedroom and work room, but when she went downstairs she said, 'What, in the mother of Jesus?' and burst into tears.

Jackie took hold of her. 'Looks as if we've been burgled darling.'

Anyone who has ever been burgled knows it feels like a personal assault, an intrusion into the private recesses of one's life. Aideen felt immediately as if she had been worked over. Jackie was intensely annoyed about his satchel being emptied. He was particular about anything concerning his work, although he didn't have a strong sense of possessions in any other way. They had just picked up the table and corrected the chairs, when Ronan and Ethna came down.

'Knock, knock, can we come in?' asked Ronan. He was standing in the kitchen doorway, with Ethna huddled behind him like a poorhouse waif.

'There's no one going to stop you, wait now 'til I make some coffee. Or would you prefer something stronger? I've some brandy,' said Aideen.

'I'll take the brandy,' said Ronan.

'Good idea, I'll join you,' said Jackie.

'Coffee for me, thank you, Aideen,' Ethna mumbled, barely audibly.

'What on earth happened?' Jackie asked both of them.

'It was terrible' said Ethna. 'Yer man, yer man I told you about, Aideen, fired a shot at me.'

'What man? Sorry, I don't understand'

'The man from the Nort, you know, the electrician.'

Jackie said, 'Wait a second. Start at the beginning.'

Ronan took up the narrative, 'We were in bed, so. We heard some shots, Ethna went to the window and saw someone running into the house. I got up. Ethna put on her dressing gown and went to the door. She pushed on the light and saw yer man. He fired a shot but it went into the ceiling. She says it was the same man who came in the morning. Must have been casing the place, I'd say. The police came to the scene pretty quickly, but they didn't come here until we phoned them.'

'When was that?' asked Jackie.

'They were only after having left a minute before you came. Said they would be back.'

They duly did arrive back at around 12.30, asking to see Aideen and John Wilson. There were three of them, one a senior superintendent. They were none too friendly and insisted Jackie and Aideen accompany them to the Central Police Station. Once there, they were ushered in to see McQuire who was wearing a well-cut suit and a silk tie. It was quickly apparent to Jackie that this was not an ordinary policeman.

McQuire said he would come straight to the point. But

he didn't. He rambled on about very serious events, important consequences for the nation. Could not have guerrilla warfare in the streets of Dublin. He tried to insinuate that Jackie and Aideen were somehow responsible. Arrests had been made, he told them, one man was dead. The police had reason to believe the shootings had taken place on Miss O'Connor's property. There could be serious consequences for her if a satisfactory explanation was not found. Aideen appeared to be shaken by all this.

But Jackie's anger smouldered and grew. He jumped up and burst out, 'Oh, come on, don't be ridiculous. Miss O'Connor's flat is raided and wrecked, and you are trying to imply that she is somehow responsible. At the time of the break-in we were sitting next to the Taoiseach at dinner!'

McQuire subtly altered his approach. 'Look, this is not a normal interview. You can see we are not being recorded. There is no intention of bringing charges, what charges would I bring? But I'd like to know what it is about your apartment that makes it so interesting to both the IRA and the Protestant paramilitaries. '

Aideen and Jackie said nothing. McQuire then came to the point. 'Could it be the report addressed to William Carstairs, and presumably in your possession, Mr Wilson? What exactly is your relationship with Mr Carstairs, Mr Wilson?'

'I never met Mr Carstairs in my life. The report that you are on about, was given to me by Dawson for safekeeping, in case anything happened to him in the course of his diving. This, as I understand it, is standard practice. I wish I'd never seen the damn thing. It's been nothing but trouble.'

'What do you mean by that?' McQuire asked quickly.

Jackie then blurted out things he later felt it would have been better not to have said. 'First, I am hijacked from the island by the Army which is interested in the document. Then my friend's flat is raided and more people are killed. It's ridiculous. It is not as if the document says anything. It is all hypothetical.'

'Yes, yes, but what is this about the British army?'

Jackie looked at him through narrowed eyes, sighed and said. 'You probably know anyway, but my brother is a colonel in the Royal Irish Regiment. He was very interested in the document, had me air lifted out of Rathlin and taken to the army barracks. '

'Did he now?' said McQuire stroking his chin, 'Okay you two can go. I will arrange for you to be dropped back, as it's late.'

'Don't bother, we'll walk,' said Jackie.

'I ought to tell you that the break-in at your place will not appear in the newspapers. A top-level notice has been slapped on it. (He hoped this was true.) You'd be well advised, Miss O'Connor, not to write about it yourself or to discuss it with your colleagues. Also I hope neither of you is planning to leave the country. We'll want to talk to you again.'

'No, we are not planning to leave the country. We'll see ourselves out,' Jackie said sardonically.

Once they had left the room, McQuire picked up the phone and dialled McGuinness at the Dial.

'There is definitely something going on. The Army, who have now got a copy of the document, picked Wilson up. You've now got Carstairs and the Army involved. Something is happening on that two-bit island. What is it? What'll we do? We can hardly use McCall again. You read about Williams getting topped?'

'No,' said McGuinness in his most menacing tones. 'Leave it with me, goodnight McQuire.'

Outside the police station, Aideen spoke: 'Bit hasty, weren't you? It's rather late even for a midnight walk.'

'Naagh, do us good. It'll only take half an hour and we can wind down.'

McQuire was premature in assuming the press had not got hold of the story. One of Aideen's colleagues, Frank Collins, coming out of a nightclub in Dame Street, spotted them leaving the police station. He would phone them in the morning. He was a crime reporter, a good one. He also knew McQuire.

Jackie and Aideen walked home in silence, but Jackie, instead of calming down, was boiling up. He finally ignited with really deep-seated anger. Once inside the flat, he hurled his coat across the room. He almost ripped his bow tie off and threw that across the room too. He started to expostulate. 'I am really fed up. I am fucking fed up. I am totally, utterly, pissed off.'

He roamed around the room, kicking the furniture, throwing things over. He took off his jacket, threw it to the floor and stamped on it. He took off his shoes and threw them at the partition. 'This has gone far enough, these stupid people of yours, these stupid people of mine. What in fucking hell is going on?'

Aideen just gaped open-mouthed. She had never seen him lose control like this.

'I'll tell you what is going on. I am going to get to the bottom of this. I am going to find out just what is going on. I am sitting there. All of a sudden, I am yanked off Rathlin. I am interrogated and insulted by my own brother. I come down here and I am treated like something from a zoo. Finally we are carted off to the police station, because our possessions are ransacked.' He started waving his finger. 'I'll tell you something, Aideen, my love. I am going to get to the bottom of this. I am going to find out what is going on.'

'You said that before. Sure ye are, me darlin, but not tonight. You come here now and hold me while you're hot.'

She was almost as tall as him in her high heels. He put his hands on her backside and kissed her hard on the lips. She wrapped a leg around him and put her arms up to his shoulders. He unzipped her dress and tore her knickers off. He threw her roughly on to the bed. She threw her legs open and he virtually pounced on her. He penetrated her. Because of the drink he was slow to come. She never had that kind of problem. She had an orgasm within minutes and writhed and turned. He kept going. She had another orgasm. By the time he had come, after 15 minutes, she had come three times.

'Jesus, you're wonderful, that's never happened to me before.'

'What hasn't?'

'The multiple orgasm. You ought to get angry more often. Come here.' She rolled on top of him: 'You know you're a great lover.'

'You're not so bad yourself.' He meant it. The abandon, the totally giving over of herself, was exciting. Then he went rigid. 'Aideen. We have got to find out what the hell is happening. It's like one of those thirties novels, we seem to be the centrepiece of something we don't know about and cannot understand. '

'Jackie, I'm scared.'

'Yeah, well don't be scared. Be angry, get even.'

'Sleep on it, Jackie. Think what to do.'

But Jackie slept fitfully, waking up every hour, going to the toilet often. At eight o'clock in the morning, he gave up and rose. He made himself some coffee, took some up to Aideen in bed and woke her up. She was dozy.

'Sure, Jackie, you know you're very good in bed.'

'Aideen, can you please try and think of something else, you sex maniac.'

'Like what?'

'Like, what we are going to do?'

'What are we going to do?'

'Do you fancy a long sea voyage?'

'We've been told not to leave the country.'

'To hell with that, do you know anyone in Londonderry?'

'It's called Derry, just Derry. Yes I do, I've a very good friend, Kieran. Why, are you thinking of taking a cruise to Derry? It'll take a long time. But why not, I'll have you all to myself.'

'No, I'm not thinking of taking a cruise to Derry. It was something that Brian and Fergus said the other night. Have we got an atlas?'

'Next door.'

He went next door and pulled a *Times* Atlas off one of the shelves. He flicked through the pages. 'Here's what we are going to do. Get your man in Derry to find a Maureen Dawson. She is known as Molly. Your friend's a journalist, presumably, he should be able to track her down through the telephone book or the electoral roll.'

'It's a Sunday, sweetheart.'

'Yes, but, even in Derry, Sundays are not what they were. If he finds her, we want to know everything about Dawson, what he worked in before, particularly in Canada. Secondly, do you think either Brian or Fergus would be prepared to drive our - your - car for us up to Derry? You and I, meanwhile, will go up to Carlingford where I am hoping a very good friend will meet us with his boat. We can then proceed to Rathlin.'

'Derry and Carlingford, are in opposite directions, Jackie. You are not making any sense.'

'Wait now 'til I make a phone call.' Jackie went to his briefcase and pulled out his battered address book. He dialled a number in Bangor, County Down. It rang several times. Finally it was answered. 'Peter, is that you? It's Jackie Wilson here. I am sorry to ring you so early. Are you going out today?'

'Hey, Jackie, whaddabouchee, how you doin?' boomed the harsh but friendly Ulster voice. 'No, I'm not as a matter of fact. Why, what's up?'

'I wonder if you would mind coming down to Greenore or Carlingford and picking me up and taking me back to Rathlin. You remember we went fishing off Carlingford peninsula for tope that time.'

'Why do I have to come right down there?' A note of hesitation creeping into his voice.

Jackie decided to come clean and appeal to Peter McClean's sense of adventure. They had known one another since childhood. He had kept in touch as Peter, a huge Ulsterman, had developed his freezing business, his stores and other food interests, like mussel and oyster beds in Strangford Lough. But he had maintained his interest in sea fishing. With the help of the Northern Ireland Tourist Board he had bought himself a Bertram 33ft twin diesel, capable of 24 knots. The idea was he would take out tourists who were going to come because of the peace process. It had not worked out quite as well as he had hoped, but he had kept the boat. He was a very larky kind of bloke, was Peter, very keen on the outdoors and adventure.

'The thing is, Peter, I need to get back to Rathlin but I do not want to re-enter Northern Ireland. I will explain when I see you. There is nothing illegal involved. I am not going on a smuggling run.'

'I should hope not,' Peter said mockingly and continued, 'Well, now, let me see. I won't be able to get down 'til later. I've some things to do this morning and I've to meet someone for lunch. But that's okay. I can run down on the tide. The forecast is for a four, possibly freshening to a five or six. I mean to say, what is it you have in mind, Jackie? How long are we going to be away? Who's paying? A sordid point I know, but time is money.'

Jackie thought that Peter had not become moderately rich by doing favours for people, even childhood friends. He said, 'Don't worry about the money. Depends on how long it takes us to get to Rathlin. Let's assume we get there sometime Monday, then no reason you wouldn't be able to leave Monday afternoon. I could take the ferry back. If not, I could always phone you.'

'That'll be okay. Better make it Carlingford, under the castle. I never like getting into Greenore, 'specially when it's a neap tide. I'll see you in the Park Hotel near Carlingford any time after six. We'll do Rathlin overnight. It'll take the better part of the night. Will I bring wee John along as crew?' John was his elder son.

231

Jackie thought for a second, then said, 'Better not. I've got my friend Aideen with me. She can crew.'

'Aye, you're a lucky devil, so you are, be seeing you.'

'Yes, we'll be there late this evening.' He went back into the bedroom.

Aideen sat up in bed drinking her coffee. She had taken the rest of her clothes off at some point and was nestling her coffee between her firm round breasts. 'Would you ever tell me what's going on?'

'Now, where was I? The atlas...' He flicked over to the index and looked up the Shetlands. He traced an arc around from the Shetlands to the west down into the Atlantic. It swept far to the north of Rathlin, but not too far.

'Jackie, what in the name of Jesus are you doing? Will you tell me what you are thinking.'

'There used to be a saying, what you don't know, can't hurt you. All will become clear in due course. Now, will you phone your friend in Derry and get him started. Will you then phone Brian and Fergus and see if they want to come for an early lunch at the Unicorn. I suggest we both keep our respective appointments, you with Brogan and me with Sweetman. I assume your appointment is still on. What time is it, ten to nine? Yes, you would have heard by now if not.'

'Jackie, this is rather irritating. What are we going to do?'

'Trust me, just trust me. Now where are the papers?'

'They should be on the doorstep.'

'Right, why don't you make yourself decent and join me downstairs.'

'I feel like being indecent again. I can't get enough of you - but I suppose I'd better wait 'til after mass.'

'Yes, that's right, you'll feel a lot better when you've unburdened yourself to your friendly local priest. Get rid of your guilt and you can start again with a clear conscience.'

'You don't confess at Sunday mass, you blithering idiot.'

Jackie opened the front door and was hit by a ray of sunshine. The nice clear weather was holding for a second day, although it was still quite cold. He gathered up the newspapers, thinking that you needed a trolley these days, and went down to the kitchen. He made himself another pot of coffee and quickly scanned the papers.

Ten minutes later Aideen came down in her dressing gown. 'Well?' she asked.

'Your papers are screaming civil war; ours seem rather more concerned with a punishment killing in the North. Peace process breaking down all over the place. We are not mentioned though.'

'Look, I'd better get ready to go to mass. Will you be able to get yourself into town?'

'I should think so.'

'What do you want me to ask Brogan?'

'I don't know. He's only a businessman. Why does he want to see you anyway, what's it got to do with him? And who's this sinister McGuinness?'

'Brogan's rather more than a businessman. Apart from being extremely rich, he is very much a player in the Northern Ireland process. He's very close to the Ra and to the Government. If there is anything untoward going down on Rathlin, you can bet your bottom dollar he knows about it.'

'In that case, ask him what the heck is going on. Why am I, and now you, being chased from pillar to post over some document which doesn't amount to a row of beans?'

'I see you're not interested in the political implications of last night's shootings. I'm a journalist, remember.'

'Yes, of course I am interested, but there's a mystery here that we've got to crack. Why is everyone so interested in this document? I think it's beginning to dawn on me why. But I need to root about a bit more.' Jackie was now starting to attack the problem with a zeal typical of those who repressed themselves in other ways.

Aideen said, 'I ought to read the papers, but I am running late. I'll run a bath. Quick now, let me have a look at the papers, especially mine.' She scanned the papers, went and had her bath and at 9.20 presented herself to Jackie in her tweed suit, pearl earrings and necklace. Jackie smiled.

'It's all right now, Jackie Wilson, I know what you are thinking. I can hardly go to mass in my jeans, let alone interview Brogan. I must get on, anyway. See you in the Unicorn.'

'Yes, okay. 'Bout twelve. Oh, have you phoned your friend in Derry and Brian and Fergus?'

'No, I've written down the numbers. There they are, there on the table, look. You do it.'

'Right, away with you.'

Jackie phoned Kieran in Derry, introduced himself and explained his problem; Aideen sent love, sorry she hadn't phoned herself. Kieran was very amenable. Any friend of Aideen's was a friend of his, Sunday was a bit difficult as he couldn't get at the electoral register, but there was always the phone book. He would see what he could do and get back to them either on Aideen's home number or on her mobile.

He then phoned Brian. Fergus was with him, as it happened, and they were just on their way to mass. Yes, they would be happy to join them for lunch. They would normally go to somewhere in Dame Street, but the Unicorn was fine.

Jackie had about an hour to kill before he was to meet Sweetman. Lovely. This was the first moment he had had to himself since the world started going topsy turvy three days ago. He would put some Handel on the CD player, *Ode to St Cecilia's Day*, run himself a hot bath, wash away the sins of life, as Aideen was fond of saying, and have a good think.

Once in the bath, with the strains of the 'double double beat invites us to war' in the background, Jackie began to try to arrange his thoughts methodically. What was the connection between his brother and Carstairs? Could it be, as Sweetman indicated, that Carstairs and Charles were planning something which would damage the peace process? He would soon be able to get some clarification from Sweetman on this. Certainly he would need to press him on the matter. The key to the jigsaw was the wretched document. Clearly everyone wanted to get hold of it, the British army, the IRA, the Protestant paramilitaries. The question was why, since, as it stood, it was obviously bogus. Maybe there was something hidden in the text, some sort of code, or maybe only the numbers were important. Or maybe everyone was mistaken. Maybe the key was indeed a document, but not the banal document he had.

The more he thought, the more Jackie inclined towards the 'there is another document theory'. It must be right to return to Rathlin. There was no point in him driving up into Northern Ireland. As he had seen at Lisburn, the helicopters would pick them up within minutes. But by boat, he and Aideen could do a bunk and hopefully get to Rathlin without anyone knowing. Carlingford, where Gerry Adams once had a weekend caravan, was right on the Irish border. The border runs right through the middle of the Lough.

If Brian and Fergus could be persuaded to drive to Derry in Aideen's car it would provide an excellent diversion. He was sure that the Garda would put a bug on Aideen's car. Even if they didn't, the helicopters would find them. But they would have done nothing wrong. They had merely borrowed Aideen's car. How were they to know there was a bug on it? It could well be that the Garda would not let the two of them get that far, but Jackie was gambling curiosity would get the better of them. They would want to know why Aideen was going to Derry, of all places. They would be safe in the knowledge that it only required one call to the Police Force or the army and the car could quickly be traced. Instant extradition was easier than was commonly thought, if you had the right connections.

In any event, Aideen and Jackie would be far away by the time the two were picked up. If Brian and Fergus managed to get to Derry, so much the better. It was a question of persuading them to do it without giving too much away. Well, he didn't know what there was to give away just yet. He would offer to pay for a room or rooms at the Everglades Hotel. He was pretty sure they were gay but this had never been vouchsafed. It was no concern of his anyway. The world he inhabited did not acknowledge many prohibitions on homosexuality. How they slept was none of his business. Jackie's attitude here was one more example of the juxtaposition of his liberal outlook on social mores for other people, stemming from his work, and the stiff reserve about his own behaviour, arising from his upbringing.

There is a saying in anthropology that within every myth there is a hidden truth. Beneath Jackie's reined-in irritation about being robbed was a burgeoning anger that his brother was involved in some kind of profound betrayal. Despite this growing emotional involvement, he was still approaching the situation rationally, as a problem to be solved. He decided that the next step should be to investigate Dawson's condition. He seemed to have been forgotten in all the brouhaha, yet he was the one with the answers. Or perhaps his wife was.

He got out of the bath and phoned the Dalriada Hospital. It didn't help. After taking some minutes to get through, there was then a further delay while he was connected to the Sir Edward Carson Ward. The sister said she didn't know how Mr Dawson was, and who was it phoning anyway. He would have to speak to the doctor. The doctor was not there. Could he phone back after two o'clock? He hung up in a mild fury. The nurse did not tell him that Dawson had shown the first, faint, signs of coming around.

He was aware that something that Brian or Fergus had said

lurked at the back of his mind. But it would not declare itself. Maybe his appointment with Sweetman would help sharpen his recall. He dressed and went out. When he got to Bewley's, just before 11 o'clock, Sweetman was waiting. 'Morning, old bean. How are you? What will you have?'

'I've been drinking coffee. Yes, some more coffee I think. Nice morning.'

'Yes, it certainly is. I'll just go up and get you some coffee. How do you take it?'

'White without sugar, thanks.'

He came back and sat down awkwardly as if he didn't know how to get the conversation started. Jackie was in no mood to help him out.

Sweetman said, 'Stirring times, eh?'

'What do you mean?' Jackie shot back.

'The shooting last night?'

'What do you know about it?'

'Only what I read in the newspapers.'

'Which is?'

'Seems to be some kind of tit-for-tat, wouldn't you say?'

'So it would appear.'

'When we met yesterday, you, ah, said that you, ah, would give me a peek at the document.'

'Was it only yesterday? It seems a lifetime ago.'

'It's always like that when there's a lot happening.'

'Yes, I suppose it is.'

There was a silence before Sweetman spoke again: 'It would be interesting to get a look at the document. It could explain a lot of things.'

'I've already told you the document is false. It's a lot of rubbish.'

'Yes, of course, and I am sure you are correct, but seeing is believing, as they say. I wouldn't mind reading it for myself.'

'That will not be possible, I'm afraid. Because I don't have it.'

'You didn't bring it, you mean.'

'No, I mean I no longer have it.'

'How's that?' Sweetman's face was a study in concern.

Jackie started to explain. 'What you read in the newspapers this morning was only half of it. If I tell you something, will you reply to me honestly?'

'Of course.'

Some chance, thought Jackie, but felt there was no point in not going full frontal and in return trying to get what he could out of Sweetman. 'What did not appear in the newspapers this morning was that Hughes was almost certainly shot after robbing our place, well Aideen's place.'

'What?'

'Wait.' He held his hand up. 'It seems that the Prods raided the apartment looking for the document and ran into Hughes. There was a chase and Hughes was shot. Now, Oliver, I am not supposed to tell you this, but the plot thickens. I want your absolute assurance that this is confidential and it won't get back to the Garda that you heard this from me.'

'Of course, of course.' Sweetman's assurance was about as solid as a sand castle. But Jackie felt he had to proceed along this route if only to get something back. 'It seems that the Protestants caught Hughes in the act and he was shot. They got the document. But then the Garda picked them up straight away. Don't ask me how. Anyway at one o'clock this morning we are down at the police headquarters. We are told it is being regarded as a terrorist offence. We are not to say a thing. The document is now in the hands of the Irish government.'

Sweetman gave a low whistle. He only said, 'Well I'm buggered,' but he was thinking fast. Back to the drawing board, the original supposition was right. There is something going on which could contain the wherewithal to launch some kind of coup. He probed. 'That is most interesting John, most interesting. There clearly is something afoot. Can you remember? Can you really say there was nothing in this document of interest?'

'I have told you, it's rubbish. It's all speculation. There is nothing of any value.'

'Then why in God's name is everyone killing everyone else to try and lay their hands on it?'

'That's what I don't know,' said Jackie.

'What did it say exactly? Try and remember will you?'

'It merely said there was money to be made out of salvaging bullion from the ocean. It mentioned one ship. I can't remember the name of it now, something Royal, which was thought to have millions in sunken bullion, jewels, gold pieces from the Caribbean on board. But it didn't say they had found it. It's false, I'm telling you.' Then, almost as an afterthought: 'Perhaps it is written in code or it's a cover for something else, but I can't think what else.' He almost added, 'but I intend to find out.' But stopped himself.

Sweetman had ceased listening. He missed the last sentence. He was now too deep into his conspiracy theory. He had enough, he felt. The salvage was the key. This would enable Carstairs and the other Wilson to realise their plans. Had he actually seen the document he would have realised, like Jackie, that the paper was a sham, and he would have thought things through a bit more. But at least the raid and robbery had allayed the suspicion that Jackie Wilson was involved.

'What you told me about confidentiality also applies to me. If I tell you my thoughts, I want your absolute assurance that it will not rebound on me.'

'Of course, I will not break a confidence.'

'When we spoke yesterday, I pointed you in the direction of

something funny going down on Rathlin. My information, well suspicion really, is that Carstairs and your brother are planning some kind of coup or military takeover when the British troops pull out. It was not clear where Rathlin came into it, but your document provides the answer. They would need money to launch a coup. They would need it to buy weapons.'

'That's too fantastic,' Jackie said, but he found himself going on, 'Charles would never be involved in anything like that. He is in the British army.'

'That's not the point really. He is an Ulster Protestant and he is a Colonel in the Royal Irish Regiment. He will be staying on after the pull-out by our troops.'

'I just can't believe it.'

'Strange things happen at sea, old boy, passions are running high.'

'It's too unbelievable.' Jackie thought of the barns, done up and empty. He thought of his brother's anger. His desire to get his hands on the document had seemed beyond reason. Perhaps it was not so incredible. 'But Oliver, Dawson didn't actually find anything. It's not as if he has money in the bank.'

'Wouldn't need to, old man. Carstairs has any number of business associates in Scotland who would front up some money and/ or arms. Well, I must be going, can I give you a lift anywhere?'

He got up and put on his coat, which had been draped over another chair.

'Er, no, no thanks, I've a bit of time to kill. Thanks anyway.'

'Not at all, keep an eye on that brother of yours.'

He left Jackie staring into the middle distance.

Chapter

18

Aideen, meanwhile, was sparring with Diarmuid Brogan in his offices opposite the Dial. She had got through the flimsy security easily enough. Brogan was alone in his penthouse. He was in a tweed sports jacket. He greeted Aideen warmly with a kiss on both cheeks.

'My, you're looking well, Aideen.'

'Now, don't you try and seduce me now.'

Brogan smiled and put his finger to his lips. 'Careful now, the place may be bugged. I'm very good at bugging according to the media.'

'You're very good at flirting, you bugger.' They both laughed. She had had an affair with Brogan when he first became rich from business and was a man about town. She was young, in her early twenties. It hadn't ended badly. In fact, it hadn't really ended at all. She was still fascinated by him and he by her, although they were not sleeping together in what Brogan called these difficult times. She knew that he could not help but flirt with any woman he fancied.

'How's Jeananne?'

'She's very well, sends her regards.'

'The hell she does. You're a messer.'

'And you're beautiful and desirable, come here. You know she means nothing to me.'

'Oh, oh no you don't, not now.' She got up and ran behind the sofa. 'Jesus, but yer incorrigible, Diarmuid Brogan.'

He tried to distract her. He moved to go one way round the sofa. She went the other. He turned around and grabbed her from behind. He moved his hands to her breasts. A frisson ran through her. 'Diarmuid, oh please.'

'Does that mean please don't, or please do?' he whispered in her ear.

'It means please don't lead me on, you old stoat, not at the moment.'

He let go of her. She turned around and put her arms around his neck and kissed him. He put his hands on her buttocks and pulled her closer to him. She hung there suspended indecisively for a few moments, then pushed away. 'Come on now, Diarmuid, you're messing. We've business to attend to. This'll get us nowhere.'

'Depends where you want to go.' He let her go. 'Okay, what shall we talk about. First some coffee? I'll have to make it meself. How do you take it, white? You're a great kisser, you know that.'

She sat down on the sofa and fumbled in her bag for her notebook and a pen. She thought she would go through the motions. She was supposed to be interviewing him. She closed her eyes, and said to herself, Jesus, Aideen, you're a whore, you're just anybody's. Jesus knows what would have happened if he had persisted. She still felt sexually aroused and a little shaky.

As he emerged from the little room where he'd made the coffee in two mugs, he said, 'I thought we might talk about yer boyfriend, his document and what the feckin' hell he's got to do with all this killing. What the feck are you doing with the likes of him anyway?'

She was surprised. 'You know what I am doing with him. But how do you know about the document?'

'Aideen sweetheart, I make a point about knowing these things. I am concerned about the situation in the North.'

'Of course, stupid of me, you'd be the first to know.'

'We've managed to keep it out of the papers. By the way,' he pointed his finger at her, 'don't you go pouring everything out in that rag of yours just yet. This could all be serious. If I am to help you at all you have to be completely straight with me.'

'Then if you must know, I think I might be in love with him.'

Brogan thought, in love with his cock more like it, but said nothing. As if reading his thoughts, she said 'I know what you are thinking, it's another of my passions, but he is a very nice person.'

'I am sure he is kind to animals, and helps old ladies across the road. So does Gerry Adams. Look, he is an Ascendancy Prod. His brother is senior in the British army. He has documents addressed to William Carstairs. William Carstairs, for Jesus sake. What are you playing at? Where's your allegiance to our Republic?' He was in his best barrack-room lawyer mode. He was playing her mercilessly. First arousing her, then knocking her all around the room verbally.

'He does not have anything to do with Carstairs. He just happened to be on Rathlin Island, and a man called Dawson who was diving for wrecks gave him some papers for safekeeping. In the event, they turned out to be addressed to William Carstairs. He has just got swept up in this.'

'Ah, I see. He just happens to be the brother of an army officer and he just happens to be carrying papers for William Carstairs after three Police Force men were killed. Pull the other leg, Aideen, it's got bells on.'

'I'm telling you, Diarmuid, he doesn't know any more than you do. He thinks the report is made up. It's completely bogus he says.' She was now like a witness at a trial who had broken down under heavy questioning by a canny QC.

'Does he now? What does he think that Dawson and Co. were really up to then?'

'He doesn't know. He says perhaps the report is in sort of code, that they were really doing something else.'

'But what else?'

'Sorry, don't know.'

She tried to shift the conversation around to other things like the drug situation but Brogan was not having any of it. He constantly brought the conversation back to Jackie, the document and what it could all mean. After a while he said, 'I'm sorry Aideen, I'm really not in the mood for a conversation about the state of the world. You'll have to forgive me. Let's meet again when circumstances are a little better.'

Before she went, he had one more attempt to get her to reveal what she knew of the document. But she didn't have any more to say about Dawson's papers. She knew no more than Jackie did and certainly less than Brogan. As she was being seen out of the door, she said, 'Oh, by the way, I saw Edward, your driver, last night. He was at the Shelbourne, meeting a friend of yours. Seemed familiar from the old days, but I couldn't put a name to him.'

Brogan said, 'Oh you mean Alex.' Then he stopped himself. 'It was no one, no one you know. 'Bye, Aideen, we will see each other again soon, I promise.'

Out in Kildare Street, Aideen was feeling decidedly shaky and thought she would go to Buswells for a drink to steady herself. It was after twelve o'clock, so she would be late for Jackie, but no matter.

Brogan buzzed McGuinness and called him in.

'Well?' said McGuinness, even before he was through the door.

'She knows feckin' less than we do. Says the thing's in code, for Jesus sake. What'll we do now?'

'I've been thinking. Morris all along seemed to know more about things than he let on. As if he knew about Rathlin, or at least knew someone there who knew. Perhaps if we got back there and found that someone, they could tell us what is going on. Remembering, of course, what MacPhee told us.'

'How are we going to do that? McCall is too risky, far too risky. He probably won't play anyway. You see one of his boys was topped. At least I assume it was one of his boys.'

'McCall has his price, as always. Sure, he's in too deep not to play ball now.'

'It's too risky.'

'Not as risky as doing nothing.'

*

Aideen sat by herself at a table in the downstairs bar of Buswells. Tom, the barman, had attempted to make conversation. Unusually, she had nothing to say. Wasn't it terrible the goings on in Dublin last evening? But Aideen sort of mumbled, 'Yes, terrible,' and took herself off with her large gin and tonic and her thoughts.

Jesus, I'm terrible. I'm a real whore. He only had to touch me and I was off and running. Poor Jackie. No, what do I mean, poor Jackie? He probably wouldn't give a damn. He's a cool fish that one. She was surprised to find she was trembling slightly. Not that anyone would notice, but shaking a little. I've got to control my libido. No, why the hell should I. I like sex. No reason to be ashamed of it. She took a large gulp of her gin and it hit at the back of her throat. That's better, she thought. Why, oh why, was everybody so interested in Dawson's document. It was, as Jackie said, pretty tame. She caught Tom's eye. 'Large gin and tonic, and go easy on the tonic, Tom.'

'My, what are you celebrating, on yer own as well.'

Then it came to her. It was Alex MacPhee, the businessman from Scotland. She remembered him now from before, when Diarmuid was in politics and messing around with restaurants and oil and gold mines. She looked at her watch. Twenty five past twelve. Better be getting on. She gulped down the gin and made her way to the Unicorn. When she got there, the three men were sat huddled at a corner table.

Brian got up and said, 'Ah Aideen, perhaps you will tell us what yer man is up to.'

'Hello Brian, Fergus. Sorry to be late, Jackie. Diarmuid pestered me about you and your...'

'Why don't you tell me about that later,' Jackie quickly cut her off. 'We've already started, I'm afraid. Why don't you order.'

'What's he been telling you, Brian?'

'Wants us to drive to Derry for him and then come back again. Perhaps meet up with a friend of yours. He's prepared to stand us a night in the Everglades.'

'Well, what's wrong with that,' Aideen said chuckling.

'Just about everything. First we have work to do in the morning. Second he's not explained why he wants us to go, other than to have a friendly chat with your friend. Third, if we wanted to have a Sunday night out in a hotel, I can think of lots of places I'd prefer to Derry. Neither of us has any association with the place.'

Jackie said, 'It's all perfectly legal.'

'I should damn well hope it is,' said Brian

Jackie had thought carefully beforehand what he would tell them. Least known, soonest mended. He didn't want to go into detail about Rathlin. He wasn't really putting them in danger. If the police picked them up, they were merely borrowing a friend's car. How was anyone to know there was a bug on it? If indeed there would be.

'Come on be a sport, it'll help us a lot,' Jackie said.

Brian turned to Fergus: 'What do you think?'

'May as well, I've not a lot on tomorrow, nor have you, if I recall.'

Brian found himself agreeing. 'Okay, then. How'll we get the car?'

'We'll drop it at your place around six o'clock. Aideen knows where you live, I assume.' Aideen nodded.

Brian said, 'On top of everything else, you want us to drive up in the dark. Oh well, in for a penny, in for a pound.'

They began to eat.

'Brian, or Fergus,' Jackie said, 'one of you was telling us at dinner the other night about the oil. How it stretches round from the Shetlands to the Atlantic. There's none off Northern Ireland I suppose?'

'None that I've heard of. The so-called Atlantic Arc is just that. It swings right out into the Atlantic. Why do you ask?' Brian replied.

'Just wondered.'

Then Fergus added in his quiet way, 'They did have a look before the Troubles started, but I don't recall that they found any, unless there is something you know that we don't.'

'No, I was just thinking about the family fortunes,' he laughed. The lunch broke up amiably and Jackie insisted on paying. ''Bout six o'clock then,' he said.

Outside, Brian said to Fergus, 'Now, what was that all about?'

'I don't know. But it'll make a change,' Fergus said, but he was thinking he might just have an inkling what Jackie was up to.

*

McGuinness had left Brogan and gone to phone a number in Northern Ireland. When he got through he was told that McCall was in the Republic, in Dundalk. Bloody smugglers, thought McGuiness.

When he finally got through to McCall he found him in an agitated state. He wanted no further dealings with McGuinness. Two of the people involved in the last operation, including McGuinness' own man, had been killed. The very top brass of the IRA were on to him. It was his neck on the line if there were any further embarrassments. No, he could not do another operation. There was no possible way. McGuinness cajoled, pleaded and threatened. It was unfortunate that McCall happened to be in the Republic. McGuinness was influential with the Ministry of Justice. It would only take one telephone call to Dundalk and McCall could find himself in the local lock-up. 'Smuggling's a grave crime you know,' McGuinness threatened.

'Come off it, McGuinness,' said McCall, while thinking that, for all sorts of reasons, it would be extremely inconvenient to be arrested in the Republic.

McGuinness went on, 'Look now, it's not that we want another team to go in and make a mess of things. What we are thinking of is one man, say, who could get on to the island and find some contact who can tell us just what is happening. You see, from the way Hughes behaved, there has to be some person who is involved in events apart from this fella Dawson.'

'I see,' said McCall ruminatively. 'Well, if you put it like that then I might reconsider.' After a pause, he continued, 'Right now, I have a very good man. A planner. No convictions. Just the boy. Very good on ideas. You say all he has to do is find a contact on the island?'

'Yes. We want to know what it is with this document. Straight in, straight out, no shooters.'

'Well now. I'll mull it over. But the Ra in Belfast is not to get a smell of this, not one single sniff, understood?'

'Absolutely.'

'I'll be in touch. Usual terms?'

248

'Yes.'

McCall put the phone down. He thought he might just get away with this. It was, after all, not a full-scale operation. No one was to be executed. It was just intelligence gathering. Oliver was a bright young man interested in exactly this kind of backroom work. Yes, it was worth another throw. From where he sat, he didn't have a lot of choice, although once back in the North he might reconsider. But probably he wouldn't. The money was very useful. He was getting curious.

What he could not know, because Active Service Units of the IRA were not in contact with one another, was that the Provisional IRA in Dublin had been contacted at a very high level about the events in Ballycastle. And they had been contacted by someone on Rathlin. As a result the decision had been taken to activate a Republic-based Active Service Unit. It would be almost a day before the members of the Active Service Unit could be contacted and briefed. But, despite the ignorance and probable fury of the IRA leadership in Northern Ireland, at some point the group would be zeroing in on Rathlin, along with McCall's freelance operative.

*

Oliver Sweetman had gone, in a state of some excitement, straight from the meeting with Jackie to the embassy in Ballsbridge. He got on the scrambler to London and, luckily, got straight through to Sir Roger Jones.

'Oliver, dear boy, you seem rather agitated.'

'The thing is this, sir. I now think my original supposition was correct. I met with John Wilson, that is Lord Strangford, and he had lost the document. It seems that all the shooting and fuss last night was about the document we were discussing.'

'You were discussing, Oliver.'

'Yes, sir. Anyway, a Protestant gang and a Provisional IRA man shot it out trying to steal the papers from Strangford. It appears they are now in the possession of the Irish government. What they say, it seems, is that this fellow Dawson, and, by extension, Carstairs, are looking for sunken bullion. This would provide the wherewithal to launch the coup. As I said before, I would not exclude Wilson's brother, Charles Wilson, from the dirty work.'

'It all sounds a bit fantastic, Oliver. The PM is not keen on any further deterioration of relations with Dublin at this delicate stage. Why don't you get someone to go and have a look? Why don't you go yourself? No, I suppose that is not such a clever idea. But there must be people. Haul in Five if you have to. Keep me posted.' He hung up.

Somewhat crestfallen, Sweetman put down the phone. Sir Roger obviously thought he was barking mad. But he would not be put off. He would send someone. It hurt to have to collaborate with MI5 but there was little choice.

*

Frank Collins, the journalist, had got on to the phone immediately after mass. Yes, Mr McQuire wouldn't mind a drink after lunch in Dalkey. They could meet in the Rose Bar overlooking the little harbour. Make it about three. They could walk along the shore. Collins had not said what he wanted to talk about, but it was not hard to make a good guess. Still, there was no harm in having a little chat. They couldn't trace it back to him. Anyway, Collins had been a good boy in the past, never betrayed confidences.

McQuire was still smarting over Brogan's curt dismissal, coming on top of the insults from McGuinness over the years. He was sick of them. He particularly resented the nasty jibes and innuendoes about his pension. Now he had Brogan humiliating him. Brogan was playing with fire. He was chancing to a ridiculous degree.

*

Contrary to popular rumour, and unlike the Rev Ian Paisley, Carstairs worked on the Sabbath. He managed to stay calm as he read the Sunday papers. There was no mention of Dawson or himself in any of the newspapers. There was no way Watson and the others could be traced back to him. He had covered his tracks well. The payments had gone out from Scotland, through a convoluted system. It was doubtful whether Watson even knew who he was working for, or so Carstairs liked to delude himself.

He decided to phone MacPhee. He got through easily. MacPhee was off-hand. Yes, he supposed the shipment would have to go ahead on Monday, as planned. Had he heard of the change of destination for the cargo? No, he had not, but he agreed it seemed sensible in the circumstances. He left the arrangement of these things to others. But he could not guarantee his further involvement beyond the shipment unless there was proof positive that the oil existed in the right amounts.

MacPhee did not tell Carstairs that he had already ordered an intensive search of the *Northern Star* to find any data that might have been taken aboard from the bigger oil vessel. He would have had that ship searched too, had he known where it was. Still less did he mention his little chat with Diarmuid Brogan. No, MacPhee would bide his time, see who emerged with the data, then pick the winner. Let Carstairs have his little coup if he wanted. It would all come to nothing without the black stuff. In the meantime, like Carstairs over Watson, he had satisfied himself that his involvement was strictly above board and legal. There was no law against salvaging bullion. Heck, half his business was about salvage.

Carstairs ranted on for some minutes. Everything would be all right. He was sure that the data would turn up. Events had moved too far for weak nerves now.

'I look forward to the proof, William. Goodbye,' said MacPhee dryly.

Carstairs put the phone down and muttered, 'Damn you, Dawson.' Like Jackie Wilson, Carstairs could not know that at that moment, that Sunday morning, Dawson was showing the first faint signs of a return to consciousness.

Carstairs did think of phoning the hospital. But he dismissed the idea, feeling that his instructions that he should be the first to be contacted were explicit enough. He went back to the newspapers. He would have heard if there were any developments.

*

Driving back to Aideen's in the Renault, Jackie said, 'I was sorry to cut you off there. But the less Brian and Fergus know, the better. There is no law that says they cannot borrow a friend's car and drive to Derry. How were they to know we were under surveillance? We were told not to tell anyone what had happened. They'll be all right. How did it go with Brogan anyway?'

"Oh, it was a rant. He knows about Dawson's document, predictably enough. What was I doing with an Ascendancy Prod? Where were my loyalties to my country? He kept on and on about the document. What did it mean? How come you had it? He was suspicious that it should be given to you, of all people.'

'Why?'

'Well, as he said, you are an Ascendancy Prod and your brother is in the British army.

'What did you say?'

'That you were non-political and that you got swept up in events by accident. You happened to be on the island. You thought the report was fabricated. He then banged on that if it was made up, why was everyone getting killed. He wouldn't talk about anything else. In the end he saw I didn't know anything and shoved me through the door.'

'Did he make a pass at you?'

'Of course he did.'

'The bounder. I'll have him horsewhipped.'

'You're not jealous are you, Jackie Wilson?'

'No. Now did he say anything else?'

'No. But there was one other thing. You know I ran into Edward, his chauffeur, at the Shelbourne. The man he was picking up was familiar, but I could not put a name to him.'

'Yes, you said.'

'I've remembered who it was.'

'And?'

'It was Alex MacPhee. Mean anything to you?'

'No.'

'He's a Scottish businessman. He was involved with Diarmuid, oh, in all kinds of things, restaurants, gold mines, oil, before Diarmuid went into politics.'

'Oil, that's interesting.'

'Yes, What is this oil thing?'

'It's nothing at the moment, but..'

She didn't let him finish. 'The thing about MacPhee is, he became a raving Unionist. He hardly got involved in Scottish politics, but he became immersed in Northern Ireland. He got friendly with the politicians. It was often said he supported their cause with his money.'

'What on earth is he doing with Brogan?'

They both said together, 'If I knew that, everything would be simple.' This was one of their catchphrases.

As they got close to the flat, Aideen asked, 'What are we going to do now?'

'We are going to hole up for a couple of hours 'til it gets dark and wait for lines we have got out to come back in.'

'You sound like Sherlock Holmes.'

As they went up to the door, he slapped her bottom and said, 'Come on let's see if your friend Kieran has come up with anything.'

*

Kieran had tried every Dawson number in the phone book, some eleven names, and drawn a complete blank. He had even walked up the steep terraces of Waterside on the east side of the Foyle, past the bright whitewashed terraced houses with clean windows, pristine net curtains, and scrubbed doorsteps. Every now and again, there would be a huge Union Jack or a mural of King Billy on his white horse, on the gable of an end of terrace house. No kids playing in the street here, no yapping dogs. This was the Protestant heart of Londonderry and it was Sunday. Everything, apart from the church bells clanging, was silent and ordered. Having elicited no response from the last house he knocked at, although the curtains moved next door, Kieran descended down the hill to the Everglades Hotel. The duty manager was an old friend. It would do no harm to have a couple of jars.

'Whaddabouchee, Kieran. You having a jar?'

'Damn right I am, Willie. I'll have one of those Steinlager beers.' Kieran explained what he was trying to do.

Willie said, 'Now's there a funny thing. We use to have a Maureen Dawson work here. She worked in the office, in accounts. Known as Molly.'

'You what? How old?'

'Difficult to say, fortyish. Didn't do herself any favours, the way she dressed. A bit of a school ma'am. She left here some months back. Returned to her maiden name I think. Never saw any husband, or any fella actually. She didn't socialise.'

254

'Where do I find her?'

'Wait on now, I'll go and see what we've got.' After a few minutes he re-emerged with a piece of paper. 'Here you are now. She goes under the name of Molly Stewart. Lives up there on Waterside. In one of the wee terraced houses.'

'By herself?'

'I wouldn't know about that,' replied Willie.

'Thanks, Willie, I'll go up and see her. I've just been up that way, actually.'

'There's a telephone number.'

'It would be better if I went to see her, I think.'

'Right you are, but I would leave it a while. It's nearly one o'clock, she'll be having lunch. Why don't I stand you lunch here, then you can go up.'

After a good roast lunch with a liberal amount of wine taken, Kieran climbed back up the hill to St John's Road. He knocked on the door, and was answered by a tall, broad-shouldered woman. Willie was right. She was probably about forty but had the mien of an older woman. She was one of those Protestant matrons, whom early middle age did not suit. There were no roles for forty-something women on their own, so she, like others, hurtled towards a safer, older, persona, where she could take her place in the tearooms and church committees.

She wore a neat, two piece, navy blue suit over a high-necked pink cashmere jumper and the inevitable string of pearls. She had a stern, cross face, beneath hair coiled into a bun. She was not unattractive, with nice round facial features and a good figure. But she had locked any joie-de-vivre very firmly away, so she came across as dowdy.

'Yes,' she said sharply as if she had spent a lifetime fending off door-to-door salesmen.

Kieran explained who he was and what he wanted, and she said she had nothing to say on the matter. Kieran persisted. Seeing he was not easily going to go away, and anxious to avoid the neighbours peering (the worst of all possible fates for a woman in her single situation) she relented.

'You had better come in, but only for a minute, mind.'

He walked into a neat sitting room with a chain store three-piece suite, stripy wallpaper. There were few adornments on the walls, apart from a photograph of the Queen and Prince Philip.

'I suppose I should offer you some tea,' she said, softening a little in the face of this handsome, genial young man.

'That would be very nice.'

'Wait now, I'll make some tea. Have a seat.'

He sat on the sofa and waited. There were no books to go and inspect. Minutes later she emerged, holding a silver tray with a silver teapot or, rather, silver-plate teapot with silver-plate milk jug and sugar bowl, and two matching floral-patterned bone china cups and saucers. No steaming impromptu mugs, tea taking was a sacred ceremony, which had to be done properly.

'How did you find me?'

'I cannot tell a lie. Through the Everglades Hotel. You are Alan Dawson's wife, aren't you?'

'I was.'

'You heard what happened to him?'

'Yes, I've been contacted by the police.'

'Are you going to see him?'

'No point, he's in a coma. He probably wouldn't want to see me anyway.'

'He doesn't live here?'

'Heavens, no! Perish the thought. We went our separate ways some time ago, and good riddance.'

'What does that mean, if you don't mind me asking. Are you divorced?'

'Separated, though he tells people we're divorced. It means I wearied of his fantasies, his get-rich-quick schemes, his boy's own adventures, whatever you like to call them.'

Kieran said, 'It said on the news that he was diving for wrecks with a police team.'

'Diving for wrecks, phooey,' she replied. 'He can't even swim. He's never dived in his life.'

'What does he do then?'

'He calls himself a mining engineer, but I suppose really he's a geologist.'

'How do you mean?'

'When things started to go wrong here, we went off to Canada. He finally began to sort himself out and took a degree in Toronto. He started out in mining and switched to geology, same thing really, I suppose. I supported him. The thanks I got were he took himself off to Alaska and the Yukon, saying they were no places for a woman. Eventually I got tired of it. If I was going to be on my own, I might as well be on my own in my own home.'

'This was your married home?' Kieran asked.

'Hell no, this was my mother's home. She left it to me.'

'When you says things began to go wrong here, what do you mean?'

'It's no secret he was involved in the UDA, and other loyalist groups.'

'So what did he do in Alaska?'

'Looked for oil, apparently. I am not entirely sure. But he worked for one of the smaller oil exploration companies.'

'So what was he doing on Rathlin?'

'I really have no idea.'

'Thanks for talking to me and thank you for the tea.'

'You're welcome. But I hope I am not going to be in the newspapers. Mercy no.'

'No, don't worry.'

He made his way back down to the Everglades.

*

Frank Collins had arrived on the dot of three o'clock, but was on his second pint of Guinness before McQuire showed up. He came in at a rush, and looked around to see who he knew and didn't know. He did not recognise anyone at first glance. He apologised to Collins, 'Sorry to keep you. I had to nip into the office. What'll I get you?'

'It's no problem. No, look it's my shout - what'll you have?'

'I'll take a pint of stout with you.'

They talked aimlessly about the shootings and killings. Collins asked McQuire whether he thought this was the start of a loyalist campaign. McQuire said he didn't know. After a while he suggested they drink up and walk along the shore. The daylight was beginning to fade. They walked along in the gathering grey. It was starting to get cold and McQuire put his collar up. White gulls wheeled and crawed. At the end of the harbour, McQuire looked around. There was no one else about. They stopped and leant against the sea wall.

'Now Frank, what do you want with me?'

'Saw Aideen O'Connor coming out of your office late last night and wondered why.'

'Have you spoken to her?'

'Yes.' he lied.

'What she tell yer?'

'Not a lot.'

'The thing is Frank, Hughes was killed by the Proddies in her flat. Well, not in her flat exactly. But they were all looking for the same thing. Her boyfriend, the Prod lord fella, had some documents

258

belong to William Carstairs. They were about bullion, sunken treasure, off Rathlin Island.'

Frank Collins was small. Staring up at the tall large McQuire, he looked like a latter day version of Oliver Twist. His mind raced to take all this in, while at the same time wanting to know more.

'What, I mean, who?'

'That's enough for you now. Usual ground rules, anything gets anywhere near me, I'll have your guts for garters. Oh, there is one other thing. The man Hughes was not in the IRA. Used to be. A clever fellow like you might put two and two together and find out what the shootings had to do with the Ballycastle business.'

Having walked back, Collins got into his car and phoned his office on his mobile. There was nobody of authority around. The night editor was just about to arrive. He looked at his watch. Quarter to five. Damn. Better drive in, he said to himself.

*

After speaking to London, Sweetman had rung Charles Wilson. To say the colonel was upset was putting it mildly. He was annoyed that Sweetman had not obtained the document, but he was incandescent that its contents were common knowledge. If a British spy could find out what was going on, then it must be all over the place. He would have to ring Carstairs and tell him, as well as ask about the shootings. They did make better sense after what Sweetman had told him. He did not relish telling Carstairs. Fortunately he was unavailable.

Sweetman made another call to Northern Ireland. This time it was to MI5. There was the usual fake politeness. After he had explained his dilemma, his contact in Northern Ireland agreed to send someone to Rathlin.

*

Aideen and Jackie had been back in the flat half an hour when Kieran rang. He passed on everything Molly Dawson had told him.

Jackie said, 'Thanks very much, Kieran, you have been more helpful than you know. Oh, by the way, two friends of Aideen's may be coming up to stay in the Everglades. We told them to look you up.' He put the phone down on Kieran, and turned to Aideen, 'That's another piece of the jigsaw. Dawson was a geologist, an oilman, not a diver. It looks as if he was looking for oil. The sixty-four-thousand-dollar question is, did he find it?'

Aideen said, 'What'll we do now, then?'

'We wait. We wait until it gets dark then we drop the car off at Brian's. Then we get a taxi to the airport and hire a car. We will be less conspicuous there. We will drive up to Carlingford and take ship to Rathlin Island. There are a couple of Gards in a car at the end of the road. I suspect they will have bugged your car. So when we go, I want you just to take your handbag, stuff a pair of jeans and a jumper in and everything else including your mobile in your pockets. I'll do the same. No suitcases. I don't want them to think we are going on a trip. Okay?'

'Whatever you say, Jackie. What'll we do until then?'

'We have a nice quiet time in front of the television. I can't take any more excitement.'

*

Full consciousness came to Dawson like an aircraft landing. First it was a faint speck in the air, then it was a fly-like drone until it took shape, finally it was a monster touching down with all engines roaring. The process of coming round had taken several hours. He remembered everything up to the car coming at him and his futile shots. But he had not realised that the other three were dead. Nor had he appreciated the extent of the furore that had been caused.

By five o'clock in the afternoon, Dawson was demanding to be released. The sister was worse than useless. She said she did not have the authority to release him. He would have to wait for the doctor. When would the doctor arrive? She didn't know. She would phone and ask what to do. Dawson, in his pyjamas, spoke to the policeman downstairs. He learnt that Carstairs had visited twice and he was to be contacted if Dawson improved. The policeman said he could probably help him liberate his clothes and possessions. The sister came back to him and said the doctor would make a special effort to drop by.

By half past six, the doctor had come and examined him. He strongly urged Dawson to stay in overnight. The doctor said that though Dawson seemed alright you never knew with these concussions and comas. After a quiet night, they could run some more tests. But the doctor couldn't stop him if he really wanted to be gone. After what the policeman had told him, Dawson felt events were getting out of control.

Just after seven o'clock, he finally got hold of Carstairs, who was both relieved and angry to hear Dawson had come round. He explained he had been to Rathlin but only found report A, as he called it. There was no sign of the other report. Dawson explained where he had put the blue floppy disc. Carstairs fumed. It was vital, absolutely vital, he had possession of the report. He would drive straight up and meet Dawson.

But the latter had other ideas. 'There is no way of getting across to the island this evening. In fact, on a Monday you would have to wait for the boat to come over, load up with the shopping and mail, and then wait for it go back. In any case, you would attract too much unwelcome attention. It would be better for me to get across and pick up the disc. I'll be in touch as soon as I have retrieved it. I know exactly where it is.'

Carstairs was not so sure. He felt he would have found it if it were there. But there were still Police Force men on the island, so nothing could go that badly wrong. Dawson announced that he would be signing himself out. He got his clothes and possessions, including his mobile phone, and within half an hour was checked into the Marine Hotel.

Chapter
19

At 5.30, Aideen and Jackie began to put their plan into operation. She stuffed a sweater and some jeans into a big bag, together with her mobile phone, some make-up and a change of underwear. Jackie put on his boots and the clothes he had arrived in. They walked up to the car. The two Gards in their patrol car on the corner immediately radioed their divisional headquarters. The two from the house were at the car. Were they to follow them. No, came back the reply. No need. The car is bugged. We'll just see where they go. No point you getting into the traffic.

Aideen drove the short distance up Baggot Street into Kildare Street, left into Molesworth Street and right into the narrow South Frederick Street, where Brian had a two bedroom apartment on the top floor of one of the tall, thin Georgian houses. Aideen was surprised to find she was puffing after she had climbed the three floors. Georgian houses were all very well but it would be nice if they had lifts. Brian and Fergus greeted them with glasses outstretched and drinks offered. Half an hour later they were on their way. The bug was able to register two people had got into the car and it had stopped in South Frederick Street. Two people had got back in. They drove off across the Liffey towards the north.

Half an hour after that, a tall thin man carrying a satchel-cum-briefcase slipped into the swirl of pedestrians around Trinity College.

He walked across the Liffey, up O'Connell Street and ordered a taxi outside the Gresham Hotel to take him to the airport, which was a fifteen-minute drive on the main road going north. Stay on it and it leads to the Carlingford peninsula and Dundalk, the last town before the border.

Some minutes after Jackie had left, Aideen slipped out into the darkening night and walked round to the Shelbourne taxi rank. This might be the tricky part. The general public knew Aideen through her television work. A taxi driver might recognise her and wonder why she was driving to the airport. But nothing had appeared in the newspapers. As far as the public was concerned she was a free agent, just. The taxi driver did give a double take of recognition but said nothing. He drove her to the airport.

*

Frank Collins had been trying for two hours to phone Aideen on her home number and on her mobile. The mobile was off. He left messages for her. Collins then popped out to the pub, although he knew the editor was different from his predecessors and didn't like drinking on duty. But he was lucky, by the time the editor finally appeared, he was back in the office. The editor at first pooh-poohed the story, but Collins was persistent. Eventually they agreed to run a story suggesting that all might not be what it seemed. The recent killings, rather than being straightforward tit-for-tat, were perhaps caused by an elaborate business scam centring on Rathlin Island. The man shot in a Dublin street was an ex-member of the IRA and not an active one. The editor didn't want to mention Aideen's involvement, since he rather liked her, but if she didn't answer her phone, it was her bad luck. He would have to go with the story anyway. Collins was absolutely sure of his source.

*

Jackie arrived at Dublin's airport a few minutes before Aideen. He tipped the taxi generously and waited a minute for it to pull away before entering Departures. He then went downstairs to Arrivals, crossed to the row of car hire desks and hired a Vauxhall Carlton. He went back to Arrivals, bought some newspapers and settled down to wait in the corner bar for Aideen. She arrived some ten minutes later. He bought her a gin and tonic. She was nervous and he found it infectious. They sat on stools at the bar and said little to each other. Finally he said, 'We better be going.'

*

Dawson, having checked into the Marine Hotel, decided he would go to the Harbour Bar. Amazingly, he found it open. Only a jagged slice of glass remained fixed behind the bar where the mirror had been. This and the pock marks in the wall testified to the earlier carnage. The place had been thoroughly scrubbed and smelt vaguely of disinfectant.

'Billy, whaddabouchee. Where's Ginty?'

'Mr Dawson, I'm glad to see you, so I am. Ginty's nerves are still at her. Sure it was terrible, so it was. They never gave them a chance.'

At this, Billy glanced nervously beyond Dawson to the long bench and table behind the door, where two men were sitting silently with pints of Guinness in front of them. Dawson half turned round. One of the men was about his age, the other a lot younger, probably around 25 at a guess. The elder man seemed vaguely familiar, although he certainly wasn't local. Ballycastle was a small place and, through his visits over the months, Dawson had got to know everyone who drank in the bars. Out of season it was unusual to come across strangers. Ballycastle wasn't on the way to anywhere, apart from Port Rush and Port Stewart, and there was a quicker and easier way to get to these seaside towns by the main road through Coleraine.

'Evening,' said Dawson, 'Nice night.'

The elder man stared fixedly at Dawson and replied tersely, 'Certainly is that.'

The soft southern accent floated across to Dawson. He was going to ask where he was from, but the hard look put him off. He turned back to Billy. 'Now Billy, I want to hear everything.'

The older man looked at the younger one and nodded. They got up and walked out, leaving their glasses half full. The older man, whose name was Noel Kelly, tossed a short 'good night' over his shoulder. Outside, without saying anything, they separated. They, with the third member of their Unit, were staying in different guesthouses.

'Who were they, Billy? They weren't very friendly, were they?'

'Search me, Mr Dawson. I never saw them before. They were asking about boats to Rathlin. Funny thing, another man I never knew before was in an hour ago asking about the boats to Rathlin. Young fella, so he was.'

'Did he have a Free State accent too?'

'No, he was from the Nort, seemed pleasant enough.' Billy then launched into a long description of how awful it all was and how Ginty would never be the same. Place has been crawling with police and those press people, although some of them seemed to have gone away.

Dawson took this in, then pushed out into the night. He passed two of the journalists who were on their way to the Harbour Bar. They would dearly have loved to interview Dawson but they had no way of knowing who he was. Perhaps the men from the south were journalists, Dawson thought. No, couldn't be. In their anoraks and jeans they looked more like oilrig workers. But the elder one was eerily familiar. Dawson decided he would go on a little pub-crawl to see if they had moved on anywhere else. First he would check the Marine Hotel's register.

He drew a blank. There were half a dozen journalists still registered. They had the names of their organisations alongside their names. Dawson heard braying noises and squawks from the bar. He went in, a group was standing around the bar, noisily amusing themselves. These must be the journalists. No sign of the two Dawson had seen in the Harbour Bar. He went to several other bars, but all the patrons were local, men he knew. Each time he asked whether any strangers had been in. He got the usual response; plenty, journalists all over the place asking questions. In one bar, where Dawson was known, he was told that some of them had been inquiring about him. They had been directed to the hospital.

At half past ten, when the pubs had closed down, he returned to the Marine Hotel. They were still serving drinks and the gaggle at the bar was still at it. Dawson sat down in a corner. He had been drinking stout all evening, but after several pints he felt bloated. He ordered a whiskey. No one bothered him. He heard his name mentioned but could not catch what was said. He finished his drink, got his key and went to bed.

*

There are two ways to get to Carlingford, the small town on the peninsula of the same name. You can drive up to Newry in Northern Ireland and come back down along the northern shore. Or you can turn off onto the little road through Ballymascanlan and Riverstown around the southern shore and under the mountain, as the hill was known. This was what Jackie called the scenic route. As the point of the exercise was to avoid crossing the border into Northern Ireland, there was very little choice. Jackie drove through Ballymascanlan and around the peninsula. He went past St John's

Fort, which was lit up, through Carlingford and to the Park Hotel.

It was just after 9.30. He and Aideen walked into the hotel. The bar was all plastic formica surfaces with a pineapple holding the ice cubes. Peter was propping up the bar at one end and there was a smattering of people at tables. Most of the locals would be at the huge Ballymascanlan Hotel for the country and western evening. Peter saw them coming towards him and got up. He enveloped Jackie's hand in his huge paw and pumped it vigorously. 'Jackie, whaddaboucheee, it's good to see you, so it is.'

'It's good to see you too.'

'Let me introduce you to Aideen O'Connor.'

Peter was a thoroughgoing Protestant, but he was scrupulously polite to his friends' friends and to ladies, even when they had Irish names. 'I'm very pleased to meet you ma'am', he said.'

'Don't call me ma'am. It makes me feel like a matron. I'm glad to meet you too.'

They got drinks and Jackie explained to Peter what he had in mind. Because of the shootings, the Irish authorities had wanted them to hang around in Dublin. This was not convenient. He did not explain why, but impressed on Peter it was a matter of extreme urgency they get to Rathlin. There was nothing illegal and Jackie would settle all bills.

'Right you are, Jackie. No time like the present. Let's be going.' As they settled up, Peter said, 'It's a good ten minute walk, might as well drive.' Jackie immediately thought that if anyone found the hire-car at the harbour, they would cotton on to his intentions straight away. He had become very detective-like. But then he just as quickly thought, what the hell, you can't cover your traces completely. He had hired the car for a week, so they might not be looking for it.

At 10.15 they were on board Peter's *Sea Eagle*. As a fishing boat, it had lots of free board. But there was also a little cooking galley down below under the wheelhouse and two sleeping berths.

Once on board, Peter, as was his wont, took control. He switched on the cabin lights, told them to stow their gear below and got out the charts. He switched on the radar. When they were cast off he would switch on the echo sounder. He got them to look at the chart showing depths and rock formations.

'It is a clear night, a full moon in fact, and the forecast is good. There is a south-westerly, around force 4, which should help us and the tide will turn around midnight. I reckon we should make good time. Get there around seven or eight in the morning. Is that alright?'

'That's fine.'

'Jackie, I suggest that you and I share the watches, four hours on and four hours off. The lady here can have a cruise. We will pretty much hug the shoreline, though we might have to go out a bit around Belfast Lough, because of the ferries and cargo. Alright? Right.' Peter switched on the engines, 'Right, Jackie, you hold her and I'll cast off.'

He scampered ashore. He untied the aft rope and threw it on board. The stern of the boat swung away from the none-too-sturdy wooden jetty to which it had been tethered. He untied the bow rope, gathered it up and stepped back on board, as the boat parted company completely with the pier. He went back into the wheelhouse. He then put the boat into reverse, backed slowly into the marina, spun the wheel around, turned the boat full circle, then pushed out into the channel. On the starboard bow were the green and red navigation lights of the channel leading to Greenore, to port the lights of Newcastle. The sky above was a rash of white stars. There was a full moon.

Once the boat had curved past Cranfield point, Peter set a new course. 'Now, Jackie, you take over. Keep on this course, it is about 22 degrees, what we used to call north-northeast. This should keep you clear of Killough and away from Dundrum Bay. You'll need to alter course after Killough, come round a bit. Wake me if you have any problems. Goodnight.' He disappeared down to the berths.

'Oh Peter, can we just get our pullovers.' Aideen had a jumper, Jackie didn't have a pullover, but he had a heavy shirt he could put on. Jackie took the wheel. He switched on the echo sounder, which Peter had forgotten to do. 'Let's see if there are any fish underneath us.' On the shore there were orange lights strung out like Christmas decorations in little occasional strips, signifying the small towns along the coast, Kilkeel, then Analong.

Behind them the Mountains of Mourne were like black shadows, brooding and sinister. You could just make out the sheer white cliffs of Maggie's Leap and the seaside town of Newcastle tucked in under the Mournes. From this distance at sea, it was just a blurred orange strip, like a smear of marmalade.

'Well this is very romantic Jackie, the stars, a full moon, nice night.' They both felt a peaceful calm wrap around them.

*

Brian and Fergus got as far as Enniskillen, on what had been a fraught journey. They were not used to this kind of thing. Driving over the border, through what was still essentially bandit territory, felt intimidating even though there was not the intensity of checks there had been previously. You could still feel the tension in the border villages. They had attempted to stop in Belturbet, just before the border. But the chill silence which greeted them in the pub made them hurry on. There had been a cursory check just inside the border by an army patrol, a RIR patrol in fact. They had emerged from the bushes, their faces blackened and in full combat gear. They wanted to know why they were driving to Londonderry. Wasn't this a strange way to go? The army did not get a satisfactory answer, but let them go on anyway.

In accordance with a request from Dublin, the helicopter picked them up north of Enniskillin, on the road to Omagh. With the close links between the Police Force and the RIR and the greater cooperation between the Police Force and the Irish Gardai, information could be quickly relayed down to Dublin. The car registration checked out. There were two men in the car.

Two men. Pick them up, went the order. Just before Omagh the two men ran into a RIR roadblock. But they were taken to the Police Force headquarters in Omagh. After questioning, during which Brian was virtually shaking and sobbing, it became clear that the two men knew nothing about why they were going to Londonderry. They were sternly warned that they were under suspicion as they had failed to give a satisfactory answer as to why they were driving someone else's car across a national border. They would be detained overnight.

C4 in Dublin was informed, they in turn notified the Gardai. Detectives went round to Aideen's apartment. The two had flown the coop. McQuire told the Minister of Justice, who alerted the Taoiseach. First, though, McQuire contacted McGuinness, who phoned Brogan. What did it mean, Brogan asked. McGuinness wasn't sure, but he assumed that Aideen O'Connor and her boyfriend had fled the country. If they were somehow going back to Rathlin, then Brogan was covered. McCall had agreed to send a reliable man. They would find out once and for all what Carstairs was up to. If it were some kind of plot to take over Ulster by means of a coup, they would spike his guns.

When he put the phone down on Brogan, McGuinness had a moment of doubt. He knew that he and Brogan thought alike. Ever since they first got wind that Carstairs was devilling around on Rathlin, Brogan, the greatest nationalist around, had seen clearly that there must be something beyond a business angle. If there really was some kind of wealth attached to Rathlin, oil or whatever, and Carstairs intended to use it to mount a coup, how could Brogan stop him, even with all his money. The IRA might well think that, with the British troops gone, they could easily take over. But they couldn't defeat the RIR any more than they had defeated the Brits. It was the Brits that had fought them to a standstill and not vice versa. The IRA was in the Assembly. The Irish Government would not send in the troops. They didn't have the troops to send in. Not really. Besides, the Irish Government was cock-a-hoop that, with the British troops gone, they had effectively won.

No, the only thing was for the British troops to stay and see off any Unionist rebellions. How did you get them to stay? Find out what Carstairs was doing and prove it. But time was short. McCall's man had better come up with something this time.

*

Dawson spent a very restless night. He woke up at 3 am and couldn't get back to sleep. Who were the men in the Harbour Bar? At seven o'clock he fell back into a fitful sleep. Just after eight o'clock, he woke up and switched on the radio. He heard,

'Finally, one of the main Dublin newspapers is carrying, as its lead item, a story claiming that the murder in Dublin appears not to have been a sectarian killing after all, but one resulting from a complex tale of industrial espionage. It seems the murdered man, who has been named as Patrick Hughes working under the alias of Dominic Morris, has not been a member of the IRA for some years.'

'According to the story, he was killed during an attempted armed robbery. Allegedly he was after some papers in the possession of Lord Strangford. The documents concern sunken bullion, which could be worth millions, and is thought to be lying off Northern Ireland's coast. The robbery is thought to have taken place at the flat of Miss Aideen O'Connor, the well-known Dublin journalist.

Police were last night seeking information as to the whereabouts of Miss O'Connor and Lord Strangford.'

'Jesus Christ,' said Dawson. Those newspapers sure know how to distort things. Four men dead and all they are trying to do is make sure it is nothing to do with the peace process and tit-for tat killings. Then it hit him! The man in the bar was an IRA man. He remembered him from the old days. What the hell was his name? God, he was a bit long in the tooth for this kind of thing. Dawson picked up the phone and called Carstairs. 'Have you heard the news?'

'I most certainly have.' He then started fulminating against Dawson. Why on earth did you ever give the document to someone so untrustworthy? The place is crawling with journalists and God knows whom else. It...

Dawson interrupted, 'William, William calm yourself. There is nothing in the story in the newspapers that we need worry about. It is just the old tat about sunken bullion. Nobody is going to take that very seriously. In fact it serves our purposes. It throws everyone off the scent. The police will be out looking for John Wilson and his floozy. Nobody will mind me slipping across to my own room to get my own property. But something more important has come up. I am almost totally sure that I have identified an IRA unit here in Ballycastle. I recognised one of them from the old days. They were asking about the Rathlin boat.'

'You what? Mother of God, where is this all leading?' expostulated Carstairs.

'I'll handle it. I want the name of a responsible Police Force leader, if you know what I mean. And I do not want you up here under any circumstances.'

'Why is that, may I ask?'

'If there is any kind of shoot-out, it would not do for you to be seen here. Think about it. Leave it to me. I will get the disc.' Dawson was feeling bad about leaving unfinished business on the island and he wanted to sort it out himself without Carstairs faffing around.

'Okay, I take your point. The man you want is Chief Inspector Marshall. Wait now, I'll give you his number. He is thoroughly trustworthy. Now, I want to hear as soon as you have the disc.'

'Yes, yes, okay.' Dawson put down the phone and rang Chief Inspector William Marshall. He explained the situation adding that, besides armed Police Force men, some marksmen would probably be needed. If these guys in Ballycastle were who Dawson thought they were, then they would be very professional. There would be no mucking around. Perhaps the SAS should be brought in.

Marshall disagreed. 'I don't think we want the SAS messing in this. Leave it with me. I can get some marksmen and the necessary Police Force men.'

*

Jackie caught sight of the South Lighthouse at Rue Point first. The red flashing light was just visible in the murky dark, as the boat ploughed serenely along in the pre-dawn calm and the first gulls wheeled over the boat. To their left, Fair Head, rising 600 feet, was the highest point along the Antrim Coast. It was grey against a dark skyline.

The boat wheeled round into Slough-na-Marra (Swallow of the Sea) the whirlpool south of Rue Point. Peter did not give it a wide enough berth and they felt the boat being tugged by the ebb tide. Peter swung out and then into Church Bay. Jackie could make out the familiar landmarks, the church, the manor house and the pock-marked basalt cliffs behind. The smell of the sea, the crowing of the guillemots and the changing light lifted Jackie's spirits. Peter gently edged the *Sea Eagle* alongside the quay. On the shore were only Gerry and two helpers, loading parcels on to the *St Iona*. The three Police Force men, who had been left behind on the island and would normally have been found on the quay, were still asleep in the diving centre.

As the *Sea Eagle* tied up in front of the *St Iona*, Gerry stopped what he was doing. 'What on earth?'

Peter jumped ashore and fastened the bow line. 'Morning,' he said.

Gerry was so amazed to see someone tying up at this time of day that he was speechless. Then he saw Jackie and Aideen come ashore. Gerry didn't listen to the news so he knew nothing of Jackie and Aideen's situation. 'So I'm not good enough for you, Jackie?'

'Of course you are. It's just we were in a rush.' Jackie then turned to Peter and said, pretty guilelessly in the circumstances, 'Why don't you come up to the house when you have tied up?'

'No, that's alright. You get away now. I'll make some tea and get my head down for a bit.' Peter then asked Gerry, 'Can youse get out alright?'

'Yes, I'll be going in a wee minute,' Gerry replied.

Jackie and Aideen trudged along the quay, up past the manor house, around the bay and through the wet grass. As they reached the guesthouse door, Gerry was pulling out of the bay towards the mainland. When Jackie went up to his room, the house seemed empty and silent. He was surprised to find that the door of his room was unlocked and that his trunk had been moved. He dumped his things and walked along to Dawson's room. It, too, was unlocked. He opened the door and Aideen followed him in. Sitting on the bed were Tony McHugh and Declan Brown. Behind them stood Siobhan.

Jackie started. The door was closed behind them and Tommy Lawrence, who had been behind the door, levelled a 12-bore shotgun. In the small room the barrel of the gun was virtually in Jackie's back.

'Looking for something?' said Tony and held up a blue disc between his fingers and thumb. He answered his own question. 'You have come back for this, I presume. You think us islanders are stupid, don't you? You think we don't know what Dawson was up to. His employer, Carstairs, rented the barns. He is planning to import arms. But it's alright. Gerry will bring some men from the Ra back with him. You see, the man killed in Dublin, Patrick Hughes, was Siobhan's brother.'

Jackie looked at Siobhan. She was expressionless.

'All that stuff about gold coins on the seabed. Oh, yes, we read it alright. It was just baloney. Carstairs was planning some kind of coup. It's all on here.' Tony waved the disc.

Jackie thought he was bluffing, so he merely asked, 'What does the disc say?' The reply showed he was right.

'That's what we don't know. Can't translate it on the computer at the diving centre. Don't know the system. But we are pretty sure it details a coup of some kind.'

Aideen then spoke, 'Your brother was not in the IRA - he left some time ago. He was working freelance, and I've a growing feeling I know who he was working for. Who is coming across?'

Tony looked round at Siobhan, 'Who did you phone?'

'A number in Dublin.'

Aideen said, 'I think you have phoned the wrong people. The IRA will be glad to get the disc, but it won't affect the others who are also after it.'

Jackie quickly butted in, 'Besides, I don't think the disc does talk about military things. Supposing I told you I think it is a drilling survey, that Dawson was looking for oil, that he found it. Supposing I told you there is enough oil out there to make all of you richer than the Arabs. Supposing I told you that if the IRA gets hold of the disc and it gets down to Dublin, you'd never get a penny of the oil revenues and that Dublin will grab it all.'

276

'I'd say you were bluffing and codding me,' Tony said.

'There is one way to find out. I know what system Dawson used. It was an old Zywrite system. Let me go next door and I'll transcribe the disc for you.'

Tony looked around the room, 'Declan, Tommy, what do you think?'

Siobhan spoke first, 'There's no harm in it. Gerry'll not be back for a couple of hours at least, probably longer.'

Declan said, 'May as well.'

*

As Gerry pulled into the harbour at Ballycastle, he was surprised that no one was waiting on the quay to greet him. Usually there would be a cluster of people gathered to help him unload and to put the post and other packages on to the boat. Today there was no-one at all. The Police Force had cut off the area and there were two marksmen crouching behind the sea wall near the telephone booth. Three men came into view, carrying bags and walking down the empty road towards the left of the quay. Suddenly an amplified voice cried 'Stop, armed Police. Throw down your weapons. Now.' But instead, the leading man reached into his bag. There was the sharp crack of a rifle. The bullet ripped into his shoulder, spinning him round with its force.

Marshall and Dawson watched from the Marine Hotel, with a largish crowd gathered behind them. 'Oh my God' said Marshall, 'We shot first. There'll be hell to pay for this. I hope these guys really are from Pira.'

The two other men, with their hands in the air, were now surrounded by Policemen in flak jackets. Uniformed officers attended to the wounded man. One summoned an ambulance. Chief Inspector Marshall walked out and spoke to the two stony-faced southerners.

'You are being arrested on suspicion of belonging to a terrorist organisation. Take them away.' They made no reply.

People flooded out of the Marine Hotel, except for the journalists who started hitting the phones. Gerry had flung himself to the ground when he heard the megaphone. He got up now and Dawson helped him. 'Well, it is all happening today,' Gerry said, 'Guess who just arrived on the island? Jackie Wilson, no less, and his floozy. Nice looking girl.'

'You're not serious,' said Dawson.

'I most certainly am. What's all this shooting?'

Dawson turned on his heel and went to look for Chief Inspector Marshall. His mobile phone rang. For some reason he always looked at his watch when it rang. Ten past ten. It was Carstairs. 'Look, the news just said that a taxi driver had taken the Irish whore to the airport. They are thought to have fled the country.'

'They've left the country alright. They're on Rathlin.'

'They are what? I am coming up.'

'William don't, there has been a shooting.' But Carstairs had hung up.

Dawson found Marshall. He explained what Gerry had told him. Marshall said he would phone his officers on the island and have Jackie and Aideen arrested. Dawson said he'd better get over as soon as he could. Marshall said he would go too. It would be best to vet all the passengers getting on board Gerry's boat.

*

On the island, Jackie was coming to the guts of the report. There was a long preamble about seismic tests, permeable rocks, sedimentary rocks, cenozoic structures. But Jackie knew enough about the subject to realise that, without actually drilling the wells, it was impossible to know whether the oil was there. He reached the crucial passage and read.

'Our tests have benefited from recent technological developments like horizontal drilling. The fields in the Rathlin catchments are broad, flat and thin. In the old days, exploitation would have required a large number of vertical shafts each cutting through just a few feet of oil-bearing shale. With computer-controlled drills, it is now possible to bore sideways through hundreds of feet of porous rock, reducing the number of wells needed to a handful.'

Dawson had drilled three wells. The first, right on the median line between Rathlin and Scotland had flowed at 10,000 barrels per day. Not a gusher, but promising. He had gone miles out into the Atlantic to drill a second well to try and establish the extent of the field. This had been called Tiger Lily and came in at 4,000b/d.

Finally, he drilled a third in between and hit paydirt. It had flowed for hours at 20,000b/d. This meant there was probably two billion barrels of oil in place. This field was big but Dawson had also identified at least another ten structures. This could mean something like ten billion barrels of oil, which made it a very substantial oil province indeed. Jackie whistled.

Aideen, standing behind him, said. 'Quick now, print it out,'

Tony came in. 'Well?'

'It is as I thought, you're swimming in oil.'

Siobhan rushed in, 'Tony, the police are moving. They look as though they are coming here.'

Jackie said, 'They are after us. Damn, how do they know we are here? Tony, you've got to help me get away. If I can get to Scotland, I will be able to prove something which should help you keep the oil.'

'Oh, no, how can I trust you. The Ra will be here soon.'

Siobhan said, 'Let him go, Tony. The girl stays here.' Siobhan then dashed downstairs, threw open her own door and spoke to her young son. 'Tommy, come here now. You're to go down to the boat along the quay. Walk quietly past the policemen who are coming up here. Wake up the man on the boat. Tell him Jackie wants to leave urgently. He's to be ready to cast off. Go now! Right, now, Jackie, you take the disc and your things and go out back. Once you hear the police arrive, walk round and down to the boat. The rest of us will just wait.'

The police knocked on the McHugh's house first and were told by Siobhan's other teenager that they were all next-door. They were let in and Tommy did the same thing he had done to Aideen and Jackie. He closed the door on the two policemen and levelled the 12-bore at them.

'What's this?' one of them said. 'We've come for John Wilson and Aideen O'Connor.'

'Miss O'Connor is here but Mr Wilson has gone,' Tony said.

'Gone, gone where?' asked the policeman.

'Gone to Scotland, if you really must know,' replied Tony.

'You can get into serious trouble, you know.'

'Never mind, you can just come into the room here and sit down.'

Jackie heard all of this from the little backyard. He calmly walked round to the front of the terrace then broke into a run, arms flailing. Peter had been surprised by the small boy's message, but had set the engine running. Jackie hurtled the last few yards, picked up the bow rope, passed his briefcase to Peter and then jumped on board.

'Where to, Jackie?'

'Scotland, I think.'

Chapter
20

The trip to Campbeltown towards the bottom of the Kintyre peninsula was usually one of Jackie's favourite journeys – the slightly mysterious islands of Islay and Jura off the port bow, the skipping, squawking seabirds, the sweeping mountains faintly visible on the mainland, and, on the right day, the sun dancing on the water - all usually left him with a sense of well being.

Today though, he was sombre. He knew that Carstairs and his friends would be pretty quickly after him. He knew also he would have a difficult job convincing Peter to collaborate further in his plans. But Peter would have to be persuaded if Jackie were to get the documents he needed and then proceed to London with them. He regretted now letting everyone on Rathlin know that he was headed for Scotland, since that would cut his lead-time. The journey passed mostly in silence with Peter not even bothering to ask where Aideen was, or why they were going to Scotland. They arrived in the harbour in Campbeltown, a little town of stone houses with a sort of village green near the sea. Peter tied up and asked, 'What now?'

Jackie looked at him and quietly whispered, 'Let's go and have a coffee and a talk.' They walked past the new terminal where the *MV Claymore*, the ferry which ran across to Ballycastle during the summer months, was now laid up for the winter. They cut through a side street and went into the Ardschiel Hotel and asked for some coffee.

'Now Jackie, what is going on?' Peter demanded.

Jackie paused before saying, 'I had better level with you. I badly need to get to Glasgow and then to London. But before I do that, I have to go to Ayr. What I want to do is hire a car and drive across and I want you to come with me.'

'You'll have to do a bit better than that, Jackie. You said I'd be going home today and here I am in Scotland. I've got pressing business in Ulster and you are looking to me as if you are in trouble.' He had no way of knowing what had happened in the guesthouse, but had obviously picked up that Jackie was in flight. He still didn't ask about Aideen.

'Look.' Jackie hung his head, thought and then continued. 'This will all sound fantastic and amazing. But I think there is a plot involving William Carstairs to launch a coup. I think he has discovered oil and wants to declare an independent Ulster.'

Peter said, 'I don't think an independent Ulster would be a very good idea.' He was a Protestant but he wasn't particularly rabid politically. He liked the status quo in Ulster. It was good for business. Peter was an adventurous sort but his main interest in life was making money.

On a fugitive instinct, Jackie said, 'One more day, no, two more days. There is nothing illegal in what I am doing. I have broken no laws. I will make it worth your while. I will pay you a daily retainer and all your costs.'

That clinched it.

'Okay, I'll do it. I haven't had an adventure like this in years. I'll have to go to the harbour master and explain I'll be gone for a couple of days,' Peter replied.

Jackie reflected that he might not know what he was letting himself in for, but said, 'Right, here's what we'll do. We will hire a car to drive to Glasgow. It will take four hours to drive from here right around the peninsula to Glasgow, but I need to go to Ayr first. You will drop me off at Claonaig. There I can get the ferry to Arran, cross the island and get another ferry back to the mainland on the other side. I will then do my business in Ayr, get up to Glasgow and meet you at the Central Hotel, in Central Station. How does that sound?'

'Bizarre, if you really want to know. But in for a penny, in for a pound,' said Peter.

'Good, it's nearly twelve o'clock now. If we are being followed, they will not get across for at least two hours, by which time we should be well on our way. There is a little place just along the road called Campbeltown Motors, which hires out Peugeots. I hired one before and drove around the islands. You get your things and join me there, Peter.' Peter went to his boat to pick up a bag and his driving licence.

Jackie went to the phone. Yes, the Argyll Land Record office was in the South Argyll County Council Offices in Wellington Square in Ayr. Yes, they were open every Monday until five o'clock. Yes, they would look out the documents he wanted. Some deeds and claims went back to the twelfth century.

Jackie walked along the seafront, past the little art deco cinema, until he came to Campbeltown Motors. He hadn't reckoned on the intransigence of the proprietor, Angus MacGregor. He had a car but was curious why anyone should need one this time of year. There was no drop off anywhere but in Campbeltown. Where had Jackie come from? There were no ferries to Northern Ireland at the moment. His suspicions were further raised when Peter walked in and hailed Jackie in his broad Ulster accent.

Jackie pleaded that they had been fishing, and, even as he said this, he realised that it sounded ridiculous. He pointed out that Peter's boat was moored in Campbeltown so he would have to return. But Angus was having none of it. Finally, he agreed that they could have a car, provided his young employee, Gareth, went with them and drove some of the way. Gareth would have to be properly accommodated if they stayed in Glasgow. And he would like the cash in advance. Angus made a mental note to talk to the local constabulary.

*

In Ballycastle, police were assembled on the jetty as if it were the Normandy landings, or so one local wag cracked. Gerry had been persuaded that he must return to Rathlin as soon as the police were ready. This was a very serious matter. Marshall and his cohorts vetted all the passengers and in the process weeded out McCall's man.

It took them just under an hour to cross to Rathlin. If Dawson had chosen to look, he would have spotted Peter's boat on course for the Mull of Kintyre. Gerry saw it, Marshall, seeing him looking, saw it too. Marshall had taken the precaution of requesting a police launch to come to Rathlin. These launches were used against drugs and arms dealers. They were not big, but they could make 36 knots. The nearest one was in Port Rush, maybe three quarters of an hour away.

Dawson and Marshall were mildly surprised not to find any constables on the quay, or any strange boats. Gerry still said nothing. Dawson strode out towards the guesthouse like some latter-day General MacArthur in the Philippines, intent on claiming back what had wrongfully been taken from him. Marshall and a clutch of plainclothes and uniformed police followed.

Dawson burst into the guesthouse and bounded up the stairs to his now crowded room. There he found Tommy, Declan, Tony, the three police officers and Aideen. Siobhan had gone next door.

Dawson said, 'What the...?'

'It's alright, Dawson, we know everything,' Tony said. 'There's no point. We know everything. Wilson has your disc. We know about the guns, the oil. Wilson's away to Scotland. You'll never catch him now.'

Aideen, unseen, secreted the hard copy from the disc in her bag, as Marshall in the doorway said, 'Right now, everyone downstairs.' Once in the bigger living room, Marshall asked the police officers what had happened. They couldn't tell him very much. Simply that they were told to come to the house to hold Wilson and the lady. But Wilson was not in the house, and they were jumped. Marshall said to Dawson. 'Mr Dawson, a word, if you please.' Once outside, Marshall blurted, 'Well this is a fine mess. What does he mean, oil?'

'Oh, nothing, nothing.' Dawson's mind was on fast forward. He walked around in a little circle, his head down. He looked up at Marshall and said, 'Look, I do not know how privy you are to Mr Carstairs' plans, but he recommended you, so you must know something. Suffice it to say that Wilson has got a floppy disc which belongs to me and which contains vital information about the future of the province. It is absolutely essential that I catch up with Wilson. God, I don't even know where he's gone.'

'Ah, well I can help you there. I saw a boat off in the distance. Must have been Wilson's. It was heading on a course to the Mull of Kintyre. It's the closest spot in Scotland to Ulster.'

'What the hell is he doing in Scotland. How am I going to get there?' Dawson asked

'You could take the police launch. See, it's pulling into the harbour now.'

Dawson looked quizzical. Marshall enlightened him, 'I took the precaution of ordering up a boat. I had a feeling that it might come in useful. Now, you must understand that there is nothing

I can do officially in Scotland, unless we invoke the Prevention of Terrorism Act. That would involve the top brass in Glasgow. But it so happens one of my colleagues has a relation in Campbeltown. He's also a policeman. He should give you a lead. If you hurry, Wilson won't have too much of a start.'

'Why are you doing this?' Dawson asked.

'Let's just say tribal loyalties. I owe Mr Carstairs a few favours.'

'You will have to keep the islanders here and what about the girl?' Dawson enquired.

'It's getting difficult. I am getting slightly beyond my remit. Obviously, the McHughs and the others know too much, and the O'Connor girl knows much too much. I can keep them here for a day or two, but the press are going to be hiring boats and my superiors are going to want to know what's going on.'

Marshall then went and fetched Detective Sergeant Jimmy McCreel, and the three of them walked down to the police launch. Marshall conferred with the skipper. It was agreed that the boat would deposit the two officers, as Marshall called them, in Campbeltown and return immediately to Rathlin.

Marshall slowly walked back to the guesthouse and mused that he was getting out of his depth. He would have a lot of explaining to do. He could hold the islanders for illegal detention of police officers. But what about the girl? What would he hold her on, and for how long? Fortunately his own police officers - those he had left on the island - didn't know much. But something would leak soon. 'I hope you know what you are doing, William Carstairs,' he muttered to himself.

*

There are two ways to get from Campbeltown to Tarbert at the top of the peninsula. There is the A83, a good road of almost motorway standard. It's straight and flat and runs the length of the west coast of the Kintyre peninsula. It is a distance of 38 miles and takes under an hour. The east coast road facing the Isle of Arran is a B road, the B843. It is full of Z bends and steep climbs and descents. In parts, it is just a single track. It goes as far as Claonaig, then cuts across to Kennacraig, where it rejoins the A83 for the last few miles to Tarbert.

Gareth was a little surprised when Jackie insisted they take the B road. It was indeed very scenic, with the trees and bushes turning wonderful russet and gold colours. Sheep ambled across the road. But the journey passed in a tense silence. Forty-five minutes after they had set out from Campbeltown they arrived in Claonaig. They had passed only two cars along the way. The village was as if in hibernation, not a soul was on the street. Jackie for a minute wondered whether the ferries were still running.

He made Gareth stop the car. Gareth looked startled. Jackie quickly got out of the car. 'Right Peter, I'll see you in Glasgow, Central Hotel.' The words just came out. He instantly regretted saying them in front of Gareth.

'Right you are Jackie. Come on Gareth.' Gareth engaged the gears and veered off to the left, Jackie picked up his bag and followed the sign to the Isle of Arran ferry to the right. After half an hour Jackie could see the incoming ferry off in the distance. Good, if this small ferry were running, the bigger one from Brodick on Arran to Ardrossan on the mainland would be too.

*

Dawson and McCreel arrived in Campbeltown about 40 minutes after Wilson, Gareth and Peter had left. McCreel walked briskly up Anne Street followed by Dawson and knocked on his cousin's house. His cousin, who was also called Jimmy, but Jimmy MacTaggart, greeted him warmly. 'Come in, come in, Jimmy,' he cried. A tall, upright man in a white shirt and plaid tie, Jimmy MacTaggart looked every inch what he was, chief constable for the Kintyre peninsula. He introduced the small man with suspicious eyes, Angus MacGregor, to his cousin and McCreel, in turn, introduced Dawson.

When McCreel had finished explaining why they were in Campbeltown, Angus MacGregor said, 'There, I told you so, Jimmy, didn't I tell you. I knew there was something funny about those two.'

'Aye, you did so,' replied MacTaggart.

Dawson told them he needed a car. Jimmy MacTaggart got out a map and showed Dawson the route Wilson had indicated he would take with Gareth. Dawson asked if it would it be possible to radio ahead to the police at wherever and have Wilson's car stopped. There was a police station at Inveraray but MacTaggart's jurisdiction didn't run that far. He could try ringing and asking a favour but there were no guarantees.

Dawson cut short MacTaggart's musings. He said, 'Okay, why don't you try Inveraray? We had better be going. Can you give us a car? Can you go and get it, Jimmy, and come back for me. I've an idea. Thank you for your help, Mr MacTaggart.'

Dawson rushed into the street. He pulled out his mobile phone and tried Carstairs' numbers. He finally got Joe on the telephone car. Carstairs' Rover was in a little car park opposite the Hilsea guesthouse up the hill from the Harbour Bar, very close to the spot the Cortina was parked on that fateful night. Carstairs was down on the quay. Joe would fetch him.

Could Dawson ring back in five minutes? He could. When he made contact, there was the inevitable explosion. Where the hell was Dawson? Why was the island cut off? What in the name of the saints was going on?

Dawson very firmly told Carstairs to be quiet and listen. He explained that Wilson had fled the island, although his girlfriend was still there. For the minute, Marshall was holding her and some islanders who knew too much. Jackie Wilson was on his way to Glasgow and he had the disc with him. Carstairs would have to get an army helicopter to intercept Wilson.

He said, 'Don't argue William. Just do it. You have got one hour. I'll give you the details. You're to intercept a red Peugeot 205 registration ELM 746 between Inveraray and Loch Lomond. You've got one hour,' he repeated.

Charles Wilson was initially dubious that a helicopter could be raised. Questions would be asked. Carstairs impressed upon him there was no choice. Wilson thought quickly and said he could get one on a pretext of going to Rathlin. It would take time. Carstairs insisted they didn't have time; Wilson agreed to see what he could do.

*

Jackie had managed quite easily to get a taxi at Lochranza. The ferry crew wondered what he was doing in Claonaig without a car and so did the taxi driver in Lochranza, but few questions were asked. As he was driven the 15 miles to Brodick, Jackie thought how very different these Highland settlements were. Lochranza was picture-postcard, with whitewashed houses beside a lake against a mountain. Brodick was nondescript, just a front of mostly modern bungalows and guesthouses, with the odd old country hotel. The next ferry was at 14.10. But this was a big ferry capable of carrying 50 cars with a restaurant and bar. He felt he was leaving the isolation of the depopulated Highlands, where he could be easily spotted and merging into the greater bustle of the mainland.

*

The helicopter caught sight of the Peugeot considerably east of Inveraray. But the problem was that when Colonel Wilson saw the car it was turning off the main road onto the narrower road to Garlochhead. There were few other cars, but there was nowhere the helicopter could land. It hovered over the little car like a giant wasp, descending then rising, dancing around it. It couldn't go too low because of the trees, but each time the helicopter lowered itself, Gareth gave a turn of the wheel and nearly had them in a ditch. Finally he stopped in one of the little bulges on the side of the road built for overtaking. Peter immediately said, 'Give me the wheel.'

They changed places, Gareth was shaking. Peter drove as fast as the road would allow, the helicopter hanging like a malevolent cloud. Finally they reached Garlochhead. There were other cars and still no place to land. Houses lined either side of the road. The pilot said to Colonel Wilson, 'Look there is a big green on the map behind the hotel. Do you think they would mind us landing on their lawn?'

'Too bad if they do,' Wilson replied.

*

Jackie felt a little more relaxed when he arrived in Brodick and bought his ticket, but the feeling was short lived. With an hour and half to kill before the boat was due to leave, he went into a pub - the Queen's hotel - for a drink and something to eat. There were some young men playing pool and four girls eating fish, chips and peas, with one doing her nails at the same time. Above the bar was a large television set. A newsreader was relating the events of earlier that morning in Ballycastle. Jackie caught sight of Carstairs being pursued by reporters. Although Jackie would not know him from Adam, there was also a shot of McCall's man, Dominic. Jackie surmised that by now the police would have got over to the island and that Aideen and the others were probably under arrest. It was a racing certainty that someone would now be pursuing him. Carstairs and Dawson couldn't let him get away with the disc.

Tension crept back into him as he boarded the boat. He found himself looking to see whether that man had a false moustache or this woman was wearing a wig. He tried to work out which of his fellow travellers could be plainclothes policemen. He bought himself a beer and sat in a window seat, well forward where he could survey the entire bar and watch anybody coming into it. He jerked his head suddenly this way and that to make sure no one was staring at him. There was a group of businessmen becoming rowdy at the bar. No one seemed the slightest bit interested in Jackie.

*

When the helicopter landed in the grounds of the King William Hotel, five soldiers ran around the side and fanned out across the road, their automatic rifles ready. Colonel Wilson walked into the dining room through the large double doors; diners dropped their knives and forks in surprise at this apparition. He strode on through to reception, announced he was looking for terrorists and said he would need to commandeer a room for possible interrogation. Peter was drawing up to the soldiers as Wilson walked to join them. Peter had not been much involved in the violence but he knew better than to break through an army roadblock. He and Gareth got out and Gareth put his hands up. Charles Wilson walked towards them. The smirk on his face evaporated when he saw there were just two of them. 'Where's John Wilson?' he demanded.

'He went another way,' Peter said. 'He took the ferry.'

'What the hell do you mean,' came back Wilson.

Gareth, who was shaking violently, blurted out. 'He said he had to go to Ayr. I heard him say that.'

Colonel Charles Wilson said, half to himself, 'Oh nice one Jackie.' He then told his men. 'Take them inside. There should be a room waiting.' Then he phoned Dawson, who though thunderstruck, said the best thing to do was wait for him to reach Garelochhead. Charles Wilson sat on a garden wall on the side of the road and lit a cigarette. Whenever Dawson arrived it would not be a moment too soon. It would not be long before the local police would be poking around. He had no authorisation for being in Garelochhead. He would be in trouble with his superior officers and the Scottish police. Come on Dawson.

There were few cars and Dawson came along after about 35 minutes. Charles Wilson flagged him down and explained what had happened. It was as if someone, or something, had sent an electric jolt through Dawson. He saw immediately that Jackie Wilson had sent them the wrong way, like some brilliant rugby player. He was miles away. Dawson had no hope of catching him.

'We'd better talk to the others.' he said. They went to the hotel, and were pointed out the room. One soldier was outside, two others were inside. Dawson walked straight up to Peter and hit him with his right fist directly on the mouth. Peter was a big man. He swayed backwards but he did not fall over. Nor did he retaliate. Dawson shook his hand as if he had caught it in the door.

Gareth started babbling with verbal incontinence. 'He said he was going to Ayr... He told us to meet him in Glasgow... He said to be at the Central Hotel.'

'Why should he go to Glasgow,' asked Dawson. 'Why should he go to Ayr? What the hell is he doing?'

Peter, who was rapidly beginning to tire of this adventure, answered before Gareth could, 'We don't know. He didn't say. I think he is heading for London.'

I bet he is, thought Dawson, then said to Charles Wilson, 'Colonel, a word please.' They quickly agreed that the Colonel would vamoose with his troops as soon as possible. Dawson would go to Glasgow and wait for Jackie Wilson there.

Charles Wilson was leaving through the front entrance when two uniformed policemen arrived.

'Good morning officers,' he said. 'Not a bad day.'

Chapter

21

Jackie passed through Ardrossan easily enough. The town was essentially one long main street with some old stone buildings. He found a taxi firm, said he wanted to be driven to Ayr and was in Ayr in 40 minutes.

Like all seaside towns out-of-season, it had a slightly desolate air as if it had been wrapped up and put away for winter, at least along the seafront. As it was only twenty to four, Jackie had time to buy one or two things. At the Tourist Information Centre, he learned that inside the Gaiety Theatre there was a theatrical shop.

He found the theatre and bought a selection of makeup and hairpieces. It was crude stuff, but it would do. Next he went to a men's outfitters and bought a pair of smart grey slacks, a Burberry's raincoat and a trilby hat. He also needed a pair of shoes as the slacks clashed with his boots. His credit cards were taking a hammering, but it was all in a good cause.

He then made his way to Wellington Square and the Council Offices. These were housed in a huge building, almost like a castle. It was similar in style to the town hall in Belfast, solidly Victorian, a confident building, but if anything rather grander than the one in Belfast. The Ayrshire Archive office was on the second floor along a cream coloured corridor. He banged on the door to be greeted by a frail-looking lady with a surprisingly strong handshake. She introduced herself as Catherine McBean, and said, 'Mr Wilson we've been expecting you. You've cut it fine mind, we'll be closing dunoo. I've managed to find the court order you mentioned. There is a copy. The Letters Patent to which it referred is earlier, sixteenth century. It is too fragile to photocopy. But you are in luck, one of our archivists here, Mr Creighton, has been translating from the Latin. He was worried about further deterioration, so he has copied several of these very early documents on to new paper. So you have not got the original. But you have got the content of the original. I hope that will do.'

'Yes I am sure it will,' Wilson said as he began to read.

The Letters Patent would be straightforward, that really was not in contention. He glanced at the text: *I James by Grace of God* .... He would read that later. The court finding was what mattered. *Know all men by these present that at the court held in Ayr on the May 28 in the year of our Lord .....* He skipped quickly to the finding, which was in favour of the plaintiff.

Mrs McBean said, 'Now I must stress that the court order refers to the Sheriff's Court. We have a different system to that in England. There may have been an appeal, which would have been heard in a higher court in Scotland. You would be well advised to contact the Scottish Records Office in Edinburgh. Here's the number. Also, you must remember that the Letters Patent were issued before the Act of Union with England.'

'Yes, yes,' said Jackie, anxious to get away, now that he believed he had found what he wanted. 'How much do I owe?'

'Auch no, we do not charge. But you can make a donation to the local charity if you wish.'

Jackie quickly signed a cheque and was on his way. He walked to the station, another Victorian structure which contained a hotel. Opposite was a statue of Robert Burns, Ayr's favourite son. He bought a ticket to Glasgow and asked whether he could buy a berth on the overnight sleeper to London.

'Ye, you could, but it's fully booked.'

'What about first class?'

'Aye, there's space available. But it'll cost you £105.'

'That's okay.'

'The train leaves at 11.54 but you can board from ten o'clock.'

Jackie took the tickets, slung his satchel over his shoulder, picked up his bag and boarded the commuter train. Twenty minutes later he was walking across the concourse at Glasgow Central station. He walked through the back door of the Central Hotel and asked at reception for Peter. The two receptionists looked at one another, then one of them said surlily, 'He is in room 105 on the first floor. There's the lift or you can walk up those stairs.'

As Jackie walked up the stairs he turned to see her raise a phone. He walked along the corridor and knocked on the door of room 105. Peter said, 'Come in, the door's open.'

It didn't sound quite right. Jackie pushed the door tentatively. Peter was standing across the room. His eyes swivelled to the right to behind the door. Jackie pushed the door right back. It didn't go back very far. Dawson was standing behind with his small Biretta pointed to the ceiling. Jackie dropped his bag, pulled the door towards him then slammed it back as hard as he could, throwing his weight against it. Dawson dropped his Biretta. Peter strode across the room and hit the dazed Dawson full in the face.

'That makes us even,' Peter chortled. 'Quick Jackie, run for it.'

As Jackie ran along the corridor, McCreel burst into the room. Dawson had picked up the Biretta and was struggling to his feet. With the gun he beckoned Peter to move further back into the room. As his senses returned to him, he yelled to McCreel, 'Quick, follow me,' and started running along the corridor.

Jackie bounded down the stairs and rushed for the back door, almost knocking over an old lady. Dawson and McCreel were in hot pursuit. Too hot. They ignored the receptionist's shout of 'back door' and rushed out of the arched front door on to the street. This gave Jackie another two minutes. Dawson and McCreel turned right and re-entered the station through the main entrance. There were people walking in all directions. A gap in the crowd appeared. 'Look. There,' shouted McCreel, catching a glimpse of Jackie disappearing between platforms three and four. Dawson went along one platform and McCreel the other. Their heads bobbed up and down looking in each carriage, but the trains were commuter ones, there was standing room only. They could not see which train Jackie boarded.

Dawson finally saw Jackie, but it was too late, the train had started to pull out. 'God damn it to hell, where does that train go?' he said to no one in particular. It took a moment to discover it went down to Ayr by way of Troon and Prestwick, then on to Stranraer. When Dawson and McCreel returned to the hotel they found two angry police officers, two frightened receptionists, a now virtually whimpering Gareth and a deeply unhappy Peter.

The police officers were too junior to deal with the matter. McCreel was similarly too junior to involve the Glasgow Special Branch. After much telephoning – the police from their car to their bosses, McCreel to Marshall, Marshall to his superiors, Dawson to Carstairs, Carstairs to Charles Wilson – it was agreed that no charges would be laid. Dawson was allowed to keep his gun. The Scottish police would check all the stations down to Stranraer and the car hire firms. They would also keep a watch on the last train to London that night, the night-sleeper. For Dawson was convinced Jackie would now try and make his way to London. But he had a feeling he could double back to Glasgow first. So it was agreed with Carstairs that Dawson would hang on in Glasgow and hold on to Peter until it was certain Jackie had left Scotland. Charles Wilson would proceed to

London, lest his brother should surface at the family flat. Dawson would join him there if there were a sighting.

By the time this was all arranged, Jackie had alighted at Ayr. He checked the time of the last train to Glasgow and walked down to the Antrim and Galloway Hotel, a small pub, and asked for a room. He then went to a McDonald's, had something to eat and booked into the multiplex cinema next door.

After an hour watching a Hollywood extravaganza, he went back to the hotel, shaved and bathed, changed into his new clothes and walked to the station. He put a bag of his old clothes, including his precious boots, in a left luggage locker. He carried a small plastic bag he had taken from the hotel, full of the make up and other bits and pieces he had bought at the theatre.

*

Dawson and McCreel had gone into the station at ten o'clock, which was the earliest opportunity travellers had to join the train. They stood with two police officers checking the identities of passengers. After half an hour Dawson got bored with this and went off to the bar of the Central Hotel. McCreel went with him. He said he would be back directly. He asked the police officers to keep checking.

At twenty past eleven the train from Ayr arrived at Glasgow Central station. Jackie went straight into the men's toilet on the platform. At 11.45 exactly, he emerged wearing a small moustache and glasses plus his trilby hat. He did not have to pass through a ticket barrier. But he had to cross a hundred yards of empty concourse. He almost tiptoed. As he approached platform one, Dawson and McCreel were emerging from the hotel. One of the police officers suddenly turned around and said to Jackie, 'Excuse me sir, going to London are you? Do you have any identification?'

Jackie pulled out a passport with the name The Lord Strangford on it. The policeman was looking for a John Wilson in corduroy trousers and a coloured windcheater. It was as well he did not look closely at the photo, or ask him to remove his hat. 'That's alright sir, thank you.'

Just as Jackie's back was disappearing down the platform, Dawson emerged on to the concourse. He went up to the police officer. 'Any luck?'

'I'm afraid not.' They stood around for another ten minutes. Then the police officer said, 'Looks like that's it. The last person to board was a Lord.'

Dawson's ears pricked. 'What?'

'Yup, Lord Strangford, some minutes before you arrived.'

'That's him. Quick.' They ran along the platform. The train was pulling out. For a second time that day Dawson had run after a departing train. The police in London were contacted. The train would be met at Euston.

Chapter

22

But Jackie did not get off at Euston. He had gone straight to his couchette, got rid of his make-up and gone to sleep. He woke at five o'clock in the morning and waited. When the train slowed down at Watford junction, Jackie threw open the train door and rolled himself on to the platform. He bumped along a little but did not seriously bruise himself. He went towards the station exit and heard the great long sleeper grinding to a halt as the open door set off the emergency alarm system.

It was half past five. There was no-one on the ticket barrier and few people about. He looked for a taxi but there were none. He phoned Mrs Vernon's husband, Tim, his old friend from the days of environment campaigns. The answering machine was on. 'Dammit,' said Jackie out loud. He decided to go for it anyway.

'Look Tim, I have to see you on matters of utmost urgency. I have discovered plans for a coup in Northern Ireland... someone has found oil off Northern Ireland and wants to use the revenues... the Republic is also involved... but Rathlin Island is not what it seems... I have to see you and your wife'

There were still no taxis. He waited. Around six o'clock the ticket office on the Underground showed signs of life. He bought a ticket to Notting Hill Gate. He would go to the flat.

At six o'clock Tim Vernon woke up and started to make his

wife a cup of tea. He switched on the answering machine and played Jackie's message. He played it again. He took his wife up her cup of tea. When she came down half an hour later, dressed and raring to go, he played her the message. 'Well?' she asked. 'Sounds like a crackpot to me. What is he talking about? A coup? Oil? Who is he? How did he get our number?'

Tim replied, 'He is a very serious person, a Lord, in fact. He comes from Northern Ireland. I trust him. We used to be involved together in various campaigns.'

'He sounds like a loony. You speak to him if you want. I'm off to run my department.' She took the remnants of her toast to the sink and walked out past the police guard to her official car. At Tim's insistence she had not moved from her modest house in Oxford Gardens. It was one of Tim's rare victories. A minute after she had gone, the phone rang again. This time Tim answered. It was Jackie. He had got off the tube at Oxford Circus to phone. 'Tim, where do you live?'

He gave the address, then asked, 'Jackie, what is this all about?'

'I'll explain everything. It is vital I see you and that you believe what I have to tell you.'

Jackie went back down the Tube. He caught the Central Line to Notting Hill Gate, then walked down to Ladbroke Grove, turned right along it, went past Ladbroke Square, up the hill until he came to Arundel Gardens. His family once owned the whole house. But now they had just the top two floors of the tall, terraced building. Mrs Samuels looked after the house, sent on any mail and kept it clean. Jackie let himself in.

'Hello, anyone here?' he yelled. No answer. He put his satchel down in the hall and went into the drawing room. He walked over to the window and looked into the street. When he turned around, Charles was pointing a 9mm Browning pistol at his stomach.

'I've been expecting you. You've given us a merry chase. Now I'll just take the disc with the vital information on it,' Charles said.

Real anger welled up in Jackie. 'You traitorous bastard.'

'No, you're the traitor. You would see your country, your heritage, sold down the river to the Irish Republic. You mix with those Taigs. Everything our family represents, eight hundred years of history, and you would see it given away, at the whim of some wishy washy government.'

'You'll never get away with this. I know about the oil. I know about the coup plans.'

'You do, but no one else does, only your lady friend and she is well taken care of.'

'You fucking bastard.' Jackie lunged at Charles, the gun didn't go off and they fell backwards. They rolled around. Charles, the stronger, quickly got on top of Jackie and starting hitting him, dropping the gun in the process. Jackie reached out for the gun and, holding it by the barrel, smashed Charles hard in the temple. Charles put his hand to his face. Jackie rammed the gun butt into Charles face at the bridge of his noise. Charles rolled off. Jackie hit him once more and Charles lost consciousness. Jackie threw the gun down, picked up his satchel and was through the door. He hailed a taxi. It stopped. The driver wound down the window. 'Not taking you mate, the state you're in.'

Jackie started walking as fast as his legs would carry him past the old Virgin Records headquarters, past the Library and the Portuguese cake shop. At the fish and chip shop he caught sight of himself in the window. He had a black eye and a bloodied cheek. He kept walking, turned into Oxford Gardens. Tim's house was towards the end, on the corner of St Helen's Gardens. It had a high wall around it. He knocked on the door. A policeman answered.

'I've come to see Tim Vernon,'

'Oh yes, and I'm Napoleon the third.'

'Look it's most important, I've got urgent matters...'

At this point Tim appeared and said, 'That's alright, Bill. Jackie, for God's sake, what on earth has happened to you? Come in, come in.'

'It's a long story, Tim, we haven't got a moment to lose.'

Once inside the house Jackie pulled out some papers and said. 'You start reading this. Do you have a computer with a printer?'

'Yes, in my study, just there, look. Would you like some coffee?'

'Yes please, white without sugar.'

Tim put the kettle on and started to read the passages Jackie had copied out from McCahan's local histories. Tim read, 'In 1617, George Crawford of Lisnorris, in Ayrshire, commenced an action against Sir Randal MacDonnell, claiming that in 1500 Rathlin was granted to his ancestors by James IV of Scotland. His case was that:- All cosmographers account the Hebrides or Aemonae insulae to belong to Scotland, like as all of them consider Raughlin to be one of the same, that the island belonged to John, Lord of the Isles, by whose forfeiture it fell to the crown of Scotland, that James IV. A.D.1500 granted it to Adam Reade and his heirs; that his grandson, Adam Read, dying A.D.1575 seized of it, left four daughters; that Henry Stewart, the husband of the eldest daughter, claimed it and also obtained from the King a new grant of it; that he afterwards sold his title to George Crawford.' Evidently, the case turned on the question of whether the island belonged to Scotland or Ireland.

Jackie emerged with a clutch of printouts.

'So?' asked Tim. 'Here's your coffee, by the way.'

'Now read this,' Jackie said, as he pulled out from his satchel the documents he had obtained in Ayr: *Know all men by these presents that, in the court held on Monday 28th of May in the year of our Lord 1617.....*'

Tim read through until he came to the end which said, 'I

therefore find in favour of the plaintiff.'

'So?' asked Tim.

'Now read this, well, don't read it all, just the bits I've marked,' Jackie said giving him Dawson's oil report.

Tim read, then said, 'So?'

Jackie said, 'I'll start at the beginning. Before I do, could you get your policeman friend to go and check on my brother. I might have done him a serious injury. Here's the address.'

'Hold on a second, I'll ask. He doesn't like any extra-curricular work.' Tim disappeared and came back five minutes later. 'He'll do it. Now.'

'Right' said Jackie, 'The beginning. William Carstairs. William Carstairs, the Protestant leader.'

'Yes, I know William Carstairs is a Protestant leader. I've met him,' interjected Tim.

'Look, we'll get on faster if you don't interrupt. In a nutshell, William Carstairs is planning a coup with the Royal Irish Regiment, including my brother Charles Wilson, and, probably, the Police Force of Northern Ireland. He has found oil, lots of it, off Rathlin Island. This will enable him to declare UDI and turn Ulster into another Brunei. Once the British troops have gone, they'll never go back. International oil interests will see to that. The fly in the ointment is that, as I have just shown you, Rathlin Island is technically part of Scotland.'

'That's ridiculous. What about the Law of the Sea and all that?'

'The Law of the Sea does not apply where there is a constitutional limbo. There is enough constitutional uncertainty over Rathlin to delay removing the troops.'

'Betty would never do that. It's her life's work. Her dream.'

'Well her dream is about to become a nightmare. I'm telling you Carstairs will be in charge before you know it. The troops are due to start leaving any day.'

'You are serious aren't you?'

'Very.'

Tim picked up a telephone and punched in one digit. 'Lucy, this is Tim Vernon. Tell my wife I am coming in to see her with a friend. Tell her it is of the utmost urgency. Whatever she has got on, she must cancel it.'

Lucy, Mrs Vernon's personal assistant was so taken aback she just muttered into the phone, 'Well alright, if you insist.'

As Tim was getting out his car, Bill returned. Bill told Tim that the man's brother was alright. He had another fellow with him, a big guy with red hair. He said his name was Dawson. He didn't want to make a fuss but wanted to know where your friend was. The gentleman here. 'I didn't tell him,' he said..

Tim and Jackie arrived at the Northern Ireland Department's offices just by Admiralty Arch, near Trafalgar Square, after an age looking for a parking meter. They were, somewhat to Tim's surprise, shown straight into Betty Vernon. She was sitting at a long table, with her Permanent Secretary, Sir Timothy Avery, her Deputy Under Secretary, and two other officials, whom Tim assumed to be from MI5 and MI6. Betty Vernon said, 'Now what's this about?'

Tim told her. He was still surprised she had been so willing to see them. Jackie was invited to tell the meeting what he had already told Tim. He also told them about his brother and Dawson and where they were.

'Do you have the documentation?' Sir Timothy asked quietly. Jackie handed over the documents he had found in Ayr, his own jottings on Rathlin and the Dawson oil report.

'Fine, could you now leave us for a moment?'

It was more like three quarters of an hour. As Sir Timothy finished one document he passed it around until all at the table had read everything. When they had finished, Betty Vernon said, 'It looks kosher. I can't bear it. The troops will have to stay. Years of work for nothing.'

'Perhaps not,' Sir Timothy said. 'There is a way to keep the peace process on track, but we will have to move fast. The Prime Minister is in Australia. He will have to be woken. We must contact the Deputy Prime Minister, the constitutional lawyers and the energy department. We will, I fear, have to be economical with the truth.'

Tim and Jackie were called back in. Sir Timothy Avery spoke for the group: 'Sorry to have kept you. You have done a great service to your country, Lord Strangford. Thank you. You need to know that an arms cache has been discovered at Port Rush. A coup was in the offing. We can nip it in the bud. We are going to be very busy. Not a word to anyone, especially about the oil. Do not worry about your brother. We will have him picked up. We would put you under protection, but I do not feel that will be necessary. Perhaps you could come back later this afternoon.'

Betty Vernon looked crushed, like a woman who had just lost a child. Jackie and Tim did as they were bid. They went to lunch in a pub in Whitehall. They walked in St James Park. They visited the National Gallery. At about five o'clock they returned to the Northern Ireland Office and were told to go to the Vernons' home. Perhaps they should buy themselves something for supper.

They retrieved the car with a parking fine on it and drove to the Vernons' and waited. At eight o'clock Betty Vernon arrived with Sir Timothy. They sat around the kitchen table. Sir Timothy said on the ten o'clock news there would be an item that would say that Mrs Vernon would make an important announcement on Ulster in the House of Commons the next day. Charles Wilson and Alan Dawson were in custody. He was not expecting any further arrests. They ate the pizzas Tim had bought, watched the ten o'clock news and then Jackie decided he wanted to go to his own flat.

The next morning the newspapers were full of speculation about what Betty Vernon was to announce, but nobody was near the mark. Jackie realised he didn't know himself what was to be said. He spent a restless morning in the Portobello Road, drinking too much coffee and finally arrived at Tim's, as arranged, at 12.30pm for lunch.

At two o'clock Betty Vernon rose to her feet in the House. She announced that British troops would be pulled out of Northern Ireland, as planned, but due to constitutional uncertainties that had come to light about the position of Rathlin Island, and whether it constitutionally belonged to Scotland or Ireland, 1,000 British troops would be stationed on the Island. A further 2,000 troops would be placed in the Mull of Kintyre. The Irish government and the main nationalist parties had been informed and they approved. The peace process would continue. The Assembly would re-convene. The measures were interim and would be reviewed in due course.

Jackie could not believe his ears. He said, 'Is that all?' He was suddenly aware of a presence in the room.

Sir Timothy Avery said, 'That is it, Lord Strangford. The Irish Government and the nationalist parties have been told that this is the only way to avoid a military coup. A rebellion will not now take place. Your brother has been arrested along with Mr Dawson. There will be further changes in the Police Force of Northern Ireland and the Royal Irish Regiment. These changes will be announced over time. Mr Carstairs has been apprised of the position and no further action will be taken against him. It seems a certain Mr Alex MacPhee was involved in funding Mr Carstairs. No action will be taken against him either. No one, least of all the Irish Government, has been told about the oil. Some of the islanders will talk, but no one will believe them. We have the only proof. Please do not talk about the oil; it will only cause unnecessary tension. Oh, and your lady friend, Miss O'Connor, has returned to Dublin. Good day to you.' He turned and left.

Chapter
23

Jackie spent the rest of the afternoon in a daze. Tim had just shrugged when Sir Timothy made his announcement. He didn't know what to say. Jackie said he had to go. He tried to ring Aideen, without success, and then walked up and down the Portobello Road in a stunned state.

He couldn't quite believe what had happened. It was a gigantic cover up. Yes, a coup had been averted. Yes, his brother had been arrested. Yet he could not help feeling that he had been betrayed. Surely they could not go ahead with the Peace Process now. Well, obviously they felt they could. Supposing someone found out? He wandered around like this, arguing the merits of the government's course. He should have felt relieved, but he just somehow felt very, very deceived and let down.

At six o'clock he went to his flat and watched the news. The experts hauled in to explain what was going on seemed at a loss to explain what indeed was going on. One kept saying the important thing was the Peace Process was continuing. Troops on an unknown island were neither here nor there. No one even hinted at oil. Jackie tried again to ring Aideen, with no more success. He felt hungry. He went out to a Chinese restaurant and then went to the cinema at Whiteley's. When he came back there were no messages on the answering machine. The world had forgotten him.

The next morning he went out and bought all the English newspapers. They were baffled. One tabloid headline screamed, 'Which Island?'. The more serious newspapers said the whole thing was perplexing, but as the Irish government had agreed, then it must be assumed that the Peace Process remained on track.

Had Jackie bought the *Irish Times*, it would have confirmed that, as Sir Timothy had told him, everyone, including Aideen, was now off Rathlin Island, and no charges had been brought against anyone.

Jackie made several more calls to Aideen at her office and at her home. The office knew nothing. He only got the answering machine at her flat. He rang other people. Peter in Northern Ireland was frosty and wanted to know when Jackie was going to settle up. Finally, around six o'clock in the evening, he got hold of Brian in Dublin. He was decidedly cool. He did not complain about the mess Jackie had gotten Brian and Fergus into, but he was off hand. Yes, he had seen Aideen. He had no idea why she was not returning his calls. Well, yes, he did have an idea actually. Jackie should read the *Irish Times* the next day and then he would discover for himself. He strongly advised Jackie not to visit Dublin. Feelings were running high. He hung up.

Jackie tried to ring Aideen but again without success. He decided to go to another film. It would keep his mind off things. Had he stayed in and watched *Newsnight* on the television he would have got a glimmer of what Brian was talking about. It had news of the first edition of the *Irish Times*.

It was only when he switched the radio on the next morning that the full blast hit him. The news bulletin reported the newspaper was carrying a headline saying 'The Greatest Betrayal Since Judas Iscariot.' An article by Aideen O'Connor said the Irish government had been betrayed and would probably fall. The Peace Process was in tatters. It was unlikely the British troops could be pulled out. A return to violence was imminent.

Jackie rushed out to Holland Park and bought the *Irish Times*. Aideen did not actually work for the *Irish Times,* but her article was all over the front page. It said the British government had deceived the Irish government and told them that, unless they agreed to the Rathlin plan, there would be a military coup by Protestant leaders and the Royal Irish Regiment. There were indeed plans for a coup, but what the Irish government was not told, was that the Protestant group planning the coup had discovered oil off Rathlin Island to finance the rebellion. The article then went into detail about how much oil. The piece ended by saying the British government had manipulated the peace Process to get its hands on the oil.

Jackie rang Aideen when he got back to the flat. This time she answered. She seemed a bit groggy.

'Aideen, what on earth! How could you? What have you done?'

'Oh it's you. I am sorry, Jackie, I just could not let the Brits get away with it.'

'I suppose that Brogan put you up to this?'

'Not exactly. But he's here. Why don't you ask?' She passed over the phone.

'Hello, soldier,' said Brogan. 'Well, I think things have worked out rather well. You've stopped a coup. I'm in bed with the lovely Aideen once more. The troops will have to stay for the minute, but the Brits won't dare try and get their hands on our oil now. A good day's work all round.'

Aideen grabbed the phone back. 'I'm sorry ,Jackie. I've just reverted to type. I'm a whore, but I'm Ireland's whore. You're better off without me. Where will I send your things?'

'To hell with my things,' he yelled and slammed the phone down.

Stewart Dalby is a publisher, editor, journalist and writer but not necessarily in that order. As a journalist he has been a news editor, foreign correspondent and travel writer for *The Financial Times*. He was a war correspondent for *The Observer* and various American publications and broadcasters. He has written about Ireland for *The Spectator*, *The New Statesman*, and *The Economist* and about collecting and alternative investments for *The Guardian*.

He is part owner of an Internet business and editorial director of a group of e-newspapers specializing in natural resources, has travelled and worked in almost 100 countries and contributed to anthologies of travel writing. He has also briefly been a fishing charter boat skipper in Ireland, a stockbroker in Hong Kong and an investment analyst in Brighton.

Married with three daughters, he divides his time between much loved homes in London and Sussex between the South Downs and the Sea. This is his first novel.